blue
rider
press

she poured out her heart

Also by Jean Thompson

NOVELS

The Humanity Project
The Year We Left Home
City Boy
Wide Blue Wonder
The Woman Driver
My Wisdom

COLLECTIONS

The Witch
Do Not Deny Me
Throw Like a Girl
Who Do You Love
Little Face and Other Stories
The Gasoline Wars

she

poured

out her

heart

JEAN THOMPSON

BLUE RIDER PRESS

New York

blue
rider
press

An imprint of Penguin Random House LLC
375 Hudson Street
New York, New York 10014

Copyright © 2016 by Jean Thompson
Penguin supports copyright. Copyright fuels creativity, encourages
diverse voices, promotes free speech, and creates a vibrant culture. Thank you
for buying an authorized edition of this book and for complying with copyright
laws by not reproducing, scanning, or distributing any part of it in any
form without permission. You are supporting writers and allowing
Penguin to continue to publish books for every reader.

Blue Rider Press is a registered trademark and its colophon
is a trademark of Penguin Random House LLC

ISBN 978-0-399-57381-1

Printed in the United States of America
1   3   5   7   9   10   8   6   4   2

BOOK DESIGN BY AMANDA DEWEY

This is a work of fiction. Names, characters, places, and incidents either
are the product of the author's imagination or are used fictitiously,
and any resemblance to actual persons, living or dead, businesses,
companies, events, or locales is entirely coincidental.

Think about it, / there must be higher love

∽

"Higher Love"

STEVE WINWOOD AND WILL JENNINGS

o r d i n a r y

Somebody should tell her he's not worth it."

It took Jane a beat or two before she could say, "Who? Tell who?" She had been lost in looking at the apples, her vision gone greedy at the wealth of them. They were piled and heaped in bins, all the different kinds: Jonagold, Red Delicious, Braeburn, Fuji, Pink Lady, Honeycrisp, Winesap, McIntosh, Rome. The names promised an extravagance of tastes. Granny Smiths were bright chartreuse, Auroras were yellow, and the rest were all shades and textures of red. Deep and polished, or striped and freckled with green and gold, or blush-stained. Row on row on row, all the apples in the world. She was thinking of nothing, nothing at all. Her eyes had taken her out of herself. And when Bonnie said what she did, it took an effort to pull herself back to normal conversation.

"Who?" Jane said. "Tell who?"

"Over there. Don't look."

Directed, then forbidden, Jane managed a sideways glance: A young couple, eighteen? Nineteen? The boy worked here, he wore the usual blue shirt and cap and he was standing next to a cart of produce boxes that needed unloading. The girl was thin, tense, wearing glasses, neither pretty nor unpretty. Jane saw what had drawn Bonnie's attention, since the two of them were having an argument.

You couldn't hear them, but it was plain enough from the girl's beseeching face and the boy's impatience and bluster. Something along the line of, Where were you last night? And, I had things to do. And, Well, are you coming over tonight? And, I don't know. Maybe. Maybe not. Depends.

At least that was what Jane imagined them saying. Bonnie gave her an elbow nudge and Jane dropped her gaze. After another minute or two the girl gave up and left, walking fast through the whooshing automatic doors. Even from behind she managed to look entirely miserable. The boy called out to one of the other boys working, again something Jane couldn't quite hear, something along the lines of, You believe that? Yeah, well she needs to quit doing whatever shit it was she did—the boy getting louder as he walked away from them, swinging his arms to show the extent of his exasperation and belligerence. He had an unremarkable, coarse face, and his voice had a braying tone to it, and Bonnie was probably right, he wasn't worth it.

"Why are women such idiots?" Bonnie said, throwing a plastic tub of lettuce in the cart. "I want to kidnap her and deprogram her."

"You could probably catch up to her in the parking lot."

"She'll have to figure it out for herself. A few more years of degradation and self-abasement."

"That sounds nice," Jane said.

"Shut up, please. I'm being wittily bitter. Witterly bitterly."

"Mhm." Somewhere, she had a grocery list. It wouldn't be much help, since she'd gotten into the lazy habit of writing "fruits and vegetables," instead of anything particular. The kids would probably eat apples if she sliced them up. She chose three of the ordinary red ones, McIntosh. Separated out and sealed in a plastic bag, there wasn't any magic left to them.

Bonnie trailed along behind her, giving baleful, disinterested looks at the celery and cabbage. It was all right to ignore her when she got herself all worked up like this, and in fact Jane knew she was meant to provide a certain going-about-her-business calm, while Bonnie had herself a little tantrum over her latest crash-and-burn love affair. Jane had already been through the escalating phone calls, detailing the events leading up to the final rupture, and had invited Bonnie over for coffee and a round of agreeing with all the terrible things Bonnie had to say about Patrick, whom Jane had never met. The tantrum could not be taken entirely seriously, just as Patrick could not be taken entirely seriously. When Jane said she had to get going on her errands, Bonnie surprised her by asking if she could come too. "I don't want to be home so he can find me if he comes looking for me. Which he won't. So I don't want to be there waiting for him to not come over. You know?"

Jane knew. It was hard not to. Bonnie always told her such things. They'd known each other since freshman year of college, and there was still that quality of late night dorm room oversharing, at least on Bonnie's part, because Jane's life had gotten so married with kids, nothing steamy going on there. This, at least, was who they had agreed to be for the last ten years or so, even though by now there was an air of performance to it all. Bonnie was pushing past the age when she might have been expected to settle down. Instead there were still guys like Patrick, who was such an amazing brute in bed, but had some issues, in the past but still the recent past, with substance abuse. You were meant to be loyal, you were meant to be supportive, but honestly.

Loyalty? Even now?

You could run out of patience with playing your part, especially when it was assumed you wanted to hear all the lurid, depressing details because your own life was, you know, dreary and conventional, while Bonnie was a *grande amoureuse*. I mean, please. Patrick had even borrowed money from her, though Bonnie wouldn't say how much, since that seemed to be more embarrassing than the sex stuff.

Bonnie said, "Is this the kind of occasion when it's appropriate to send dead flowers? I could do that. He'd get the message."

"I hope you didn't let him take any naked pictures. You know, revenge porn stuff."

"No," Bonnie said, but not right away, meaning she had to think about it. For a moment her face lost its indignant, focused quality and wavered. Then she regrouped. "Not unless he had some hidden camera system, and I don't think he's bright enough."

Instead of asking why it had seemed a good idea to invest (in all senses of the word) in a man who was either too dumb or too untrustworthy, or both, for purposes of basic peace of mind, Jane said, "I forgot olives, would you go back and get a jar of olives? Kalamata. Pitted."

Bonnie said sure and sauntered off, and Jane watched her go, thinking that Bonnie should probably cut back on her drinking, it was making her gain weight. Or maybe Jane should wish that on her.

Jane steered her cart out of the main traffic path and rummaged her purse until she found the grocery list. If she didn't arrive home with the right brand name products, her spoiled rotten children would whine. So that there must be Fudge Stripe cookies and Goldfish crackers and macaroni made with fluorescent orange cheese, and so on. Of course, calling them spoiled was a cover for her own pleasure in buying such items for them and satisfying their passionate, trivial desires. It was a Mom thing.

She wondered if Bonnie would ever have kids. She talked about it from time to time. She hoped to God that Bonnie was using birth control. And if she wanted kids, she could find a sperm donor, or latch on to the next incarnation of Patrick and get herself a baby that way. Both of them were collapsing into their nervous late thirties now. Biology closing in. They were stale dated. All those calcifying, unreliable inner parts. Babies didn't just come along when you wanted them to, lots of things went wrong. Nobody's fault. Menopause would come down like the lid of a box for both of them, and there would be one less impossible worry.

Stop thinking thinking thinking.

People ended up doing pretty much what they wanted to, didn't they? In spite of anything they said. Watch their feet, not their mouth. Bonnie liked her life of high drama and dingy heartbreaks, it gratified something in her and she didn't want to change. Bonnie considered a lot of men "boring," meaning they weren't alcoholic or unavailable or in between jobs. She didn't intend to settle for an ordinary, draggy life, like Jane's.

But it wasn't fair for Bonnie to want everything.

Jane consulted the grocery list one more time. She had procured "fruit" and now had to work on "vegetable." Something she might be able to sneak into a plain lettuce salad, shredded carrots, maybe. The kids ate frozen corn and frozen broccoli with glop sauce. That was all she had to show for her efforts. Fine. Let them eat cake. Hadn't she set herself on a track for what she'd wanted, hadn't it all come to pass? She had. It had. Difficult to remember these days, when she was at the service of her family from eyes open to eyes closed, that she had willed it all into being. Her son was eight, her daughter six. Her husband was a husband. What else could you expect? You couldn't pick and choose your problems. They were ordinary too, no matter how exquisitely they pained you.

You had to make your peace with ordinary, since it was most people most of the time. Nothing more ordinary than this oversized temple of food, its well-engineered lighting and whispering air and all the buy-me colors, and her grocery list, now getting grubby around the edges. The apple aisle was right behind her but she was done with spacing out in front of produce displays. She selected the shredded carrots, and some red and green peppers that she might be able to hide in tacos, and then she backtracked to the liquor section and picked up a bottle of the Frangelico that she liked and her husband didn't. Then it depressed her that she was attempting the consumer cure for whatever ailed her, not to mention the expense, not to mention, hello, alcohol, and she put the bottle back.

All right, enough, Jane told herself, her corrective for useless, fanciful thoughts, summoning up this droll self-awareness, *see how amusing I am being, speaking to myself as if I were my own misbehaving child.* But the charm was not working. *I will not be able to go on. I will not be able to do and say all the things that are expected of me, minute by minute by day by day, with no end to it. I will fall down and not get up again. I will open my mouth and black croaking noises will come out.*

As if the force of these thoughts had literally pulled her head around, she found herself staring up at the ceiling of the store, which she could not remember ever looking at with any particular attention, and now she was surprised to find it so large and vaulted, equipped with all sorts of trusses and grids and catwalks and spotlights and rigging, like some vast, mechanical sky.

Bonnie couldn't tell which kind of olives Jane meant, since there were a couple of different brands, and she herself didn't spend a lot of time thinking about olives. She took both bottles back with her so Jane could suit herself. And make a particular kind of face at the inferior olives, as if, how could anyone imagine her taking such a deficient product home? The Jane standards were unforgiving and mysterious, and Bonnie had given up trying to fathom them. Jane cut out recipes from magazines and went through phases when she tried to get her family to eat mashed root vegetables or grains popular at the time of the Pharaohs, which usually ended with the kids pitching a fit and getting cereal for dinner instead.

Bonnie had to admit, she herself wasn't much of a cook. Her refrigerator was usually full of hinged styrofoam boxes, the remnants of different meals out. Once in a while she roasted a chicken with lemon and rosemary, her one foolproof recipe. Patrick was such a shit. And she was so screwed.

She'd had her reasons for Patrick, the usual ones, having to do with lonesomeness and boredom and good old sex. And some less usual ones, like not wanting to give the impression of being so stupidly available, just hanging around and waiting for the next time.

Not that there was going to be a next time, except you never really knew that, did you. In spite of all the promises and good intentions. You set yourself up for the endless possibilities of next time.

Surely he knew about Patrick by now. Let him wonder what she was up to. If he ever did such a thing as wonder about her. She was such a total fucked-up mess.

You did not want to believe that you were a terrible person, and on the one hand you could list your virtues: kind to animals and those in need, good sense of humor—did that count?—positive energy, hard worker, etc. etc. But the other hand was a big smashing fist.

Bonnie shook her head loose from her crummy whiny downer fest and looked around to see if anybody was watching her, as if her forehead was a billboard advertising stupidity and shame. But no one was paying any attention to her. They milled around, dazed and unhungry, shuffling their coupons. Whatever else she was, whatever else she'd done, at least she wasn't somebody who thought that pricing value packs of chicken parts was entertainment.

She started back with the olives. Sometimes you needed to take stock. Reassess. Do inventory. It was never too late. People did it all the time. Got over their addictions, left (or joined) cults, rebuilt their credit, and so on, and she could do that too. And although she had not been thinking about the superficial stuff, the appearance stuff—more like, the milk bottles representing souls in the Catholic religion classes, with the milk gone black and foul from various venial and mortal sins—she caught a glimpse of herself in a display mirror that stopped her cold.

What had she been thinking? Her hair looked like ass. She'd gone red this last time, a considered, middle-of-the-road red, but it had faded to a pinky carrot color and her part showed gray. There was lint on her jacket and her shirt gapped open where it pulled across her boobs, a sloppy look she hated. It was one of her favorite shirts, black, western style, with an embroidered yoke and pearl snaps. She wore it because she liked the idea of being a cowgirl, in a humorous, jokey way. And now she couldn't wear it anymore, because it made her look like, like, she tended bar in a bowling alley or something.

Her makeup had been just fine when she'd put it on. Or had it really?

Her eyeliner was sinister, reptilian. Thank God the mirror wasn't full length, or she would have seen what was wrong with the rest of her.

Bonnie headed to the cosmetics shelves, looking for first aid. Not that she could do anything about the hair except buy a hat. Not that she wanted to meet Jane at the checkout lane with a box of hair dye in her hand, an admission of vanity gone wrong. She got out her compact and smudged some of the eyeliner so it looked a little less like pavement striping. Found a tester for some solid perfume and rubbed it on her wrists. It smelled like vanilla. Somebody in products marketing had decided that everyone should smell like vanilla.

Maybe she should start wearing plaid skirts and cashmere sweaters, get her hair done in a country club bob, wear little gold knots in her ears instead of gypsy chandeliers. Clean up her act, literally.

Would that help? All this while she'd carried on like she was some kind of female pirate, as if she was allowed her excesses because she was a creature of tempestuous moods and passions and sensibilities, like an opera diva or an artist. Except she was not an artist. Had never wanted to be or tried to be. She had enthusiasms, but no real talents. Mostly she bought things that were meant to demonstrate her quirky and individualistic tastes. Mostly she had stupid affairs. She was a diva of fucking.

Then, having beat herself up to the point where it no longer mattered how repulsive she was, she hurried to meet up with Jane, because Jane's husband, Eric, had taken the kids out for some enforced daddy time, and it would not do to be there when they got back.

Jane was standing in the open space by the deli. She had taken a step away from her shopping cart and was doing nothing at all, except looking up at the ceiling. Staring, really, with her head back and her mouth falling open. Was there a bird flying around up there? Something trapped?

Bonnie walked up to her, checked out the ceiling, saw nothing there, said, "So what is it, huh?" And Jane jumped out of her skin, like she'd been surprised in some woodland solitude, and for the briefest moment her face was hard and angry and crazed and she stared at Bonnie like she didn't recognize her, or maybe she did but she hated her and *she knew? Did she?* . . .

The next instant she was Jane again, and she said, in her usual voice, "I never noticed how big this place is. Warehouse big. I mean, you know it from walking around, but . . ."

Jane shrugged. She didn't seem especially embarrassed at spacing out and babbling. "It's just a long way down," she said, as if that was an explanation.

"Don't you mean, a long way up?" Bonnie suggested, deciding to play it wise-guy cool, a sidekick.

"I suppose." Jane looked at the jars of olives that Bonnie presented. Selected one and put it in the cart. Bonnie left the other jar next to a display of fancy cheeses. Jane pushed the cart forward, then let it go. It wheeled a couple of feet forward on its own, then stopped.

"Hey, Jane?" Still keeping it all in humorous sidekick mode, but a little concerned now. "Earth to Jane."

Jane roused herself, caught up with the cart, and attached herself to it again. "Sorry. Sorry. I think I have everything. Now I just have to decide what to fix tonight."

"That's why I don't ever cook," Bonnie said. "I don't think about meals until I'm hungry." Relieved that everything was back to Jane-normal. Maybe Jane was taking some kind of new antidepressant? Bonnie knew she had prescriptions, she'd taken a lot of different meds in the past for whatever Jane-depression she suffered from. It was hard for Bonnie to tell what might be wrong because Jane had always seemed pretty much the same to her and had for all these years.

Although there had been that one time, requiring hospitalization, which they were careful not to talk about.

But for now, at least, the little spell of weirdness had passed, and Jane was once again scrabbling around for her grocery list and her checkbook and whatever else she needed. She was always doing that, making sure she had one thing or another, her wallet, phone, keys, as if the different parts of her got lost in her big mom-style purse.

"There he is again," Bonnie said. She meant the boy they'd seen before who'd been having the fight with his girlfriend. Or maybe she just thought she was his girlfriend. He was a jerk. And the girl was one of those pitiful types. Sometimes you hated people you didn't even know. Why was it all so important, the endless stupid back and forth that wasn't even love after a while. Or never had been. The boy was in line at one of the self-checkout lanes with a bottle of pop and a bag of some greasy snack food. His face was thick-featured, expressing absolutely nothing. What was inside his head? Car parts, probably.

"It's hard to tell, isn't it," Jane said, nodding at the boy.

"Tell what?"

"If he's worth it or not."

Bonnie shrugged but didn't answer, and they moved to the checkout lane and waited their turn. They seemed to have arrived there at one of those cresting times when everybody in the store was jammed together up front. In the next lane, a little girl about five years old was squatting next to a display of tiny bottles, each filled with a different flavor of sugar water, red, green, orange. One by one, she stuck them in her mouth, tried to pry the cap loose, then put them back on the rack.

The child's mother was busy unloading her groceries, as well as managing the baby strapped into a carrier, and an older boy who was pestering his mother about something he wanted and didn't get. Were you supposed to say something? Jane didn't seem to notice, nor anyone else. The child was oblivious, too young to know she was doing anything wrong. Fine, let it go, let everybody catch little kid germs. Why did anyone have so many children anyway? It didn't seem necessary.

Their line moved slowly. Of course they had chosen the wrong one. The mother and children moved toward the door in a straggling group. The woman ahead of them was buying not only groceries but clothes on hangers, and there was a price check that kept everyone waiting. Jane said, "You know something? Every once in a while, I mean every once in a long long while, I get these flashes where I think, this is going to sound so, anyway, sometimes I think I can see the future. Little corners of it."

Jane ducked her head, as if she was either self-conscious or proud of saying such a thing.

"Really?" Bonnie said, meaning, *what brought that on?* She had no idea.

Jane began setting groceries on the belt, arranging the frozen items together, then the meat, then dairy, produce, and so on. "Uh huh. Out of nowhere. Very unreliable. But when Robbie broke his arm at school? The day before, I knew it was going to happen. I mean not know know, because of course I would have done something. Kept him home or told him to be careful on the monkey bars. It was just this random thought that popped into my head from nowhere."

"Wow," Bonnie said. "That's . . ." She meant to go on, say wasn't that remarkable, and something about the mother-child bond, but the idea of knowing the future filled her with an unreasoning dread, as if the future was a lurking thing waiting to catch you off guard. Why dread, why so fearful? Why not believe in a better tomorrow, a brighter day? What was wrong with her? The best she could manage was, "Well, so what do you see happening, Miss Psychic?"

"Like I said, it's not very reliable. More of a, I don't know, like when you think you see the lights flicker? And you wonder if the power's going out?" Jane put the divider bar at the end of her groceries and smiled an unexpected, impish smile. "Silly! I don't even know what I'm going to make for dinner."

jane

When Jane was nine years old, she was diagnosed with a heart defect and spent a lot of time in doctors' offices and in hospitals, undergoing tests and treatments, echocardiograms and scans, catheterizations and surgeries. The diagnosis brought her some relief from her bullying father, who believed in vigorous sports as character builders and pathways to success in life. He believed there was no reason Jane couldn't keep up with her two brothers, why she could not take to something, soccer, volleyball, or lacrosse, why she could not be a team player. Why her tennis lessons and swimming lessons and gymnastic lessons always ended in tears and mortification. "You want to give up? Huh? You going to quit every time something doesn't go your way?" Jane passed out and cracked her head on the cement of a swimming pool deck.

The doctors and nurses had long experience and training in dealing with children, unlike many parents, and they tended to her in ways that were both jolly and soothing. Jane felt weak and strange but not really frightened. So many people and voices and lights revolved around her. On this and subsequent visits to the hospitals and clinics, it was as if something rare and important lived within her chest, something worth a great deal of attention and concern. A doctor sat beside her bed and explained the functions of the heart to her, and how they would take hers apart and put it back together better than new. He used a pink plastic model with all the veins and arteries sticking out in a way that resembled a bug's legs. And Jane knew that her heart did not look like this at all. Her heart was smooth and it had a pretty heart-shape, and it was made of heavy shining glass, like a paperweight, and it beat in its own secret code.

Once she was through with the round of doctors and surgeries and had returned home, her family treated her with caution that edged into a kind of resentment at having to do so. She was special only in the sense that she was deficient. The certainty of being extraordinary faded.

At school she was a dutiful student, quiet and tidy, the kind teachers did not worry about. She had nice hair, her best feature, long and sandy blond. Her face was freckled, her eyebrows sparse and surprised-looking. In the later grades, when boys started up with their smutty talk and harassment, she was most often overlooked. The first two years of high school she had a boyfriend, serious, brainy Allen, who read philosophy and said things like, "What is rational is actual and what is actual is rational." Or, "No man's knowledge can go beyond his experience."

He latched on to Jane, it was all his doing, and it flattered Jane to be singled out and chosen. They kissed in basements and outdoors on chilly park benches—they were too young to drive—and Jane let him feel around inside her shirt, although she couldn't say why this was meant to be meaningful for either of them. It made her self-conscious that she didn't have that much to grab on to. She was just grateful that she'd managed to get herself kissed and fondled, since other girls her age had started so much younger and by now were making jokes about blow jobs.

Jane wondered if there was something wrong with her that she didn't get more excited about having sex, the prospect of having sex with Allen. He was her boyfriend and one thing was meant to follow the other. But the only times she felt anything lowdown and agreeably carnal were when she got caught up in a movie or television show and could imagine herself as somebody else, the girl in *Dances with Wolves*, for instance.

Allen was in the habit of carrying breath mints when they were together, crunching them and offering some to her, then, once prepared, taking off his glasses and leaning in, gusts of hot peppermint enveloping her from his open mouth. In *Dances with Wolves*, the white people had turned into Indians, and so they were allowed to jump all over each other and roll around passionately in the grass and dirt.

Allen said, "I feel like we ought to give some thought to the future."

"Oh?" Jane said, keeping her voice light and neutral. She had no idea what he might say next, but she felt apprehensive. They were watching television in the family room at Jane's house. Her parents had gone to bed, but there was always the possibility that they might descend the stairs, or else one of Jane's brothers might come home. Her brothers regarded Allen with a certain amount of mirth, and it was best not to give them any opportunities. So that this evening, like others, was spent unbuttoning and buttoning, melding themselves together and then pulling apart, their moist skins making a smacking noise. The future? "Yeah?" she ventured.

Allen said, "I've been trying to find a term that would convey the idea of 'God,' but without the religious context. 'God' as a comprehensive, unifying principle, 'God' as unquestioned rightness and authority. Except, secular. Not-God. It isn't as easy as you'd think."

"What are you talking about?" Jane had started out impressed by Allen's intelligence. Then she got used to it, and now it often annoyed her. "What does that have to do with the future? Future in general or me and you future?"

"Me and you. See, people say, 'in the eyes of God' meaning, an alternative to state-sanctioned, as in, 'married in the eyes of God.'" He gave Jane a cunning, sideways look.

"What?"

"But if we don't want to go all religious, we can just say we're married 'in the eyes of the universe.' I think it's a reasonable alternative."

"Married? Who said we're married?" It didn't seem like the kind of thing you had to argue about with somebody. "That's crazy. Anyway, you didn't even ask me!"

"I guess I just figured . . ." Allen began. "I mean, we've been hanging out for more than a year."

"Hanging out," Jane repeated. She supposed that was what you called it. She and Allen didn't do a lot of boyfriend-girlfriend activities, besides the kissing stuff. No date things, like football games or parties. They studied together, they watched movies on video, and sometimes they accompanied Allen's grandparents to performances of the symphony, where the grandparents were patrons. These did not feel like dates either, even though Jane dressed up and Allen arrived at her front door with the corsage his grandmother had made him buy. They climbed into the vast backseat of the grandparents' Lincoln and Jane answered the grandparents' questions about what she had been studying in school while Allen, inspired to friskiness, attempted to work his hand or foot across the chilly expanse of upholstered seat that separated them and burrow undetected between her knees.

"I'm not getting married, or pretend married, what a stupid idea. Why do you even want to?"

"So everything would be all settled." Allen was sulky now. Clearly he had expected her to go along with it. He gave her a peevish look. Maybe he was not as smart as everybody thought.

"You want to, like, do it, but you don't want to have to bother with talking me into it or anything."

"You're a very conventional person, you know that?"

As always when somebody told her she was one or another thing, Jane kept silent. She never thought of herself as conventional, or whatever other label was placed on her, but other people seemed to view her so much more clearly than she did herself. Allen grabbed her hand and shoved it into his crotch. Jane yelped and pulled away. She thought she had felt his penis squirming around beneath his clothes, ready to break loose, attack.

"You're just afraid nobody else is ever going to come along," Jane said, meaning it to be scornful and sarcastic, but then she realized she was right.

And for a long time after Allen, nobody else came along for her. She got excellent grades and was admitted to the state university as a general education major in the humanities. She didn't have clear vocational plans; she figured she could find some way to support herself if she had to. Meanwhile, she signed up for classes in art history and political science and American literature, meant to enrich her being with knowledge much as a layer of fertilizer might be spread over a field.

Her roommate was going through sorority rush and spent a lot of time on the phone with other rushees, comparing their prospects. There were good houses and less good ones. Which house had a reputation for being sluts, which had the best parties, or partnered with the hottest fraternities. Which one was for joyless dreary types going for high grade point averages, like Jane over there on her side of the room, writing a paper on Walt Whitman. Most of the time she and the roommate politely ignored each other, but on this night the roommate said, "Do you want to go to a mixer? There's a guy somebody knows who needs a date. You wouldn't have to dress up or anything. Just don't wear your glasses."

She could have said no. She was so clearly one scant step better than no date at all. But so far Jane's new life at college was turning out to be too much like her old life at home, narrow and unremarkable. She told her roommate sure, she'd go. She fluffed her hair out and put on mascara and presented herself for inspection. Her roommate scrutinized her. "Why don't you wear my red sweater?" she suggested.

She'd been having trouble with her contacts, and without her glasses, the world was an agreeable soft-edged blur. It was November and pleasantly chill. They walked to the party through pools of light from the old-fashioned streetlamps, and underfoot were heaps of red and yellow maple leaves, and around them all the houses and apartments were busy with people coming and going on their way to their own amusements. And for once she was a part of it.

"So who is this guy, my date?" Jane asked, trying not to think foolish, hopeful thoughts. Her roommate, who was still no more friendly than she ever was, said only that he was this guy from Valpo who was in town for the weekend, a friend of Candy's boyfriend Josh. Jane did not find this helpful information. She didn't know Candy or Josh. She wasn't even sure where, or what, Valpo was. She had to wonder why it was so important for the weekend guest to have an escort, why he couldn't tough it out alone. She walked on in silence. For her paper on Walt Whitman, she had been reading certain titillating lines about a lover who "settled your head athwart my hips" or "plunged your tongue to my bare-stript heart." There was some argument that Whitman was gay, but what did it matter? There had to be other people who felt that kind of thing. It couldn't just be poets.

At the frat house, a DJ was playing a mix of rap songs, boom boom boom and fuckety fuckety fuck. Red Christmas lights were strung along the walls. The noise was terrific. They wandered around in the crowd until the roommate found Candy and Candy's boyfriend, and then Jane was introduced to her date. The roommate vanished, borne away by her overexcited girlfriends. The date's name was Tim. He brought her a red plastic cup of beer, which she drank down fast, though it tasted sour, like something she had already vomited back up.

The music kept playing at terrific volume and it was impossible to hear anything else, so she and Tim mostly grinned at each other. "Where are you from?" she shouted at him, but he just kept saying "Huh? What?" He had buzzed hair, like he might have been in ROTC or a punk band. He was tall, which she liked, and after she drank two more beers she kissed him, standing up against a wall while the music thumped and brayed. He was a better kisser than Allen. He put both his hands on her backside and pulled her up so that she was riding him, a slow grinding dance, which felt sort of good, in a hopeful way. Other couples around them were also entwined and grappling, and she understood why she, or some other female creature, was necessary, for who could be alone in this paired-off frenzy of mating? It was like the nature program she'd seen on an education channel, a lake full of copulating fish, their tails beating and thrashing the water.

"Want to go upstairs?" Tim asked, and she did, mostly. *I know what I'm doing,* she told herself, although it was not possible to know what was beyond your experience. Should she tell him she was a virgin? Would he be more or less likely to regard her with contempt? Would he change his mind? It would probably be worse to tell him she was a freshman.

Jane tripped and fell against him on the stairs, which set them both to giggling, and gave them an opportunity for another friendly hands-on interlude. At the top of the stairs they felt their way along the walls, Tim trying the doorknobs of different rooms. They were all locked. "Well crud," he said, perplexed. Finally one door opened. It was dark inside and they bumped against furniture. "Hold on . . ." Tim felt along the door frame and flipped a light switch, then turned it off again. Jane saw flashbulbs behind her eyes. At least they knew where the bed was, more or less. Jane backed into it and sat, her legs sticking straight out, and Tim tripped over them and they fell into the mattress in a tangle and Jane hit her head on a wall but that was all right because her head was not quite attached to the rest of her by now. She reached up and felt his bristly hair, which was softer than she'd imagined, and then his face was up against hers and his big wet tongue was slathering around inside her mouth.

She didn't dislike this, exactly, but she wasn't transported by it either. She wished everything would slow down so she could take her time with each different sensation: hair, tongue, and so on. But she was losing track of the sequence of events, there was a blinking, staticky quality to her understanding, because her pants and underpants were now off, and Tim was tickling her down there in a way meant to be pleasing, she guessed, but was perhaps too energetic for that, and anyway it was embarrassing, like a doctor's appointment. Her sweater and her bra were still on, which seemed like a mistake: perhaps she should call it to his attention?

"You ready?" His fingers were inside her. At least that made sense. Ready? Excuse me, I don't understand the question. He didn't wait for her to answer, but rolled away from her and put her hand on his penis, which felt like a skin-covered tube with a doorknob on the end. It was so comical! How did men walk around with this branch sticking out of them? She'd only seen pictures before, not the actual item, and it could be argued that she wasn't really seeing this one now, it was too dark in the room.

She had no idea what she was meant to do with it. "How . . ." she began.

"Medium hard, and fast," he directed her, moving her hand up and down, and then she did get the hang of it, a little, and he began breathing and blowing in a loud, alarming way, and then he'd landed on top of her, impossibly heavy. She had to try and reclaim different parts of herself and wiggle loose. Really, there was such a great deal of him, so much in the way of flopping legs and smothering chest. She felt sorry for him, having to inhabit this big, unworkable body.

"Almost forgot." He caught his breath, laughed a little, swung his legs over the bed, and started feeling around. "Give me a sec here, I need my party hat."

Had he gone crazy or something? A hat? A small crinkling, tearing sound and God she was so dumb. She hadn't given one thought to precautions, or all the dire consequences, the warnings that were meant to scare you off, well, too late. She could just barely make him out, sitting and working away at getting the condom on, and she would have liked to see that part, just from curiosity. "Uh, thanks," she said. "It's very . . ." She wanted to say something like chivalrous, but that was stupid. "Cooperative of you," she finished, which was also pretty stupid.

"Safety first," he said cheerfully, and then he was back on top of her, prodding at her with the doorknob end of his thing, and at first it wouldn't go in and then he took hold of himself and it did, a little, and she yelped.

"S'OK," he said, but it wasn't, it hurt, it didn't seem to fit right, and this was beginning to seem like an all around bad idea, shouldn't they talk about it first? He pushed in farther and Jane went *Owowow*, and he raised himself up on his elbows and said, "How about you make less noise and move more?"

He didn't sound mad or anything, more like he was trying to be encouraging. As always when given instructions, she tried to follow them. Moving made it a little better, at least he wasn't just poking at her, but it still didn't feel that good, not something you would do for fun or because of overwhelming passion. Maybe she was frigid. She'd worried about that and now she was pretty sure it was true.

How long was this supposed to go on, anyway? He kept on lifting and spreading her, and she didn't want to be rude or anything, but it really did hurt, she was getting chafed, and she had to pee, she'd been having to for a while now, all that beer. Just when she was about to tell him he had to stop, he snorted and sped up like he was trying to turn her inside out and then he made some of his own noise and that seemed to be it.

She waited a minute, then two. He was flopped on top of her, not moving. "Hey," Jane said, from underneath the dead weight of him. "I have to get up." She felt messy down there, something was leaking out of her. She wondered if she'd already peed. "I have to go to the bathroom. Sorry."

She'd imagined it would be just as tricky for him to get himself out of her as in, like a cork in a bottle, but of course that wasn't how it worked. His penis had deflated in amazing fashion. "Lemme . . ." he said, and she guessed he was holding on to the rubber so it wouldn't come off or spill. There really were a lot of purely awful things you had to think about. He said, "I don't guess there's any Kleenex or anything, oh well . . ."

"I could bring you some," she said, wanting to be helpful.

"No, I got it . . ." He rolled over and tended to himself. "You don't want to let that thing dry on you. You only make that mistake once."

"Oh yeah, ha ha." One more hideous piece of new knowledge. "I really do have to get up now."

"Sure." He leaned down and gave her a brief, smacking kiss. "Hey, this is going to sound really awful, but would you tell me your name again?"

"Shannon," Jane said. Shannon was her roommate's name.

"Hurry on back, Shannon."

It took her a fumbling long time to find everything: pants, underpants, shoes, and another spell to get it all together and find the door. It was one more embarrassment, still sitting there after she'd said she was leaving. "If you need a light . . ." he offered, but that was the last thing she wanted, "No, I'm OK," she said, and in the end she escaped with her underpants wadded up in one hand.

The hallway was darker than she remembered, although the music was still going on, had been playing the whole while. Her legs were shaky. She felt *ravaged*, and she was going to have to decide if that was anything you might eventually feel good about. It was at least better than *deflowered*, which was a completely ignorant word. You might be able to put ravaged on a T-shirt, like the ones you saw people wearing, bragging about how drunk they got at such and such a party or a bar crawl. I got *ravaged* at the Pike Fall Frolic! She had no idea where the bathroom was, but it wasn't going to matter in about two seconds.

Here it was, a wall of urinals and three stalls, each with the doors half torn off and hanging loose. She didn't even want to think about the kinds of things that went on here.

She was lucky, the bathroom was empty. She checked herself, found only a small amount of pinkish blood. Washing her hands at the sink, there was a bad moment when the mirror made her wonder if she had been permanently marked or disfigured, but no, it was only the unaccustomed mascara, which had smeared into black, vampish rings. She scrubbed at them with a brown paper towel.

Back in the hallway she hesitated, not remembering which way she'd come, or which door was the right one. Why hadn't she tried to wear her contacts? She was bat-blind. There was some commotion ahead of her on the staircase, voices shouting, an argument or a good time, and she turned and retreated, still lost. A door opened behind her and a boy stuck his head out. "Hey, where you going?"

She fled. Down a back staircase that led to an empty, institutional kitchen, dim lights above the stainless steel tables, a door marked EXIT in glowing red. Beyond the door, a wooden landing with stairs leading down to a line of dark green rubber trashcans, and that was where Jane came to rest.

No one had followed her. No one was watching. She had ejected herself cleanly. Music still beat beat beat from the party. Other music from other parties boomed, a dull noise, like detonations heard at a distance.

She might have felt bad for Tim, still waiting for her to come back, but decided he really didn't have anything to complain about. She walked to her dorm, feeling cotton-mouthed from the drinking. . . . Beyond worrying about whether or not what she'd done had been success or disaster or brave or idiotic or totally out of character, well yes it was, loomed the fact that it had happened and could not be undone. Actual, if not rational. She found herself thinking of Allen in an unexpected and sentimental way. He'd gone off to college at the University of Chicago. Jane hoped some kindly girl would take him to bed before too much time went by.

Her dorm wasn't far. But once she reached the front door, she didn't go in. It wasn't likely that her roommate was back yet, she might be out all night, but Jane wasn't in the mood to see anybody she knew, not just yet. She circled around to a small sunken garden, bare now except for a ring of boxwoods around its dry fountain. Jane sat down on one of the stone benches, and only when she heard the scratch and saw the flare of a cigarette lighter did she realize she was not alone.

She jumped to her feet. A girl's voice said, "Easy there," and Jane tried to make her feeble eyes work in the gloom. "Didn't mean to startle you. Sit back down, jeez."

Jane sat. The girl was across from her, on the opposite side of the fountain, and Jane couldn't make her out. "Or if you want to be alone, I can split," the girl offered.

"No, that's all right." She did want to be alone. She'd get up in a minute and go inside.

They sat in silence for a time. The girl was smoking some kind of tobacco with a heady smell, and she was using . . . Jane squinted. "Is that a corncob pipe?"

"Uh huh." The little orange fire glowed when she inhaled. A corncob pipe was just one more bizarre thing.

More silence. Jane shifted on the cold stone of the bench. Her invaded parts felt sore and unquiet. She couldn't have said that she missed Tim, but it was a sadness to be alone after being so, whatever it was they'd been. Some version of together. But not entirely together, which was another kind of sadness.

"Rough night?"

"Oh . . ." She had forgotten that she was not, technically, alone. "I guess, I lost my virginity tonight." Why say it? Because she wanted to say it out loud, to somebody, so she could believe it herself.

"Really? Wow, congratulations."

"Yeah, I guess so. Thanks."

"So, not like it's any of my business . . ."

"No, that's OK," Jane said. "I guess I'm still processing it."

"Uh huh. Boyfriend?"

"No, just, more like, a date." That sounded pretty bad. Well, maybe it had been pretty bad. "It wasn't all that much fun."

"Never is, the first time," the girl said, making it sound like she was some kind of expert, a sex researcher, maybe, who went around interviewing people. "Too nervous."

"Yes," Jane agreed, though she'd been more bewildered than nervous. It was reassuring to think that it was just something you had to get through. "It didn't feel especially . . . sexy."

The girl tapped the pipe bowl against the bench and a piece of glowing ember fell out, flared, then darkened. "Oh let me guess, he didn't exactly care what was going on with you. Most of these guys, they're just intervaginal masturbators."

Jane laughed, a squawking sound that she tried to make more ladylike. She sniggered and giggled and hiccupped. "Inter . . . vag . . . oh boy." Perhaps it was something you could laugh about.

With the pipe gone out, the girl's face was easier to see, or at least to locate. A pale, nodding shape. "Yes, just a collection of supercharged, wriggling sperm."

More giggling and squawking. Jane tried to get herself under control. If she kept on laughing, she might end up on some kind of jag, laughing or crying or both. "So, not like it's any of my business, but when you, you know, the first time . . ."

"He was my high school boyfriend. And we'd already spent so much time messing around in all sorts of different ways, I mean, we'd arranged and rearranged our parts so much, when it finally went in it was, whoa, did we just do it? It wasn't like the earth moved or anything. That's from Hemingway, isn't that dumb? What a big barrel of crud that guy was."

Jane didn't say anything. They hadn't gotten to Hemingway yet in class.

"Anyway," the girl went on, "promise you won't buy into the notion that it's some tragic loss. That's just more patriarchal bullshit and commodification of women's bodies."

"I won't," Jane said, feeling as if she had sworn a kind of oath, although to what she was not entirely certain. "Thanks, it helps to talk to somebody who's . . ."

"Depraved?" the girl suggested. "Ah, you just needed a little pep talk."

Had it all really happened? She knew it had, but the very unlikeliness of everything made it hard to fathom, as if she was still up in her dorm room, padding around in sweatpants, and had never gone out and had sex with a stranger. And then talked all about it with another one. Maybe she'd been smarter than she knew, picking a boy she'd likely never see again, keeping it separate from anything fond or emotional. She'd give the borrowed sweater back to her roommate, and if asked how she liked Tim, she'd come up with something about how he seemed nice enough but she'd lost track of him as the evening went on. She stood, ready to go upstairs and get on with it. "Hey, my name's Jane."

"I'm Bonnie," the other girl said, and she stood up also, close enough to a streetlamp for Jane to see her sharp, vivid face, and Jane felt the peculiar inner thrum and hum that told her something else was going to happen here, though she did not yet know what it was.

bonnie

By her senior year of college, Bonnie took to saying that she couldn't wait to get out of the playpen of school and into the real world, even though she did not have any particular destination in the real world.

She had begun college as a Spanish major, since she'd taken Spanish in high school. She thought that perhaps she could go to Spain or South America to study, end up living an expatriate life. That sounded dangerous and glamorous, like Ava Gardner in *The Night of the Iguana*. But her Spanish was not really good enough. Her accent twanged, forever Midwestern. In literature classes, she found herself having to read everything in English to keep up, and even then she didn't much like *Don Quixote*.

Sophomore year she changed her major to psychology, but that disappointed her also. It was mostly behaviorism and statistics, and trying to predict what a rat in a box might or might not do. She had expected to learn about primal drives, the unconscious, dreams and archetypes. But Freud and Jung were now the grandfathers installed in comfortable chairs in the back room while the party went on without them. The courses Bonnie took were all about experiments, and stimulus and response, and, although this was left unsaid, the application of these findings to make more people buy more things.

She found a home in anthropology, where anything and everything human could be studied. She liked the expansiveness of it, trying to figure people out from every conceivable angle, archaeology and biology and culture and linguistics. She liked the assumption that you actually could figure them out.

"You're never going to get a job," Jane said. "There are no jobs called 'anthropologist.' You'll have to go to grad school." Jane was six credit hours away from a degree in public health. There was a clear answer to what you did in public health: improved population-based health services and worked to eradicate disease. "Syphilis and gonorrhea," Bonnie suggested, when she wanted to annoy her. "Pants down for Nurse Jane!" But Jane had interviewed with nonprofits and AIDS organizations and public health programs. She would use her critical thinking and writing skills to craft proposals, grants, public education campaigns. Soon, no doubt, she would be getting job offers, deciding between different rollouts of the Real Job gravy train and functional adulthood.

Clever Jane. Feckless, unemployable Bonnie. Jane, industrious ant, Bonnie, fiddling grasshopper. That was her, yup. But she wasn't ready to give in without an argument. "I can do historic preservation. Environmental issues. Museum work. I'm a generalist."

"You could still do something with computers."

"I'm not one of those business guys." They were class of 1999. The dot-com bubble was still bubbling.

"I didn't say start a business. I said learn a few things about programming. Add to your skill set. They always need people who know computers."

"And when I was heading off to college, one of my aunts told me I should advertise on the dorm bulletin board to do people's mending and alter hems, because people always needed that."

"You're not the mending type," Jane agreed.

"I don't think I'm the computer type either."

"Well you better figure something out, if you don't want to have to move back home."

"Now you're just being mean," Bonnie said.

It was the beginning of their final semester, and they were sitting in the living room of their campus apartment. Outside it was bright and snowless January, the nothing-landscape of the Midwest in winter, brown grass, sticks of trees, pavement. Their apartment was on the third floor of a midrise building of tan brick. An identical tan brick building was visible across a courtyard. Both buildings, and all the other apartment buildings on the block, were occupied by students. Twenty minutes before classes started, the street doors opened and lines of students hitched to backpacks filled the sidewalks.

Bonnie and Jane had lived here more than two years, and although they had put a lot of enthusiasm into decorating and arranging the space, by now it was overfamiliar to the point that neither of them really saw it anymore, and with its stacks of books and CDs and plants and candles and the framed Gauguin prints leaning against the wall so as not to violate the prohibition against putting holes in the walls, it looked a great deal like the apartments of everyone else they knew.

Bonnie was bored with saying she was bored, and waiting for her jobless future to land on her. If nothing else came through, she was going to move to California, where exactly she did not know, and get a job in a bookstore or a coffeehouse or more likely both. The prospect was mildly panic-inducing, but it was a talisman against the used-up feeling of college life.

Bonnie's mother and stepfather, who had paid for her education, wanted to believe it had all been worth it, if not in a strict dollars and cents calculation, at least so they would not have to keep worrying about her. Bonnie's stepfather was a sculptor of large, landscape-sized, beaky-looking metalworks, the kind commissioned by enlightened corporations and civic bodies. Bonnie's mother handled the business end of things, keeping the books and wheedling clients. They wanted Bonnie to have some tangible accomplishment, not just be a student of the human condition, which was the unfortunate flip answer she'd given them the last time they asked. Bonnie liked to make fun of the stepfather's sculptures; she considered them ugly and overpraised. But they were kind of a big deal, getting respectful mention in art journals and bringing in handsome amounts of money. It was confounding, it put her into a false position to be sniping at something massive, tangible, and successful when she had nothing of her own to set against them.

At any rate, she would not be moving back home after graduation, inhabiting a spare bedroom and listening to everybody else's ideas for what she should do with herself. Grad school would be better than that. Of course she had not applied to grad school, so that wasn't an option either.

Jane said, "I don't suppose we could clean the place up some while we're waiting to graduate, you know?"

Meaning, it was Bonnie's turn to vacuum and dust and scrub the toilet. It always seemed to be Bonnie's turn, but that was because Jane was so tidy. Jane wore an apron and rubber gloves to do the dishes, scrubbing away like a housewife on speed. She wiped down refrigerator shelves and even cleaned the top of the refrigerator, which Bonnie regarded as something like the free space in bingo.

"It doesn't look so bad."

"There may not be standards around here, but there are limits."

"All right, fine, memsahib. There shall be clean."

"You know, one reason to get with the program on jobs is so you can hire a maid."

"But most elevated memsahib, do you not understand? Maid will be my job."

"So funny," Jane said. She stood up from the couch and started straightening a toppling pile of magazines. "Jonah's coming over tonight." Jonah was Jane's boyfriend. They were probably going to get married sometime, if she could get Jonah to go along with it.

"Really not much point in cleaning up ahead of time, is there."

"Just do it, please?"

Jane was stomping around the room, or Jane's version of stomping, and looking all furrowed and put out, and Bonnie ventured to ask, "So how is Loverboy?"

"He's just great. Rolls out of bed in the morning, watches SportsCenter, shows up in class, goes home, plays video games, shows up here, eats whatever I put in front of him, and then we go to bed."

"Yeah?" Bonnie prompted her.

Jane gave her an irritated look. "Not everything is about sex, you know."

"My mistake."

"I really do love him, I just wish he was more . . ."

"Don't look at me, I don't want to get in trouble." Jonah had a body like a teddy bear and a halo of dark curly hair. He had trouble with his aim when using the toilet. There were any number of things Bonnie might wish he was more of, or less of, but it was not always wise to express these.

"We're really comfortable together."

Bonnie waited for it.

"Maybe too comfortable," Jane added, after a beat or two.

"You mean, bored. So all right, what do you want to do about it?"

"I don't know." Jane stopped her pissed-off circuit around the room and stood, swaying a little. She was wearing a pair of unfashionable, waist-high jeans. She had a boy's meager butt and hips. She'd cut her hair short, a blond fringe. It made her look like a Scandinavian athlete who excelled in some minor winter sport. "I guess when we graduate, we'll end up going off in different directions anyway."

"Leave it up to inertia," Bonnie suggested.

"I thought I wanted to marry him."

"No, you just thought you wanted to get married. Uh oh, here it comes. Don't give me the look of loathing. Don't tell me this stuff if you don't want to hear my opinion."

Jane sat down on the orange tweed chair they'd bought for a joke, no longer funny. "You think I should go ahead and break up with him now?"

"I think we need the wisdom of the elders here," Bonnie said, getting up and going into her bedroom.

"Oh God, not the stupid comic books again."

Bonnie returned with a handful of tattered and gnawed-looking magazines. "Here we go. 'From the strange turmoil in a woman's heart comes the question, "Can I Forget You?"'"

"Crap." Jane slid deeper into the orange upholstery.

"This is from 'Love Diary,' January 1950, Quality Romance Publications, illustrated. Here's one about a lumberjack. Do we know any lumberjacks? 'Though I shrank from the look in his eye, in my heart I desired his kisses, and I knew that I was . . . Afraid to Love!'"

"I'm begging you, stop."

"'Dear Diary, I can't understand what's happened to me! I thought I had my emotions under rigid control . . . that no one could turn me away from the kind of life I chose for myself! But then along came Jack Banton . . . a big, burly galoot . . .' Do people say that anymore? Galoot? '. . . and all my plans were blown sky high!' You should see this guy, he looks like a gay pin-up. And she's got these pneumatic tits. She's yelling at him 'Did you hear what I said? Take your hands off me!' Then he says, 'Take it easy, sister! I guess they forgot to tell you in finishing school that up here in the north woods, women don't give the orders!' Now honestly, doesn't that give you a little retrograde thrill?"

"Sure. Domestic violence always does."

"See, she thinks she's in love with her city-slicker boyfriend, but then Jack dives into the river to rescue her from a log jam."

"What's she doing in a log jam?"

"Unclear. So he pulls her out of the river and takes her back to his cabin, and would you believe he has a bookshelf full of Shakespeare and Thackeray. He's a self-educated diamond in the rough!"

"The Thackeray is overkill."

"Agreed. Well, you can guess the rest. She breaks up with the city slicker. His name is Jonah."

"It is not."

"Now, what have we learned from this story?"

"We should head for the north woods and jump in a river."

"Correct. OK, here's another: 'Office Cinderella.' 'Just be patient, Sally. When we're married I want to support my wife! I don't want to share her with a boss!'"

"It's hard to find great guys like that nowadays."

"How about this one: 'Gee, Ruth, I thought you understood. I'm crazy about you, but well, a guy doesn't like it when a girl is smarter than he is about everything.'"

"Sound of vomiting."

"This is from 'Western Love Stories.' 'Can a girl be a sheriff and forget that she is a woman? Lucy performed her duties very efficiently until she had to arrest Dave Ringo, and then she was all woman.' Dave Ringo! I bet you money that's not his real name."

Jane wriggled herself upright again. "Maybe you could get a job as a sheriff."

"I think I'd like that. These comics have some great ads. The 'Up-And-Out Bra,' with a testimonial by Miss Doris Harris, Wichita, Kansas. Her new, attractive bustline has given her poise and confidence. Or perhaps, Jane, your problem is tormenting foot itch?"

"Why did you buy these wretched things?"

"I swear, the only thing that's changed in fifty years is reliable contraception. Don't get me wrong, that's not nothing. Why aren't there any romance magazines for men?"

"They're called pornography."

"Seriously, don't men fall in love? Are they embarrassed about it? What about love poems and love songs, do they write them just so they can get laid? It's very discouraging."

"Don't forget to take the garbage out," Jane said, getting up.

So Bonnie resigned herself to cleaning. After Jane left for class, she started in on the bathroom, clearing away all the shampoos and styling products and skin scrubs and toothpaste, the eyelash curlers and lip gloss, all the products with hopeful names, meant to evoke, variously, meadows, jungles, deserts, breezes sultry or fresh, innocence or ripeness. Vanity vanity vanity. Would she be any happier with blotchy skin and fuzzy hair? No. It was one more discouraging thing.

Bonnie took a sponge and Comet to the shower, and yes, there did seem to be more of her own hair clogging the drain than Jane's, as Jane often noted. She had thick, coiling dark hair, always falling forward into her eyes. There was too much of it, just as, it sometimes seemed, there could be too much of Bonnie.

"You're like, a sexual predator," Jane told her once, meaning it mostly, but not entirely, as an insult. "Why thank you," Bonnie had answered, because what else could you say, really. By now she knew she was different from most women, not even necessarily more juiced up, because how did you measure such things anyway, but willing to go to greater and more outlandish lengths, have the wrong kind of boyfriends and the wrong kind of sex and go about things all wrong so that more often than not her romances ended in wreckage and despair.

She wouldn't have said she was in love with every one of them, but often enough she was, and often enough love, or keening lust, or mad impulse overwhelmed her in ways that confounded and embarrassed her and led her to all manner of bad behavior, including, but not limited to, drama, indiscretion, urgent phone calls, reckless trysts, peering through windows at night, crying fits (on sidewalks, in bars, in a hospital emergency room), outlandish couplings (including in a parked VW Beetle, but that was only the once), and breaking and entering (once or possibly twice, even if that particular time she had not meant to go inside, only heave a chunk of rock through a glass door).

These were the things that she had told Jane, or that Jane had witnessed, although there were some further incidents that Bonnie had not shared.

What was wrong with her? She was always too impatient to sit back and wait for boys to come calling, or those who did call didn't please or interest her. She was too full of longing, she wanted what she wanted and saw no reason not to pursue it, and of course she scared the crap out of most guys. Not one of whom was a burly lumberjack who owned a shelf of Great Books. Laugh all you wanted at the old, sappy stories with their cartoon faces and cartoon hairstyles, and all the while sex like a dog under the dinner table, fed in sly handfuls. Hilarious, cornball, a triumph of repression aided by industrial-strength lingerie! But everybody wanted the dream, the fantasy, the happy ending, and in spite of it everybody wanted the dream, the fantasy, the happy ending, and that included her, no matter how much she mocked them.

Jane thought that Bonnie was too often unrealistic, that she expected too much. "You put so much energy into chasing these guys, you keep trying to turn them into something they aren't. Maybe you should just calm down some. They don't have to like, make your toes curl every time, do they?"

How funny it was that they had met on the occasion of Jane's single most transgressive act, the removal of her virginity by some drunken character she couldn't have picked out of a police lineup. Which must have scared Jane away from doing anything so bold ever again, because instead she had a series of boyfriends, each more dreary than the last, the soon-to-be discarded Jonah the latest.

Anyway, it was time to get her head out of her ass, stop thinking about boys, in comic books or out of them, and figure some way to make a living.

Bonnie moved on to the kitchen. The stove needed degreasing. The inside of the microwave looked like a miniature crime scene. She hauled the kitchen garbage out from under the sink and started a new bag. Set the morning's oatmeal bowl to soak, swept and mopped the floor. She wasn't enjoying it, exactly, but there was an energy to it that carried you along. She would have sung a work song, if she'd known any, something about hoeing cotton or hauling in fishing nets.

She took the garbage down to the outside bins, not bothering to lock the apartment door behind her, and when she came back, and was wrestling the vacuum cleaner out of the hall closet, she looked up to find a man standing in the passageway.

"Hey!" she said, more of a yelp than a word. At first glance Bonnie took him for a student, but no, he was older, rougher and shabbier, tall and thin, with his hands jammed into the pockets of his coat. The coat, she noticed, as if this were important, was the same kind as her old high school boyfriend once had, with a facing of soiled fake sheepskin. "Hey, what are you doing?"

"Terry live here?" he asked, looking not at Bonnie, but at the floor near his own feet. He had a long, hollowed-out face, and droopy blond hair.

"No, you have the wrong apartment." She waited for him to do something, say something. "So you need to get out of here."

"Terry back there?" he asked, nodding at the rooms behind her and taking a step toward her. He was between her and the door. Bonnie shoved the vacuum cleaner into the hallway and that checked him. He took one hand out of his pocket. He held a knife with a short, thick, sharp blade. Bonnie's brain spun like a dial. She could almost hear it making clicking sounds. She was unable to fathom the idea of the knife, of it actually doing something to her.

So out of pure and stupid reflex she said, "Would you at least get out of the way so I can vacuum?" And bumped the machine toward him.

He took a few steps back. "Go on," Bonnie said. "Give me some space here." She stooped down, plugged the vacuum in, turned it on, and advanced on him. It was an old machine and it made a lot of racket, vrooming and hooming.

Together they rounded the corner and Bonnie ran the vacuum energetically over the nubby carpet. The man watched her. The hand with the knife hung at his side. Bonnie was aware of some bodily process happening to her from the skin out, a coldness, a quivering, traveling inward in rapid waves, until her heart was squeezing through some painful cold.

The vacuum went quiet. He had pulled the plug.

Bonnie wheeled behind her, retreating into the kitchen portion of the main room, and opened the refrigerator. "Hey, you want a beer?" As long as she kept moving, talking, she felt, nothing bad would happen. "Bud Light OK?" She took out two cans of beer and set one on the counter closest to him. "Come on, man, have a drink with me."

He looked at the beer can, then down at the knife in his hand, as if asking its opinion. His long, oddball face and long hair made him look as if he'd been stretched out, like kids' clay. Bonnie sat down at the kitchen table and opened her own beer. "Make yourself at home," she said, idiotically.

He picked up the beer with his free hand, then laid the knife down on the counter to open it. The kitchen was small, and he stood maybe ten feet away from her. Only the dinky table was between them. Bonnie raised her beer and sloshed some into her mouth, swallowed. She watched him drink, then he set the can down again, next to the knife. He wasn't looking at her, he still hadn't looked directly at her. His face had a blank, unseeing quality, or else he was seeing something nobody else did, submerged beneath layers of murky impulse. "So who's Terry?" Bonnie asked, trying to nudge him toward the surface. "Do I know Terry?" Man or woman Terry? Did it matter? Her heart hurt. It was bruised from all the work of beating. The advice of a million dopey magazines, generations of true romance, slipped into a groove in her dumb brain: Show an interest in what he says! Be an active listener! But why was it always the girl who had to make all the effort at conversation? She said, "I'm really thinking you need to check the address again."

He took another drink. It made him cough and sputter, as if it had gone down the wrong way, and he leaned on the counter, trying to recover. "Whoa," Bonnie said. "Easy there."

His jaw worked as he tried to set himself to rights. "Goddamn," he said, still coughing.

"Sometimes it helps if you hold your breath." She demonstrated, puffing her cheeks out.

"Goddamn sheriff took my dogs away and the county had them put down."

And what did the moron magazines tell you to say to that? Like dating advice or makeup ads were enough to keep you from getting raped and murdered in your own kitchen. Bonnie felt her face attempting a number of false emotions all at once: sympathy, interest, indignation on his behalf. See, nice person! Friend! Not that he was paying any real attention to her. There was something wrong with his mouth, something loose, like a baby's.

Bonnie started to say she liked dogs, and that's when the man said, "Stupid bitch." Spitting the words out like seeds.

Who did he mean? Her, Bonnie? The sheriff? Somebody else, maybe even an actual female dog? And because there was no way of knowing, and what difference would it make anyway, Bonnie said, "She shouldn't have done those things she did."

"Goddamn," he said again, and this time it sounded like agreement. He lifted the beer can once more and drank it down. Bonnie got up and fetched another from the refrigerator. She put this one a little farther away on the counter, so that he'd have to take a step away from the front door. A part of her mind was working furiously, wondering if she might be able to get to the door, or scream, and would anyone hear, and when was Jane due home, and how would that even help, since Jane would just stand there pie-eyed, a born victim.

But another part of her was curious in spite of or because of everything: who was he and what made him crazy and dangerous and had he always been that way. She said, "I guess she made you real mad. Hey, what's your name? I'm Bonnie. Are you hungry? How about I fix you a sandwich? Turkey and Swiss OK?"

Rattling on. He didn't answer, just opened the new beer and drank from it. He watched as Bonnie moved around the kitchen, yanking bread, plates, the rest that she needed. She made up the sandwich with plenty of everything, mayo, lunchmeat, cheese. Cut it nicely on the diagonal and emptied a bag of potato chips into a bowl. "Here you go," she said, setting it all down on the table and moving out of the way, just a bit closer to the door. "Oh, wait. Napkin."

Now he was looking at her, which might or might not turn out to be a good thing. He picked up the knife and the beer and sat down in front of the sandwich, stared at it. "Whadja put on this?"

"Just mayonnaise."

"Mayonnaise's all right I guess," he said, and bent over the plate, using both hands to get as much food as he could into his mouth.

Bonnie said, "Do I know you from someplace? You go to the bars or anything?"

He didn't answer, still working on the sandwich. You saw guys like him on campus often enough, panhandlers or criminals or both, homeless or close to it, hanging around because students were stupid and careless and easy pickings, well she sure was, why hadn't she locked the damned door behind her and taken her keys? She tried again. "You from around here?"

He was eating the chips now, crunching them by the handful. She was running out of things to feed him, inane questions to ask him. She ducked around the table, keeping it between them, and ran water in the sink. "Mind if I clean up some?"

He didn't answer. He was sucking bits of food from the inside of his mouth. Bonnie opened the cupboard under the sink and put on Jane's big green rubber gloves. It was comforting, putting this extra, protective layer over her skin. "Yeah, it's my turn to, you know, shovel the place out." He wasn't paying her any particular attention; why should he? She was just some random body, currently making noise. Beneath the sink were the usual scrubbers and sponges and soaps, when what she really needed was a baseball bat, or the sort of things they made weapons out of on television, batteries and matchsticks and chewing gum. All she could find was a spray bottle of some vile mildew remover Jane had bought for the bathroom. It had a reassuring trigger grip and she set it out on the counter with one green-gloved hand. "Not that most of the mess isn't mine. Not all of it. Most."

The man shifted around in his chair and the plates on the table jumped. "You sure run your mouth a lot."

"I do. Nervous habit." Was he angry? She guessed she should shut up now but she couldn't stop, because they might be the last words she ever said, aside from those things he might soon make her say. "I really think men and women speak different languages. I bet if you did a scientific study you could prove it. Because men aren't socialized to talk about emotions, relationships, I get that, but see, women can't leave that stuff alone, we want men to pay attention to us. The right kind of attention." Not the breaking and entering and assault kind. "I mean"—Bonnie's breath ran out; she stopped her babbling to pry her lungs open—"did you and her have some kind of fight? What happened?"

"Her and her big deal friends."

"Ah," Bonnie said, nodding.

"They was always against me."

Right, because what could any fair-minded person object to? "They ganged up on you," Bonnie suggested.

"The law took her side too. Like a man doesn't have a right to live under his own roof."

His hand on the table was a fist now. Behind her back, Bonnie made a green rubber fist with one hand. She said, "But there must have been things you liked about her; it wasn't all bad, was it?"

He didn't answer right away, but gave her another glance that had some seeing in it. Like, what was Bonnie doing here in the middle of his righteous grievances? Bonnie said, "I mean, maybe the two of you could make up." Unless he had already murdered her. "A fresh start. Sort of like cleaning house." She picked up the bottle of cleanser and waved it around. "Everybody cops to their share of the dirt, you know?"

He said, "How is it a woman always thinks she can talk her way out of anything."

She was quiet then. He tipped the can up to empty it. A little of the beer dribbled past the loose corner of his mouth. He wiped at it with the back of his hand and pushed his chair away and patted at the pockets of his coat, looking for something. Not the horrible knife, it was right there in front of him on the table. Cigarettes? Her high school boyfriend, the one who'd had the same kind of coat, had smoked, and they used to argue about it because Bonnie said the smell got into her hair and clothes. They'd gone round and round about it. Of course the cigarettes were just an excuse to argue about everything they couldn't put into words, how their bodies bewildered them, now impossibly close, now separating into two contrary creatures, so that there was always longing and always the confusion of feeling. They had been so young! His name was Eddie. Where was he now, she didn't know; he'd moved away and she'd lost track. She would have liked to find him again and tell him, what, what, what had she learned in all this time? She burst into sudden, noisy tears.

"Now quit that," the man said, annoyed. "It's not needed."

"It doesn't have anything to do with you." Bonnie reached for a paper towel and blew her nose.

"Oh, hah."

"I don't care if you believe me or not. I was thinking about my very first boyfriend, well not very first, but the first important one, and how we really did love each other but we were too young and I guess angry to know it."

"What a woman means by 'love' is 'give me all your money,'" he pronounced, sneering.

"That is so unfair. And I'm sorry, I don't believe you. You wouldn't be so"—so criminally vicious?—"upset if you and whoever she is hadn't started out with some kind of love." The crying had clogged up her nose. She reached for another paper towel and honked into it.

"She sure didn't seem to mind driving my car. Emptying out my wallet."

At least he was having an actual conversation, not just muttering grievances. Bonnie said, "Well, I never took anybody's money. I never went out with anybody for their money."

Sneering again. "Then somebody got himself a good deal."

"Wait, I get it. You think women trade sex for money! That is totally, totally insulting!"

"Yeah," he said, but it was as if he was losing patience with talk. Maybe she should not have said "sex."

"So you're mad because things didn't work out, and because it cost you money."

"None of your business."

"I'm just trying to figure things out," Bonnie said, and then there was a silence. She would scream, if she had to. Scream and scream. He rubbed at his eyes, yawned. Maybe he was just sleepy? Or on some kind of crazy-making drugs? She should have thought of drugs right away. She watched his head nod lower, hoping he'd just nod off.

But he jerked himself awake and said, "I allow that a mother loves her child. But that's the whole of it."

"You are so, so wrong."

"It's all about what a woman wants to get off a man. And what a man wants to get off a woman," he said, looking Bonnie over in a nasty way, which she pretended not to notice.

"All right, so, there's no such thing as unselfish love. There's just greed and lust and narcissism."

"What the hell's that mean."

"Narcissism? That's basically when you're in love with yourself."

"You learn that in college, huh?"

Ignoring him, Bonnie said, "According to you, everybody who thinks they're in love is either a liar or a fool. That's nice. That's real healthy."

"You can shut up any time now."

"No, see, I get it with all you guys, love is unmanly! Because it involves loss of control, sure! Think of all the crazy things you do when you're in love, you like, humiliate yourself and talk baby talk and, well, I'm not even going to tell you some of the things I've done. It's so much easier to say it's all about sex, because that involves these fantasies of conquest and domination—"

He actually put his hands over his ears then. Bonnie went on, half inspired, half just making noise. "—and I guess that's why you go looking for women you can victimize, because there's not any emotional component, the part that's so difficult if it's a true peer relationship. I don't suppose you have any gay male friends?"

"Who you calling gay?" he said, the blurry look coming into his eyes again, and right then the door to the apartment opened and Jane and Jonah came in.

"Hey," Jane began, and then the two of them stopped short, taking things in. They had been to the Karmelkorn shop and they were both holding bags of popcorn, as if they had just walked into a movie.

Bonnie grabbed the mildew remover, aimed, and pulled the trigger. The bottle sputtered. A little foam dribbled out and over her rubber glove, and they all stared at that.

The man cleared his throat. "OK if I use your bathroom?"

"Sure," Bonnie said. "Thataway."

He got up and squeezed past Jane and Jonah, who shuffled together to give him room. He left the knife on the kitchen table.

The bathroom door shut behind him. "Really?" Jane said. "I mean, he's kind of on the scabby side. Where did you meet him?"

Bonnie hissed at her to shut up. The toilet flushed. "Open the front door, stay out of his way."

The man came back into the room, looked around at the three of them as if he'd asked a question and was waiting for the answer. "Bye," Bonnie said melodiously. "Take it easy."

He took his time leaving. When he was gone, Bonnie said, "Shut the door, lock it!"

Jane looked out into the hallway, then closed the door and turned the latch. "No offense, but I kind of hope you broke up with him."

Jonah wandered over to the kitchen table, munching popcorn. His cheeks bulged as he chewed. Bonnie supposed she ought to be grateful to him, since only a male presence had scared her visitor away. But he was so perfectly and willfully dull, such a well-kept animal. Was it wrong to expect so much more from a man? He picked up the knife. "Hey, what's this?" he said, through crumbs.

Bonnie said, "Would one of you knuckleheads call the police? Never mind. I'll do it myself."

This was how she came to work in the field of crisis intervention.

jane gets married

That May, for some number of days, if Jane woke at a certain time and the weather was clear, the bedroom walls were lit with her own private sunrise. The house was a rental, but the landlord allowed them to paint, and Jane had chosen this pretty cream color for the room. Now, on these mornings, the cream took on shades of apricot, rose, and gold, one melting into the other, washes and tints of unnerving beauty, the colors of heaven. Jane watched from bed, as still as if she had sighted a rare bird on a tree branch. Because it was for a few moments only, this gift of light, nothing you could hold in place. Even as she tried to fix it in her mind, make a memory of it, the sun brightened and flared, or went behind a cloud, and then it would be time to get up and go about her day.

Eric would already be up and gone, making his early hospital rounds. He was a first-year resident and he worked punishing hours. Jane had the house to herself a lot, which she understood was necessary, given the high seriousness of medicine. She was bored rather than resentful; they had not had any other kind of married life together so there was nothing else to compare it to. They were trying to put together some time off next month, a break from everything hasty and rushed and undone.

This was now her life, her world, herself. So much had changed. Even the air in her lungs felt different, breathing in so much busy newness.

.   .   .

They had been married in cold December, the week before Christmas. December was the only free time she and Eric had to get married and move seven hundred miles away, given all the complications of Eric's work schedule. The date was the closest they could come to obliging everyone else's travel and holiday plans. Still, their families greeted the invitation with an undercurrent of exasperation. No one said it quite this way, but a wedding was one more claim on their time during this busy season.

"Don't come if you can't fit it in," Eric told his relatives, meaning it. One of the things Jane admired about him: he said what he thought, he wasn't forever worrying about what people thought of him, like she did. Jane assured her family that it was only a little old wedding, nothing grand, and would not seriously inconvenience anyone. They were paying for everything themselves. Jane was twenty-five, Eric twenty-six. It had not seemed right to ask her parents for a wedding at this age, although it was true they did not have much money. Eric's medical school loans were going to be around for a while. But Jane did not want battles over what things cost, or her many mistaken choices regarding dress, music, food, and so on. It was surely not the last occasion her family would feel entitled to boss her around, but one of the big ones. Eric, like most grooms, just wanted to get things over with.

In the end, everyone came. They found a Methodist chapel that was available to the unchurched, along with a pastor who made the most tactful references to God, along the lines of God equals universe. There were not enough guests to fill the sanctuary, so they were seated in the choir stalls on both sides of the altar, and eyed each other like the fans of two opposing football teams. A guitarist and a fiddler, friends of theirs, served up winsome Appalachian tunes. Eric wore a suit, Jane a lace skirt and a frilled blouse. She carried a bouquet of evergreens and Christmas roses. She had one attendant, a nineteen-year-old cousin.

Bonnie had been emphatic about not standing up at the wedding. "I'll do whatever else you want. I'll laugh at your dad's jokes. I'll dance the Hokey Pokey—"

"No one will be dancing the Hokey Pokey."

"—but I'm sorry, you know weddings make me itch. People should just go to the courthouse and recite the ordinance. Weddings are all about the commodification of women, with these awful subtexts of submission and subordination. I'm really happy for you, by the way."

"Thanks," Jane said. "Just show up, OK?" It was actually something of a relief not to have Bonnie as a member of the wedding party, since now she would not have to worry about Bonnie drinking too much, or wearing something with fringe or feathers, or flirting with a randy old uncle, or rather, she might still worry about such things but they would not have official, ceremonial status.

As it happened, Bonnie was no problem. She wore a printed jersey dress, drank her portion of domestic champagne from a plastic glass, and did indeed laugh at Jane's father's jokes. True, she did ask Jane, as she was making herself ready in the church basement, "Want me to talk you out of it?" But that was just another joke, ha ha, meant to steady Jane as she was being fussed over by her female relatives.

"Now Bonnie, don't even say such a thing," said Jane's mother, dabbing at Jane's face with a Kleenex. "What was that horrible movie? With what's-her-name?"

"*Runaway Bride*," Bonnie said. "Julia Roberts. It's all right, she really did get married in *Steel Magnolias*. Of course, later she died."

"You're not helping," Jane's mother said. "Don't mind her, Jane dear. She's only trying to be funny to soothe your nerves."

Jane lifted her forearm to deflect the Kleenex. "Please don't do that, unless I have dirt on my face." In fact Jane was, if not entirely nerveless, distracted. The day after tomorrow she and Eric were renting a U-Haul truck, loading it with their boxed belongings, and moving themselves from Chicago to Atlanta, where Eric had already begun his residency, and Jane would start the job that had been found for her at Emory. Any honeymoon would have to be deferred. So that instead of approaching her vows in the proper bridal swoon, a part of Jane's attention was still given over to checklists with subheadings like Bank, Utilities, and Packing Tape.

Jane's mother and the attendant cousin and the cousin's mother, Jane's aunt, did their best to prod at her and perfect her, but there was no veil or train, no borrowed pearls or something blue, just Jane in her pieced-together costume, wishing, mildly, that she was not the center of attention. "Do you want a 7UP to settle your stomach?" Jane's mother asked, and Jane said no thanks, and her mother took this to mean that Jane needed something else instead, a Diet Coke? Perhaps her mouth was dry? It wouldn't do to get up there and not be able to recite her vows. "Cough drop? Maybe just an ice cube to suck on?"

"Xanax?" Bonnie offered, wriggling an eyebrow to show that she had some on her. Jane shook her head.

"Go on upstairs and tell them I'm ready." Bonnie gave her a finger wave and headed out.

"I wish I'd thought of Xanax," the aunt said. "It really hits the spot. All I have is aspirin. Alex, it's time to put that thing away," she said to her daughter, who was still hooked up to her iPod.

"I'm fine," Jane said stolidly. In her mind the fuss of getting married was just that, because the hard part of things, finding Eric, the two of them finding each other, had already been accomplished. But she did feel a tug of anxiety, wanting to see him, wanting to make sure that in spite of everything, plighting their troth, buying rings, signing leases and all the rest, he had not somehow decided he'd made a mistake and changed his mind. "Let's move," she said, getting a good grip on her bouquet.

They passed through a hallway filled with stacks of retired hymnals. Up the stairs. Jane and the cousin hung back while their mothers took their seats. Jane tried to see around her cousin's now-unencumbered ear, saw nothing but the half-lit sanctuary and its rows of vacant pews. The musicians took up a new tune, not "The Wedding March," but some Scotch-Irish stand-in. Jane gave the cousin a nudge and they moved forward. And there Eric was, all dressed-up and handsome in his gray suit, outright grinning at her. Jane grinned back. The rest would be easy. A walk in the park. "Dearly beloved . . ."

Later, at the reception (pizza and homemade cake at a friend's apartment), Jane and Eric stood, arms entwined, happy, tired, gamely smiling. There was a sense that perhaps they had done something extraordinary and important, but that they would have to wait until they were alone to be certain. Eric's parents—her in-laws! She had in-laws!—kept drifting up to them and attempting conversation. Eric was their only child, and they felt bereft. "I can't believe we're going to have to spend Christmas without you," the mother-in-law said.

"Mom, it can't be helped. Anyway, it's practically Christmas now."

"Well it's not Christmas Christmas," the mother-in-law said, tearily, giving Jane an aggrieved look. Jane, mortified, smiled harder.

Jane's father and brother sat on the couch, watching a basketball game while her mother roamed the kitchen, looking for things to clean. The musicians were off-duty, and someone had put on a hip-hop tape, probably trying to get rid of the parents. Bonnie strolled up to them, glass in hand. "Why don't you do the cake thing?"

The cake was chocolate, and the baker had aspired to three layers but settled for a lopsided two. Some of Eric's old soccer club friends had procured a cake topper in the shape of a soccer player fleeing, being tackled by a bride in full dress. Good old Jane laughed along with everyone else. But why was it assumed that she was the one catching Eric? Even if he was a doctor, even if that was how everybody saw it. Wasn't there some more refined tradition, in which the gentleman pursued the lady, paid her court, won her hand, and then was congratulated on his good fortune?

"We're not going to feed each other cake," Eric announced, in case anyone was expecting it. No one seemed to be. Their friends were all smart, modern. Not that many of them had married yet themselves, but they were not inclined to follow a lot of used-up customs like smashing cake into each other's faces, or the groom taking off the bride's garter, even if Jane had worn such a thing as a garter. Jane supposed she might have to throw her bouquet, though there wasn't much clearance in the apartment. She would worry about that later, along with everything else she had to worry about. Now she concentrated on cutting an acceptable slice of cake, Eric's hand on the knife alongside her own. The cake was delicious, everyone agreed, and if it was a bit crumbly, that didn't interfere with taste.

The family members ate their cake and began to migrate doorward. "Call us," Jane's mother said, kissing her. "Oh, I wish you weren't going so far away!"

Oh, but she was glad she was. She was ready to be someone else, not the focus of everyone's worry and exasperation, Jane the difficult, the delicate, the droopy. Someone she could only be in her new estate, one half of this new and splendid creature, a married couple.

The parents, both sets of them, shook hands with each other and said they'd be seeing each other again before too long, and then retreated to their own cars to nurse their private opinions of each other. Behind them, the party loosened up, grew louder. Jane took off her shoes, Eric his tie, and when a slower, smokier song came on, they danced in the center of the small living room, to general applause.

They collapsed onto the couch, breathless, happy, beginning to think about the end of the evening, of going home together to the packed-up apartment and making love. They squeezed hands, meaning they wouldn't stay that much longer.

The best man, one of Eric's med school friends, said that he guessed he should propose a toast. That was what you did at weddings, even one as marginally traditional as this one. "To Eric and Jane," he announced, holding his plastic cup on high. He was a little drunk, as were they all. "They go together like, wait, I got this. Like . . ." He shook his head owlishly.

"Like Bonnie and Clyde," someone suggested.

"No, not them."

"Roy Rogers and Dale Evans. And maybe Trigger."

"You guys, just let me finish, OK?" The best man lowered his glass to take a drink, then stopped himself and raised it again. "Eric, Jane, the two of you are meant to be together, because who else would put up with Eric? Jane, don't let him get away with any shit. I know you think he's a nice guy, but soon the scales will fall from your eyes. Jane, I don't know you that well, but there's probably something wrong with you too."

Somebody said, "What exactly are we drinking to here?"

"Alcohol and happiness," the best man declared, but the group voted to edit that to just happiness.

"To happiness!" They toasted, drank, and cheered. The maid of honor had departed along with her mother, but Bonnie stood up next.

"I'd give you guys advice, but you can sum it all up as: 'Men are stupid, women are crazy!'"

And they all drank to that too. Bonnie sat down next to Jane on the couch. She'd been dancing and she smelled of cologne and sweat. Her hair had broken loose from any gels or sprays and assumed its default position, falling into her eyes. "So how does it feel?"

"Brand new," Jane said. But it was more than that; she felt as if she were carrying something both heavy and fragile, and if she lost her grip, it would shatter. "God, I wish we weren't moving right away," she said, because she didn't want to talk about what was closest and keenest, so she fell back into perfunctory complaints. "There's still so much to do."

"Want me to come over after work tomorrow?"

"Thanks, but we have to take some boxes to Eric's parents, stuff we don't have room for."

"It really is a shame you won't get to spend Christmas with them."

Jane gave her the shut up look. A new, cautionary thought came to her. "Honey," she said to Eric, sitting on her other side, "your mother isn't expecting us for dinner tomorrow, is she?"

Eric groaned. "I'll call her. Remind me."

Bonnie leaned around Jane to talk to him. "Hey Eric, I have this pain in my ass, do you think it's serious?"

"Probably. I expect you'll have to have surgery. A radical ass-ectomy."

The music started up again and Bonnie had to shout to be heard. "So, can you recommend a good ass man?"

Jane said, "You don't have to answer that. In fact, better you don't." The two of them got along famously, like a pair of thirteen-year-old boys.

Whatever Eric might have said, he was interrupted by another of the med school friends coming up to talk to him. Bonnie sat back again. "It can be so difficult to find good medical care," she remarked.

Eric was the first of Jane's boyfriends that Bonnie liked. This was hard for Jane to get her mind around. Did that mean Bonnie had been right all along when she disapproved of the others? "He's cute," Bonnie pronounced, after she'd met Eric for the first time. "He looks like an intelligent chocolate Lab." And he did, a little, with his friendly brown eyes and upturned nose. "And he's a bit arrogant, which I think you have to be if you're going to be a doctor and do all those life and death things."

"Self-confident, not arrogant," Jane said.

"I meant, arrogant in a good way. He's a solid guy. Not one of those weedy, whiny ones who you'd end up supporting because they're so terribly unfulfilled."

Bonnie, as always, was some combination of irritating and accurate. Eric was, if not arrogant, at least ambitious, diligent, focused. Each step of medical training was a competition, everything scored and ranked, everything depended on admissions, or rejections. Eric took to it all, thrived. Jane had never known anyone like him.

"You mean," Jane said, "he's not like Adam." Adam had been her last serious boyfriend before Eric.

"Adam was not what you would call a man of action."

"More like an action figure," Jane agreed.

"Wasn't there something wrong with his gums? I always insist on good periodontal health, no matter what else is lacking."

"Someday," Jane told her, "you're going to fall in love with the really, really wrong guy."

"But meanwhile, there are so many delightfully wrong guys out there for me."

She and Bonnie didn't see that much of each other these days. Bonnie lived in the city, in Wicker Park, and spent her days doing training and simulations for cops and firefighters, also the occasional ride-alongs when they had to deal with the dope sick, the pillheads, the unmedicated homeless or people who were blasted out of their minds on street drugs or alcohol, or some combination of all of the above. She had her share of war stories. The naked guy, the Jesus guy (there were several of these), the guy with a dozen fishhooks impaled in his face. The mother holding a knife to her baby's throat, the guy pulling behind him a stuffed cat on wheels. The job was a good fit for Bonnie. She had an affinity for the outlandish and the downright dangerous, she was unafraid of them, she spoke their language. She could help people who didn't especially want to be helped. She was dating a cop at present but she had not brought him to the wedding because, she said, he was not the kind of guy you took to weddings. Jane wondered what was wrong with this one.

Jane, meanwhile, lived in Evanston and worked for a nonprofit that was doing a study of blood banks. (She was a vampire, Eric teased.) She distributed questionnaires—*How does your facility do outreach? Do you target specific populations?*—she gathered data, she wrote reports. She got used to the sight of blood, at least, as it was stored in refrigerated plastic units, those cold liquid jewels. She had friends from work and often on weekends they went out for drinks or dinners. From time to time she took the sort of classes that were meant to give you a better mind in a better body: tai chi, journal writing, cookery.

Sometimes she was lonely, sometimes she was merely alone. Her occasional boyfriends were just placeholders, nobody you might consider as the companion of your life or even a considerable portion of that life. Because she did want to get married, she did want kids, all the things everybody wanted and you did not wish to miss out on them.

But at odd and unpredictable moments she might have a sensation— the shadow of a sensation—as of something sliding away beneath her, jarring loose—the familiar become strange. Had her repaired heart sprung a leak, begun sending electrical short circuits into her brain? She wondered, but she didn't tell anybody. She didn't want to get caught up in some medical juggernaut of CT scans and EKGs and galvanic skin responses, all the tests that ruled things out but ruled nothing in and ended up with a prescription for anxiety medication. What would she tell them anyway? They wanted a list of symptoms: dizziness, blurred vision, palpitations. You could not say, it is a different life trying to nudge this one aside. I am meant to be living that different life. Who would understand that, if she could make no better sense of understanding it herself?

∞

The sunrise colors began so imperceptibly, she could never catch the exact moment when the wall began to change. It broke over her and over and over and over, every day, for a suspended instant of ecstasy.

∞

She and Eric met when they were both standing in line for the bathroom at a party, and although Eric was ahead of her he stepped aside when the door opened. "Ladies first," he said, bowing her in, and she guessed that was polite, even gallant, but she didn't like the idea that he was standing outside and hearing her pee. She had to run water in the sink before she could go. Of course he was right there when she came out and she blushed and tried to walk sideways past him. But he said, "Wait for me, OK?" She retreated far enough so that she would not have to listen to his toilet noise. He emerged perfectly cheerful and untroubled. When she found out he was a medical student at Northwestern, that made sense: bodily things would have no mystery or shame for him.

Much later, once everything was settled between them, she asked him, "What was it you liked about me? Why did you tell me to wait for you?"

"Because," Eric said, "you were about to get away."

At the party they sat on a back staircase. He talked. She talked. Jane was a good listener, she'd had years of female practice, but Eric wasn't bad, for a man. He laughed, he nodded, he asked questions. He'd grown up in Highland Park, where his parents still lived. He'd wanted to be a doctor for as long as he could remember. He was still at the beginning of his training and had not yet decided on a field, but he was leaning toward cardiology. Jane said as a matter of fact, she knew a little about cardiology, and told him the story of her childhood heart condition. "That is really something," he kept saying, wonderingly, and if offering yourself up as a medical curiosity was not the usual way of piquing a man's interest, well, you did whatever worked.

Jane thought he was good-looking, in a normal, ordinary way, like those figures who fill in the background in beer commercials. She liked his hair, brown and worn curly/shaggy. He had a kind of ease or confidence—which Bonnie would later call arrogance—he seemed to know exactly what he wanted. And what he wanted, strange as it might seem to her, was Jane.

"I'm so glad you're not a nurse," he told her once. "I'm up to my neck in nurses day in and day out." So that was one of her attributes: not a nurse. In the most roundabout way possible, Jane inquired about his past girlfriends. He looked at her seriously. "I have a confession to make. I wasn't a virgin when I met you." Jane threw a pillow at him.

He mentioned the old girlfriends from time to time, but not in any way that Jane found very helpful. His high school girlfriend, he said, had confounded him some years later by going Goth in a big way. A girl he dated in college had a pet ferret. And so on. Certainly not, the girl who broke my heart, or the one who got away, or the gorgeous, sexually depraved one. She guessed that was gentlemanly of him, but also disappointing. Had they left no mark on him, had he simply said good-bye and gone on his blithe and untroubled way? He was incurious about Jane's past sweethearts, which was just as well, since there were not all that many of them and none of them made for interesting anecdotes. The one who helped himself to my groceries. The one who watched football. Or maybe that was true of all of them. What kind of a mark had they left on her? Dismay, mostly, and disappointment.

After the first time she and Eric made love, Jane apologized. "I guess I'm just not really a physical person."

Eric, dozing and drowsing, stirred. "What?"

"I'm not . . . I'm sorry I'm not better at this." She had bundled herself in the sheets, hiding her sorrowful body away. He wouldn't want to have anything to do with her now.

"What are you talking about? Hey!" They'd been lying side by side on their backs, and now he rolled over toward her. "I don't have any complaints. So I guess you do."

"No, I didn't mean that, I just . . . I've never been exactly passionate." She was horribly embarrassed. She shouldn't have said anything, except that she was certain she'd never see him again, now that her dismal sexual self had been revealed.

"You're apologizing because you didn't have an orgasm?"

"Ahh, oh . . ." She was an idiot to have said anything. She hadn't meant orgasms, she didn't even care about that. She just didn't have his kind of enthusiasm. He deserved better. Then again, she was aware that men did not necessarily notice what might be going on with you, as long as you were compliant.

"Come here." He tugged at the sheets, unwrapping her.

"You don't have to . . ." Jane began, but he was already busy, rubbing, stroking, licking.

"Just relax," he murmured.

She was not relaxed. She was waiting for it to be over. Even though she wanted all the kissing and holding and lying in bed next to him. She liked watching and touching his body, which was slim and compact and not so large as to make her feel overwhelmed. She was OK with all that. The rest of it she was accustomed to go along with, which was all right because it usually didn't last that long.

He was still diligently working away at her. "How's that?"

"It's fine," Jane said, because it wasn't *not* fine. But if there was some goal involved, she was falling short of it. She put her hand on top of his, stopping him. "I think I need a break."

He did stop then, and folded his hand over hers. "You have to tell me what you like."

Did she? Was it something else you had to work hard at? They hadn't known each other very long. She thought she would like talking to him and watching movies on television with him and eating take-out and having someone to tell if she had a bad, or a good, day at work. She would like trying to imagine what he was doing at different times of the day, and dressing up for him when he was coming over. But that was not what he wanted to hear. "I like being close to you," she began. "I just have trouble being in the moment."

"Are you . . . afraid or something?"

What should she say? He was being nice, he *was* nice, and it came to her that he was concerned for her, he was asking if she'd had anything horrible happen to her, like had she been raped or abused. It would be easier if she had been, or maybe she could make up some story. But she couldn't be that dishonest.

She said, "I guess it's mostly nerves." Which was only a little dishonest.

"I just want to please you," he whispered. He slid her hand down to his penis, which was poking around again in an amiable way, and at least Jane knew what was expected of her here, and that was all right too, as long as you didn't have to do it every time.

This was pretty much how things would continue between them, for some number of years.

They weren't able to spend that much time with each other, since Eric's schedule of clinical rotations was taking up more and more of his hours. He was finishing his last year of medical school and everything depended on applying for residencies and where he got in. But they talked on the phone every day and when they did get a night or a weekend together, it had the feel of a holiday. For Valentine's Day Eric gave her yellow roses edged with coral. Jane gave him a book of funny cartoons about doctors. She grew more used to the idea that he found something about her desirable. And she was crazy about him. Oh yes.

Jane involved herself in the intricacies of his application process, asking intelligent questions about residencies and offering encouragement. So much strategy and effort went into trying to get matched with your top school, where you might spend the next five years or more, where your career would be molded and minted. There were personal statements, interviews, performance evaluations; there was an implacable computer process that sorted everyone out. Then, on one dreaded day in March, the word came down and people either rejoiced or wept or gritted their teeth and made the best of it.

Even buoyant Eric felt the stress of it. "Of course everybody wants Johns Hopkins," he said gloomily. "And Duke. I shouldn't even have them on my list." Jane served as his cheerleader and morale officer, telling him she was sure he'd get one of his top choices, and that wherever he ended up, he'd make it work. She couldn't tell if Eric believed her or even paid attention. "What?" he'd say, after Jane delivered one of her exhortations. "What?" When he came over he sat hunched in front of the computer, searching for one more clue, one more advantage that might help him calculate his future. She found herself looking at him critically, not even liking him very much at such times.

That was just as well; she was clearly an interim girlfriend, a convenience. Someone to keep him company in his occasional off-hours, before he picked up stakes and headed off to his triumphant future. He didn't want to stay in Chicago, he said, which Jane took to mean, he didn't want to stay with her. And why would he? He was on the fast track. He would end up with some Highland Park princess, one of those shiny-haired, high-powered girls who had been smiling nonstop since the eighth grade. Jane would turn into another line in his personal résumé: the one who hung around blood banks.

Jane asked him if he wanted her there when he got the residency news, and Eric said no, he wasn't going to put her through that. He wanted to be able to break dishes and curse and sulk. Then he'd suck it up and call her. "You need to be more positive," said Jane. She found it hard to remember her own last purely positive thought. "You're going to be just fine."

"Yeah, it's all sunshine, lollipops, and rainbows."

He was impossible. "Bye," she said. "Talk to you later." She hung up. She thought it was unsurprising that Eric would not handle rejection well; he had hardly ever been rejected.

She waited to hear from him, feeling both nervous and deadened, as if everything reached her through a layer of cotton padding. The phone rang and she picked it up. "How do you feel about Atlanta?" Eric's voice said in her ear.

She didn't feel anything about Atlanta. He sounded excited. "What happened?"

"Emory. They aren't top ranked in cardio, I might have to go some-where else for a fellowship, but they were pretty high up on my list."

"Congratulations," Jane said. She was happy for him, in a sad way. "I told you it would work out."

"Listen, I need to hang out with some of the guys for a while, then let's go for dinner. I'm going to make a reservation someplace killer."

"Sure," Jane said, funereally. "That would be great."

"Oh man. What's that thing they say, the weight of the world . . ."

"The weight of the world has lifted from you."

"That's it. Seven o'clock, OK?"

The weight of the world had been transferred over to Jane. It felt about like she expected. She reminded herself of all the things she did not care for about him. His sense of humor could be juvenile. He had a terrible singing voice and never missed a chance to sing. He clearly shared everyone's high opinion of himself.

Just for spite, Jane took extra care with how she looked. She had grown her hair out long enough to pull up in a pouf. She chose a black dress that, when properly engineered and arranged, gave her some cleavage. She was surprised at how good she looked, once she got past her usual rituals of making critical expressions in the mirror. She thought she benefitted from the kind of makeup that allowed you to draw an entirely different face over your own.

"Wow, you look amazing," Eric said when he arrived. He kissed her, she kissed back. He'd dressed up too, in a jacket and tie, shaved and damped down his curls. Even so, a residue of exhaustion showed in his face, in the gray skin beneath his eyes. She felt sorry for him, in spite of her own sense of dreary grievance. He'd been through a hard few weeks, and plenty of hard weeks and months and years before that, so much work, finally paying off. She wouldn't spoil things for him. She would be good company, happy for him. Go through the motions. It wasn't as if anyone ever noticed the difference.

They went to a restaurant in the city that Jane had only read about, one of several owned by a famous chef, a place that served things like bison, persimmon emulsion, artichoke fritters, saffron-infused desserts. The menu a parade of marvels. "I hope you'll like it," Eric said, and Jane murmured that she was certain she would. The only complaints anyone might make would have to do with decadence and waste, since it was all so viciously expensive. You half expected to see the cast of *Les Misérables* pressed against the windows.

Jane thought Eric's parents must have given him money to go cele-brate. Eric was always vague about them, but she gathered, from a remark or two, that they were people of means, even if Eric said he had largely (vaguely) financed his own way through medical school. Some of his confidence undoubtedly came from growing up with money, the solid fact of it backing everything up. But the residency was something that he had accomplished on his own, fought his way to.

He talked about how his friends had managed with their matches. Not bad. He would not have to feel guilty about his own good fortune. "Tell me more about Emory," Jane kept saying, or, "Tell me more about At-lanta." He was excited about everything, which was a good way to start out. He said he'd no doubt be working at the huge public hospital, Grady Memorial, the one with the ER called Grady Knife and Gun Club. The prospect energized him. He loved the tough stuff. She felt how dearly she would miss him.

"When does all this start?" she asked him. Although she knew very well when it started. Graduation was in June, and the residencies began soon afterward. She just wanted to feel good and sad about it yet again. He began to answer, but was interrupted by the waiter, who set in front of them terrines made of different exotic sea creatures.

When the waiter left, Eric said, "You could go with me, you know."

Jane had picked up her fork. Now she put it down again. "What?"

"There are about a million different health careers there. I mean, the Centers for Disease Control, for starters."

He was waiting for her to say something, maybe, "Centers for Disease Control, really?" Jane looked around her. The restaurant was one of those minimalist temples of gastronomy, all tile and sleek leather and industrial lighting. Nowhere soft for the eyes to land. Hunger of any sort unknown here. She burst into noisy tears.

"Hey, hey," Eric said. "What's the matter? Jane?"

She couldn't stop. She had invested so much in the idea of her own failure and unlovability.

"Don't cry into the terrine. You know, the chef hates it when people add salt."

That made her laugh, hiccupping, although she was still bawling. The waiter stationed himself a discreet distance away in case the lady needed special attention, a taxi, say, or perhaps she wanted to change her order.

When she was able to speak again she said, "I thought when you left town, that was it."

"Oh come on." He made a scoffing face.

"I didn't know what you wanted. You didn't say."

"I didn't want to even talk about it until I knew where I was going to end up. Here, drink some water."

She drank, and fished around for a Kleenex in her purse. "Am I blotchy? I get blotchy when I cry."

"You're fine." Eric waved the waiter away. "So . . ."

"We should talk more about this," Jane said, picking up her fork once more. She was slowly realizing that she had actual power here, she was free to say yes or say no. Why would she consider no? This was what she wanted, wasn't it? But didn't people first decide to be together no matter what? She didn't like the idea that the computer program had determined her future as well as his, that if it had sent him to Pennsylvania, say, he might not be asking her to come along. But maybe he had wanted to be certain he had been matched, that he had something to offer her. Exactly what was he offering her, anyway?

Jane called Bonnie the next night. "Eric's going to Atlanta for his residency and he wants me to come with him." Although he had not actually said anything about wanting; you had to extrapolate that.

"Yeah? You going?"

"I don't know yet. It just came up last night."

"Are you getting married?"

"That part didn't come up."

"I trust," Bonnie said, "that you have told him the instructive story about free milk and the cow."

"I'm not a cow." It wasn't what you'd expect to hear from Bonnie. "Since when did you turn into some marriage booster?"

"You know I'm not. But if you're going to up and quit your job, and live somewhere you don't know anybody else—you don't, do you?—so that pretty much everything depends on Eric, how do you want this to end up? You want to get married, don't you? You love him all goo-goo, right?"

"Yes. Sure. But . . ."

"But what, tiresome girl?"

"He hasn't asked me."

"Well go out there and get him to marry you. It can't be that hard, people do it all the time."

"I don't know." She didn't even know what she didn't know, except for that sense of something sliding away beneath her and life tilting sideways. "If I don't get married. If I never get married. I'd be this whole different person. Does that make any sense?" Jane waited.

"Well," Bonnie said after a time, "I guess so. But that's how it works. You can't be everything. Nobody can."

"All this is happening just because of *his* job. *His* swell career. I'm just a component of it."

"It's never too late to discover feminism, Jane honey."

"Dr. and Mrs. Nicholson. It sounds so fifties." She wasn't even sure she believed in all her objections, but it seemed important to register them.

"Then don't change your name. Marry somebody else. Be a doctor yourself."

"What if we get married and move to Atlanta and things don't work out?"

"Then you'll at least get something from it. Train fare back home. Never mind. Don't get married. Hitchhike on down there with him. Throw caution to the winds."

"That's what you'd do," Jane said.

"Need I say more?"

. . .

Jane stood in the apartment's hallway, her back to the crowd, and tossed the bouquet over her shoulder. There was some whooping and scrabbling, because the men were in on it too, clowning around and pretending they wanted to catch it. But when Jane turned around, Bonnie was holding the roses, wagging them back and forth. "How is this supposed to work? Do I get a prize or something?"

Everybody gathered around to wish them good-bye, good-bye. Bonnie hugged her and told her she done good, and Jane did not see her again for a long time.

∞

The rose, the gold, the leaping sunlight: did everyone see such things as she did? The beautiful seeing filling you up so entirely that there was no room for the rest of you? She didn't think so, but how would you know? It was nothing anyone ever talked about.

∞

They walked out into a swirl of snow that had already coated the streets and sidewalks. Cars passed by on muffled tires. Veils of moving snow dimmed the streetlamps. It was as if it had all been arranged for them. Their breath sparkled with frost and once they were far enough away from their friends' apartment they stopped and kissed, the first private kiss of their marriage. It was cold, but not brutally so, and once they reached their car and started it up and the heater began to work, the cold only sharpened their pleasure in being warm and enclosed.

They went slowly, since you had to drive with care on the unplowed streets. Neither of them felt the need to say anything grand or important-seeming. When they arrived home and climbed the stairs and unlocked the door and went inside, they remembered too late about the carrying over the threshold part, and there was nothing to do but laugh about it. It wasn't as if they hadn't gone in and out and in and out, separately and together, for months and months, and any good or bad luck involved must have already been sealed.

They removed their wedding garments, hanging them in the almost-bare closet. They turned out the lights so that they could open the curtains and watch the snow falling in the high window while they made love. The snow sifted down and down.

Some trick of reflection made the sky beyond it almost white. After they had finished, they lay quiet, watching, until they both sighed.

"I hate to say it, but . . ."

"Yeah."

They got up and dressed in their ordinary clothes, jeans and sweat-shirts. There was still so much to be done to get ready for their trip.

It was Jane's apartment, but Eric had moved in for the last months of school. After graduation he had gone down to Atlanta on his own, taking only what he could fit in his car. It would be easier that way, he told her. He was going to be swallowed whole by the new routine and the new schedule. Better he go alone and tough it out for a little while, sleep in a dorm or on somebody's couch, then look around for a place for both of them.

There had been some unhappy discussions. Of course they would get married, he said, when pressed. It was only a question of when. So, when?

Jane made some trips to Atlanta. Eric went back and forth to Chicago. Their relationship had always had its share of time apart, but inevitably their time together now took on the unnatural quality of needing to pretend the time apart did not matter. Jane was not sold on Atlanta; it was all so brand new and hyperdeveloped, the whole of it could be picked up and set down several hundred miles away without anyone noticing. In October, Eric asked her when she was going to be visiting again, and she said she wasn't sure. Two weeks later Eric bought a ring and came to Chicago.

It had all come together in the end. He had just needed reminding that there was more to life than work. He would need further reminding. She knew that. Every marriage had its stress points, everybody signed up for their share of good and bad. You could say she was fortunate to know ahead of time what the issues would be.

Although she could not help thinking there was a great deal he had taken for granted.

They still had a lot of the kitchen to pack up, and the bathroom to be cleaned out, and all the cumbersome wedding presents they had begged people not to give them, things like blenders and casseroles, that now had to be dealt with. It did not seem unglamorous of them to be doing this on their wedding night; rather it felt as if the real, serious work of the marriage had begun, and they would undertake it together.

Jane started in on the kitchen while Eric took the framed pictures and mirrors off the walls, bubble wrapped them, and slid them into over-sized boxes. They turned on the radio for some noise and found a station that played jukebox hits. ZZ Top, Tom Petty, Roy Orbison. Eric sang along in his loud, blissfully out of tune voice: "Cause you doon't love me, so I'll aalways be, crahahaing, over you, crahahain . . ." Jane wiped down the refrigerator shelves and pretended they had been married for years and years and Eric's singing was by now an established joke, something that no longer bothered her.

She filled a black plastic garbage bag with unwanted refrigerator odds and ends, jars of mustard and half-eaten applesauce, dead vegetables. She carried the bag out the kitchen door to the trash—they were the first floor of a four-flat—and when she turned to go back inside, she found the door had locked behind her. She'd forgotten to flip the latch, which she'd done a time or two before, and as before, she called herself an idiot.

Jane rattled the back door and knocked, but of course Eric was busy with his oratorio and didn't hear. She wasn't too worried; eventually he'd miss her and come looking for her. Or if she had to, with some effort, she could go out of the yard to the alley and around again to the front of the house and ring the buzzer.

The snow had slackened to a sparse, thready shower. Two or three inches had fallen, not the first snow of the season, but the biggest so far. Colder air was filtering in behind the snow. Jane tried knocking again. Waited, rubbing her arms for warmth.

She left the back step and walked around to the side of the house where, if she balanced on a window well and pulled herself up, she could see into the living room. The curtains were open and the old-fashioned wooden blinds left plenty of space to see in. Here was Eric, bent over one of the packing boxes, using great gobs of tape to put it together, taping over tape, then reinforcing the seams crossways. So this was what his face looked like, singing without sound. His mouth making shapes, shoulders pumping, tossing his head with rock star gusto. She had to smile; he was ridiculous. And although she had believed herself to be thinking fondly, playfully about him, as if this too were a joke they might tell years later—*did you know your father locked me out of the house on our wedding night?*—there was a coldness in it too, as she watched and waited for the moment when he realized she was no longer there.

b o n n i e ' s   c h r i s t m a s

Bonnie's stepfather, StepStan, was raised sort-of Jewish, and he cele-
brated an aesthetic holiday known, informally, as Christmukah. The
Wisconsin homestead where he lived with Bonnie's mother took on a
new aspect. An old GM half-ton truck sitting in a field beyond Stan's
studio was outlined and criss-crossed in multicolored lights, the world's
trippiest ride. Some number of Stan's sculptures were set about the property, towering structures of anodized or case hardened or polished metal
in the shape of spheres, wings, ribs, cages. These too were bedizened
with special lighting effects, on one occasion, twirling red and green, on
another, electronically programmed displays of starry blue-white lights
going off like flashbulbs. Metallic ribbons were strung on wires, bumping and clanking together. The effect was not always festive. Often it was
as if a crew of Jurassic Park dinosaurs had decked themselves out for the
holidays.

One year there had been a twelve foot high metal stick figure with
jointed arms that swung back and forth, and a triangular red Santa hat,
but this looked disturbingly like a hanged man, and it was not repeated.

Indoors, Bonnie's mother, Claudia, tried to represent the traditional.
There was always a tree of some kind, and candles and felt decorations,
and a menorah, and an old carved wooden nativity set that had belonged

to Grandma Somebody, its colors gone soft with age. Stan liked to add the occasional figure to the set. One year there might be a small rag doll among the shepherds and magi, a calypso mammy-figure in headscarf and hoop earrings. Or a plastic Batman, or a squadron of army men. That Stan! He was such a kidder!

A week after Jane's wedding, Bonnie headed north across the state line for those portions of the holidays that her family observed, eating and gift giving. She made a trip to a north side bakery for *mandelbrot* and macaroons, and to the liquor store for wine and spirits, God forbid they should ever run short. She bought a number of all-purpose gifts, books, mostly, and wrapped them up to distribute as needed. You could never tell who might or might not show up. In addition to Stan and Claudia, there would be, most probably, Bonnie's older brother Charlie. (Their BioDad lived in New Mexico, and neither of them had seen him since they were little kids.) Their half-sister Haley was supposed to be there, along with her husband and twin babies. Beyond that, perhaps some assortment of Stan's children from his previous two marriages, who were technically Bonnie's stepbrothers and -sisters, although she hardly knew them. And anyone else Stan and Claudia might be cultivating or paying off with hospitality.

Jane once spent three days with Bonnie's family over the holidays, and later said, "Well, I see you weren't exaggerating."

It had not been easy for Bonnie to get time off at Christmas. If anything, the crisis meter spiked during the holidays, as families collided and people went off their meds and the alcoholics stepped up their game. There was always some sick-making headline in the middle of the news coverage of midnight mass and the charity dinner. A beaten child, a murdered wife, somebody robbed and shot dead while picking up the sweet rolls for Christmas morning breakfast. Of course some of this was just run of the mill crime, as her cop boyfriend, Denny, pointed out. Meat and potatoes, head-banging fun. But somebody in her office had to be on call and nobody much wanted to do it, and in the end Bonnie had to make extravagant promises to her co-workers before she was off the hook. There was no reason for her to stick around; Denny would spend Christmas with his wife and kids and that was just the way it was.

Although now, fighting traffic and thirty miles of sideways snow on the Tollway, she wondered if it might have been better to stay in town and tough it out. Not that she was inclined to mope and pine overmuch about Denny, who had been a stupid idea from the get-go and they were probably pretty close to through with each other. He was just the cop iteration of all the other bad boys in her life, and totally full of himself. She could have made some excuse to her mother about working. She could have called around to her friends and found somebody to go out for drinks on Christmas Eve, or a movie Christmas Day. It wouldn't have been so terrible.

But here she was, racing a snowstorm and hoping she could outrun it before she had to turn off the interstate and onto the two-lane. Snow was beginning to sift across the pavement in wind-driven, snake-like ropes. Her car, a little Dodge product, was good enough for city driving, not so great out in serious weather. She guessed if she ran off the road, she could eat pastry and drink the liquor until somebody showed up to tow her out of the ditch.

Her luck held, and by the time she reached Madison the storm had taken itself elsewhere. She kept on 39 north for another hour, then turned west onto the county road, two lanes but decently maintained. The snow pack on either side looked like it was there to stay. Just as the light was fading in a cloud-muffled sky that had no hint of color, she made the last turn and climbed the ornery hill that led to Stan and Claudia's. It was not Bonnie's childhood home; she wasn't sure she had such a thing, with all the ruptures and dislocations involved. But it was where whatever combination of memories and DNA she could call her own resided, and she guessed that was why she had to keep coming back.

At least she'd arrived at the right time of day to see the lights. She slowed the Dodge at the crest of the hill to take it all in. Stan always tried to top himself year after year, just like, Bonnie had pointed out, every-body with icicle lights on their gutters and inflatable Santas on the roof and spiral cones meant to represent trees. This year, he'd gone in for holograms.

Here was a new sculpture, a solid steel wall almost house-high. It was set up as a kind of screen, pulsing from blue to violet and then quickly through the spectrum, settling on a burnt orange. This gradually extin-guished itself, turning once more to blue. And just in that last flare of light, a herd of galloping deer! She had to watch the cycle one more time to determine that the deer were, in fact, projected shadows. It was quite lovely and Christmas card–like. Perhaps Stan was losing his edge.

She drove downhill along the S-curve road to the main house, past a few more eruptions of colored lights that reminded Bonnie, unworthily, of the special effects at old Polynesian restaurants. A number of cars were parked out front, some of which she recognized, some not. Her mother had been vague about the holiday schedule when Bonnie had last called. "I think we'll have a few people stopping by. Oh, I don't know. Whoever Stan runs into. Whoever Charlie brings. No point in planning ahead." As usual, there was the chance of at least one thundering party while she was there.

Bonnie parked and hauled her luggage up to the front door. The air was already biting cold, and she didn't want to have to go out again. The house, as her brother Charlie liked to say, practically screamed "Artist in Residence." It was a long, rambling structure with a dramatic roofline, sided in reclaimed barn wood. You approached the front door along a curved portico that gave the effect of walking through a barrel. The main room had a twenty-foot ceiling and an L-shaped fireplace. Around the fireplace was an expanse of severely modern couch seating. People at the far ends could only wave to each other.

Entering and dumping her bags, Bonnie heard a man whose voice she did not recognize say, "But design in itself is not sufficient. Design does not replace reality. Design must be a reflection of life yet also be itself. As is true of all living things."

"I couldn't agree more," Stan said. "Unless, of course, you're talking about the idiotic decompositionists. Then all bets are off. Bonnie! You look like the orphan of the storm. Come here and warm yourself by the fire and be taken into our collective bosom."

Still wearing her coat, Bonnie advanced into the room. The fire popped and snapped, but the room was so huge—a goddamned Viking mead hall, Charlie called it—that it hardly seemed to heat any of it. She nodded at the guest she did not know and allowed herself to be embraced by Stan, a process involving more enthusiasm and whiskers than she cared for. He wasn't a big man, but he was gut heavy and muscled, used to hauling chunks of metal into place. Released, she took a step back and said, "I like the deer. I thought they were the real thing."

"The real thing, although not replacing reality. Bonnie, this is Franklin. My blended daughter, Bonnie." This last being Stan's clever joke about blended family.

Bonnie shook hands with Franklin, who rose slightly from his seat and then fell back again. He had a jowly, dark-bearded face, severe eyebrows, and a head that was perfectly bald except for two fringes of dark hair that resembled earmuffs. One of Stan's art guy friends. They tended to come in two varieties, the happy drinkers and the melancholy ones. She put Franklin down as melancholy, but maybe that was just the eyebrows. "Nice to meet you," Bonnie said, then, turning to Stan, "Where's Mom?"

"In the kitchen, attending to her womanly chores. So you liked the lights? The little deary deer?"

"I did. I like representational, I wish you'd do more of it."

"Representational," Stan said, "is interior decorating. I just put it outside." He spoke dismissively, but Bonnie knew he soaked up praise of any kind. Artists, in her experience, were all attention whores.

"What's the structure, the tall one, is it headed somewhere?" Stan often had partially assembled pieces on the property so he could trouble-shoot them.

"Kansas City. Guy there wants a waterfall for his stately home. They all want waterfalls. They're big on fake nature. Are you going out to the kitchen? As long as you're passing the bar . . ." Stan wagged his empty glass at her.

Bonnie collected their glasses. She paused on her way to contemplate the Christmas tree, which stood, as always, in the juncture of two windows. It was an ordinary enough Douglas fir, probably purchased from the Kiwanis lot in town. And it was decorated with an ordinary string of multicolored lights and some gold bead garlands. But the rest of it had an unsettling, Druidic air. Sheets of moss and lichenlike growths draped the branches, also a number of twigs and dried leaves. A large black crow sat on the topmost perch, its yellow eyes glittering.

She put the packages of sweets on the dining room table and draped her coat over a bench. Like every other piece of furniture in the house, the table had some design pedigree she couldn't remember, like the chairs in the shape of artful gnarled branches, like the enormous glass globe suspended lights, like the bathroom vanities made of pickled wood and the sink basins of volcanic stone. Jane, and anyone else who she brought home with her, always marveled, surprised that there was so much money to be made in giant metalworks, that Bonnie herself had that kind of money, though they didn't always put it so crassly. Bonnie shrugged it off. It was Stan's money, or more accurately, his mercantile grandfather's, and Bonnie's access to it was controlled by Stan's whims and by a system of legalities that resembled plumbing, complete with capped pipes and shut-off valves.

Claudia was standing in front of the stove, enveloped in a cloud of fragrant steam. "Hi Mom."

"Honey! Did you just get here?" Her mother turned and embraced her with one arm. She held a wooden spoon in the other hand. "Were the roads horrible? I was so worried."

"They were fine." Bonnie had to bend down to get her mother's welcoming kiss. She wasn't tall, but Claudia was a shorty. "What's for dinner, you need any help?"

"Cioppino. Pasta. I got it under control. Go find out if Frank is allergic to any seafood. He just showed up and I already had dinner planned."

"Showed up from where, exactly?" It wasn't like they were in the middle of a flight path.

"New Jersey, maybe? He lost his job, or something else bad, I forget. Stan's going to help him. Isn't that nice of him? Are you starving? Do you want wine, there's some open. How about you put some salami and antipasti stuff on a plate and take it out to them, so they don't get too carried away." *Carried away* meant drunk. "There's olives and breadsticks and mozzarella. If they want anything else, they can come fix it themselves."

An idle threat, Bonnie knew. Claudia fed the multitudes. Bonnie took a platter from the cupboard and ate salami and cheese as she put the food together. The kitchen had a six-burner Wolf range with a custom hood and mosaic backsplash, a central island with its own bar sink, and a separate butler's pantry. It had been designed so as to console Claudia for living out in the Wisconsin wilds. Bonnie couldn't cook her way out of a Glad bag. It was one more piece of mirthful family lore.

She fixed Stan and Franklin their new bourbon and waters, brought it and the food in to them, and interrupted the conversation long enough to learn that Franklin would eat whatever was put before him. She went back to the kitchen and relayed this to Claudia. "Who else is here, I saw a bunch of cars."

"Charlie brought some friends. They're in town playing pool, they'll be back later. Haley and Scott and the babies are down in the family room, that's where they're staying. You haven't even seen them yet, they're precious. You're in Haley's old room, I hope that's all right." All the while she was talking, Claudia was opening cupboards and drawers, stirring, tasting, chopping. She cooked, she ran the house, she kept up her looks with yoga and antioxidant facials. She tracked Stan's commissions and managed his money and arranged for his appearances and interviews and believed in his genius as if it were a religious vocation. "Talk to me, how was the wedding? Did Jane look happy?"

"You know, she did." It was a mild surprise to realize this. "Kind of a small scale thing, but that's what they wanted." Hoping to steer the conversation away from weddings, which might lead to difficult questions, like when was she going to have one herself, Bonnie said, "Whose idea was that tree? It looks like Hallowe'en."

"It's a woodland theme. It goes along with the deer."

"I liked the deer. But why do you have to have a Christmas tree with a dead bird on it?"

"It's not real, it's papier-mâché. You just got here, try not to criticize." Claudia ran water in the sink and shut it off with a snap.

"I'm just saying. For once, couldn't you have candy canes and snowmen? A corny, all-American Christmas? Would that kill anybody?" They used to have such things. Her earliest memories, pre-Stan.

"When you have your own household, you can decorate whatever way you want to."

"Shot through the heart," Bonnie said, clasping her chest and staggering back in mock affliction. "Spinster daughter put in her place."

"Don't be silly, nobody says that anymore, 'spinster.' And please tell me you're looking for a new job. I can't stand thinking of you in the middle of all those crazy drug users."

"I'm not in the middle of them. The cops are. I only see them if they get arrested and there's an intake process." This was not entirely true. There were times she put on a vest and aided an officer at the scene, although they were always careful to keep her out of harm's way. She thought about Denny, who, whatever else was wrong or inconvenient about him, was the very model of To Serve and Protect, right down to being Irish, and she felt a little wayward pulse of horniness. "I just got here, try not to criticize."

"I'm not criticizing, I'm worried. Every horrible news story I hear from Chicago, I wonder if you're involved. Now don't go mocking me, you know what I mean. I just want you to be more—settled. Happy." Her mother turned as if to give Bonnie another hug, but the flame under a skillet flared up and demanded her attention.

Meaning, Bonnie supposed, that she should find a megalomaniac man of her own and devote herself to his care and feeding. But Claudia was content, to all appearances, with being a handmaiden to the artist. Here was her kitchen kingdom, with its collection of gourmet salts, its espresso machine and Le Creuset pans and the glass fronted china cabinets with the Craftsman details. What did Bonnie have to show for herself? A collection of matchbooks from cop bars.

"Mom, I'm fine. My job is fine. I'm glad I'm here." Three lies in a row. "I'm sorry I started in about the tree. It's actually pretty funny. I'm going to go see Haley, meet the chillun, OK? Call me if you need any help."

As Bonnie headed downstairs she heard her mother say something about "pretty funny," but she didn't wait to hear the rest of it.

One of the babies was screaming bloody murder, and a moment later the other one started up in solidarity. "Now, now, Aunt Bonnie's here," she announced. The screaming redoubled.

There was another fireplace in the family room. Scott, Haley's husband, was trying to get a small, sulky fire to burn. "Hey Scott. Merry Christmas."

"This chimney won't draw."

"HalfHaley! Merry Christmas."

"I wish you would not call me that." Haley was sitting on the couch, a baby on each side of her. Their faces were red with screaming. Their legs and arms flailed in infant fury.

"Sorry. So these are the kiddos? Very robust. What's the matter with them?"

"I ate some chili that turned out to be too spicy and now they both have gas."

"Oh dear," Bonnie said, bending over the sofa to get a better look. She was not one of those people who naturally took to babies. She preferred children who were somewhat older and more articulate. "This must be . . ."

"Leah. That one's Benjamin." The babies wore identical striped onesies and striped knit hats. Their tiny faces were clenched like fists. They were three months old. Haley looked unhappy, overtired, and still saggy from baby weight. Actually, all four of them looked unhappy. Even Scott, who had a naturally furtive expression that made it hard to tell.

"They're amazing," Bonnie said, wondering if that expressed sufficient admiration. But no one was paying her that much attention.

"We should have stayed home," Haley said. They'd driven in from Colorado. "It's too much hassle. But Mom and Dad insisted."

"Well, you know, first Christmas, first grandkids." Bonnie had to raise her voice to be heard above a particularly penetrating bout of screaming. Although this was only a first for Claudia. There were already some Stan-Grands. "When did you get here?"

"Lunchtime. It was Mom's chili. So we didn't exactly get off to a good start."

"Your dad kept calling Leah 'Layla,'" Scott put in. "And Benjamin, he was 'Boris.'"

"Get used to that," Bonnie told him. "He means it affectionately." Mostly.

"Mom never nursed any of her kids, did you know that? So of course she wasn't thinking. Scott had to go out and find formula. Plus I'm leaking all over."

"That's . . ." Bonnie was at a loss. Too much information, but she couldn't say that.

Haley didn't notice; she was still recounting grievances. "Not to mention they make a total mockery of anything religious." Six years younger than Bonnie, Haley had dropped out of college to live in a Christian commune. "Hippies at prayer," Stan called them. Scott worked as a carpenter. Most of the commune's men seemed to be carpenters.

"I wouldn't say mockery. More like, disregard," Bonnie said, trying to put the best face on it. None of them had been raised with any sort of religion, unless you counted Stan as the high priest of Art.

"You think? Remember the party where they had the chorus line of nuns?"

"They weren't real nuns," Bonnie said. Going all Christian was probably an irresistible way for the child of a rebel to rebel, though Bonnie congratulated herself on finding more interesting paths. At least her sister's commune wasn't the kind where the women had to deck themselves out in ruffled prairie dresses. Both Scott and Haley wore a lot of flannel shirts. It was hard to see anything overtly pious about either of them, only a certain morose seriousness.

"Whatever. Our kids are going to be raised differently." Bonnie was sure of that. She envisioned the home-school lessons, the joyless indoctrinations. "Scott," Haley complained, "all you're doing is making a lot of smoke."

The babies were still going off like alarms. Smoke alarms? "Can I do anything?" Bonnie asked. "Tell them bedtime stories?"

"Here, walk Benjamin. Sometimes that calms him down."

Haley handed over one of the squalling bundles and Bonnie draped it over her shoulder.

"Wait a minute," Haley said. "Burp cloth."

Bonnie jiggled and patted at the baby. "Hey little man." He was having none of it. His sister's wails were diminishing, but he was one of those kids who was going to cry himself into complete exhaustion. "Go for it," Bonnie murmured. What were you supposed to do if they screamed themselves insensible and stopped breathing? She paced up and down in front of the full length glass windows. It was a walk-out basement and there was a steep, snow-covered slope just beyond the glass, leading down to the woods. It looked delicious out there, dark and crisp and blue-cold. She put her forehead to the sliding glass door, just to feel the coolness.

"I give up," Scott said, turning his back on the fireplace. "The wood's wet or something. I wouldn't bother except it's too cold down here for the babies. They could get pneumonia."

"Not to mention we have to sleep on this sucky fold-out couch," Haley added. "Mom and Dad seem to think we live in a barn, well, we don't. We have our own cabin with kerosene heat and a composting toilet."

"Trade," Bonnie said, shifting the baby to her other shoulder. "Take your old room back, I'll stay in the basement."

"They won't like it," Haley said. "We're down here so nobody has to listen to us."

"They don't have to like it. It's a health and well-being issue. Child welfare." She was taken with the idea of having the basement all to herself. She'd get the fire to burn, sneak up to the kitchen and raid the refrigerator. Not to mention she'd have her own bathroom. "Is there a crib? Can I help you move stuff?"

"We didn't set up the crib yet," Scott said, looking hopeful at the notion of sleeping elsewhere. "I guess it's still in the garage."

"You don't mind the fold-out?"

"Think of it as my Christmas present."

"Well . . ."

"Why don't you guys take the babies," Bonnie said. "I'll get your suitcases together. Don't worry, you've got them outnumbered, four to two."

She stayed downstairs and gathered up infant paraphernalia, keeping an ear out for sounds of negotiations and protest overhead. The babies' noise masked most of it. The crying had a heartbroken quality now, as if they had realized there was no easy way out of their small, hurting bodies.

After a while, hearing nothing, she grabbed a quilted bag with BABY spelled out in patchwork letters on the side, full of diapers and tiny garments, and ventured upstairs. The kitchen was empty. The broth for

Claudia's fish stew simmered, and the counter held small saucers of chopped mushrooms, parsley, strips of red and green pepper. It looked like one of Grandma Somebody's recipes. (There was also a Grandma Somebody Else, but she did not cook.) Some new commotion was going on in the main room. There was a back passage and a half flight of stairs you could take to the bedrooms, and she chose this route, wanting to lay low for a time. She guessed she felt a little guilty for disrupting Claudia's arrangements. At least the babies had stopped crying. Maybe they really did want to be upstairs.

Ahead of her in the hallway, someone was running water behind a bathroom door. Bonnie hurried to get past it, but the door opened and she nearly collided with a man coming out.

"Jesus!"

"Bonnie?"

She staggered back against the wall. "What are you doing here?" She was afraid she might faint, actually up and faint.

"I came with Charlie," the man said. "And Diane," he added, after a moment.

"Sure." Bonnie nodded. Nodding made her head feel tilted. Waves of vicious heat dizzied her. "Jesus, Will," she said again, attempting to sound lighthearted, humorous.

"Charlie didn't think you were coming."

"Got that wrong."

"We're only staying the one night." He had backed himself into the bathroom in an attempt not to crowd her. "So, wow, did you . . ." He pointed at the BABY bag.

"Yeah, don't worry, it's not yours." He looked stricken. "God no, that's a joke. It's my sister's. She has twins."

"Twins. Amazing."

"I guess Charlie didn't mention it. "

"I guess not."

"He isn't, you know, a reliable source of information."

"Yeah." It was as if they were locked into a death spiral of stupid con-versation. "Look, I gotta . . ."

"Yeah, see you later, I guess."

They nodded, grimaced, and hurried off in opposite directions.

Oh Jesus Jesus Jesus oh shit.

Bonnie got herself down the hallway to Haley's room, mercifully empty. She dumped the BABY bag, closed the door, and stood on the other side of it, waiting to see what she would do next. Because you had to do something. You couldn't just stop, freeze frame, end of story. Or you could, but only if you managed to fall down dead on the spot.

At one time she had thought he was the goddamned love of her god-damned stupid fucked-up life.

Had he been? Was he still? Did that ever change? Should you want it to, since no further good was ever going to come of it? You ought to be able to put things behind you and move on, sadder but wiser, etc. Espe-cially since the alternative was all this pointless mooning around and self-dramatizing and tearing of hair and rending of garments and being entirely shallow and witless and worthless.

Her stomach heaved. She grabbed one of the diapers from the bag and threw up into it.

Once she was finished, she listened again at the door and, hearing nothing, made her way back to the bathroom. She rinsed the diaper in the toilet, threw up a little more from the sick-making smell of it, and hid the mess away in the bottom of the wastebasket. She ran cold water in the sink, cleared her mouth, and wrung out a washcloth to blot her face. At least she looked the part of the haggard, cast-off lover. All she needed was a ragged shawl.

But nobody else knew that was what she was. Or what he was to her. They'd kept it a secret from everyone, especially the pretty, pretty girl he wound up engaged to this summer. Was no doubt still engaged to. Un-less they'd gone ahead and gotten married. She thought she would have heard, but maybe not.

Because he might have been the love of her life, but she was obviously not the love of his.

She heard laughter, a great rolling wave of it, from the main room. She smoothed her hair, used the mouthwash she found in the medicine cabinet, and willed her face in the mirror into its usual wry, skeptical expression. In the kitchen she poured white wine into a water glass, enough to keep her going a long time. Then she walked out to join the party.

∞

Two years ago. More than two, August. Every morning the city woke up to heat haze and the same forecast, two, six, ten days in a row, hot and hotter. Bonnie's air conditioner couldn't keep up. Bonnie and Will drank cold beer and ate popsicles and took showers with towels that never quite dried. In bed they lay in the grand ruin of the sheets. A rotating fan sent a current of silky air across them. Outside, buses coughed exhaust. Somebody's radio played at headache volume, tamped down by glass and the window air conditioner.

Oh holy God, the way they'd had each other. It was not quite a memory. It was still in her skin. She stayed as still as she could to keep what they'd done from receding, minute by minute by minute, into the past. A losing fight against time and an already-forming sense of loss. The fan revolved once more. The small wind passed over their salt skins. He put his mouth to her ear. "I have to go . . ."

If only you could stay in bed forever! But sex was the opposite of forever. So insubstantial, and yet it was the root and branch of everything, seed, flower, tree. It was ravishment and chiming skin. She was always getting it mixed up with love, or maybe you were supposed to. And what happened when the sex got tired or went stale, because of course that happened, in spite of everyone's best efforts. She didn't know. She hadn't stayed around for that part often enough to know.

Will had not stayed around. He was moving to Phoenix to work for

Honeywell. An engineer, he would work in aerospace technology. It was all set up before they met. Phoenix, another hot place. "I'll find an apartment with a pool. And a swamp cooler. You can get used to weather." What was the name for that hollowed out space beneath the collarbone? It should have a name. She wanted to open his shirt and rest her two hands there. Confound everybody in the nice restaurant where he'd taken her to say good-bye. He was leaving in two days.

Bonnie wasn't going with him. His plans were complete. They did not include her. He was excited about his brand new life, all the splendid possibilities. Bonnie was something that had already happened. Why secret? Why not tell people? Well, he was her brother's friend, it was a little embarrassing. Good Time Charlie. She didn't want Charlie knowing her business. He talked about all the wrong things to all the wrong people. So they kept it on the down low. Who would they tell, anyway? Then, as time went on, they liked having a secret, an *intrigue*, like something out of an old French scandal, everybody dressed up in wigs and satin. Not that there was, technically, anything scandalous. They were both healthy, unattached, of age. But what they did with and to each other was meant to be secret.

"I've never been to Phoenix," Bonnie said. She'd ordered a salad that was composed of a great many confusing things: slices of egg, beets, olives, knobs of cauliflower. Every so often she raked through it with her fork, but that only brought up more alarming ingredients. Was that bacon? No, an anchovy. She hadn't been paying attention when she'd ordered. She was waiting for him to say she could at least come visit him and he wasn't saying it.

"It has a lot going for it. Did you know that it's the sixth largest U.S. city?"

"I did not know that."

"Golf is huge there. You can play all year round."

"I bet."

"Don't hate me," he said, switching tones. "Would you rather it had never happened? I don't."

"Yeah, great memories. I can never have too many of those."

"You're angry, you're hurt. I wish you weren't but you are. I'm sorry if you thought it was going to end some other way."

"I guess I wasn't thinking about the ending." Bonnie gave up on the salad. She could say she was going to the ladies' room and just leave, spare herself this part. But she wouldn't. Soon enough she wouldn't be able see or hear him at all.

He reached across the table and took one of her hands in both of his. "You are the most amazing, lovely person."

Bonnie snatched her hand away. "Don't make me hate you."

A heaviness came over his face. "You aren't being fair. Come on, we never had enough time. It's not like we even know each other all that well."

"So when you tell me I'm 'amazing' and 'lovely,' that's just something you pulled out of your ass?"

"You know I mean it," he said, and then they were both quiet for a while.

Bonnie looked down at her salad. It looked back. She said, "How long is enough? Is there some established minimum? OK. We could make more time. But you won't. You could but you won't. It's only Phoenix, it's not like you're going off to war."

"I can't ask you to leave everything and move out there. It's not fair, I'd feel responsible for you."

"You could stay here," Bonnie said, in a smaller voice, and she watched him go miles and miles away without ever leaving his chair.

Some of the things she knew about him: Where he grew up (Pennsylvania), his parents' names (Wade and Virginia), siblings (two sisters), the dog, a terrier, who slept on his bed when he was a kid, the shin splints he got running cross-country, his sensitivity to insect bites, fondness for terrible crappy science fiction, his beautiful squared-off handwriting, how particular he was about his car and how you were not allowed to tease him about it, his sense of fair play when it came to competitions of all sorts, his devotion to those incomprehensible, to her at least, calculations and computer models and metrics which made up his profession. His mouth, his hands, his voice. How he whispered, "Wait, wait," while he teased and stroked his way into her. How, when leaving, he always looked up at her window so they could wave good-bye.

∞

Charlie said: "You remember Diane, right? Well, they broke up for a while, then when he got out to Arizona they started up again, long distance at first, your basic hot and heavy rendezvous, and I guess they decided to just go for it, kind of a surprise, you never know, but they seem real happy."

It was true that Bonnie had her well-articulated objections to marriage. But she would have married him. "My ex," Will had called Diane, with a raised and wriggling eyebrow, as if he might have said more, except for gentlemanly restraint. Nice girl, everybody said so. Pretty. Lacking in some respect? Too smiley-anxious? Needy? Clingy? Maybe all that meant was that she had demanded he take her seriously.

Coming into the large and laughing room, Bonnie spotted them first thing. They were sitting together on the hearth. Don't look. Claudia was saying, "'Have a Holly Jolly Christmas' is not a carol. A carol is something like *'Adeste Fidelis.'*"

"What's that?"

"'O Come All Ye Faithful' in Latin. Not that any of you heathen are aware of that." Stan, who liked to demonstrate that he knew a thing or two about a thing or two. He was sitting in his oversized leather chair. It made him look both regal and stunted, the king of the dwarves.

"So, 'Frosty the Snowman' and 'Grandma Got Run Over by a Reindeer' don't count either? Mom, all those years, you let me believe. You suck." This from her brother Charlie. He was standing at one end of the fireplace, throwing pistachio shells into the flames. He wore an old, too-small Christmas sweater, a joke one, with panicked gingerbread people being scooped up by a big Santa hand.

Claudia said, "Where did I go wrong with you, Charlie?" Only pretending to be displeased. She loved it when her men acted up. Scott and Haley, along with the babies, were bestowed at one end of the sofa. Presumably they had an opinion about sacred music, but they were keeping it to themselves. Other people standing around, who were they? And that sad sack Franklin guy.

"Bonnie!" Her mother turned and extended an arm, draping it around her. "You used to love Christmas carols, 'Silent Night' and 'O Little Town of Bethlehem.' She had the most precious little voice," Claudia informed the room. "She had just the slightest bit of a speech defect, so it was 'Thilent Night.'"

"Yeah, precious. Hi Charlie."

"Hi Bon. So, everybody, this is my sexpot sister."

"Nice."

"Charlie," their mother scolded.

"It's OK, Mom. Nobody believes him."

Haley said, "Honestly, Charlie. Some things are not funny."

"Did you want to be the sexpot sister? I didn't think so. Hey Bonnie, this is Jack and Irina and Sam and and . . . oh, you know these guys."

"Nice to see you again," Bonnie said, in her most comradely voice. Will said Nice to see you too. Diane gave her one of those great big smiles, like she'd been waiting all day for whoever she was smiling at to show up. But that was the worst Bonnie could say about her. Hers was a purely technical hatred.

Charlie poked at a log with a fireplace iron. The log broke and sent red sparks shooting out onto the rug. "Sparks fly," he said, to no one in particular.

Stan said, "How about you quit messing with the fire? It was burning just fine."

"Well it just got a little stirred up."

"Claudia," Stan said, "do I hear the dinner gong?" He was not a big fan of his stepson's theatrics.

"Table's already set, I just have to . . ." Claudia already halfway to the kitchen.

Bonnie crossed the room and went to sit next to Haley and the babies. She couldn't tell if Will watched her, but Franklin seemed to be looking at her ass. Creep. Thanks, Charlie, for that one. "They fell asleep," Haley said, as Bonnie sat down. "Right in the middle of all the commotion. They were exhausted."

"They look like somebody flipped their Off switches," Bonnie said, examining their tiny, slackened faces. "And fortunately, they're too little to remember any of it."

She'd meant, the gas pains, but Haley rolled her eyes and muttered, "I wish I could say the same." It always took Bonnie a little while to get used to seeing Haley again. They resembled each other, but in an inexact way that cast both their faces into doubt, as if one or the other was the imperfect version. "Scott, please go see about that crib so we can get them settled." Scott got up and went looking for his coat. Bonnie wondered if he'd always been so compliant, or if it was a new dad thing.

"You know," she said, "I don't think I've brought a boyfriend home with me since high school. They'd have to be made of pretty stern stuff to handle it all." Will certainly didn't count as a boyfriend. He was there under entirely different auspices. "I guess once you're married, they have to show up. Did your in-laws meet the babies yet?" Scott's parents were missionaries in Lagos and had not been able to leave their posts.

"No, but they're hoping to get back this summer. Of course we send them all kinds of pictures. And they write the sweetest letters. They're so strong in their faith."

Charlie left the fireplace and retrieved his glass from an end table. "The Lord loveth a cheerful drinker." His friends, a rat-faced girl and the two hipster boys, looked particularly out of place, as if they'd been expecting a party with a DJ. Charlie always did cast a wide net. He was almost thirty, and managed a bar in Lakeview, but mostly Stan paid him money to stay away. Will was an old friend from college, back when Charlie had briefly gone in for college.

Will and Diane—Bonnie could see them without turning her head— were having some whispered conversation. Bonnie hoped they were rethinking their plan to stay the night. Diane stood up and left the room. She wore a red sweater, a short suede skirt, patterned tights, and high boots. She was one of those women who looked good from behind. Was there a ring? Bonnie couldn't tell. She got up and went to sit next to Will, close enough to make him look at her with lurking dread. Chicken-shit. "So, how's Phoenix?"

"It's good, yeah, real good." He didn't seem to believe she was going to put him through this. Believe it. "How's things with you?"

"Never better. Processing those who are a danger to themselves or others just as fast as they surface. I'm still in Wicker Park. I can't remember if you ever saw the place. Nothing fancy. Just where I hang my hat. You must tell me all about your golf game. Does Diane play?"

"A little. She just started."

"Give her time. I bet she'll really, really get into it."

No one was paying them any attention. Will dropped his voice. "Can't you just leave it?"

"Not yet," Bonnie said, at full, cheerful volume. "Maybe later. I haven't decided yet." She had drunk quite a bit of the wine by now, but something tight within her was keeping her from feeling it. She didn't know what she wanted from him, but something other than this limp-dick, skulking fear.

Fear of her? It made her furious. She wanted him to be worthy of all the feeling she'd invested in him. All those times when the very fact of his absence had made him so spectacularly present, when the edge of her longing was so sharp, she could have cut herself on it. Was his face different now? Weathered? Sure, the desert sun. She was staring. Don't.

Looking up to address Charlie, she asked him, "Where are all of you sleeping tonight? Curled up next to the fire?"

"The studio. We brought a bunch of foam mattresses and stuff."

"That's great! It can be like, your clubhouse."

"You can hang out with us if you want to stay there too."

"Slumber party! Maybe I will," Bonnie said, just to watch Will flinch.

Stan said, "If anybody breaks anything, I will weld their ass to a post."

"Don't worry," Charlie said. "We're all art-lovers."

"If you think I'm kidding, boy . . ."

"Naw, Stan. We know you never kid around."

Crisis intervention time? No, Stan just shook his head and growled into his drink. Charlie grinned. Charlie was putting on weight. Drinking, Bonnie guessed. Of the three of them, he'd always been the one with the looks, taking after the BioDad. Their mother's beautiful boy. He used to have a pirate's lean, dark face. Now he looked like a fat pirate. He wheezed when he laughed. Nobody ever stayed the same, was the same person you fell in love with.

Bonnie drank some more of her wine, waiting for it to do its thing. She wanted to be drunk enough to aim herself like a weapon. Diane was walking back toward them. Will stood up to meet her. Bonnie stood up too. There was indeed a goddamn ring on her left hand. A sparkler. Hooray!

"I understand," Bonnie said, "that congratulations are in order. So, congratulations!"

"Thank you." Diane smiled up at Will, who smiled back in return, a little curdled.

Charlie said, "They look good together, don't they? Like, I don't know, two sportswear models."

"Ah." Bonnie nodded and took a step back as if appraising them. Who wouldn't want to marry Diane? She had dark gold hair and skin like peach ice cream. And Will! It broke off another piece of her heart every time she looked at him, still handsome, and only someone who had known him before would have noticed the claw marks of age. The two of them did look good together; she couldn't stand it, why hadn't she kept her distance, kept her mouth shut? She'd overestimated her capacity for righteous indignation. She should fall on her knees in front of them. No, her face. Get over it. Diane was explaining that they hadn't set a date yet, there was still so much to think about. "Ah," Bonnie said again.

"Did you see the nativity set?" Charlie asked Bonnie, tugging at her sleeve. "Come on."

Bonnie followed him. Had she looked like she needed to be called off? Just how flipping obvious had she been? She flushed, then went cold. But Charlie only seemed impatient to show her the annual prank. The nativity set was arranged on a side table. The same old splintered and faded cast of characters, the camel who by now resembled an ordinary cow, the Angel of the Lord with its open, surprised mouth, Mary and Joseph posed in reverent parenthood over the small wooden manger and the Holy Child, here represented by Mr. Potato Head.

"Oh, too much. Don't let Haley see it."

"We could add Mrs. Potato Head, then there'd be twins."

"This family," Bonnie said, "is just one big practical joke."

"Yeah. Happy Christmukah. So what's with you and Will?"

"Nothing," she said, too fast.

Charlie shook his head. Not buying it. "OK, nothing now," she admitted. Her brother kept peering at her, eyebrows raised. "It was a while back. You know, one of those clean breaks so he could go off to Phoenix without any annoying entanglements from his past."

"Shit. I'm sorry."

"Yeah, me too." Over Charlie's shoulder, she saw Will and Diane, seated again, talking earnestly, perhaps deciding what sorbet to serve at the reception. She was so tired of being a moron loser.

"No, I mean, I'm sorry I brought him. Them."

"Here I thought I was being smooth."

"Maybe on some other planet you're smooth. Want me to do anything? Punch Will in the nuts? I feel, you know, implicated."

She could have told him not to pimp her out at family gatherings, but it was too late for that, and besides, he wouldn't have seen the harm in it. Her poor dopey brother in his outgrown, unfunny sweater, picking all the wrong times to be chivalrous. "Don't punch anybody. Don't say anything either. It's nobody's fault." Except, probably, her own.

"Water over the bridge," Charlie said, nodding seriously. "Wait, that's not it."

"Close enough."

"Dinner!" Claudia sang. "Now there's plenty for everybody, so don't be shy."

One of her mother's talents was the ability to put together a meal for an always expanding number of guests. There were twelve of them, not counting the babies. This dinner was like the miracle of the loaves and the fishes, although with more upscale ingredients. The cioppino was fragrant with fennel and the perfect, briny fruit of distant oceans. Claudia had made the loaves of peasant bread herself. And there was pasta with peppers and lamb sausage, and a platter of deep fried eggplant. Haley asked if she could say grace, and they all sat politely as she thanked the Lord for His bounty and for their many blessings, Amen, and then got up in a hurry to check on the babies. "I thought she was holding back," Charlie remarked. The two hipster boys sitting with Charlie looked around them, wondering if it was OK to laugh, then decided not to.

Stan took his usual seat at the head of the table, and Claudia sat next to the kitchen so she could run back and forth and not eat. Will and Diane were next to each other at Claudia's end, where Bonnie didn't have to listen to them. She was glad for that. She was tired and dismal and she wished them both a long and happy life somewhere far away from here.

Bonnie found herself sitting next to one of Charlie's friends, the rat-faced girl called Irina. Irina was a videographer, she told Bonnie, doing some commercial work, some event work, just to pay the bills, though what she really wanted was to go to Japan and make documentaries about their youth culture. The fads, the alienation, the revolt against materialism. Bonnie said that sounded interesting, although it didn't especially. To her annoyance, Franklin was seated on her other side. She didn't feel like making conversation with him, although she wondered what his story was, and how long he was planning on sticking around.

Stan looked to be in a better mood now that his dinner was in front of him. Claudia called it a blood sugar problem, but really, he was just a mean drunk. He started in on the pasta, then sawed off a portion of bread and used it to soak up the fish broth. He noticed Scott spearing different pieces of fish and dredging them up to lay on the border of his plate. "What," Stan said to his son-in-law. "Why are you playing with your food?"

"There's stuff I'm allergic to," Scott said, but he stopped fooling around with his stew and buttered a piece of bread. For a religious person, he had an unfortunate guilty face.

"Yeah?" Stan looked as if he might have more to say on the topic of finicky eaters, but instead turned to Franklin on his other side. "Let me tell you, I had no idea what I was getting into when I got married. I mean the first time, when I was young and green. Then the kids start coming. And you think, 'Wait a minute, can I just skip to the part where I'm an ancestor?'"

"Hah," Franklin said, by way of agreement. He didn't seem to be eating any of his food.

Stan took a pull of his drink. "Not that I'd change any of it. Being a part of, you know, the great chain of being."

Franklin leaned toward Bonnie and gave her a smile that had some cross-eyed effort at flirtation in it. "You remind me of my ex-wife."

"As long as I don't remind you of your next wife."

She turned her back on him. Irina was still talking about her Japanese documentary. "They have their own urban legends. Perhaps you've heard of One Man Hide and Seek? A ritual for contacting the dead. Very elaborate. Theirs is a culture of ceremonies. I'd love to film it. Not a ghost story per se, but a kind of meta-ghost story."

"That's very high concept," Bonnie told her. The wine was finally loosening in her. Drunken bad ideas were beginning to seem plausible. She'd get Will alone somewhere, fling herself at him, have one last sublime fuck for old times' sake.

Stan said, "Not that there weren't difficulties. Financial strains. Compromises. Accusations of bad faith. I wasn't selling anything yet, any of my pieces. Nothing taking off, no commissions, no matter how many hours I busted my ass. Then, around eight or nine at night, I'd come out of it and remember I was supposed to be home for dinner. Or no, I was supposed to *bring* the dinner. Wife and children, not happy."

". . . I mean, what if ghosts look entirely different than what we expect? I'm not saying I believe in ghosts, but . . ."

Haley came back to the table then. "I tried nursing them," she told her husband. "I think it went OK. Benjamin was a little fussy." Scott got up to take his turn at baby-tending. "We never eat a meal together," Haley complained. "Everything is tag team."

"Ah, try and enjoy this part. They don't stay little forever," Stan said. He looked morose, perhaps remembering his own long-ago babies.

"Are you supposed to enjoy it?" Haley said wearily. She prodded at her bowl of cioppino. "Cold fish soup. Yum."

"Because after all," Stan said, "the kids turned out all right. And the sculpture, well, the record speaks for itself. So cheer up, Haley girl. I remember when you were just a wee bit of a lump in a blanket, squalling and filling your pants. Now look at you, a blossoming Madonna. Look at . . ."

"Bonnie."

"Our own sweet Bonbon. How old are you now, twenty-six? Five. What the hell. Soon, I expect, you'll be procreating too."

"Not tonight, sorry." Why hadn't she gotten Will to impregnate her when she had the chance? Talk about a missed opportunity.

"Well, try to choose the right sire, would you? No scrub horses in the bloodline."

Haley said, "I don't know what you have against Scott, but it's very unfair to keep making these little sideways remarks when he's not here to defend himself."

"Me? Unfair?" Stan raised his eyebrows, all astonished innocence. "Did I even mention Scott? You're just oversensitive."

"In the One Man Hide and Seek ritual, a cloth doll is stuffed with rice, also the clippings of one's fingernails. The doll is sewn up with crimson thread. The rice represents innards, and the crimson thread is a blood vessel. A bathtub is filled with water and the doll is submerged in it. The ritual also requires a sharp-edged tool, like a knife."

Oh, Stan, but she'd tried to get herself a good one. There he was at the far end of the table, leaning forward and smiling at something some-body said, handsome, sun-tarnished, long gone. One arm draped over Diane's delightful shoulders. If you could kill people with a thought, she might have killed him. Or Diane. Somebody. Herself. She could move her dead self to Phoenix and haunt them.

"Make up a cup of salt water," Irina was saying. "Put half of it in your mouth, but don't swallow."

"Excuse me," Bonnie said. "But does it work, this ritual thing? Do people really see ghosts?"

"They think they do. That's the important part."

From across the table, Charlie was trying to catch Bonnie's eye. When he did, he made a pantomime of slugging Will, who was sitting next to him. Want me to? his raised eyebrows asked, and Bonnie shook her head.

Haley got up from the table again. "I'm going to put my dinner and Scott's in the fridge. We'll eat later, when things aren't so hilarious."

Bonnie jumped; Franklin had put his hand on her knee under the table. Bonnie picked his arm up by its shirt sleeve and dangled it in the air. "Whose hand is this, and what is it doing on my body?" She let the arm drop and got up from her chair. "Come on, Haley, I'll help you."

In the kitchen Haley said, "Why is he picking on Scott? Why is he all of a sudden picking on me? He doesn't even seem that excited about the babies. That's unnatural."

"Maybe they make him feel old."

"Well he is old. What was Franklin doing, feeling you up? He was teaching in some college and got fired for a sexual harassment thing. Him and Stan were talking about it."

"Nice. Bring a pervert home for the holidays." Claudia had made a Sicilian cassata for dessert, layered with sweetened ricotta and candied fruit, frosted with swirls of bitter chocolate. It lurked on the counter like a sugar bomb about to go off. "Want any help with the kids? I don't think I'm going back in there."

"Thanks, we've got it under control. And thanks for getting us out of the basement."

Haley leaned in and gave Bonnie a hug. Her nursing breasts were enormous, pressing against Bonnie like a pair of nosing puppies. "Happy Christ's Birthday. I know you think religion is all stupid but I pray for everybody. I pray the spirit will come to them."

The Holy Ghost? Bonnie said, "Sure, go ahead, what can it hurt?"

Once Haley left, Bonnie went downstairs, opened the fold-out couch, and lay on it, trying to feel either a lot more drunk or a lot more sober. The room was dark except for the path of light from upstairs, and the snow outside the windows glowed with its own cold radiance. Everybody believed in something. Stan in his own massive ego, Claudia in Stan. Haley in God, the Better Father. And Bonnie? She believed in the ghosts of old boyfriends.

But he wasn't one of her usual bad choices. He really wasn't. There was no reason they shouldn't have been happy together. Except that he didn't love her.

Some kitchen operation was going on overhead, voices, plates. She thought she heard Diane, asking sweetly if she could help serve dessert. Why sure, Diane honey, help me slice up this cake, now smile while I smash it into your face. Bad Bonbon! She got up, found the puffy coat Haley had left behind, and let herself out the sliding glass door.

The air was so cold, it made her lungs seize up. The snow wasn't deep, but it had a thin crust that resisted each step. She struggled and almost skidded down the slope into the woods. She'd fall, break her leg, freeze to death because no one inside would miss her or hear her piteous cries for help. She had the lamest fantasies in the world, and none of them did her any good. She walked around a corner of the house and watched Stan's light show from this new angle. The shooting colors, orange-red, purple-blue, rose and fell away and rose up again. They were entirely beautiful in and of themselves, no matter how self-satisfied Stan might be, or how much damage he did to everyone else. The record spoke for itself.

She turned and headed back the way she'd come. She hadn't gone that far, but she was clumsy with cold by now, and it took her longer than expected. Her fingers and ears ached. She fumbled with the glass door, alarmed now by how fast the cold was getting to her, as if she might freeze solid on the spot.

Finally she got the door open, closed it behind her, and hurried into the bathroom to run water over her hands. They burned. Her face was bright red and her eyes watered. She might have wanted to die a tragic death in the snow, but she certainly hadn't wanted to look bad while doing it.

Once she'd thawed out and turned a normal color again, she went back upstairs. The kitchen was crowded with people, all of them making some hectic effort she couldn't fathom, opening drawers, lifting things from the countertops. Claudia was going through a garbage bag, unloading vegetable peelings and fish scraps and paper wrappings. Will was under the kitchen sink with a wrench and Diane was standing next to him, looking fretful. Charlie had the broom out and was sweeping the floor one section at a time, stopping every so often to examine the bristles. "What's going on?" she asked him.

"Diane lost her engagement ring." Waiting to see what she'd say.

"Oh, that's." Dead stop. She wasn't sure what it was.

"She took it off while she was doing dishes."

Another stop, while each of them waited for the other to . . . Confess? Condole? Rejoice? "I expect it's insured," Bonnie said.

"I put it right there, in the little saucer on the sink, and I didn't even notice I didn't have it until I finished dessert, I don't believe it!" Diane kept rubbing her fingers together, all teary.

Claudia said, "It has to be here somewhere. I haven't run the garbage disposal yet, so we don't have to worry about that."

Will unbent himself from where he'd been working on the piping. "It's not in the trap or anywhere I can reach."

The others, Irina and the hipster boys, gradually gave up their effort and stood around looking ineffectual. Will said, "You're sure you put it on the sink. Not in your purse or anything."

"Why would I put it in my purse?"

"Why would you put it on the sink? Come on."

Franklin came in then, stopping in the doorway and blinking. "Diane lost her ring and we're looking for it," Claudia explained.

"Ah." Franklin nodded. He walked to the refrigerator and held his glass against the ice dispenser to chunk some ice cubes into it.

"I know it'll turn up," Claudia told Diane. "Things always do. Why don't you and Charlie and the others go get yourself set up in the studio?" She gave Diane a motherly hug. "I'll keep looking, it'll be easier without such a crowd."

"I'm never going to forgive myself," Diane said, but she let Will lead her out of the kitchen.

By the time Bonnie followed, they'd collected their coats and headed outside. The dining room table was cleared, the main room empty. Stan must have gone on to bed. The fire in the hearth had burned down to ash and embers. The Christmas tree lights had been switched off. The crow at the top brooded in the dark. She sat down on the couch and yawned. She supposed she took some small, mean pleasure in the lost ring, but nothing that changed the essential cruddiness of everything.

The front door opened and Will came in, scraping the snow from his boots. He stood in front of Bonnie, looking down. "Do you know anything about this?"

"About what?"

"About Diane's ring."

"Not a thing. How many carats did you get her?"

"Did you take it? Just tell me, all right?"

"Drop dead."

"Were you in the kitchen after she left? Did you see it?"

"I wasn't there. I went for a walk."

"It's below zero out there."

"Yeah, it was cold."

They stared at each other. Charlie thought she'd taken it too, although he would have sympathized. "Look," she said, holding out her hands and spreading her fingers. "No rings. Nothing up my sleeve."

He shifted his weight and looked away, as if he might believe her in spite of himself. "Diane asked me about you. Like she figured out something had, you know, happened with us."

"Yeah, something did. Maybe you should tell her. Whatever it is that, you know, you decide to say."

He sat down next to her. "I'm sorry."

"Sorry for what, exactly?"

He turned and kissed her then, pulling her up to him and holding her face in his hands. It was a surprise and then it wasn't; it was everything remembered and familiar and starting up all over again. Because nothing was ever over as long as you were both alive. Or maybe even then it went on and on, ghost love? It had not gone to waste, been dismissed or forgotten. It could not be undone. She leaned into him with her entire self and finally he pulled away, got up, and walked out, closing the front door behind him.

Bonnie sat there a long time. Then she stood. Her whole body hurt, as if she was coming down with the flu, as if she'd been beaten.

So she guessed she'd been kissed off.

Moving with care, she reentered the empty kitchen and turned on the light to the stairs. She got halfway down then stopped. Someone was snoring.

It was Franklin, face down on the fold-out couch, arms and legs in a dead man's sprawl. His shirt had come untucked and a wedge of fat showed above his belt. She contemplated him for a moment, then retraced her steps back upstairs.

The house was quiet. A baby started up crying, faintly, at some distance, but even as Bonnie listened, it ceased. The kitchen had been scoured down and the dishes done and put away in the course of all the searching. Hungry now, Bonnie found the leftover cake in the refrigerator, cut herself a slice, and ate it standing at the sink, looking out at the woods. The window had begun to ice over in crescents of frost.

When she was finished eating, she rinsed her dishes and washed them, and reached into the top drawer for a clean dishtowel. Something popped out of a fold of the towel and bounced tinnily on the floor.

She picked it up and examined it under the light. It was a pretty ring, sweet rather than showy, with a round-cut diamond held by prongs, and small chips of diamonds in the band.

It didn't quite fit her, but she could get it on her little finger.

She thought about her choices, the different things she might do, the different selves she might decide to be. Then she went back into the main room. She bent over the nativity scene. Mr. Potato Head's arms were white curlicues and he had cartoon-style white gloves, waving. Bonnie hung the ring on one of his outstretched hands. "There you go," she said. "Congratulations."

atlanta

She was Mamma, Mamma, Mom-mee! All day and all night, each and every day and night, forever and Amen. She'd gotten pregnant again when Robbie was only eighteen months old. Now, four months along, she moved like a sleepwalker, though her actual sleep was dead and dreamless. Ma! Mamma! Mom-mee! Her son needed everything every minute: his breakfast toast cut into squares, his stuffed Tigger retrieved from where he'd thrown it behind the couch. His nose blown, his ass wiped. He was in constant motion, slamming himself into walls and leaping off furniture and tumbling onto grass, dirt, gravel, asphalt, howling and covering himself with blood and bruises.

Everyone, that is, her husband and the other residents who were their friends, and the wives (and the husbands) of the residents, said that this was what little boys did. Eric said he'd been a tree-climber himself, big time, back in the day. Boys were just naturally energetic and into everything. Jane wasn't so sure. She didn't remember either of her brothers getting their foot stuck in an empty mayonnaise jar, as had been the case in their most recent trip to the emergency room.

The new baby swam and tumbled inside her, only inches long. It had been not much more than a bubble of blood and a few ambitious cells, but now it had grown enough for the sonogram to determine it was a girl. And everyone said, wasn't that just perfect, a boy and a girl. A pigeon pair, it was called, did she know that? Jane did not. The extent of her ignorance was vast, profound. Perfect? Were they serious?

She'd wanted children. They both did. She and Eric had talked it all out. Of course you did not know what to expect. You took what came. You held hands and jumped over the cliff together into this grand adventure of adulthood. But did you ever stop falling?

Eric was such a good father. The everyones agreed. He was cheery and helpful and patient, running Robbie's bath and telling him stories and fetching Jane a pillow when her back hurt. Of course he had to work his killer hours, coming and going, and then he'd have a day, or a day and a half off—except for those times when he was on call—and the house would transform into a kind of brightly colored and hectic Dad-dyland. It was a little bewildering, and perhaps a little unreal. But Jane and Eric were determined to make the best of things, and not to let the marriage drift, and now the joke was, with two babies so close together, they had certainly not wasted any of their precious time.

There were no doubt easier ways to be married, less demanding schedules for sure, but this was the deal they'd signed on to. You put your head down and scrambled to get through the maze of doctor world, to get the children birthed and launched, and eventually, surely, it would get better. The two of you would reunite on the battlefield and lean on your swords and congratulate each other on surviving. The old war stories, now fond reminiscences. Remember when Robbie got his foot stuck in the mayonnaise jar? Except that Eric would not remember it entirely the same way she did since he had not been there.

Only a few of the residents had families underway or planned. A number of the wives were doctors themselves, or had their own busy jobs. So that stay-at-home Jane had managed to become a subset of a subset. The other mommy-women were considered her friends, although fellow travelers would have been more accurate. The mommies were like military wives left behind on base while the wars were fought elsewhere. Jane would have liked to get to know some different people, different kinds of people, but where was there time or opportunity for that?

Atlanta didn't feel like home. It didn't feel like much of anything, just a place they had landed for now. When they were first exploring it they'd gone to a historic house and World of Coca-Cola, and they'd eaten in a couple of celebratory restaurants. But those were tourist things. The survey research job at Emory, which might have helped to ground her in the place, only lasted a few months and was not renewed. Jane learned her way around well enough to get to the grocery and the bank, the shopping mall, the doctor and dentist. All the while, the city itself escaped her. It was too big and spread out, a whorl of freeways and skyscrapers, always seen on the horizon, like the Emerald City of Oz. They didn't even live in Atlanta itself, but in one of its all-purpose suburbs. Eric and the other residents worked downtown at Grady Hospital, where the real Atlanta went about its business of living and dying.

One of the mommies in their group had a little girl who was a few months older than Robbie, and they arranged some play dates. These did not go very well. The little girl was bossy, and her speech was better than Robbie's, so she called him stupid, and poop-head, as her mother made too mild objections, and usually the session ended in tears when Robbie hauled off and chunked some plastic toy at her. But when the two women did manage a conversation (the children's truce holding, the iced tea or Coke or wine cooler poured out), they often gave Jane pause.

"Are you going to stop at two, or keep going?"

There was no need to ask two what; everything was about babies. "We haven't decided," Jane said, although they had. Two children were enough for them. It was a nosy question, but Jane guessed it was the kind of thing women were supposed to talk about when they got together in henlike groups.

"We'll probably wait until Bree's a little older. But there's something to be said for having one right after the other, like you. Just go for it."

There was something to be said, but it did not make for pleasant speech. In the weeks when Jane was fighting nausea, the sight of Robbie with oatmeal or pink meat paste smeared and crusted all over his face, hands, clothes, etc., had often made her stomach empty on the spot.

"Anyway," her hostess continued, "if you decide you're through after this one, you can go ahead and schedule some work down there. You know?"

Jane didn't. She must have looked particularly clueless, because the other woman put down her glass and smirked. "Rejuvenating the vag. Get things back to where they were. Oh don't look so shocked. It's just a little tuck here and there. The magic of modern medicine."

"I'm sorry, I guess sex is the last thing I've been thinking about."

"Well it's not the last thing the guys are thinking about. If they could make their penises bigger, don't you think they would?"

The thought of ever again using her body for any sort of pleasure (that is, someone else's pleasure) was alien. She was at its mercy. And her body was, if you could say such a thing, single-minded. It existed only to serve the child within her and the child without. Her body dragged her from one place to another. She was not tired. Tired had been months ago. This was some other condition, a weight in her limbs, a haze in her head, her eyelids falling shut without warning. Between this pregnancy and the last one, she'd had every form of discomfort and every wretched symptom, so much so that Eric said she must have read all the textbooks and memorized them. "Don't," she told him, "joke about it." She was swollen, constipated, seeping, itching. Gaseous and plagued with heartburn. She made constant, ignominious trips to pee. There was a lot she wasn't looking forward to, up to and including childbirth. With Robbie her breasts had enlarged, pulling her forward. She'd had hemorrhoids and varicose veins. She felt like she'd been pregnant for the last five years.

What was the matter with her? There were women who loved being pregnant, who sailed through any distress and nested comfortably throughout. But Jane felt submerged. As if she was being dissolved. Absorbed. Something. It was all wrong, or maybe the way she felt about it was all wrong. Although she was a mother, she did not feel motherly. She loved Robbie, his damp eyelashes after tears and his breath at night and his warrior's heart. She already loved the baby inside of her; she was only waiting to find out exactly how. But it was not a comfortable love. They took too much of her. They would always do so.

It wasn't anything she could tell anyone else, certainly not Eric. He adored Robbie, of course, he was excited about the new baby, he spoke often of how lucky they were. Which was true, in so many objective ways. She was a part of Team Eric now, and the team was accustomed to winning out. He could not be blamed for anything, except, perhaps, his certainty that things would always go well.

One night they were having a late supper of sandwiches while Robbie slept on the carpet in front of the television. He'd wrapped and twined himself in his favorite blanket so that he appeared, at first glance, to have successfully strangled himself.

Eric said, "We need to switch him over to a big boy bed pretty soon. He's already climbing out of the crib. How about for his birthday? We could make it part of the occasion."

"Sure."

"Then there's time for him to get used to it before the baby comes. So he doesn't feel like he's being kicked out when we move the crib."

"Sure."

"Not much of a conversationalist tonight, are you?"

"Perhaps," Jane said, "we could talk about something other than babies."

They both worked on their sandwiches for a while, waiting for another, nonbaby topic to emerge. Eric smoothed his hair with one hand in what had become a sorrowful, unconscious gesture. His hairline was receding. He made a lot of mortified jokes about it. Jane was almost glad. She didn't want to be the only one whose looks had taken a beating.

"Well," Eric said, "I could tell you about the bowel resection I observed today. But maybe that's not exactly a dinner table story."

"We generate enough of our own bowel stories around here," Jane agreed.

He reached over and patted her stomach. "I do a rotation in urology next. That should be good for snappy repartee."

"Ha ha," Jane said. She was in a white, white room. No, she was not in anything. There was only the beautiful floating white. There was a sound that might have been a buzz or a hum but was neither. It was the most curious thing, not to be anywhere. Where did you go instead?

"Honey?" Eric was leaning over her. "You fell asleep."

Had she? She didn't think so. It was something different, more un-earthly, more beguiling and transporting. But because it would alarm him if she said this, she yawned and stretched and said, "Really? How long was I out? I'm sorry. You were saying something."

"I said, once the baby's born and we feel we can leave her on her own for a day or so, I want you to tell me something you'd really like to do, somewhere you'd really like to go. For a getaway. A special treat."

"Would you come too?"

"If you want me to," Eric said gamely. "Or it could be something just for you. Like, a spa day."

"That would be nice," Jane said, as she was supposed to. And it was sweet of him. He wanted to express his appreciation and concern. Jane could have her depleted body lotioned and steamed and kneaded. Maybe get the vag resurfaced. Come home relaxed and beautified and ready for a merry time between the sheets. "A spa day, that sure would be some-thing different."

It wasn't Eric's fault. She had to be fair. No one had forced her to ac-cept the life he'd offered her, and she would have been desolated if he'd passed her by. Any normal woman would have been content, or at least, would have been a better, if burdened, wife and mother. But she had always known, even as it shamed her, that she was not entirely a normal woman.

She called it the white room. It opened itself to her at her times of greatest fatigue and stress, some bodily limit reached. When Robbie in his car seat squalled and writhed at a traffic intersection and her hands locked on the steering wheel and she couldn't move and the white room pulled her in. How long did she sit there? When she opened her eyes again, Robbie was still screeching and the milk she'd bought was still chilled in its carton. The traffic light was still red, although whether it was the same light or the next cycle, she couldn't tell. Nobody behind her. She'd been weightless, diffuse, a state one might think of as non-Jane.

Was she going barmy from exhaustion and pregnancy hormones? There was probably some reasonable physiological explanation that she didn't want to hear. So she did not bring it up to her obstetrician, a smart, delightful young Indian woman who was expecting her own first child. She did not feel mentally ill, but then, maybe that was a backwards proof of being mentally ill. And there was something deeply, deeply pleasurable in these episodes of non-Jane, like another woman's secret drinking.

The white room erased sadness, fear, pain. It was pure anesthetic. She came back to herself, the world, her unhappy body, with regret. It always seemed as if she had a choice.

Leave poor old droopy hangdog Jane behind and paddle around in the ether. She guessed it had become her kind of spa.

She didn't think anyone would have noticed. After all, most of the time she was easy enough for people to ignore. But one morning Eric asked her if she thought she was depressed.

They were in the kitchen. Robbie was in his booster chair, eating fistfuls of cereal from a bowl in front of him. Half of his face was still swollen from climbing headfirst into the empty bathtub. "Depressed?" she echoed back, stalling. "No, just, I'm tired a lot. You know."

"Sure. But you seem kind of like you've . . . checked out."

"I don't know what you mean."

She knew exactly what he meant. There was a brief, obstinate silence, broken by Robbie.

"Maaaama!"

"What, honey?"

"More cereal."

"More cereal, please." Jane reached for the box and shook it over the bowl.

"Shouldn't he be eating with a spoon by now?"

Wordlessly, Jane picked up the spoon from the floor where Robbie had thrown it and presented it.

"Did you do that, big guy? Huh?" Eric ruffled his hair and mugged until the little boy giggled. "Pitch a fastball? Huh?"

"Eric."

"Sorry. Don't throw your spoon, OK? It makes Mommy sad."

Jane said nothing. This would be the pattern of the future. The two of them united in manly understanding, tiptoeing around her unreasonable fussy self. Robbie looked so much like Eric. Except that Robbie's hair was blond. Eric said he'd been a blond baby and that Robbie's hair would get darker, just as his had. And then, in time, fall out. Now that was a depressing thought. Was that depression? Was there a difference?

Eric poured himself a cup of coffee. He never had his coffee at home. He was making an effort. "There's this really good guy. A family practice guy." He waited for Jane to react.

"I think I have enough doctors, thanks."

"I'd like it if you'd just go talk to him. Maybe he could write you a prescription."

"I'm not taking anything that would hurt the baby."

"Do you think I'd let you? I've asked around, there are some perfectly safe drugs that might help."

"Help what, exactly? And ask who, people who know me?" From Eric's irritated look, she saw that this was the case. She hated the idea of him communing with their medical friends, telling them how peevish and fumbling and out of it she was. "Thanks."

"I wish," he said sadly, "that you at least wanted to be happy."

"Maybe I am happy. For me. I wish you didn't feel like you had to fix me."

"Fix," Robbie said. "Fix me!"

"Fine," Eric said, giving up. "Be happy your way. Don't let me stop you."

She thought how much of her marriage, her part in it, went back to her fear that he would realize he'd made a mistake in choosing her. That he had fallen in love with her on false pretenses.

∞

She sat across from Dr. Cohen in the examining room. He had already gathered and assessed Jane's observable and measurable characteristics. Weight, height, allergies, the composition of her fluids. He believed, he said, in a holistic approach, and so there was this talking stuff. "I understand," Dr. Cohen said, "that you might be here somewhat under protest. Is that right?" Smiling a twinkly smile to show Jane that he understood that she was a reluctant patient, and he didn't hold it against her. He was sixty? North of sixty? Gold, rimless glasses, a lot of lopsided curly gray-black hair. Maybe he was an old hippie, he'd recommend aromatherapy or herbal teas.

"No, but it was my husband's idea. I agreed to it."

"To keep the peace."

"Pretty much." She tried to sound straightforward, unsurly. "Maybe he told you. He thinks I'm depressed."

"It doesn't matter what he told me. You're my patient now, with all the rights and privileges thereof." Jane gave him an inquiring look. "It means I won't share information with your husband."

She nodded. At least that much was good. She tried shifting in her chair to get comfortable. She was starting to gain weight faster now, and while she wasn't showing yet, she felt bulky and slow.

"Before we talk about depression, what that is or isn't, why don't you tell me how you're feeling these days."

"Extra super pregnant."

"Are you having a hard time with this one?"

"I don't know. Is it supposed to be easy?"

"I'm pretty sure my wife would say no. We had three of our own."

Jane looked around for pictures of them. But no, he'd have them in his office, not here. The same as Eric had his pictures of her and Robbie. "I'm uncomfortable. Tired. Normal, I guess. It's hard to catch up. Rest up. Our little boy is almost two."

"Robbie. Your husband bragged on him up, down, and sideways."

"Oh yes. Proud papa." Small talk. She waited for him to do his doctor thing so she could oh white. Oh lovely pure nothing. Oh gratitude and whiteness and blessedness.

"Mrs. Nicholson?"

Her eyes opened. Dr. Cohen looked, something. Concerned. Blurry. "Hmm," Jane said, because it was an easy sound to make.

"What happened just now?"

"Sorry. Fell asleep."

"Do you have any history of epilepsy?"

That meant, seizure. Was that what they were? Jane shook her head.

"Let me get you some water." He stood, went out into the hallway, and came back with a paper cup. "Here. Take your time."

She drank. She took her time. "Are you all right?" Dr. Cohen asked. "Do you feel like talking?"

"Sure," she said agreeably. She became aware of the everyday sounds of the office building rushing in, as if her ears had just been turned back on: footsteps in the hallway outside, an elevator chiming, voices. Dr. Cohen's big cloud of hair crinkling. "How long was I, whatever I was?"

"Less than a minute."

"Do I have epilepsy?"

"I don't know. It's possible."

"It doesn't feel like epilepsy," she said, stubbornly. As if she knew all about it.

"Tell me what it feels like."

"It feels . . . beautiful. Peaceful. More than that. I can't explain it right. Something exciting. A sacred feeling. Like my head turns into . . ." She might have said heaven, but settled for ". . . a cathedral."

"And how long has this been going on?"

"Not long. A few weeks." It seemed important that she explain and reassure him that it was no big medical deal. "It happens mostly when I'm tired. Stressed." She couldn't keep herself from asking. "Did it look weird? Was I moving around or making sounds?"

"No, if it was a seizure, it's what we call an absence seizure. It's just what it sounds like. Someone blanks out, loses focus, then comes back to the present."

She wasn't sure she wanted it to be a disease, something ordinary. "Do I have to have tests or something?"

"I'd like to hold off for now. Estrogen increases the electrical activity of the brain, did you know that? Let's see if you have the same problem once the baby's born."

"It's not a problem," Jane said, but softly, so that Dr. Cohen had to ask her to repeat it.

"It would be a problem if you were holding a baby. Driving a car."

She shook her head. "It makes me happy."

"How so?"

"I'm not there anymore. Anywhere."

"I don't understand why that makes you happy."

Jane shook her head again, but carefully, as if it were full of something that might spill.

"I wish you would try to tell me."

A space of silence. Jane said, "Because I'm living the wrong life." It was as if she hadn't known it until she said it.

"How is it wrong?"

"Not so much wrong." She retreated. "But not always good at it. I mean, fall in love, get married, have kids? Everybody does it." The doctor was only sitting there, watching her lurch from one incoherence to another. She tried again. "Do you ever see people—patients—who aren't friends with their bodies? I don't mean, they think they're too fat or anything like that."

"I see plenty of people who are ill, in pain, and they aren't on good terms with their bodies."

"No," Jane said. "This is different. I mean, feeling separate from your body. Being not really in it. I'm sorry, I'm not explaining anything very well."

Dr. Cohen looked as if he was at least making an effort at understanding. "But we're always in our bodies."

"I'm not. That's what happens. I get to leave."

"And be nowhere."

"Yes," Jane said, aware that she was sounding unstable, or maybe just eccentric and comical, as if she'd claimed to be the reincarnation of an ancient Aztec princess. "You asked me to tell you what it feels like," she reminded him.

"I did." He shifted in his chair, rocking backward. The diplomas on his wall were all from New York State. Was anyone really from Atlanta? "OK, here are some possibilities. Pregnancy stress. Hormone overload. Some sort of neurological deficit or abnormal brain activity. Psychological issues. None of these conditions are mutually exclusive, that is, you might have some of them or all of them."

Jane stayed silent. She was either sick or crazy or else just one of those broody females who were always at the mercy of their glands. She shouldn't have said anything.

"Or else," Dr. Cohen continued, "and again, not mutually exclusive, that is, perhaps caused by one of the above, perhaps not, you're having a mystical experience. A connection with the absolute. Like Saint Teresa of Avila, or a Zen master."

"Wow, you really are a holistic doctor."

He laughed. "I try to keep an open mind."

"Well . . . I'm not very religious," Jane said.

"You did use the word sacred."

"I guess I did." *Sacred.* She didn't think she'd ever spoken the word out loud before in her life. "But I don't think I'm a saint, or a Zen master. That sounds a little grand. I mean, I could just have a brain tumor."

"Exactly." He seemed pleased, not at the brain tumor, maybe, but at her grasp of the way this might work. "Or epilepsy, or some other seizure disorder. Seizures have been associated with ecstatic feelings and religious visionaries throughout history."

"It all sounds very complicated," Jane said, though what she meant was, it was worrying.

"I'd like to keep monitoring you. Let's have you come in next month. No tests or medication for now, but you could keep a record of how often you have these, let's call them events. And it would be desirable if you didn't drive. And if you avoided getting overtired or stressed."

Jane just looked at him. He shrugged. "I only said, it would be a good idea."

Her appointment time was up. Jane could tell. Doctors, even the nice ones, were so intent on keeping to their schedule that they turned abrupt and twitchy and made conversation-ending statements. She stood to go. "What should I tell my husband?"

"Whatever you choose to tell him." Dr. Cohen stood also. They shook hands. He really wasn't any taller than Jane, unless you took his hair into account.

"Can I tell him you said I wasn't depressed?"

"Let's talk about depression next time."

A neighbor was watching Robbie, and on the way home Jane put aside mommy guilt for long enough to stop and get a sandwich at a take-out place and eat it at a picnic table next to the parking lot. It was March, and already there were hints of heavy, syrupy warmth in the air. Trees were in bud, and also the yellow arcs of forsythia, and other blooming things she did not know the names of. The baby would not be born until August. It was going to be a long, hot, pregnant summer.

She thought her brain was probably fine. The problem was always her heart, which they'd patched and shored up all those years ago, but had never been at home inside her.

The white room was the one place where she could be alone. That was all she really wanted.

The baby inside her fluttered. She was wrong. She was never truly alone.

When Eric asked her, as carefully as possible, how her appointment had been, Jane said she thought it had been helpful. Eric didn't push it any further than that. Jane tried smiling more often. And, as if cautioned, the white room remained closed to her, at least for now.

The following week, she got a call from Bonnie. "Hey, girlfriend."

"Hey yourself." Always a surprise when Bonnie called. Always some effort required for Jane to bring her energy level up a few notches so she didn't sound like a big drag. They weren't really that close anymore. Except that then, in a matter of minutes, they were. "Are you still the toast of the town?" Jane asked, aiming for sprightliness.

"More like just toast. How are you feeling?"

"Great. I'm having twin elephants. I wanted you to be the first to know."

They talked for a time, catching up. It never took that long to fall back into the old dorm room griping. Bonnie said she was through with men, meaning, Jane guessed, she was between boyfriends. She said that men were no longer necessary for the perpetuation of the species, thanks to scientific advances in cryogenics and assisted fertilization, you know, the way they did things with bulls and racehorses. Jane said that the guys she knew were still hung up on doing things the old-fashioned way.

"Counterrevolutionaries," Bonnie said. "Czarists. We'll smoke the last remnant of them out of the hills." Then, "Listen, I've got a few days off coming up. I was thinking of a little Atlanta jaunt."

"Oh." Surprised. "Well, that's great. But you know, we're not a real fun vacation destination these days. Robbie, don't." He was climbing the arm of the sofa, trying to pull a lamp over onto his head. Jane scooped him up and deposited him back in the toy zone on the floor.

"I'm not coming to have fun. I'm coming to see you."

"Thanks." A suspicion lit up her head like an old-fashioned cartoon lightbulb. "Did Eric call you?"

Bonnie sighed. "He's worried about you."

"Maybe he ought to be."

"What? OK, he shouldn't have tried to be slick. Me neither, I'm sorry. He didn't want you to feel you were being manipulated."

"Even though I totally am."

"So forget the bad motives. We'll hang out with the rug rat. Drink from sippy cups. Finger paint. Make fun of your husband."

"Listen, I can't stay on the phone." Robbie was mobile again, careening down the hallway out of sight. "It'll be good to see you, let me know when you're coming, bye."

That night she said to Eric, "Bonnie's thinking of coming for a visit."

"Is she?" Jane watched him pretend mild surprise. "That'll be a nice change of pace for you. She always peps you up."

"She's a peppy kind of a girl," Jane said, but she left it at that. How mad were you supposed to get? Would she like it any better if he didn't care about her?

She'd seen Bonnie only once in all this time, and that was when Robbie was a few months old and they'd made the arduous trip back to Chicago for Christmas so that the grandparents could view him. It had been a hectic visit, Robbie already a wriggling, vocal infant, and their two families competing for equal time and attention. Bonnie was skipping the holidays with her own family—it was a new tradition, she'd said— and came by Jane's parents' house on Christmas afternoon. She'd looked older, in a way that Jane realized was a reflection of herself. Neither of them yet thirty. Not exactly over the hill. Just something other than what they'd been.

Bonnie, meanwhile, had become, in a local sense, something of a well-known figure. Crisis intervention was very up and coming, an important tool in urban policing. "As opposed to, say, just shooting people," Bonnie said. Jane's parents were impressed that she'd been interviewed on one of the Chicago news programs, and they'd taped it to show Jane. They cued it up in the family room and Jane's mother brought out coffee and Christmas cookies. Bonnie murmured that it wasn't really a holiday classic. But here she was, looking cool and savvy in a white shirt and a leather jacket, a streetwise professional talking knowledgeably about demographics and distressed populations and the new skill set required of officers in the field as they adapted to changing conditions, etc. "You're so *articulate*," Jane's mother said, and Bonnie and Jane traded weary looks, since it was a habit for both their mothers to find in the other those remarkable virtues that their own daughters lacked. Bonnie's mother liked to point out how polite Jane was.

A time or two a case Bonnie had been involved in landed in the newspaper. She sent these along to Jane, and Jane read the heartbreaking, infuriating details of people who did not seem willing or capable of even the lowest common denominator of responsible behavior. Not every crisis was resolved happily, of course, and Jane thought that would be the hardest part. When crazy, or crazy drugs, or a vicious, unfettered mind won out, in spite of your best efforts. She thought it would have to take a toll, if you did it long enough.

For her Atlanta visit, Bonnie made Jane promise not to go to any trouble, and Jane said that was easy enough to comply with. Especially since there was no other place to put the potty chair except in the bathroom that Bonnie would be using. Bonnie said she guessed she'd meant, more along the line of entertainment, but no matter. Jane made up the guest bed in the spare room—she had not yet begun to think of it as a nursery—and put out a stack of fresh towels. She scrubbed down the kitchen and sorted and folded the backlog of laundry as Robbie threw the pieces of his educational puzzle toy one by one at the glass patio doors. Perhaps she could project an air of cheerful television sit com havoc.

Bonnie had insisted on taking a cab from the airport so that no one would have to pick her up. Jane watched Bonnie shut the cab door, hoist her suitcase, and roll it along the sidewalk. "Nice place," she said, when Jane opened the front door. "We've got to get you out of here."

Robbie was still at an age where he was fearless around strangers. He squealed and crowed when Bonnie picked him up and swung him around. "Roberto. The jig is up. There's a new sheriff in town." To Jane she said, "Go lie down and take a nap."

"But you just got here."

"And I'll be here when you wake up. Go on, I'll call you if I need you."

Jane made a few noises of protest, but the unexpected reprieve and the gravitational pull of her bed were too strong to resist. She closed the bedroom door behind her and lay down. "All right, kid," she heard Bonnie saying. "What do you have to drink in this joint?"

Jane was instantly asleep. She woke just as suddenly, as if she had slept no time at all, but the room was full of shadowy evening light. She panicked: where was Robbie? But he was with Bonnie, and then she panicked all over again, swinging her legs over the side of the bed and rushing into the bathroom because of course she couldn't live another minute without peeing.

She heard voices, one of them Eric's. Had he come home early? Or no. It wasn't early. Still fighting sleep and dread, she hurried toward the light and commotion of the kitchen. The three of them were sitting at the table, Eric and Bonnie and Robbie in his booster chair, surrounded by sandwich wrappers and paper cups. And even as she was greeted with noisy enthusiasm and Eric stood to kiss her and Robbie clamored to be picked up and held, she knew that all she'd had to do to bring about this scene of contentment was to leave them alone.

She could not shake her sense of dislocation, as if everything in the room had been arranged so as to mimic the perfectly normal. "Great timing," Eric said, showing her the plate set out for her. "We just this minute started. It's still hot."

Bonnie said, "Eric brought barbecue. From world famous something or other."

Jane checked the clock. It was almost seven, and she'd slept for most of four hours. "I guess I was really out of it."

"Or really tired. Here, I got you a mac and cheese, and a pulled pork sandwich. Is that OK? There's ribs too. And slaw. You want iced tea?"

"I was going to cook dinner."

"And we'll let you. Tomorrow. Here, I made sure they put the hot sauce on the side."

Who could ask for a better husband? How deftly, and with what a light touch, he skated over her shortcomings, smoothed the way for her. Every so often he gave Jane an encouraging smile. Jane sat down with Robbie in her lap, trying to arrange him so that he did not kick her in the stomach. To Bonnie she said, "How did you manage with him, did he run you ragged?"

"Nah. We reached a negotiated settlement." Bonnie was in on it too, playing the part of the fast-talking babe in the screwball comedy. "We ran race cars. He's a competitive little dude. Aren't you? Ticklish, too." Bonnie made a mock-lunge for Robbie, who squealed, enamored, and hid in Jane's shoulder. "Are you ticklish? Huh?"

"No-ooo!"

"Not ticklish. Good to know. Let's see, then we had peanut butter and crackers and orange juice, and we watched *Jeopardy*, and we did a little target practice in the bathroom. Don't worry, everything's all cleaned up."

"Bonnie, I didn't mean for you to do—"

"Stuff you do every day? Chill. It was no biggie. Since I don't do it every day."

"Well thank you, Mary Poppins." She shook her head to get some of the sleep strangeness out of it. To Robbie she said, "Let's eat some dinner now, all right? Can you sit up and eat your sandwich like a big boy?"

"I want play my cars."

"After you eat." Jane reached for the chicken sandwich he hadn't touched. "Here. Make sure you chew it enough."

"Don't you get to eat?" Bonnie asked.

"In a minute." In fact Jane was hungry, but the smell of the red-brown meat was unpleasant, almost swampy to her. She would have liked something clean and persnickety, like cucumber and watercress sandwiches with the crusts trimmed. She had the most useless pregnancy cravings, there was never any hope of satisfying them. "Drink your milk," she told Robbie. "Another big bite." He was good and wound up from his adventures with Bonnie. Bedtime would be a challenge. "How about we play with your cars in the bathtub?"

Once Robbie had been fed, bathed, and put into pajamas, Jane came back to the kitchen table, where Eric and Bonnie had switched to bottled beer and were chatting companionably.

"Daddy has to kiss him good night," Jane announced. She sat down and started in on the cold mac and cheese.

Eric drained his beer bottle and got up. "We're very child-centered around here. The child insists." He patted the top of Bonnie's head on his way out.

Bonnie said, "What's it going to be like with two?"

"At least the baby won't be running around for a while. Other women do it. Other women put their kids in day care and go to work every morning." She must look even worse than she felt, for the two of them to be so solicitous. It irritated her, in an unworthy way, as if she could do nothing without supervision and care. Jane had second thoughts about cold mac and cheese; she got up to put it in the microwave. "I'll be all right."

Eric came back in. "He's down but not out." From the hallway came Robbie's mournful, imperious cry: "Mom-mee!"

"Go to sleep," Jane called. "We have bedtime issues," she told Bonnie. "Because Daddy and I are, believe it or not, one heck of a rousing good time."

"She didn't used to be sarcastic," Bonnie informed Eric.

"Clearly, I'm a bad influence."

"Mom-mee!"

"Honey, it's bedtime." She was going to have to go in to him, but she wanted to get some food in her first. She took Robbie's half-eaten sandwich apart and started in on the bun. She saw the other two watching her. "I ate a very balanced breakfast and lunch."

"Maaa-mee!"

"I'm coming." If she didn't go to him, he'd get himself out of the crib and then they'd have to start all over. "Just put everything away, I'll eat it later."

Jane headed back to tend to Robbie. It came as a relief to get up and leave. She was still out of sorts, and there was something discordant about the three of them together in a room, as if any two of them would be a better idea.

She stayed with Robbie until he fell asleep, rocking him in the rocker, rocking the new baby also, the three of them heavy with sleep and warmth and there were these moments too of perfect contentment, the boundaries of her body blurring into theirs, the weight no burden, and love, for once, coming easy.

By the time she lifted Robbie into his crib, and tried to arrange his arms and legs into some peaceful position—because even in sleep he looked ready to land a haymaker punch—the others had gone to bed. The guest room door was closed. Her own room was dark, and Jane undressed and put on her pajamas without turning on a light. She left their door ajar in case she needed to hear Robbie. Eric snored breezily. When she got into bed on her side, he woke up enough to send an arm in her direction, draping over her.

Jane said, "I know you called and told her to come."

It took him a moment to swim up through his sleep and be able to speak. "Was that such a terrible thing?"

"You could have asked me about it."

"You would have said no, it was too much trouble."

"You don't know that." Jane heard her voice rise, then damped it down in case Bonnie was awake and listening. "Anyway, why was it so important?"

"I thought she'd cheer you up."

"And why is it so important that I get cheered up? I'm doing the best I can, Eric. I try not to complain, because then I'd be complaining the whole time, but this is not easy."

"You never want anything I can give you."

That stopped her, and by the time Jane came up with something she might say to him, he was asleep again.

In the morning, Eric left before anyone else was up. Jane got up next, fed Robbie his breakfast, and plunked him down in front of a Disney movie while she ducked into the bathroom for one of her three-minute shower routines. By the time Bonnie woke, she'd started the day's second pot of coffee. She'd tried doing without caffeine early on. Even Eric agreed she was better off drinking it.

"Good morning," Bonnie said, playing peekaboo around the door frame. Robbie was instantly in the fun zone, ready to pick up where they'd left off. He pounded across the floor to Bonnie and tackled her around the knees.

"Whoa there, killer. Can I get a little coffee before we get rowdy?"

"No!"

"Welcome to my world," Jane told her. "Robbie, why don't you go get your cars? You left them in your bed."

Robbie took off down the hall. "Quick, medicate me," Bonnie said.

Jane poured her a cup of coffee. "Are you hungry? We have Cheerios, toast, and . . . Cheerios. Orange juice."

"Just coffee. Eric's at work?"

"Eric's always at work."

"Huh." Bonnie wrapped her hands around the coffee mug as if in prayer, and drank it down with an intensity that Jane found theatrical. Really, it was just coffee. Bonnie still wore her hair long and mussed, and she still slept in what she called her Whore of Babylon nightgowns, limp, satiny things trimmed with lace scallops. This one was peach-colored. Its slightly draggled bottom hem was visible beneath the terrycloth bathrobe Jane had loaned her.

Bonnie saw Jane looking at her. "What?"

"Nothing," Jane said. She had been wondering who Bonnie had bought the nightgown for.

"I guess you pretty much have to be a big workhound if you're going to be a doctor. I mean, some of the stuff he's up to is pretty amazing."

"It's good you're here for him to show off to. There's no point in him trying to impress me anymore, I've made all the adoring noises I can."

"Huh," Bonnie said again.

Robbie came running back with his cars, and Bonnie did a good impersonation of yesterday's enthusiasm. She and Jane carried on a conversation punctuated by Robbie's instructions and demands. No, they had not yet told him about the b-a-b-y. They were waiting until it got a bit closer. Did they have names picked out yet? Still deciding. Grace was on the list, as were Sophie and Anna. Jane said that maybe she and Bonnie could go out and buy a few things for the new you-know. Pink things, girl things, so that she didn't have to wear all hand-me-downs, and Bonnie said sure, they could do that.

"You're being an awfully good sport," Jane said, accusingly.

"I am. Sorry. I'll stop."

"There's this whole commercial enterprise built up around pregnancy. You'll see. It's like the military industrial complex, but with babies."

They went to Target and Babies R Us and then to a boutique store that felt, Bonnie said, like the inside of a decorated womb. Everything on display was fuzzy and precious. They looked at baby dresses embroidered with ducks and with rosebuds, at petal collars and fairy wings, at tiny socks and bloomers and flower headbands. Robbie, confined to a stroller, had fallen asleep. "Just as well," Bonnie said. "It's not his kind of store." There were acres of pink, in tones of cameo, cherry blossom, flamingo; there were stripes and checks, frilled garments and sporty ones.

Jane bought two sleepers, one yellow, one with a pattern of pink sprigs, and a pink ruffled bubble dress. Bonnie insisted on buying accessories: lacy socks, a sun visor, and a pair of soft leather mary janes. "Thanks," Jane said. "She's ready for a night on the town. That's really going to happen, isn't it? She'll be a teenager and she'll want to go out with horrid boys."

She meant it to sound lighthearted and humorous, like something Bonnie would say, but it came out with too much force, as if she meant it, as if she planned on being one of those impossible mothers who made daughters' lives miserable. Maybe she was already a bad, an unnatural mother, she'd just managed to hide it so far. Then Robbie woke up and started fussing, and there was no time to decide what she'd meant or had not meant, except that of course you worried all the time that you were doing everything wrong.

Bonnie was staying for five days, and Jane had to admit, it was a help to have her there. Bonnie was always forgiving about household messes, or more likely, oblivious to such things, and so Jane didn't worry about the litter of toys or the wet towels hung up in the bathroom drying into deformed, cardboard wrinkles. Bonnie played with Robbie, with varying degrees of patience, true, but anything that soaked up some portion of his energy was a benefit. She ate what was put before her, she took her turn at washing dishes, she was as grounded and matter-of-fact as a box of dirt. Jane felt herself relaxing by inches. Eric might have gone about it wrong, asking Bonnie to come, but it hadn't been the wrong idea. Maybe she had been spending too much time alone, that is, without an adult presence. Maybe her white room episodes were just some inexplicable, boo-hoo, hormonal weirdness. Anyway, it was now her fifth month. She was ready for things to get easier.

In the afternoons Robbie napped, while Jane and Bonnie sprawled in front of the television, watching ancient black and white movies, or soap operas with the volume turned down so they could make up the dialogue. ("It's no use, Axel. Ever since the accident, I only want to have sex with vampires.") Bonnie retreated to the front porch to make phone calls to the man she said she was through with. Jane watched her bending over the phone, intent on her conversation, clutching at handfuls of her hair as she talked.

"Who is he anyway?" Jane asked, when Bonnie came back in, looking morose. "You never exactly said."

"I met him through work."

"A cop?"

"Please. I am so through with cops. I can't even watch *Law and Order* anymore."

"So who? He's in mental health? No? He's not a client, is he? Bonnie!"

"Not technically," Bonnie protested. "That would be unethical. He's more like, a friend of a client. We were both trying to get Hector into treatment. Now don't be judgmental. We didn't have much in common, but it was fun for a while. Don't. I know you think I'm an idiot."

"I just wish you could meet somebody you might want to keep around."

"I always do want to keep them around," Bonnie protested. "At least at first. Well, not this one. He was more of a fling-ette. But listen, I'm so done. From now on I'm all chastity and good works. The Sisters of the Gutter Rose."

"You shouldn't demean yourself, even as a joke," Jane said. She was tired, she realized, of Bonnie being Bonnie. Her dumb moves that she talked wise about, her delight in her own bad behavior. Just as she was tired of being herself: poor, exhausted, neurasthenic Jane, needing to be jollied along, needing allowances made for her, like some beloved but limited household pet. For both of them, identities that had been formed and sealed back when they'd first encountered each other.

Or no. Formed, but not sealed, because weren't there other possibilities, other Janes, or other Bonnies? Other paths they might have taken? There must be. She didn't believe in fate, or doom. She believed, half-heartedly, in coincidence, and even more so in accident. She had just happened to meet Eric, it wasn't the hand of God or anything. And one thing had led to another and here she was. She'd had some vague and shapeless regrets when she'd married, that sense of avenues now closed off to her, but she'd thought everyone must feel such things, and besides, she'd been convinced she was a slightly second-rate person, gawky, comical, slow, who might, with luck, fit into some ordinary life.

But perhaps she had chosen wrongly. Perhaps she was not ordinary, nor meant to be. Her strangeness somehow exceptional, powerful. A beckoning mystery, a life that would have nothing to do with her family and their claim on her, nothing to do with love, even. Only its own imperative, as when you moved a rock in a garden and beneath it found a growing thing, pale, curled, greedy for sunlight.

It confused her to be thinking this way. Did she have some prepartum depression craziness? Should she go back to Dr. Cohen and ask to be chemically sedated? Should she start reading St. Teresa of Avila?

Jane said, "Really, I know you're trying to be funny, but it comes across as defensive."

"It is defensive." Bonnie picked up the remote and cycled through the channels. "And disarming. People can't insult you if you beat them to it."

"I wasn't insulting you."

"But you worry about me. Thanks, Mom."

Jane stayed silent. It seemed like the edge of some kind of argument, and she didn't want to blunder over it.

After a moment Bonnie said, "I'm good at my job because the crazies love me and I love them. I've found my niche. Feel free to disapprove."

"It's not disapproval. But the way you live scares me."

For whatever reason, this seemed to put Bonnie in a better mood. "You know the secret of our success? You and me? Neither one of us wants to be the other." Just then Robbie woke up from his nap and started calling for her, and Jane didn't have to respond.

Eric was home for dinner that night. Jane fed Robbie early, and then the three adults sat on the back patio with drinks (iced tea for Jane, gin and tonics for Eric and Bonnie), while they grilled shrimp and corn and baked potatoes in foil and kept watch so Robbie would not upend the hot coals over himself. Bonnie was leaving the day after tomorrow and it was their last dinner together, since Eric had to cover for another resident tomorrow evening. Jane made a green salad and sliced a bowl of strawberries, and they set out plates on the picnic table under the thin early shade of a pecan tree. The air was mild and blue, the smells of smoke and cooking food were good smells. Her little boy was playing with a handful of grass he'd torn up, serious and charming. The baby inside her dreamed watery dreams. Here was ordinary life at its best, a pause in the round of worries and chores. Only a fool, or an unbalanced pregnant person, would consider turning her back on it.

Eric took the food off the grill and they filled their plates and everyone agreed it was a fine meal. Bonnie said it was nice they had a yard for the kid. Kids. Eric said yes, for sure they'd want that in their next place. The next place would be wherever they'd move for his fellowship in cardiology, a little more than a year from now.

"Would you go back to Evanston?" Bonnie asked. She was peeling shrimp and heaping up shells on her plate. "Or do you want to go farther out into the classier zip codes?"

"Evanston?" Jane said. "Why are you talking about Evanston?"

"Because of the Northwestern fellowship, duh." Eric gave her a good-natured elbow check.

"What about it?"

"I think it'll work out. Though, you know, nothing's a sure thing."

Bonnie said, "False modesty, Eric. So unbecoming. You know they'll take you."

"When did you decide this?"

"Come on, honey, we talked about it. We decided. You thought it'd be good to go back to Chicago. Of course it wouldn't be until next May or June. You said you didn't want to spend another whole summer here if you didn't have to."

"No, when did we talk about it?"

They thought she was joking, and then they did not. A pause or hitch in the air around the table, although Eric and Bonnie kept on buttering corn and peeling shrimp. Eric said, "Oh, I don't know. Three, maybe four weeks ago? I forget where we were."

"I must have been tired," Jane said. She shook her head, smiled. Humorous.

"We were probably in bed. You weren't talking in your sleep, were you?"

"No, you're right. Of course we talked about it. Another summer in Hotlanta. Killer." They were going back to Chicago. She could not for the life of her remember Eric bringing it up. "Robbie, don't put grass in your mouth, sweetie." Chicago was fine, she guessed.

It wasn't like she'd wanted to live somewhere else instead. But what condition had she been in, that she'd discussed and agreed to it without memory? What else was wrong with her?

The next morning she said to Bonnie, "I think I'm losing my mind."

"Come on."

"I mean it. I space out. I don't remember things. Like last night."

"OK, that. It was a lapse. Is it a pregnancy thing? Part of your brain goes on maternity leave?"

"It didn't happen with Robbie. I felt tired and sick a lot, but I wasn't . . ." Jane tried to say exactly what she was. "In another world," she offered.

"You space out," Bonnie suggested.

"Way out."

Bonnie rubbed at her eyes with the heel of one hand. "I've been having some eye problems. I guess it's from computers. Or age. Do you feel old yet? There's times I feel like, if I was a package of hamburger in somebody's fridge? I'd get thrown out. Well whatever you are, you don't seem deranged or anything. Maybe it's just the mind-body connection. Your body's on this amazing ride, I mean I can't even imagine what that's like, pregnant, and your mind's trying to follow along. Like, your body's a speedboat and your mind is on water skis."

That made Jane yelp with laughter, and Robbie came running up to see what that alarming sound was, his mother laughing out loud, because when had he heard such a thing? Then Jane had to leave off laughing and speak soothingly to him.

When Bonnie left the following day, insisting once again on taking a cab, they hugged and promised each other to do better at keeping in touch, and they were both genuinely sorry to be parting but also relieved, since they'd had such long practice at mutual exasperation. Although neither of them wanted to be the other, there might be times at which a part of themselves might have wanted to try on some portion of the other, the same as when they'd been roommates and had borrowed each other's clothes.

Eric started a period of intensive shifts at the hospital, and it was easy for he and Jane not to talk much. Without Bonnie they felt a sense of diminishment, as if with a guest they had been more cheerful, animated, loving, in ways that were not really false but had required some effort. Why did people get married seeking a way out of loneliness? There was nothing lonelier than two married people in a room together, she knew that now.

And yet she would have said she had a good marriage, and she thought Eric would have said the same. Good not precisely the same as happy, although there were times when they were happy. Both of them fighting the same fight, doing their best to shore up the enterprise.

What did couples do if they didn't have children? What else was worth the enormity of effort?

❧

Here is how it began: In her sixth month, Jane was fixing Robbie's lunch, trying to make his tuna sandwich look the way he liked it, a tidy square in the center of an otherwise bare plate. No garnishes, nothing protruding from the edge of the bread. Any stray bit of lettuce or celery was an excuse for a food tantrum. Eventually he would be old enough and hungry enough that he could be told to stop fooling around and eat. But for now it was easiest to do things his way, and hope that he would not be entirely and permanently spoiled.

She set the plate on the table and opened the refrigerator to pour his milk. "Robbie, come eat." He didn't answer, since he had recently learned how much fun it was to ignore her and make her shout for him, and she readied herself to call him again, in that tone of peevish worry that had come to define motherhood for her.

It felt like rain drumming on a roof, except that she was the roof.

She stood at the open refrigerator, bathed in chill, noisy air. The baby had gone quiet inside her. "What?" she said out loud, or thought she did. Her ears roared. What was wrong?

Once more, the sensation of pounding, scattered rain bearing down on her.

Pay attention.

Now.

Jane dialed Eric's pager number, and when he didn't answer, she left a message for him to call her. "Robbie, you have to come with me. Where are your shoes?" She hoisted him up barefoot. In the garage she strapped him into the car seat and jammed his shoes onto his feet. Went back into the house for her purse and his sandwich, poured the milk into his toddler cup. "Here," she said, giving him a section of sandwich. "Can you eat that? Can you hold your milk too? All right, just eat your sandwich."

"I don wanna sanwich."

"Eat it anyway." She backed out of the driveway and set off, driving as carefully as she could, since the car was behaving so oddly, as if it was floating just above the road surface.

Or no, she was not registering the feel of the tires, as if she had been wrapped in soundproofing. Here was the baby driving itself to the hospital, but that was foolish, since babies did not know how to drive.

Of course she knew the way to the ER from all her visits with Robbie. The clerk at the desk remembered them. "Oh no, what's he up to this time?" Smiling down at Robbie, who Jane was half-dragging, half-pushing. He still held a portion of sandwich in his fist and was bawling about having to walk, loudly enough for anyone to think he'd needed stitches.

"It's me, it's the baby."

The clerk's face took on a new, brisk expression. "You have your insurance card?"

Jane did. There were questions to answer. Was she in pain? Had there been any bleeding?

"Not really," Jane said, then, realizing she needed to use more guile, said, "Yes, some. Yes."

"I'm sorry honey, what did you say?"

She was having trouble talking, as if she'd been punched in the mouth. The clerk's face was round and she'd dusted it with some kind of yellow powder, like the full moon. "Moon," Jane said. Then, "Some. Sure."

She sat down to wait, holding Robbie between her knees to keep him from running off, and tried to reach Eric again. She called her obstetrician and was on hold when they came to take her back to the curtained-off exam room.

The doctor, a woman, was one they had not seen before. She was not enchanted by Robbie's presence, though she tried smiling and speaking to him in a loud, arch tone that at least made him stop fussing and stare at her. To Jane she said, "Tell me about the bleeding."

"I'm not sure," Jane said. She knew it was the wrong answer. She hung her head, embarrassed. She felt the doctor looking at her, deciding.

"What are your other symptoms?"

"Just that, I know something's wrong." With one arm she tried to corral Robbie, who was reaching for the cabinet top where they kept supplies. She noticed that she had put his shoes on the wrong feet. She tried again with the doctor. "It's the mind-body connection."

"Mrs. Nicholson, I really think you should make an appointment with your obstetrician so you can discuss your concerns."

"Please don't make me leave here."

The doctor decided, visibly, not to say anything. She took Jane's blood pressure and listened to her heart and put her hands on Jane's stomach. "I can't feel her," Jane said.

"She's asleep," the doctor said, soothing now.

"Will she wake up?"

"That depends on you."

"It isn't fair that it's all on me," Jane said, but by then the doctor had gone away.

They had left her quite alone. It was peaceful, as before. Limitless, luminous, like the inside of an infinite pearl. She floated, she flew. And it came to her that she could choose to leave everything failed and sad behind and stay here, and there would be no fear in it. She'd had no real gifts besides this remarkable one. She could step easily out of her life.

She had been so very tired. The whiteness buoyed her like water, lifting and cleansing. She had pushed and pushed, trying to fit herself into the shape that was expected of her. It had left her bruised and raw. And now there would be no need to keep trying. The whiteness blessed her. It forgave everyone for everything.

But the doctor had returned. She had a face like a moon, and like a clock also, a moon clock, and she said, You are forgetting something.

Go away, Jane told her. Leave me be.

Tick tick tick, the doctor said. How can she be born without you? Are you that selfish?

I am that tired.

You came asking for help. You wanted to save her.

I wanted someone else to save her.

But there is only you.

I am tired of me.

Yes, but it's not as easy as you think it is. Dying.

"Jane? Honey?"

They were dragging her back. She would not open her eyes.

"Honey? Can you hear me?"

The inside of her head had been scraped dry. Light beat against her eyelids. She tried to speak but her mouth was parched.

"What? I can't understand you." Eric's voice was right in her ear. She raised a hand to swat him away. "Everything's fine. Don't worry."

How fine? How not to worry? How to live in the world and not worry? "The baby's all right. There was a tear in the placenta. We've got it under control. You were bleeding internally. It's just amazing that you knew something was wrong."

She opened her eyes to a slit. Painful light blurred the outlines of the room. Eric's face hung over hers like something large and inflated. He said, "How are you feeling? Can you talk? It's all right, just rest. I have to tell you, it was touch and go there for a while. But you hung in there, thank God."

Was he crying? Would he have been sad to lose her? Of course he would. Her little boy too. She felt the baby inside her shift. Everything that tied her here, strand by strand.

Eric wiped at his eyes, smiled. A crooked smile, still wobbly at the edges. "Robbie's fine too. Well, he ran smack into a cart and put a gash in his scalp, but we were right here in the ER, so it's all good." He leaned over and kissed her forehead. "Hang in there, you're incredible. You're the absolute best mother in the world."

No she was not, but she would have to be. She would remain here, and the lives of her children would be her life. There could be no more escape into the extraordinary, into bliss, into delight. "That's my girl," Eric said. "You're a trouper. You're the best, I mean it. You're like Supermom."

accident

Bonnie's brother Charlie crashed his SUV into a bridge support on Lower Wacker with a blood alcohol of .22 and landed in the hospital and a whole lot of trouble. The woman who was riding with him was also seriously and expensively injured. One of Bonnie's cop friends called her and told her Charlie was at Mount Sinai. Bonnie drove herself there through the glassy, predawn streets. It was October and already cold enough for frost. She blasted the defroster and ran the windshield wipers in an attempt to keep the ice from creeping up like dread.

Charlie was still drunk. He'd cut his face when the airbag inflated. He had dislocated his shoulder. He had a lacerated liver and a shattered kneecap. "Hey Sis," he greeted her. "I hadda accident." His face was swollen and they'd painted his leg with iodine and put his knee in a brace. He'd vomited onto his gown, but they'd cleaned it up. He looked bloated, clammy, dissolute, shockingly bad.

"I guess you did." Although if you drank yourself blotto and then got behind the wheel, that was a different order of accident than getting hit by a meteor in your backyard. "How do you feel?"

"My knee hurts like sin. They screwed it up, I'm serious, it feels a whole lot worse now that they, what is it they do? It's bullshit. None of these people speak English, I'm all 'What? What?' Hey, how's Kelly? How bad's my car?"

"They're taking care of Kelly. Don't worry about the car right now." Charlie wasn't going to be driving anything for a long while. The party was over, he just didn't know it yet. "I have to make some phone calls, OK? Hang in there, be right back."

Claudia came from Wisconsin the next day and then there was what she and Charlie used to call Mamma Drama. No one did it better than Claudia. She buttonholed doctors and nurses, orderlies and housekeepers, vigilant for lapses in the standard of care. She wanted to read charts, she wanted to talk to the dietician about meals. Charlie, who would have otherwise laughed her off, turned piteous. Unpleasant realities were crowding in on him. He had surgery for his busted kneecap and the pain drugs further unmanned him. His friend Kelly was discharged from the hospital after her own repairs. Ominously, she would not respond to Charlie's calls.

"You don't think he'll have to go to jail, do you?" Claudia asked Bonnie, and Bonnie said he would at least have to go to court. She wanted to stay noncommittal. People went to jail for DUIs, it happened. It should probably happen more often. A good lawyer, the kind Stan and Claudia could afford, would no doubt be able to grease things so that Charlie would end up with probation and fines. But there would be lawsuits, and going ten rounds with the insurance companies, and money paid out, probably a lot of it. Stan wouldn't want to help. Claudia would talk him into it. It wasn't going to make for any happy family reunions. And Charlie? At least he hadn't killed himself or anybody else. There was a bleak sort of comfort in that.

While Charlie was still in the hospital, Claudia asked Bonnie, "Isn't Jane's husband a doctor?"

"Yes, why?"

"I'd like a second opinion."

"On what? Eric's at a whole different hospital. He's a cardiologist."

"I'd feel better if somebody we knew looked at him. I don't have full confidence in these people."

"Mom, he doesn't practice here. He's a heart doctor, how does that figure? And you've never even met him."

Claudia turned stubborn. She set her small, well-groomed chin and said she didn't see why Bonnie objected to using every available resource, this was a serious, serious situation and her brother needed her support, why was she being so selfish?

Bonnie called Jane. "He doesn't have to. It won't accomplish anything except reinforce my mother's delusions that everybody should rally to Charlie's defense."

"I'll ask him," Jane said. "I bet he will. He'll do it for you. Anyway, he likes swooping in and talking doctor-talk to a worshipful audience."

"Really, he doesn't have to," Bonnie said, wondering at Jane's tone. It was the kind of spousal snark that usually meant the speaker was mad about something else entirely. "Make sure he knows that. And it's not really for me, it's for my mother. That's not the same thing."

"How's Charlie?"

"He's still pretty banged up. At least he can't drink while he's in the hospital. I was hoping this would be enough of a wake-up call, but he's back to feeling very sorry for himself because of all the terrible things he's been through. You know, poor me, poor me, pour me a drink."

There was one of those lapses in the conversation when Jane had to cover the phone and go referee the children. "Sorry," she said, coming back. "Robbie was teasing Grace and she bit him."

"I thought Robbie was in kindergarten now."

"Only half days. Full time isn't till first grade. Listen, I have to get back to the slugfest. I'll have Eric call you, OK?"

Eric said he'd stop by for moral support. "You know I can't change treatment orders or anything like that. Anyway, I'm sure they're perfectly competent."

"Tell my mother that, she won't believe me. I think she's just looking for somebody to blame for the whole misery besides Charlie."

And so Eric made a visit to Charlie's room and endeared himself to Claudia by agreeing with her, hospitals often made mistakes, doctors too, although, he said, Mount Sinai was very well regarded. He cracked jokes with Charlie and conferred with a nurse about the medical regimen. Everything looked like it was coming along fine, he said, not allowing himself to meet Bonnie's eye. The doctors here had everything on the right track. It was just going to take a little tincture of time to heal. He wasn't wearing his white lab coat, of course, only a sports jacket and a tie. Still, he was so doctorlike in his easy authority, his confidence and bearing, there was no mistaking him for anything else.

"Oh, I wish you practiced here," Claudia said, smitten.

"No you don't. I'm really a hard-ass. I like to boss my patients around."

"Listen to you, I don't believe you for a minute. Why don't we have a doctor in the family, it would be so helpful. Why did neither of you children go to medical school?"

"Poor role models," Charlie suggested.

"Neither of them ever thought in practical terms," Claudia said, appealing to Eric. "Charlie was going to live a rock and roll life. Bonnie took a lot of courses in, what were they, ancient civilizations? And she ends up in these horrible true crime stories. You're so intelligent, darling, you just don't plan things out very well. There's no reason you couldn't have been a doctor."

"Or at least married one," Bonnie agreed.

Charlie said, "Lay off Bonnie, Mom. You're embarrassing her in front of the real doctor."

"No, really, it's great," Bonnie said. "Otherwise I get so full of myself."

Eric said, "I wish I could stay a little longer, but I've got to get home. Charlie, best of luck. Claudia, a real pleasure."

"Thank you so very much. I can tell you're a wonderful, wonderful doctor. Do you have children yourself?" Claudia asked, extending her hand for him to shake.

"Yes, a little boy and a baby girl."

"And they're both going to medical school," Charlie said.

Bonnie stood up to leave with Eric. She kissed Claudia on the cheek. "I'll be back tomorrow after work, call me if you need anything."

"I'm like, a black hole of neediness," Charlie told her. "A gaping maw." He looked cleaner than he had when he'd been admitted, but years of galloping drinking were taking their toll. His face was both puffy and shriveled. He was growing a drunkard's inflamed nose.

Eric and Bonnie walked out together, past the nursing station, around the corner to the elevator. The day shift had gone home and the halls had an empty, echoing feel. "Do they still have candy stripers?" Bonnie asked. "You know, the girls in the red and white pinafores who walk around cheering people up?"

"I think they're just called volunteers now," Eric said. "Older women, mostly, and they wear smocks. There's some younger kids who help with transport. They wear polo shirts and khakis."

The elevator came and they rode it down. Bonnie started to say something about the decline in standards, and what it must have been like when nurses wore real nurse outfits, not just pajamas, but she was sick to death of saying amusing things, and when she and Eric emerged from the building into an early dark and misty rain, she burst into angry tears.

"Hey," Eric said, putting an arm around her shoulders and guiding her away from the door, along a sidewalk with a concrete overhang. "Hey, it's OK."

"This is not," Bonnie said between sobs, "about my mother humiliating me. That's nothing new."

"It's OK," he said again. He wrapped both arms around her and Bonnie leaned into him and cried for all she was worth. She was cold, miserable, and Eric tightened his hold on her and they stood there a long time. The fine rain turned the light from the streetlamps into halos and veils. Cars rolled by on the street, their tires skimming the puddles. "It's just so sad," Bonnie said, surfacing. "My whole sad, stupid family. I mean, me too."

"I don't think you're stupid," Eric told her. Bonnie hiccupped and sniffled and let herself cry some more. She'd forgotten the comfort you could take in a man. It was so seldom offered to her, she was so accustomed to doing without it. She hung on for dearest life. Eric was tall enough so that the top of her head fit into the hollow of his shoulder, and she buried her head in the solid warmth of him and breathed the smells of his clothes and his skin and felt the rumble and pulse of his body, its secret shiftings, and it was only Eric after all so it was all right and then the next moment it was not all right and she pulled away.

"God," she said. "I'm such a mess, I'm sorry."

"You're fine." He looked embarrassed. She was an idiot. Well, everybody knew that already. "I mean, you're not fine now, but you will be. Your brother's going to get better."

"And my mother's going to stay the same. It's OK, I'm used to it."

"She's a little hard on you."

"It's just her way. A fond, doting, ultimately hostile way."

They laughed. Eric patted her on the back and dropped his arms and Bonnie turned and dug in her purse for anything resembling Kleenex. "Thank you again," she said, still looking. Giving up. Maybe she had some in the car. "For the unofficial medical consult. Hospital chaplain services. Much appreciated."

"Sure. Sometimes all it takes is a little doctor juju."

They headed out to the parking lot and Eric said he would walk her to her car, it was already dark, and Bonnie said there was no need, she was right over there, and anyway he didn't need to stay out in this rain. Not wanting to tell him how many times a week she got into her car by herself after dark, and in far worse neighborhoods. They hugged again, to show there was no harm in it, and Bonnie said to say hi to Jane. She got into her car and started the engine and the windshield wipers. Eric stood where she'd left him, watching. She backed out and tapped the horn as she drove away.

Claudia stayed in town, moving into Charlie's apartment in Lakeview and doing a lot of energetic and scandalized cleaning. Charlie couldn't manage stairs without help, he needed groceries and cooking, he needed to be hauled back and forth to doctors' appointments, he needed cheering up, Claudia said. "Try a candy striper," Bonnie suggested.

"What? Are you making a joke? Please tell me what's so funny."

"Nothing, forget it." They were on the phone. Bonnie called so she didn't have to go over there. "How is Himself?"

"He's supposed to be doing exercises, but he says they hurt too much. I think he's depressed."

In the background Bonnie heard music, some kind of Goth-punk banshee chorus. "He sounds depressed."

"I don't know why more of his friends haven't come by. There was a girl, but she didn't stay long. I know what you're thinking. I was perfectly nice to her. We have to meet with the lawyer Tuesday. I don't believe he's looking forward to it."

"The lawyer will tell you it's a very serious situation but he's going to do his expensive best to give you a good result."

"I don't suppose you want to come along," Claudia said, without much hope. "He doesn't always listen to me."

"Maybe he'll listen to the lawyer. The lawyer will tell him to stop drinking, clean up his act, go to AA, and show a judge he's changed his ways. Of course, that means he actually has to change his ways."

"Oh I don't know, honey. He's so miserable right now, I don't know if this is a good time to tell him he has to start a whole different life style."

"When is a good time? After his next DUI with injuries? What does Stan think of all this?"

"Stan is being difficult," Claudia said, primly, and Bonnie waited for her to say more about it but she didn't.

"You can't keep doing everything for Charlie, Mom. Are you familiar with the term 'enabler'?"

"Would you stop it? You always think you have to be so smart about everything, making fun of people who have actual feelings, like that makes you better than the rest of us, but you're not. You don't care about Charlie, he's only your family, not some homeless crazy person."

Bonnie let the phone slide away from her ear. Then she picked it up again. "Mom? Just who was I supposed to be, huh? Exactly how have I disappointed you, I'm really having trouble nailing it down."

But Claudia had resumed her usual ladylike and plaintive manner. "Sweetheart, I'm sorry if you're unhappy, but you're going to have to work on that yourself, because right now I'm very concerned about your brother and it's taking all my energy. I have to go now, love you."

Bonnie got off the phone and looked for something to throw or break, but what good would that do, and who would be able to tell the difference in this hellhole of an apartment? She'd lived here too long, telling herself she didn't care that it was small, unfashionable, grim, even using it as proof that she didn't care about appearances, as if she was above, or below, all that, as if she'd been playing some elaborate joke on herself. And now all she had to show for it were her little bits of artsy junk, the furniture that was, at best, funky-amusing, the kitchen with its slopped-over stove burners, the sad and messy manifestation of her sad and messy life.

She picked up the phone again and called Jane. It was eight thirty, not late for most people but borderline for moms with little kids. The phone rang and rang, and just as it was about to go to voice mail, Eric answered. "Hello?"

"Eric? Hey, I'm sorry, I thought I was calling Jane's cell."

"You are. She's trying to get Grace to sleep, she has a fever."

"Is she all right? Nothing Daddy Doctor can't handle, I hope."

"Yeah, she's . . ." The phone must have gotten away from him. There was a sudden fumbling racket.

"Eric?"

"Sorry, yeah, it spiked at 103, but you know, high fevers in kids aren't as concerning as they are in adults."

Bonnie did know that, or at least she used to know it. She said she hoped it was nothing serious, and Eric said he was pretty sure it wasn't. He sounded tired, rattled, abrupt. Bonnie said to tell Jane she called, and they hung up.

Her phone rang again a minute later. It was Jane's house phone. "Hello?"

It was Eric. "I'm sorry, I forgot to ask you how Charlie's doing."

"Oh, thanks. I guess his knee's better. And he's on some medication for his liver. My mom's staying at his place to help him out, which is sort of a mixed blessing. You know, if it's not one thing, it's your mother." She had wanted to complain about Claudia to Jane, but it would have felt whiny to do so one more time to Eric. "I'll tell her you were asking about him, she'll be all kinds of ecstatic."

"Ha, well, that's nice. I'll tell Jane, maybe she'll be more impressed with me."

"Yeah?" Bonnie said, careful to have her voice convey exactly nothing.

Eric exhaled. "Scratch that. Nobody's required to be impressed."

"I'm not sure if I—"

"No, really, I spoke out of turn. I'm glad Charlie's feeling better."

"Let me guess, Jane's freaking out because of Grace's fever and you can't convince her it's not a crisis."

"Something like that."

"Don't take it personally. It's a Mom thing."

There was the sound of water running in the sink, then he shut it off. Ice cubes. A drink?

"I wish," Eric said, "that she'd keep things in proportion when it comes to the kids. It's a fever, not the plague."

"She's very responsible. Very involved." It seemed like a good idea to say something in Jane's defense.

"Yeah, she is."

A gap of silence. "I hope Grace will feel a lot better soon. I'm sure she will."

"Yeah, thanks."

Another silence. Bonnie was ready to say good night and hang up, but instead she asked, "Are you all right?"

"It's been a long day and I'm feeling sorry for myself, but I guess I still qualify as 'all right.' But thanks for asking, that's sweet of you. I should go see how Grace is."

"Sure. Say hi to Jane."

"Will do. Good night, dear."

"Good night." Bonnie put the phone down. She didn't much like the thoughts she was thinking.

She was so accustomed to Jane and Eric being fixed points in her world, especially since they'd moved back to Chicago. *My married friends who live in the suburbs and he's a doctor.* They didn't see each other that often, but they were all busy, and it never seemed that necessary, since after so much time, they could always pick up where they left off. But you could not count on anyone or anything in life to stay the same and she ought to know that by now. So maybe Eric and Jane were having themselves a little fuss, people did that. So she and Eric had a bit of a moment, or two; it was what it was and nothing more and she needed to be stern with her fool self.

It wasn't like she didn't have enough to keep her busy. One of Chicago's Finest had lost his shit and beaten a homeless guy who had been creating the usual minor disturbance. It was the kind of cop overreaction that happened for all the familiar cop reasons of stress and one too many crumby encounters with the more combative segment of the general public. It wasn't even the worst such incident. But this one had been captured on cell phone video and showed the officer sitting astride the man and head-punching him for a solid minute, and now it was all over the place, and there was general outrage, and editorials implying or outright saying that nothing ever changed, and all the community outreach and so-called training was just a lot of noise.

It didn't do any good to point out all the times the cops didn't beat anybody up in the performance of their difficult, life-threatening duties. Or for the officer to argue that the video didn't show the homeless guy whaling away on his girlfriend, and then when the officer attempted to render assistance, the guy spitting on him and trying to knee him in the balls. Also not recorded: the homeless guy's girlfriend ("the female subject") wading in and straddling the officer's back and locking her legs around his neck (the female subject's lack of hygiene described in regrettably nonprofessional terms by the officer), and the subsequent use of pepper spray to subdue her. (Along with another departure from professionalism on the officer's part in his unsolicited remarks as to where on the person of the female subject he would have liked to administer pepper spray.)

Bonnie was good at staying calm in these difficult situations and doing what had to be done in terms of damage control. Putting it all behind her, moving forward. Anyway, she was only a consultant, an advisor, she had no power to discipline or to change policy. She made her suggestions, helped draft the press release. Stood ready to protect and defend her turf, since she was invested in the program, and she honestly believed it accomplished good things. And it did, in general; it was only when you had to deal with the unfortunate specifics that doubts crept in.

She was thirty-two now. She felt, if not exactly old, at least no longer young. When she'd started her job it was the crisis part of it that had engaged her, the proximity to what was risky and outlandish. Now she had migrated over to the management side, fund-raising, grantwriting, justifying her own existence. Patience, argument, strategy: those were her tools, the skills she'd developed over time. She achieved results in less flamboyant and more lasting ways. At the same time, she missed her younger, impulsive, unafraid self. She hadn't necessarily wanted to grow sadder and wiser. Well, she probably wasn't any wiser. That was some consolation.

From time to time she thought about getting married, having children, wondering if she even wanted to do such a thing. It wasn't yet too late. Of course she'd have to find a partner, or at least a sperm donor ha ha, but no. Bad jokes aside, she'd want a man who voiced the intention to stick around. That is, if she made an actual decision in the first place.

And where was she supposed to find this future mate, this accomplice in willful self-delusion? The men she knew (through work, through her occasional bouts of self-improvement via gyms, gallery talks, etc., through, it must be admitted, nights spent in bar-trolling) were not notable in wanting to marry. They had expensive hobbies or engrossing jobs or both. They squirmed at the mention of children. Or maybe they had already been married and were not anxious to repeat the experience. They'd already had a first batch of children with whom they were on precarious terms.

Or sometimes they were still married, although this was not always disclosed at the outset, and even then you could go along with it and be Low Expectations Girl. But Bonnie had not done so, aside from a dispiriting episode or two, not because she was so morally upright—she was pretty sure she was not —but because she didn't see why these guys ought to be able to get away with it. Not to mention the unsavory parade of cover stories and excuses. Who would have thought there were so many marriages of pure convenience out there, platonic and sexless? So many wives with so many obvious, damning character defects? Maybe it was easier back in the good old guilty days, when they just hid their wedding rings and you weren't expected to help them validate their excuses.

Jane called the first week of December to ask Bonnie what she was doing for Christmas. "Do I have to do anything?" Bonnie said. "Christmas has turned into such a misery. But"—she amended herself—"you have little kids, you get to do all the fun Santa stuff."

"Grace is too young, but Robbie's into it, big time. Of course, since we don't go to church or anything, it's basically this extravaganza of greed. We tried telling him that we celebrate Jesus' birthday because Jesus was an important person, but that sounds pretty feeble. Anyway, Eric thinks we should have a Christmas party."

"He does?" Bonnie tried to calculate a response. "What do you think?"

"People are always inviting us over, so, sure. Probably the week before Christmas."

"You don't sound entirely sold on the idea."

"It's either this or wait until the kids are in college."

"I bet the house is going to look nice all dolled up." With the help of Eric's parents, he and Jane had bought a bungalow in Elmhurst, small but charming, with a deep, covered front porch, hardwood floors, a fireplace, and a kid-friendly backyard. "I bet they have some ordinance, you can't put a blow-up Santa on the roof. Let me know if I can bring anything. I mean, something that doesn't require cooking. A salad, or bakery stuff. Italian beef so you can make sandwiches."

"Thanks. Maybe some wine."

"No, really, let me bring actual food. Jane! Don't overdo it! Back away from the refrigerator! Order a bunch of pizzas. People always like pizza."

"I just want it to be nice," Jane said vaguely. "It'll be fine. I have plenty of time and I'll be really organized. I was thinking, a seafood buffet for starters. How hard is that? It's mostly ice. Then some kind of main course dishes. And a big dessert table. Everybody expects sweets at Christmas."

"How many people are you thinking?"

"Twenty, twenty-five. Or more. I haven't got a good feel for it yet."

"You know what's big these days? Hiring a chef. They come in with their own knives and pots and pans. They take over the kitchen and you don't have to do a thing."

"Like that's going to happen."

"At least get Eric to help."

"Ditto."

"Can you hook up with a cookie exchange? You know, you bake a batch and then you trade cookies with everybody else? Don't they have those things in the suburbs?"

One of the kids was acting up and Jane said she had to go, which was the usual exit for their conversations. Bonnie hung up and wondered if she should talk to Eric, try and head off what sounded like a bad idea in the making. She was pretty sure that Eric had not demanded a seafood buffet. More likely, he'd mentioned a party and now Jane would turn it into something completely exhausting and then blame Eric for it. But that was their business, and anyway, Bonnie didn't want to find herself joining forces with Eric one more time, talking about Jane as if she was a problem that needed solving.

She didn't know anything about marriages, Jane and Eric's or anyone else's. All you ever saw were the public moments, the submerged or surfacing fights, the lovey-dovey. People did their real living behind closed doors, which was why the couples you thought were so happy ended up divorcing, and the miserable ones hung on forever. Of course there were the things Jane told her about Eric, and from time to time, things Eric told her about Jane. These were most often in the nature of complaints of the letting off steam variety, nothing that sounded fatal. Jane was too tired. Eric was too busy. The kids were good kids but they were a handful. Jane didn't appreciate. Eric didn't help. The kids didn't behave. Jane always. Eric never. Kids!

Did love get worn down over time? Did it change form like a chemistry experiment, from a fizzy potion to an inch of tar in the bottom of a beaker? Most likely she had the entirely wrong idea about it, all her stupid trashy notions. Grow up, she told herself. Nothing was as simple as she'd thought it was back in her comic book days.

She bought Christmas presents for Robbie and Grace, and for Jane and Eric, a gift card to a grown-up restaurant nearby, in case they managed such a thing as a date night. Two days after the party was their seventh anniversary. When Bonnie pointed this out, Jane said, "Really? What's that in dog years?"

"Stop," Bonnie said. "Stop with the bitter jokes. You sound whiny. Am I supposed to feel sorry for you? I kind of don't."

"All right. I need new material. Noted. Listen, I'm seeing somebody."

"You are?"

"A psychotherapist. He's got me on these antidepressants, I think they're helping. So I want you to know, I'm making an effort here."

"That's great." Bonnie tried to cover her mistake. She had assumed Jane meant, seeing a lover. "It's great that you're trying for some positive changes. Because really, you have so much going for you. You and Eric and the kids. You ought to be completely happy."

"Yes, I ought to. Oughtn't I. See you at the party."

Bonnie couldn't decide what to wear. There would probably be some women there in pants and holiday sweaters. It was, after all, the suburbs. Maybe some glammier cocktail dresses. It wasn't a night to wear too much black, or high boots with a leather miniskirt, or anything else that would mark her as an interloper. And although it was bound to be mostly couples, you couldn't help thinking there might be some cute young single doctor on the premises. Maybe not even young. Maybe not even cute.

In the end she chose a red sweater with a pretty scoop neckline, one of her fifteen different black skirts, and the kind of jewelry she thought of as aspirational. Low black heels. She thought she looked all right if not great, festive if not quite ready to compete with the Christmas tree. It wasn't a long drive to get to Jane and Eric's, a straight shot down the Eisenhower. There had been a recent snow and now polar cold had settled in on top of it. The traffic kicked up slush and Bonnie had to keep running her windshield wipers to clear the grime. Why did she always spend major holidays in transit, hurrying to whatever celebration would keep her from feeling like an isolated failure? Maybe someday she'd live somewhere big enough and nice enough to host her own parties and have people come to her.

Once she reached Elmhurst, she let herself enjoy the look of the place, all done up for Christmas with its lighted greenery and decorated windows, although the whole point of the suburbs seemed to be an attempt to look like what it was not. An English country village, perhaps, complete with these half-timbered mock-Tudors. An American small town circa 1910, but with good access to shopping and regional transport. No matter. The streets were plowed, the sidewalk shoveled, and the new snow was a clean layer of cold.

Jane and Eric's house was decorated with swags of colored lights across the evergreens in front, and electric candles at the windows. A wreath hung on the front door, and the woodbox next to it held some white birch logs, sprigs of holly, and a floppy-legged felt elf. Bonnie stamped her feet on the red and green door mat so as not to track any snow in, and knocked. Nobody answered, perhaps they had not heard her. Some kind of child-themed Christmas music was playing inside. She pushed the unlocked door open and entered.

The living room was empty except for a hulking decorated tree that took up a lot of the small space. It had multicolored lights and ropes of tinsel and some construction-paper chains that the kids must have pasted together. "Hello?" Bonnie put her bag of presents on the sofa and took a few steps inside. Had she arrived on the wrong night?

But no, they were all in the kitchen, "all" being Jane and Eric, two other couples, and Robbie and Grace, who were sitting at the table and making a mess with some frosted sugar cookies and red and green sugars. The adults were all watching them, either interested or pretending interest. Little Grace was paddling in the bowl of frosting and Robbie, who was older but not much tidier, was applying colored sugar by grinding it in with his knuckles.

"Bonnie, hey!" Eric spotted her and waved her over, giving her his usual half-hug and kiss on the cheek. "Merry Christmas!"

"Merry Christmas. Where's your reindeer sweater? Hi kids. Hi Jane. Hi." This last to the people she didn't know. Jane was trying to haul things out of the refrigerator even though everyone was in her way. "Excuse me," she kept saying. "Excuse me." What were they all doing in the kitchen? Why were the kids still up?

"Bonnie, this is Ed and Allie. Jay and Carol." Hello, hello, Bonnie said, shaking hands. Were they neighbors? Doctors? Neighbors who were doctors? She had the unhappy premonition that this would be one more goddamned party where she would be the only single person. To Jane she said, "What can I help you with?"

Jane looked oddly blurred or out of focus. Medication? She had the whole of the counter space filled with bowls and trays, wrappings of foil and plastic. "Maybe you could . . . Robbie? Grace? I said you could stay up for the party and now it's bedtime."

Neither child looked up from the cookies. Bonnie said, "Hey guys, what if I help you put the cookies away and get cleaned up? Robbie, do you still play your astronaut game?" She didn't mind, really. The maiden aunt always had to tend to the children, and anyway it would save her from exchanging what-do-you-dos with the guests whose names she had already forgotten.

Grace was no problem. She was a sweet, quiet little girl with Jane's fair coloring and nearly translucent skin. She kissed her parents good night and headed for the stairs. Robbie was still a hell-raiser and a worldbeater and required more negotiation, more cookies, before he was ready to give in. "Come on," Bonnie said. "I'll let you be the Russian cosmonaut." Robbie still considered her an acceptable playmate, although the day would come when she would be demoted to a mere female. They were both delicious children, each in their separate ways, and Bonnie was grateful to Jane for having them so she could hang out with them occasionally and not have to have her own.

Bonnie got heavy-headed, sleepy Grace settled into her pink bed in her pink pink room, then sat on the floor of Robbie's room with him and played the astronaut game. This was a made-up contest involving a model of the international space station and its crew, who were always subverting the spirit of scientific cooperation by smashing into each other and knocking each other out of orbit and into the vacuum of space, although, unlike space, there were many sound effects.

Bonnie might have been content to sit there all evening, engaging in interstellar mayhem, but the doorbell kept ringing and she knew she had to get downstairs. "OK, kiddo. How about you get in bed and take your astronaut with you?"

"My astronaut's the best! Yours is a wuss!"

"Yeah, well my astronaut got better grades in school. Good night, sweetie."

Descending, she noted that the music had changed over, from songs about reindeer and snowmen to something resembling choir music. Christmas anthems, presumably, as sung in some high church setting. It seemed like the wrong choice for a party, and once she reached the bottom of the stairs she could tell instantly that the party had not jelled.

There were people standing around in pairs—she'd been right about that part—holding drinks and plates of food. Surely some of these couples knew each other, or at least knew the person they were standing next to. But there was a general dearth of conversation, as if they were attending some sort of well-fed holiday visitation. Bonnie fixed her expression in a pleasant half-smile and made her way through the guests, looking for Jane.

Passing through the dining room, she was impressed, no, daunted, by what Jane had done with the food. If not an entire seafood buffet, there was at least chilled shrimp and pickled herring. A platter of cold sliced roast beef and fixings for sandwiches. Different bowls and trays, cheeses, salads, casseroles. Asparagus wrapped in prosciutto, mushrooms entombed in phyllo. The guests were milling and nudging each other around the table, intent on getting as much as possible onto their plates without looking too piggy.

Good God, the dessert table. Jane must have been baking in her sleep for weeks. There were frosted snowflake cookies, date bars, chocolate stars, jelly tots, coconut snowballs. Red and green cupcakes. A Bundt cake on a pedestal stand. A jar of multicolored candy canes. How had she managed to keep the kids out of it all?

The bar had been set up in the kitchen, and that was where she found Eric, drinking bottled beer and talking with a couple of other men. Jane must have been in the bathroom.

Eric waved her over. "Are the kids locked up yet, I mean, settled in?"

"Such a kidder. Grace is out like a light. Robbie might bounce around for a while."

"Thanks. I'll go check on them in a sec. Have a drink, you've earned it." He reached for a bottle of red wine. "The usual?"

"Sure." She was all about the usual. That was, of course, a self-pitying thought, and she tried halfheartedly to bat it away. The two men nearby were still deep in conversation. Neither of them had registered her presence with as much as a glance, which told her she'd dressed in acceptable camouflage. "Thanks," she said, accepting a glass from Eric. "The food looks great. I bet Jane's been cooking up a storm."

"Yeah, you bet. OK, I'm going to go check on the kids." A layer of something distant and unreadable settled over his face. If they'd been alone, she would have asked him if everything was all right, meaning it didn't seem to be, but he patted her shoulder and hurried off. She raised her glass and tried to look serene and self-possessed, rather than a stranded wallflower. She looked around the kitchen, hoping for some chore to occupy herself with, but everything had been cleared away. The sink and countertops, refrigerator and stovetop, had all been wiped down. Whatever Jane's doctor was giving her, she wanted some herself.

Trying to maneuver, she bumped into one of the talking men. Sorry, they both said. Sorry. They glanced at each other, waiting to see if a conversation would take hold. Nice party, or something like that. He said, "Hi, I'm Ron Madjiak."

"Bonnie Abrams." She extended her hand and they shook. At least he knew enough to wait for the lady, in this case her, to offer to shake. It was one of those etiquette things that nobody much followed anymore, but that she got huffy about. He was older, forties, blond and heavy-set. His wedding ring sent out a beam like a lighthouse beacon. She said, "Let me guess. You're a doctor."

He spread his hands. "You got me."

"Are you a heart guy like Eric?"

The other man leaned into their conversation. "He's *the* heart guy," he informed Bonnie. "We're in the presence of greatness. This man can unhook your wires, jump-start your battery, and put it all back inside your chest, smoother than peeling a peach." He clapped Ron on the back and headed off for the food tables.

"Wow," Bonnie said. She tried to be more eloquently impressed. "That's something."

Ron looked modestly bored. Or boredly modest. "It's not exactly like peeling a peach."

"I wouldn't think so."

"I'm the head of Cardiology at Northwestern."

"Eric's boss?"

"Mentor. Supervisor," he corrected. "He's a great guy."

"Yes, he is." It was her turn to offer something. "I'm an old friend of Jane's."

Slight puzzlement on Ron's big blond face. "Jane?"

"Your hostess." Where was Jane, anyway? And then, because Bonnie did not want to launch into a narrative of what it was, exactly, that she did, because it was all too involved and sometimes she told people she was a bartender or an aerobics instructor instead, she said, "This music isn't really doing it for me. I'm going to see if I can find 'Deck the Halls' or something."

Bonnie hadn't expected him to follow her, but he did. She knew where the sound system was inside a cabinet in the living room, and she apologized her way past a few people who were trying to keep a grip on their plates and drinks. "What we need," she said to Ron, "is something in between 'Have a Holly Jolly Christmas' and a bunch of chanting monks."

"Let's see what we can do." Ron bent over the console. One of those take-charge guys.

She was used to it in Eric, she guessed that surgeons had to have that kind of confidence bordering on arrogance. He dialed through the play-lists. Blips and squeaks of sound. Then an uptempo version of "We Wish You a Merry Christmas" with a bit of a swing beat. "What do you think?"

"Good. More energy. Thanks." Bonnie nodded, taking her leave, and passed through to the dining room. She wondered if she ought to replenish the shrimp or the meat plates. They were getting a lot of heavy use. She went back into the kitchen to see if there might be extra supplies. In the refrigerator, a number of plastic containers, plastic bags, items triple wrapped in plastic. Carefully disassembling the stacks, she turned around with her hands full.

Ron was standing behind her. "Here, let me get that."

"Thanks." She felt a mild, cautionary buzz. Where was Mrs. Ron anyway? "You know what would be great? Could you break open another bag of ice for the drink tub? If it won't mess up your hands. I mean, I know surgeons are supposed to be real careful."

"We're still allowed to fix drinks." He reached around her to get to the freezer, his arm grazing her hair. Hmm. She laughed, ha ha, at his little joke and took the extra food out to refill the platters. The party was loosening up a bit, more people chitchatting, sitting down, getting comfortable. But it didn't yet have the kind of alcohol-fueled energy that made for a rowdy good time. Why had she come in the first place? She didn't know any of these people, aside from Eric and Jane, and she was unlikely to know them by the end of the evening. Where were Eric and Jane anyway?

Bonnie squeezed her way past the too-big Christmas tree, out to the hallway and the staircase. She stood at its foot, listening. Maybe one of the kids needed something, maybe they were both reassuring Robbie that Santa Claus was real, no matter what the mouthy kid in his kindergarten class said. Turning away, she almost bumped into Ron.

"You forgot your drink," he said, holding out her wineglass.

"Oh, thank you." She took it, drank. A dreary familiar feeling overcame her. Another horndog man who would have to be entertained, chatted up, deflected, oh help. "So why cardiology? Why that instead of, say, gastroenterology, or dermatology?" A man and his job. It was surefire. She settled back to listen. The music had switched over to "I'm Dreaming of a White Christmas."

"I guess I like a challenge. Cardiac care has come such a long way, and there are constant innovations. It keeps you hopping." Ron took another pull of his drink. He was wearing a buttondown shirt with a pink stripe and a V-neck navy sweater, preppy clothes that he should have put aside a decade or two ago. You could see through the overlay of middle age to the dashing young man he must have been. She didn't much like him. She didn't much dislike him. He said, "I bet you think I went into it for the money. People think that a lot, though they don't come right out and say it."

"Well, did you?" She had only the idlest of curiosities.

"That was part of it. I don't mind saying." He smiled. Wanting credit for honesty. Oh, boredom. "But see," he went on, "there's a little more to it than that. Everybody in my family has heart problems. Father. Grandfather. Uncle. Brother. Well, the men have heart problems. Look at my face. Go ahead. See if you can spot the heart attack predictor."

Invited, she stared. He had the kind of face that seemed good-looking, until you broke it down into nostrils and chins and other less than lovely parts. "You're kind of red-complected. Is that it?"

"Nope. Earlobe creases." He pointed. "Ups your cardiac event risk by about fifty-seven percent."

"Huh." For a moment she found him interesting. "How does that work? The ear creases don't actually cause heart attacks, right?"

"No, otherwise we'd go get our earlobes ironed out and sleep better at night. They may indicate some deterioration of the tissue around blood vessels. Same thing that goes on in the heart." He tugged at his earlobe. "So see, some of going into cardiology was just self-preservation. Of course I try to live right. All kinds of monitoring and preventive care. I got after my brother about his risk factors. He didn't want to go in for a stress test. I bet him nine holes of golf. I won, and he had triple bypass surgery."

"That's kind of a nice story. I mean, not the surgery part. Good thing you're up on your golf game."

"I probably could have beat him in arm wrestling, but that might have been too much for his cardiac profile. So, Bonnie," smiling, shifting gears. Enough attractive posturing. Serious hitting on about to commence. "What do you do, when you're not going to parties?"

Who should she be? A private investigator? Organic farmer? Screw it. She said, "I'm a crime fighter."

"You mean, like a superhero?" His blond heart attack face swung close to hers.

Her and her big mouth. She really had to come up with a better script. Maybe she could get a superhero costume. Danger Girl! Before she had to answer, Eric came down the stairs. "Ron, hey, I need to steal this lady away for a minute, sorry."

He walked Bonnie into the kitchen. "Have you seen Jane?"

"No, not since I got here. What's the matter?"

"I can't find her."

They stared at each other. Eric looked away. Bonnie said, "What's going on? Eric?"

"Nothing."

"Did you have a fight? Come on, just tell me."

"No, no fight." He looked impatient at the idea.

"Did she say anything? Are your cars still here?"

"Nothing. Yes, both cars are in the garage."

"All right, we have to get rid of all these people." Her brain clicked along a practical, automatic track. "Did you try the basement?"

Eric said that he had.

"Would she go to a neighbor's? Maybe she needed to borrow something?"

"All the neighbors we know are here."

People pushed past them to get to the bar. They spoke to Eric. Great food. Thanks. Somebody asked him what he and Jane were doing for the holidays and Eric said it was all about the kids. Of course. He laughed and turned again to Bonnie. They retreated to a small porch off the back door that held mops and brooms, rags hung up to dry, a child's raincoat, a vaporizer, possibly broken, more. "How's she been lately?" Bonnie asked. "Have you noticed anything different, off?" She shivered. The porch was uninsulated, the glass windows rimed with frost.

"She knocked herself out getting the party together. But that's nothing new." Eric raised his hands, then, not knowing what to do with them, lowered them. He looked unsteady, scattered. "Should we call the police?"

Bonnie was staring out over the backyard. "Oh God," she said. "Eric."

The next minute they were outside in the brittle cold, running as best they could across the snow crust. A heaped shape in the middle of the yard. Eric reached her first. Jane was lying face up to the sky. Scraps of clothing around her. She was a pale and naked doll, arms and legs flung out to her sides. Her breasts had flattened into pools and her hips were wide white dough. "Oh God," Bonnie said again. "Is she . . ."

Eric pulled Jane up out of the snow. She sagged against him, fell back again. Eric was saying "Ah, shit, ah, ah," hoisting her up, holding her to his chest. There was not enough of him to contain her and parts of Jane kept escaping his grasp, her head of icy hair, her flopping arm. "Go, call 911, get a blanket."

Bonnie ran back, already reaching for her phone. The emergency operator came on and there was a bad moment when she could not remember the street address, one of those idyllic suburban names like

Hollyhock or Pleasant View, but then it snapped into her mind and she told them yes, an adult female, no, she did not know if she was conscious or not, breathing or not, how had she not thought to notice? Then she was inside, upstairs, snatching up the plaid blanket at the foot of Jane and Eric's bed. The stereo was playing "Have Yourself a Merry Little Christmas." In the kitchen a woman leaned toward her, mouth open as if getting ready to talk or perhaps she was already talking. Bonnie blew past her.

Now that her eyes were used to the snow light, now that she knew what she was looking for, she saw Jane's shoes not far from the back door. Black pumps with pointed toes, slung carelessly, one on top of the other, like someone too tired to put them away right. The blanket dragged in the snow, tripping her up as she ran. Eric and Jane were tangled together. He was trying to warm her with his body and breath. Jane's face rolled up to the sky. Her eyes were closed.

"Is she . . ." She couldn't say "dead." Eric didn't answer. He made a one-handed gesture that had something to do with the blanket, she should do something with the blanket. Bonnie unfolded it and held it out.

"Help me with her."

Bonnie took one end of the blanket and Eric held the other. Naked, Jane was impossible not to stare at; she both did and did not resemble herself. Covered up in the blanket, she looked like an accident victim in some country on the other side of the world, a woman pulled out of rubble from an earthquake, perhaps. Jane's head flopped forward. A frost cloud came out of her mouth. Alive?

"Did you call? Are they coming?"

"Yes." Not knowing what else to do, Bonnie bent over and picked up Jane's clothes, bra and slippery panties, pantyhose, the blue sweater dress she'd had on. None of them had frozen solid, though her own hands were so clumsy with cold, it was hard to tell anything more. Maybe Jane had not been out here very long. But then, it was only ten or fifteen degrees. How long was too long? she wanted to ask. She waited for Eric to say it was going to be all right, and he didn't. A siren wailed at some distance. Bonnie thought she should go tell them to come out back. She didn't think she'd said backyard.

But she couldn't get herself to move. Jane was shivering now, a heavy, convulsive shaking. Was that good? Bonnie couldn't remember. It had something to do with trying to maintain body heat. More frost came out of Jane's mouth. "What," Eric said. "What?"

Bonnie came closer. "What is she saying?"

Eric shook his head. "Go," he said. And she went, dropping Jane's clothes on the back porch. She went to the front door, the partygoers only now registering the approaching sirens over, what was it, one of the syrupy songs, "Chestnuts Roasting on an Open Fire."

Bonnie went to the front door, looked out to see the red emergency lights revolving and strobing in the driveway. Two paramedics in down jackets and ball caps got out, carrying gear. She stood aside to let them enter. She could have taken them up the driveway and around, it was stupid not to. Bonnie caught up to them and guided them away from the astonished guests. "Outside, out back," she told them, remembering, finally, to turn the yard light on. They were both ridiculously young men, barely more than teenagers. They had a radio and it was making some garbled noise. Bonnie watched them walk out to Jane and Eric, one following in the other's tracks in the snow, not running, but purposeful, brisk.

Then she turned back to the kitchen and the people who had crowded into it. "What happened?" someone asked.

"Jane had an accident."

"Is she all right?"

"I don't know."

They stared at her, wanting more. Bonnie said, "She fainted or something. Eric's with her."

Someone in the back of the room said, "What was she doing out . . ." Then stopped themselves.

Ron made his way through the crowd to stand next to her. She was almost glad to see him. He'd had the presence of mind to put on a coat. "I'll see if I can help," he said, heading out the door.

The guests were trying to see out the windows for themselves. Bonnie turned her back on them. She watched as the paramedics brought out some kind of stretcher or cart and loaded Jane onto it. She saw Eric and Ron standing together. The paramedics maneuvered and bumped the cart over the snow. She'd forgotten Jane's shoes; they were just within the circle of yard light.

Ron came back inside, blowing on his hands to warm them. To Bonnie he said, "Eric's going to the hospital. He wants to know if you can stay here with the kids until he gets home."

"Yes, of course."

Raising his voice, he addressed the group. "Listen, there's been an accident, but it's under control. Jane's receiving medical attention. I know Eric will get back to everybody when he has some news."

It was beginning to dawn on people that they were meant to leave. A couple of the women began bringing the food in from the dining room, wrapping it back up, and stowing it away in the refrigerator. Someone turned the music off. Bonnie ducked back outside for Jane's shoes and put them with the rest of her clothes. She couldn't bear to leave them out there, as if she would be leaving Jane herself out in the cold.

One of the women in the kitchen began explaining what she had done with the different leftovers, how she had apportioned them, what had gone into the freezer. Bonnie nodded and thanked her. People wanted to help, she got that. Some of the guests had already left. She heard car doors slamming, engines starting.

Bonnie went upstairs to check on the kids. They were both heavily asleep and with any luck they'd stay that way until Eric got home and could explain where Mommy was. Grace had one of those bubbling nightlights. Robbie's bedside lampshade had cutouts in the shape of stars. Maybe it was shock and cold catching up with her, or just pure sorrow, thinking of the two of them waking up to a world that would no longer be right, but she could have laid herself down right then and there and cried.

She came back downstairs. A last couple was putting on their coats and heading for the front door. Bonnie recognized them as people she'd met when she'd first arrived, although she had no clue about their names. The woman said, "Now we're right next door if you need anything. If Eric needs anything."

"Of course. Thank you."

"I hope it's nothing serious," the woman said, by way of asking just what, exactly, it was.

Bonnie said, "She went to take the garbage out and she must have either passed out or slipped and hit her head. I'm glad we found her when we did, you don't want to take chances in this weather."

The woman nodded. Faintly disappointed? People would think what they wanted to think. She'd have to tell Eric the story she'd put out, so he could go along with it if he wished.

The husband said, "Lucky somebody was out there looking for her." Shrewd eyes. Not inclined to believe her.

"It was like, the hand of God, wasn't it? Good night," Bonnie said, ushering them out. She turned to close the door, thinking the house was empty, but here was good old Ron coming up behind her with a drink in his hand, and this was really and seriously too fucking much.

"How you holding up?" he asked. As if she was the one needing fake solicitude and care.

"OK." She kept her hand on the doorknob.

"We're thinking it was some kind of breakdown," Ron said, not specifying who "we" encompassed. The guys at the bar? The paramedics? He and Eric?

"Ah." Her best bet right now was words of one syllable.

"You said you were old friends?"

"Right. Since school."

"I guess even when you know somebody, you never know them." He nodded, all serious, inviting her to opine, gossip, speculate. What was the goddamned matter with people? Her heart was sore with worry, ah Jane! "Fix you a drink?" She shook her head. She knew, from her negotiations training, that the important thing was to get somebody to say yes. "Anything you'd like?"

"You know what would be great?" She watched him perk up, as if she were about to suggest they settle in to watch pornography. "Go down to the hospital and stay with Eric. I know he could use some backup. It would be such a help." And it would, she meant it. But she wasn't above saying it for her own purposes.

He went quietly. Bonnie found the plug for the outside Christmas lights and shut them off. She unplugged the Christmas tree and double checked all the doors. It wasn't that late, only a little after ten. She sat downstairs in the living room for a time, waiting for something to happen, then roused herself and went to check on the kids again.

They hadn't so much as shifted in their sleep. Bonnie stood at Grace's doorway, trying to match her own breathing to the child's, soft and sweet and easy. Eric and Jane's bedroom was down the hall. A light was on next to what was clearly Eric's side of the bed, with its utilitarian pile of folders and medical journals. Jane's side was Kleenex, hand cream, lip balm, nasal spray, cough drops, emery sticks. The bed was made up with a down comforter. Eric had one of those valet stands with a coat hung over it. She didn't know that anyone really used them. It was probably something Jane got him.

She stepped into the adjoining bathroom, peed, washed her hands. How long had it been since she'd shared a bathroom with Jane? Known everything about her down to how much toilet paper she used. Now, even laid bare, she was a mystery.

Bonnie went back into the bedroom and laid down on Jane's side of the bed. She took off her shoes and stockings, her watch and jewelry, and wrapped herself up in the comforter. The pillow smelled faintly of hair.

She'd imagined that this was how she might come to understand Jane, what had gone wrong. Or had always been wrong. Was that it? She sorted through her stack of memories. Jane, the audience and straight man to Bonnie's wild and crazy act. So long ago. They'd only been kids. She'd been such an intolerable brat. How had Jane, or anyone, put up with her?

They'd wanted different things and they'd ended up with different things. Was Jane dissatisfied with what she had? Sometimes she'd complained that people didn't seem to notice her, think her worth noticing. But then, whatever the reason for what had happened tonight, Jane wasn't trying to attract attention as much as disappear entirely.

Bonnie didn't know she'd fallen asleep until she woke up. Brief panic as to where and what, the unfamiliar room, the light still on, noises she couldn't fathom. Eric had come home. She heard his feet on the stairs, stopping at the children's rooms to look in. Then he entered and sat down on his side of the bed. "Hey." He got up again, went to the door and closed it, sat back down.

"How is she?" Feeling a little stupid/awkward/weird at sleeping in his bed, but that was hardly the most important thing right now. "Eric?"

"She's stabilized. They admitted her and she'll be there at least until tomorrow. Her body temperature was 96 when we got there, which is just above hypothermia. So it was probably lower before we got to her." He rubbed at his eyes, kicked his shoes off, and lay back on the bed. "I don't think there'll be, you know, those kinds of medical issues, respiratory . . ." He trailed off, mumbling a little.

"But why . . ." Bonnie sat up. What time was it? She couldn't see a clock. It felt like the deepest darkest part of a winter night, when you can't remember there's such a thing as daylight. "What's wrong with her? I mean, why?"

"I don't know."

She waited for Eric to say something else, but his eyes were closed. "I should go," Bonnie said, trying to get herself untangled from the comforter. "You need to rest."

He reached out with one arm and found her shoulder. "Please stay a while."

"All right," she said after a moment. She lay back down, and Eric pulled her in closer to him, but she guessed that was all right since the big comforter was wadded up between them. She smoothed her skirt, which had ridden up. "Eric?" His eyes were still closed. "What was she saying? She said something to you?"

"She said, 'white.' Yeah. I don't know. Delirium, maybe." He turned over on his side so that Bonnie could see his tired, tired face, the dry lines around his mouth and eyes. There was a current of something on his breath, liquor or coffee or both, strong but not unpleasant.

"White," Bonnie repeated, but the word led her nowhere. She thought Eric had fallen asleep, but he yawned and propped his head up with one arm. "Well . . . ," Bonnie said, feeling like an elephant trying to tiptoe. "You knew she was seeing a therapist, didn't you?"

"It was my idea. Doesn't seem to have helped, huh."

"You wanted her to go because she was unhappy?"

"She's never actually unhappy. Or actually happy. You know how she is."

Bonnie nodded, although Eric couldn't see her, and although she was in the process of reevaluating whether she did, in fact, know Jane, if people were knowable, or if you only got used to them being around, got used to your idea of them, and then they flipped out and attempted to kill themselves at their Christmas party.

"There's also the possibility," Eric began, sounding noncommittal now, in a way that made Bonnie pay particular attention, "that, because, see, one of the symptoms of hypothermia, when the body starts to lose function, lose the ability to regulate itself, when the mental function is impaired, one thing people do is, take their clothes off."

"So maybe she wasn't trying . . ." Bonnie tried to find space for it in her tired head. "But, why be out there in the first place?"

He didn't answer. After a minute he said, "Day after tomorrow is our anniversary. Some celebration, right?"

There was nothing to say to that either, and then Eric said, "There's times I wonder why she ever married me. If I was going to make her so miserable."

"No, hey. It's not anything you did. It's medical, it's psychological, you wouldn't blame yourself if she got appendicitis, would you?"

Eric said, "I'm tired of always worrying about her," and then there was a silence, and once more Bonnie did not know she was asleep until she woke up. Eric was stirring too. It was still dark. They drew in close to each other, their faces together. They kissed, lightly at first, and then with intention. Eric pulled and tugged the comforter away so they lay entwined and pressed together and even though it would seem that there would be other moments later when it was possible to draw back and to stop, in fact this was the last one, and they did not.

His hand was working his way underneath her clothes, and Bonnie reached behind her to loosen her bra, though she kept her sweater on and let him pull and tug it away from her breasts. His hands were warm but she shivered. Then he was up under her skirt and she was feeling for him too. The old hungry wanting, and it didn't much matter by now who he was or why it was a bad idea, except that there was a moment when it was impossible not to think of Jane, of how she might be only imperfectly understood even when sleeping on her pillow and becoming a lover to her husband, and then there were no more such thoughts.

Eric stood up to take his clothes off and Bonnie pulled her skirt and panties off so that she was bare except for the disarray of her sweater and bra riding up around her collarbone. She liked his body, its neatness and compactness. He looked down at her and in spite of every reason not to, they both smiled. He lowered himself to lie next to her and pushed her legs apart with his hand. He wanted to see her come, she understood that without his saying it, and so she put her hand over his and guided him. His fingers entered her even as he stroked her. It was like climbing a staircase in the dark, all you had to do was find the first step and follow it up and up. Her breathing caught on something and made its way out of her in gasps, up and up, and at the very top she writhed and cried out and he put his hand over her mouth to muffle the sound.

Then he was straddling her and pushing his way inside, and now it was required of her to do him the same service, even as sparks were still going off in her and trying to kindle again. She liked the feel of him. Not huge but hard. He went slow at first. Then he couldn't help himself and sped up and pitched his weight forward and she rode along with him and at the last she pressed herself against him and used her hand and climbed those stairs all over again.

"I should go," Bonnie said, wanting to get away before the guilt smacked her upside the head. He moved the arm encircling her and she sat up and pulled the sweater down over her again and took the rest of her clothes with her into the bathroom. Here was a whole mirror not to look into. She used the toilet and washed her hands and cupped water in them to rinse her face. Her body was hectic, unquiet, her head scraped dry from bits of patchy sleep. There was a small clock with a silver frame, something that either Jane had bought as a present for Eric or Eric for Jane, she couldn't remember. It was four thirty, or a little past.

When she went back into the bedroom, Eric had dressed in sweatpants and a T-shirt.

He was standing by the door and Bonnie knew he had opened it to listen for the children.

She started to say something, she wasn't sure what, then remembered the jewelry she'd left on Jane's nightstand, oh nice touch, leaving her gaudy finery at the scene of the crime. She picked it up and dumped the whole handful of it in her purse. Then faced him again. He said, whispering, "If you could . . ."

Bonnie followed his pointing finger. "Right," she said, and stooped to take off her shoes. He opened the door for her and they soft-footed their way past the children's rooms. She followed him down to the dark living room and into the kitchen, where an unlovely fluorescent light burned over the sink. Eric opened the refrigerator. "Drink? Anything?"

She shook her head. He took a glass from the cupboard, filled it with ice, and poured out a can of ginger ale. "Here. Settles the stomach."

"Stomach, sure." Bonnie nodded and drank. She set it down on the counter. "Yup. Good stuff."

"Come here." He opened his arms and she stepped into them and they leaned into each other and that felt fine, in a sad way. She breathed in the complicated smell of him, the layers of heat, body, and sex. Then she drew back and looked at him, this ordinary man who had become both dear and confusing to her. He said, "Why don't you wait until it's light. I don't want you driving at this ungodly hour."

"I'll be all right. Better this way."

"If you think . . ."

"Yes."

And then they both began talking at once, and stopped, and Eric motioned for her to go first. She said, "I hope Jane's all right."

"Thanks." Bonnie looked at him, waiting, and he said, "I guess we should think of this as some kind of accident."

Bonnie said yes, that was probably a good idea, and she got her coat, and they kissed, lightly this time, on her way out the door, and she didn't look back as she walked carefully down the glazed sidewalk and cracked open the door to her frozen car and cranked the cold heart of the battery until it caught and the engine turned over. It took a while for the defroster to make enough headway so she could see to drive. And so she had to sit there and sit there when all she wanted was a clean getaway, and among the things she was trying not to think was that *accident* wasn't the right word at all, because an accident was something you couldn't avoid.

a vacation

If Jane opened her eyes and did not turn her head or change position, she saw a long, narrow rectangle of sky, ocean, and beach, one stacked on top of the other, like a fancy dessert. She did not turn her head or move because this was the way she had been arranged, they'd left her like this. She lay on a reclining chair under a beach umbrella. She wore a swimsuit, in the hopeful possibility that she might go in the water. And over that a gauzy caftan, plus a broad-brimmed hat and sunglasses. And of course, they'd put sunscreen all over her. Jane couldn't decide if she liked the smell of it or not, a lotion smell that overpowered the ocean one. She spent a long time going back and forth about it, then ending up at the same place without deciding, and then having to start all over again. That was the medicine they gave her, which slowed her brain down. It was thought that she needed to be easy in her mind, and everything made very calm and restful.

The vacation was a part of the prescription too, something else it was determined that she needed, and not just any vacation but a trip to this warm and sunny island (she had forgotten the name of it, if she ever knew it), a long ways away from ice and snow. And so, after their patched-together Christmas, there had been this expensive last-minute trip. She thought that Eric's parents must have paid for it. She hoped so. She hoped they were mad about spending so much. The medicine made her not care about liking people she was supposed to like.

Every so often, in the rectangle of her vision, her children appeared, walking or wading, dressed in their beach clothes and accompanied by, not a babysitter, but a buddy sitter, as the hotel styled her, a cheerful, very black girl wearing a tropical print camp shirt, her long legs in khaki shorts. She was helping Grace pick up shells and trying to keep Robbie from charging headfirst into the surf. Eric was there too, strolling along behind the group, entering the rectangle after a delay. He waded in after Robbie and pulled him out of the water, then held on to his arm as he bent and spoke to him, one more reminder about paying attention and doing as he was told.

Eric was careful not to look in Jane's direction too often, though sometimes she caught him doing so. Nor were the children allowed to disturb her. It was believed that the care and management of the children had contributed to her stress, and so they were told, many times a day, that Mommy was sleeping, or Mommy was resting. They were, however, permitted to approach her on occasion and show her the periwinkles and sand dollars and seagull feathers they had found. They were nice children. She missed them.

The hotel sitter was trying to get Grace and Robbie started on building a sand castle, for which they had been equipped with plastic pails and scoops. She pointed out a good spot, neither too wet nor too dry, and sat down with the children and used Grace's scoop to demonstrate how to dig. Jane felt sad about this. She should be the one showing them what sand castles were all about, how you built them up and then watched the inevitable, magnificent ruin when the tide came in. She could get up right now and go to them.

But her legs were so heavy, and once she got her legs in motion there would be the rest of her to haul upright, and the sun was so hot. And say she did get up and walk a careful path down to the water's edge. Would they be happy to see her, the Ghost of Mommy? Or would they be unsure, afraid, wondering what was wrong with her? What would Eric do? What would she want him to do? She rolled that question around in her head for a while, and then came up with the answer: nothing.

She fell asleep. She slept all the time now. The medicine parched her mouth and her dreams were slow, as if they were mired in glue. Were the pills supposed to make her feel better? No. They were only meant to keep her quiet and out of harm's way. She was seldom left unsupervised. There was another employee provided by the hotel, an older black woman who helped her dress and bathe in the mornings, and who brought her meals in on a tray, and who sat in a chair while she napped. It was all quite deluxe, she didn't have to lift a finger, all of it the result of the one time in her life she'd caused anyone trouble.

Of course they'd asked her—the doctors at the hospital—what had happened and how she had come to be in such an alarming condition, and she could see that their questions all had to do with finding out if she was self-harming, that is, likely to do such a thing again, and if so, what flavor of mental illness she was. She allowed as how she had been stressed, what with the holiday, the party, the kids. Perhaps more stressed than was good for her. Yes, and perhaps unhappy at times, since who wasn't? The whole housewife thing. Everyone was familiar with dissatisfied housewives, dragged down by the repetitive boredom of their routine and the bitterness with which they imagined the unrealized lives they had been deprived of. Yes, she might have been feeling unappreciated, taken for granted, etc. That hint of marital discord that allowed the doctors to feel they were able to put together the whole picture. None of this was exactly a lie, but neither was it entirely true.

She woke with Eric's hand on her arm. "Honey? We should head back to the hotel, the kids are tired."

"Don't touch me," Jane said, and he drew his arm away as quick as if he'd touched a snake, and she was glad to see the concern he did not mean wiped from his face, replaced by the peevishness and anger which he did. "I'm coming," she said, and managed without his help to swing her legs around so she sat on the edge of the chair, then stood, carefully, getting her bearings. Now there was a great deal more to look at, sky and ocean and sand all spilling their boundaries, rushing in at her. She fought against dizziness, steadied herself. Eric stood back from her and it was easy enough to read his thoughts: *Fine, go ahead, fall over, do it your way.* He was furious with her for being something broken, for refusing to be well, *even with everyone's best efforts.*

Where were the children? Jane had a moment's panic, imagining them drowned, lost, but no, they were right here, being herded toward her by the hotel sitter. In spite of all the sunscreen, parts of them, Grace's nose, Robbie's shoulders, were turning the color of boiled shrimp. "Did you build a big castle?" she asked them. "Was it fun?"

"It was super big," Robbie said. "A shark ate it." He made biting faces at his sister, who shrieked and held on to Jane's legs.

"Sharks don't eat sand castles, Robbie." This from Eric. Since the hotel sitter was there, he made his tone fond and indulgent. He was the fun-but-responsible parent, making all the tough decisions, shouldering the burdens. It was so unfair for him.

"I'm a big shark!" Robbie couldn't decide what kind of noise sharks made, so he employed a variety of roaring and snarling and showing his teeth. Grace started to cry.

"That's about enough," Eric said, since Jane was only looking on in an interested way. "Robbie, leave her alone. Gracie, he's just teasing you. I think both you guys need naps."

"If you eat a whole lot of sharks, then you turn into a shark," Robbie informed them.

"I'd like to do that," Jane said. "Be a shark. Just try it on for an afternoon, maybe."

"Thank you, Rachel, we can take it from here." Eric drew money from his shirt pocket and passed it to the girl. "Kids, say thank you to Rachel."

They did so, in a spotty, halting fashion, and the girl hugged them and headed up the path to the hotel. Jane watched her go, so lithe and mobile, her legs bounding along so effortlessly that she might have taken an extra leap, lifted her arms, and flown.

She turned back to Eric and the children. Left on their own, their group seemed diminished, straggling, untidy, Robbie and Grace clearly needing care and setting to rights. But her body refused to let her be more than a polite spectator, and so it was Eric who said, "All right, kids, let's march," and made sure they rinsed off in the outdoor shower.

The hotel was not one of the luxury places they'd passed on their way from the airport, all royal palm walks and pink stucco villas, but it was nice enough, with its own little stretch of beach, and purple bougainvillea climbing the walls. The bedrooms had ceiling fans that rotated in lazy fashion and the windows were framed with plantation shutters. Jane had to remind herself that these were not merely props to evoke the Caribbean, that they were in fact in the Caribbean. Jane lay down on the bed and left Eric to tend to the children, peeling off their swimsuits and rinsing the itchy sand from their bodies and the salt water from their hair, applying sunburn cream to their flaming skin. He made sure they drank water to keep from being dehydrated. He put them down for their naps in the bedroom adjoining his and Jane's. Jane heard Robbie complaining that he was not sleepy, and Eric telling him to pretend he was sleepy, make a game out of it, and Robbie telling him that sounded like a really really dumb game.

Eric came through the door, closing it lightly. Jane was lying on the bed with her eyes closed. She was not asleep but she wanted him to think she was. She felt Eric looking at her. Then he went into the bathroom and she heard him running water, opening and closing, slow sounds, tired sounds.

He was unhappy. She was supposed to feel sorry for him but she didn't. Maybe it was the pills. What was that supposed to mean, anyway, a husband? A man you lived with. The one who went to work in the morning and needed food and conversation when he returned. The one who jollied up the children or yelled at them to clean their rooms. One half of the genetic contribution to said children. In such ways the species preserved itself, and they were no different from swarming bugs, each bug self-importantly believing that its own little bug-life, its own bug happiness or lack thereof, was necessary to some greater good. That would be something she could tell the next round of doctors when they asked her how she was doing, and could she describe her feelings: I am a bug.

They had been here three days, with three more to go. While she rested, Eric took the children out on excursions, on a pirate boat ride, and to a sugarcane plantation. See? he seemed to be telling Jane. See what you're missing out on by being so stubborn about not getting better? He bought them hand puppets and T-shirts and picture books about tropical fish. He bought guavas and soursops and papayas, all of which he encouraged the children to eat, without success. The local drink was rum, dark and strong, and he took to drinking it as the locals did, rum and Coke, rum and orange juice, rum and water, rum and rum. At night, once the children were tucked in and Jane too was asleep, he went down to the hotel bar. Maybe he went other places as well. She couldn't have said. The room had two double beds and each of them slept in their own. In the same bed she might have been able to tell more, by his smell, or his unquiet dreams.

When Eric came out of the bathroom, Jane wasn't quick enough about closing her eyes, and he saw that she was awake. He hesitated, then sat down on the edge of her bed. He said, "I'm trying to think of what we should do once we get home."

"Do," Jane said, as if not understanding what he meant, although she did. "I expect you'll go back to work."

"If you won't . . ." He corrected himself. "If you're still going to need time to get better, then we have to decide some things."

A pool of spreading panic beneath the surface of the pill-calm. "Like what?"

"Like, if you still can't take care of yourself. Or the kids."

He waited for her to ask the next question, and when she didn't, he said, "You could go to someplace private. A nice place, with a lot of support services. A good facility."

He seemed embarrassed by the word *facility*. It hung suspended in midair, like a cartoon anvil about to drop. "Just until you felt up to it again. Somewhere you can keep getting better."

"Then you think I am getting better," Jane said, and watched him try to make that into what he wanted to say. He had changed from his beach clothes into the shorts and linen shirt he'd bought here. None of them had the right clothes to bring. He'd picked up enough sun that his winter skin had turned a bright brown. Unlike Jane and the children, he didn't burn. The new color in his face made its lines and loose flesh even out. The retreating hairline he was so worried about wasn't any big deal. She said her thought out loud. "You're still a good-looking man."

He was startled, disbelieving, cautious. *What? Does she really think? Why?* "Thank you," he said. He rested one hand on her leg before he remembered himself and took it away. "That's a nice color for you," he said, meaning Jane's sky-blue caftan.

"Thanks."

"Grace was really cute today. Every time the tide went out and sucked the sand from beneath her toes, she'd squeal and do this little up and down dance."

"Ah." Jane nodded. Remembered to smile.

"So." Eric trying to recover the thread of his talk. "I just wanted you to be thinking about it. In case you had any questions. In case that ends up being the way we decide to go."

"In case," Jane repeated.

"That's right."

"I wasn't trying," Jane began, but she had trouble getting any air behind her words, and Eric had to bend closer to hear her.

"I wasn't trying to hurt myself," she said, with a new effort. "I just wanted to be out in the snow."

"We've talked about this," Eric said. He had dropped into doctor mode, a way of sounding patient and engaged without actually being either. "You said you didn't remember."

"Well I remember now." She had not been talking very much lately and the words felt like a mouthful of bees. "I needed a break. From the party. I put my face against the glass. It was so nice and cool."

Eric was waiting for her to go on. "That's really it," Jane said. "I went outside. The rest of it was a mistake."

"Some mistake."

"It was colder than I expected. I was dis . . ."

"Disoriented."

"That's it," she agreed.

"You took your shoes off right by the back door."

"Yes, I believe that's how it happened." She could tell from his face that she had not succeeded.

"I'm sorry," Eric said. "I have to think about Robbie and Grace. I have to think about their safety."

Jane gaped at him. "You think I'd hurt them? You honestly think that?"

"I don't want to think it. But I can't stop worrying, because this thing happened, this very dangerous, dangerous . . . Jane, you were either trying to kill yourself or you had some kind of psychotic break, and I don't know which is worse, or what else it could be. Or how to explain it. I mean I know you were unhappy a lot of the time, I don't know why but you were, and I know you had a lot of work with the holiday, with the party and all. OK, too much work, I should have helped more, I see that now. But none of that adds up to . . . Jane! It wasn't a normal response to normal problems! We have to take it seriously. We have to get you the help you need." He stopped to catch his breath. "We have to work this through together."

"I am taking it seriously."

"All right then." Eric nodded as though they had decided something important. "All right."

"It might be this other . . ." She was still getting the hang of talking. "This other thing. Condition."

"What other condition," Eric said, back to doctor mode.

"What if I had a brain ah, what if I had," she tried the word out, "epilepsy."

Instantly his attention sharpened. "Why would you think you have epilepsy?"

"The doctor in Atlanta, what was his name . . ."

"Dr. Cohen?"

Jane pretended to remember. "Yes, that was it. He thought it was a possibility because I had these, he called them, episodes . . ."

"What kind of episodes? What did you tell him?"

She didn't want to say more, but it was too late not to. "I didn't think they were any big deal, I mean, not any big, huge . . . It was more like, I'd just space out." She shrugged. "So, I don't know, maybe that's what happened, I went outside for a moment and had one of these . . ." Again she trailed off.

Eric stood up. "Did Dr. Cohen run any tests? Scans? Anything like that?"

"No. I was supposed to go back, but I didn't," Jane admitted.

"I don't believe this, why not? Why the hell not go back?"

"I don't know."

He shook his head. Words insufficient to express the vast depths of his disbelief and gobsmacked incredulity. How could she be so irresponsible foolish irrational, etc.

"I stopped having the, whatever you call them. Episodes. Seizures. I thought they were gone. And there were all those problems with Gracie." If only she could stop talking, explaining things, forever and ever. "I'm sorry. I guess I was too embarrassed to bring it up."

"Jane, honey. You take the cake. The absolute, triple layer chocolate frosted cake."

She had made him happy. He was so pleased and relieved, thinking there might be a name for what she was, what was wrong with her. Here he was explaining things, as he liked to do. How it was nothing to be ashamed of, since epilepsy—if in fact that's what it was—was only a disease like any other. With many treatment options available. Advances in research. Of course there would be a process, a thorough medical process. As soon as they got back, he'd make some calls. Tempering his relief with serious talk.

She had hoped not to say anything. Because now she was ashamed of herself for her weakness and foolishness.

He said, "I think we should go out to dinner tonight. Just you and me. If you feel up for it?"

He wanted to celebrate her impending diagnosis. The receding prospect of a facility. And she would be happy along with him, she would try. She had to be a real mother to her children, not some moony invalid. "I can rest this afternoon."

"That's great. Lucille can stay with Robbie and Grace." He stood over the bed, not sure what to do with himself, then stooped and gave her a quick kiss. "I'm going to go ask about restaurants."

"Eric? No more of the pills."

He considered this, then agreed. "I'm sure there's something that would be better. We'll get you a thorough work-up." He smiled and closed the door behind him.

And still she had not told him all of the truth. How she'd walked out of the kitchen door and hoped she would be struck, as if by lightning. How she'd wanted the beautiful white nothing, if only for a moment, because the ordinary awfulness of her life had closed in so completely.

At dinnertime, Jane put on an old summer dress, left over from college, that someone, Eric she guessed, had packed for her. It was thin and green and left her arms bare. She didn't like the look of her jutting collarbones and too-pale shoulders. She was limp, pallid, like something embalmed. Instead of lying on the beach all swaddled and shaded, she should have gotten some sun. Well, too late now. Here was a cotton shawl bought from a beach vendor, red and green and yellow. Although she wasn't clever about such things, she managed to tie it around her shoulders in an approximation of tropical flair. She found some makeup in the bottom of her purse and did what she could with it, applying bits of pink and beige. She arranged her blond hair so it fanned out around her. Eric told her how nice she looked. "Thank you," Jane said. She assumed he was encouraging her for making an effort.

Of course she had not intended the rest of it. All these consequences. Who would have thought that stepping out into the backyard would result in so many serious doctor conversations, not to mention hotel rooms and sand castles and the rest of it. Had she really taken her clothes off? She didn't remember that part. She didn't want to remember it.

Robbie and Grace were plied with hamburgers and videos and left in the care of the nanny. Eric and Jane walked across the hotel lobby and out to the street. Eric said, "There's a nice restaurant at the resort just down the beach. It's not very far to walk, if you're up for it."

"That would be fine." Both of them making an effort. Maybe there was something to the idea of a vacation, of getting away from your same old habits and patterns. Maybe she could manage it. Try harder, be more of a wife to him. Will herself into normal happiness.

All along the street were people strolling or jolting along in the little open cars favored on the island. This was the tourist district, so all the world seemed to be engaged in pleasure-seeking. The tourists were American or Canadian or British or German or Japanese, expensively strolling in their sandals and straw hats, their new sunburns making them twitch and struggle delicately inside their clothes. Everything was arranged for them: the open air bars and fine restaurants and tourist buses and souvenir shops. The obliging natives. And of course there were the white beaches and the turquoise ocean and the perfect weather, as if that also had been procured for them.

Jane said, "I've never been anywhere like this before."

"You mean, the Caribbean?"

"Yes," Jane said, although she had meant, a place where so many people gathered in this hectic fashion, so determined to be carried out of themselves. It was a little frightening, like being caught up in a cattle stampede.

"I took a couple of spring break trips in college. Of course, that was Jamaica, not here. This is a lot more grown up. Well, I'm a lot more grown up."

"Ah," Jane said. It was useful to learn that this was not Jamaica. She expected that she could find out where they were without coming out and asking. Now that the pills were wearing off, it was embarrassing not to know.

"There's the resort," Eric said, pointing it out. "See? Not far." He kept wanting to take her arm and guide her, then he'd remember himself and stop. She supposed she'd have to let him, sooner or later.

The resort was several notches grander than their own hotel, with a white-pillared entry and a circular drive where automobiles could be parked and admired. Flags that Jane did not recognize fluttered on slim poles. There were palm trees and plantings of hibiscus and red, spiky plants; there were valets in white shirts and a doorman in a tall hat and braided coat. Everyone was professionally happy to see them, and guided them out to a dining terrace overlooking the beach.

Eric said, "I thought, if it wasn't too chilly, we could eat outside. Or, if you'd rather, they have another dining room inside."

"This will be just fine," Jane said, and let him pull out her chair for her. The dinner napkins had been folded into points and placed in the water goblets like bouquets. It took Jane a moment to recognize what they were. It made her nervous that there might be other such things that would confuse her.

It was early for dinner and only two other couples were on the ter-race. Below them was the resort's lagoon-shaped swimming pool. It was equipped with what Eric explained was a swim-up bar, so that guests did not have to leave the water for their daiquiris. As they watched, a man in a Speedo with the Union Jack plastered across the seat and a woman in a gold bikini held together by chains appeared on the pool deck, their hands tucked into each other's waistbands. "It's not as much of a family place as our hotel," Eric said.

The waiter was their new best friend. He brought them calamari and coconut shrimp in chili sauce, crabmeat crepes, beef tenderloin. Side dishes, things like mangoes or caramelized vegetables, kept arriving. It was a great deal of food and they ate slowly, as if not wanting to offend a host by leaving anything uneaten. The tables around them filled. The waiters lit tall propane heaters to keep the chill away. "How are you feeling?" Eric couldn't help asking her. "Are you feeling all right?"

"I'm fine." And she guessed she was, just woozy from overeating. The waiter offered coffee and dessert. They both ordered coffee and Eric said he'd try the crème brûlée. Jane watched the sunset sky. It was so wildly and unnecessarily gorgeous, a pool of gold light intersected by bars of purple clouds, that she had to keep reminding herself it was the same sun as back in Chicago.

Eric said, "I know this is coming a little late, but Happy Anniversary."

"Happy Anniversary," Jane said in turn. It was the kind of thing you toasted to, but all they had in front of them was coffee. They smiled at each other, though they were awkward about it and their eyes glanced away.

Eric began speaking, keeping his voice low in an attempt at privacy, although he had chosen this public place to speak: "I want to make it work for us. We can go on from here. Things can be better than before. I really believe that."

"I would like to think that too," Jane said. But where was the name of the island? She didn't want to ask anyone.

"A lot of it's been my fault. I accept responsibility for that." Here he paused, as if waiting for Jane to make some similar speech. When she stayed silent, he had to go on. "I've been too preoccupied with work, and

I guess some of that is inevitable because medicine is what it is. The demands on your time."

Again he waited. "Sure," Jane said. "It is what it is."

"And the kids, don't get me wrong, I wouldn't have it any other way, but they do take a lot of energy. No wonder we get crossed signals sometimes."

"I guess I worry about them too much," Jane allowed. "Get too wrapped up in all the day to day kid needs."

"That's because you're a great mom."

She liked hearing it. "Thank you."

"You just need to dial it down a little. Not make it so hard. For your own sake."

"I can work on that. Yes."

"I know you can. And we'll figure out this seizure thing, I promise."

He made it sound so easy. How things like brains could be fixed. How they would resolve to do better and then move on. He wanted it to be that easy. Eric saw her looking at him and stopped himself. "What?" he asked.

She shook her head. It was something he would not say. It was stuck far down in his throat. Or perhaps she was just imagining. She both knew him and she didn't know him. "Never mind," she said. "Sorry."

"No, what?"

He leaned forward, waiting. When she didn't answer, he said, "There's times you're a million miles away. You know?"

The waiter appeared at the table, inquiring after their well-being. Everything was fine, Eric told him, and Jane too said it was fine. The waiter left and now they were both embarrassed at having such a conversation, saying things they did not usually say. "I'm sorry," Jane said. "I know I get distracted. Spacey. But it's not like I'm thinking these involved, complicated thoughts. It's more like I'm thinking . . . nothing."

It was a feeble way to talk about it. She could tell that Eric was disappointed. "Nothing?" he repeated. "I guess that's better than some dark, scheming plot."

"I meant, nothing as in, a quiet mind," Jane said, annoyed that he seemed to be making fun of her. "Letting yourself be open to whatever comes to you."

"Like, meditation," Eric suggested.

"Yes, I suppose. A lot like meditation." Why did he think everything had to have a name, an explanation?

"Sure you don't want to try some?" He offered her the half-eaten crème brûlée, and when Jane shook her head, went back to eating it.

He was glad to have this part of things over with, and having avoided more distress or complication. She guessed she was too. They had both admitted fault and pledged to do better. But there were things that neither of them had said. Perhaps what they had really agreed to was that they could each keep their secrets.

She had become a responsibility to him. One more thing he needed to take care of.

You could say that there were times he was a million miles away too.

The check came and Eric paid it and they walked down from the terrace to the pool deck and the beach beyond. It was nearly dark. The pool and the little thatched roof bar were lit by colored lights, red and green and blue. A steel drum band was playing, a chiming sound like a carnival or an old-fashioned ice cream truck. They stopped to listen. Eric said they could sit for a while if she wanted.

"No, let's just go on back." It was all so bright and hectic. She felt bleached out just standing next to it.

"You're still tired. Come on, we can walk back on the beach." He put an arm around her. She allowed this. They were, after all, celebrating her return to their shared life.

They turned their backs on the resort and walked toward the ocean. "Nobody's out here," Jane said, wonderingly. It was true, they had the stretch of sand to themselves. Everyone seemed to be at the bars, revving up for a night of fun. The hotels and villas were lit, but once you walked toward the water's edge, there was only the deep blue evening sky and the white sand and the dark rolling ocean. The nub of a quarter moon had risen.

Eric said, "Finally, my fantasy comes true. Walking on the beach with a pretty girl. Is that a smile I see? Yes it is!"

So much lived beneath the surface of the ocean. A kingdom of weaving, waving plants, grottos of coral, schools of silvery, darting fish. And other fish in colors beyond imagining, and creatures that hid their softness within shells, or burrowed into the ocean floor. Cruising sharks. Beyond them, in the deepest ocean, whales. Undersea flowers, blind worms, translucent creatures sending out tentacles.

So much that could not be seen and yet it was as real as anything you could. In this different sky was the same snow-moon that had pierced her with its white beauty and bestowed on her an ecstasy of knowing, even as her body had given way to the cold and fallen, even as that same body now walked, hand in hand with the man who was her husband, toward their hotel.

but how are you really?

"B ut how are you really?"

"All right. You don't have to worry."

"I'm not worrying, I'm asking."

"I have this new medication, it's helping. It keeps me from stressing. Everybody says I need to manage my stress."

"So do you agree with everybody?"

"Stress is bad for you."

Bonnie waited on her end of the phone, but Jane didn't go on. Bonnie said, "I guess if you feel you're moving in the right direction. Doing something positive for yourself."

"Everybody," Jane said, "is encouraging me to think positively."

There was a flatness to her voice rather than the shades of humor Bonnie might have expected, even Jane's trademark weary, knowing humor. Medication, maybe. Bonnie said, "Well, so I'm everybody. Be positive. Do as I say, not as I do." A space of silence. "Did I tell you I found a new apartment?"

"I didn't know you were looking."

"It kind of came up around Christmas."

"Then I guess I wouldn't remember. No, it's OK, there's all kinds of stuff I missed." Mild interest on Jane's part. "Where is it?"

"North. In Norwood Park, south of Foster. Lots of cops and firefighters live around there because it's just inside the city limits. Very pleasant, safe. It's practically the suburbs."

"But you've been in your place forever," Jane said, making it sound funereal, as if Bonnie might be moving into senior living.

"Yeah, well, it seemed like a good time to clean up my act."

"I guess you'll be closer to us."

Us, Jane and Eric. She would, although damn that was not the main idea or even a good idea. "A little closer. Should be less city traffic. It's a nice place, in a four flat. Two bedrooms, has its own washer and dryer. Off-street parking. Lots of windows, natural light, big kitchen. Well, pretty big." Nothing from Jane. Bonnie guessed that compared to Jane's aspirational real estate, it wasn't much to brag about. Still, it would have been nice if Jane pretended excitement. Maybe the excitement had been dosed right out of her. "Anyway, some guys from work are going to help me move Saturday morning. Yes, I am freaking out, because I have lived here forever and the place is a total goat barn."

"Can I help? I can help you pack. Saturday? I could come over."

"Thanks, but no. There's not a lot of packing involved. It's more like illegal dumping."

The old, unmedicated Jane might have found that funny. Instead there was another silence. Bonnie was about to say good-bye and hang up when Jane spoke. "Eric's disappointed that I don't have some kind of brain disease."

"Is he," Bonnie said, carefully.

"I'm not diagnosable. I'm in a gray area, clinically speaking. Doctors don't like gray areas."

"I'm sure he just wants to be able to help you."

"It scares him when things aren't under control," Jane said, suddenly chatty. "Because he's afraid he might let himself lose control. And then who would he be?"

"You know, Jane, I wouldn't—"

"I mean, who would any of us be, if we did something that was totally, totally out of character for us? What does that even mean, out of character? Are people supposed to be this fixed-for-all-time quantity? Is that a weird thing to think?"

"No, it's interesting, really."

"It's how my medically suspect brain works nowadays." Jane's enthusiasm dropped off as quickly as it had risen. "OK, I should go start dinner. I'm trying to get us all on this low-sugar high-fiber diet. It's going over just about as well as you'd imagine."

After they hung up, Bonnie sat down on her old swaybacked couch, which was not going to make the move along with her. The apartment had been upended and turned inside out. Every closet and drawer and shelf had disgorged its secret messes, like some perverse magic trick. Some of it had been packed and sealed into boxes, but a lot of it, old papers, old clothes, dishonored odds and ends, was only waiting to be declared trash and hauled out in black plastic garbage bags. She was buying new furniture from Ikea. She was going to start over clean in a clean new space.

So many good intentions! Such an honorable fresh start! Rotten feelings toted out to the alley. Useless regrets for a moment of stupid weakness, never to be repeated. She and Jane would go on as before. Jane and Eric would struggle through this current crisis. Bonnie and Eric would keep their distance and observe the formalities. Don't dwell on it. A closed chapter. One moved on, sadder but wiser. Good old fallible human beings, same old sordid story. Not that this made you feel any better about yourself.

Eric said pretty much the same thing when he called. Of course he called her. He couldn't let it be, had to try and make it, somehow, all right. He wasn't someone who could tolerate being on bad terms with anyone. Jane said, "You remember how you used to say he looked like a Labrador retriever? That's exactly what he is. Always shoving his nose under your hand."

When he called, Jane had still been in the hospital, although out of immediate danger. The kids had been deposited with the grandparents, they'd have some sort of Christmas over there. But, he said, that was not why he wanted to talk to her. "How are you?"

"I'm all right." A few beats of silence went by. Bonnie shifted the phone to her other ear.

"What?"

"Nothing."

"I thought you said something."

"No, just fumbling with the phone."

Eric sighed. "I guess, no way this wasn't going to be awkward."

What did he want? Bonnie wasn't inclined to help him out. She stayed silent and obstinate. It was good to hear that Jane was all right. But a combination of guilt and hurt feelings and general lowdown thoughts got in the way of any heartfelt concern. Which only made things worse.

"So I feel bad," Eric said, trying again, "I mean I feel bad all kinds of ways, but I wanted to apologize for practically kicking you out of the house. It was the middle of the night and it was freezing cold. Less than freezing, zero. I was a jerk."

"No, it's OK." She did understand that part. The kids, the panicky impulse. "No biggie. I got home all right."

"I shouldn't have—"

"No, don't start. It's not necessary." She spoke sternly because in spite of herself, she was remembering his face, his hands, and yes, his dick.

"I accept responsibility," he said, in a formal tone, as if signing a treaty. "And I hope we can go back to the way things were without damaging any friendships. Yours and Jane's. Yours and mine. That's important to me."

"Sure."

"It was a mistake. But I hope we can keep it, you know, between ourselves."

"I'm not going to rat you out, Eric. For God's sake, why would I do that? Don't worry."

"It wasn't a rational fear," he admitted. "More like, I deserve to get caught, so I probably will."

"Sorry. You probably won't."

Another silence. He said, "Not that it wasn't really . . . Not that you aren't . . ."

"Thanks." She wanted to get off the phone now. Talk wasn't helping anything.

"Because you're a wonderful girl. Woman. Broad? Chickadee?"

"No, just don't. You don't have to shine me up. Why don't you worry about Jane instead? She's the one who needs you."

"All right" he said. "I'm not doing a great job here. You're mad and hurt and whatever else. I knew it wasn't going to be easy to call, but I had to. Because I do care about you. We crossed a line. That doesn't have to ruin everything from now on. So don't shut me out. Yes, I will take care of Jane. I don't need reminding. But who's supposed to take care of you?"

He hung up the phone, and Bonnie burst into tears.

She didn't need to feel sorry for herself. She didn't need to feel like she was alone in the world, even if she was. Even if it was so largely her own choice to be alone in the world. She didn't need to be made pitiful.

That was just before Christmas, the only time they'd spoken, although Eric had included her in an e-mail to friends, telling everyone that Jane was out of the hospital and back home, and Bonnie had sent Jane a get-well card, a funny one, with a puppy wearing one of those cones around its head. "Hope you're back on all fours soon!" Or maybe it wasn't all that funny. She didn't trust her judgment anymore about such things. Either everything was funny, or more likely, nothing was.

Moving day came, a bright, cold February Saturday. Her friends from work were these younger guys, Ian and Derek, two of the mechanics who serviced the cop fleet. Bonnie had met them when her Ford Escort had an oil leak. They did side jobs at Ian's cousin's North Side garage and did them cheap. The two of them smoked a lot of pot and memorized old comedy albums from the '70s, so that they were always cracking each other up with routines that nobody else but them understood.

Bonnie had promised them beer and pizza for helping. They didn't show up until ten, and only after she'd called them twice, but they got the heavy stuff, books and her bed frame and mattress, stowed away in short order. Bonnie kept finding more things to throw out rather than move. She wasn't sure they could make it in one load, even with her own car packed with houseplants and clothes on hangers. She planned on sleeping in the new place tonight and coming back to clean tomorrow.

The apartment was simultaneously emptying out and becoming more disheveled. "It looks sort of like a crack house," Derek said helpfully. "You know, where they've gotten rid of all the furniture and just throw everything on the floor."

"That's nice. How much room's left in the van?"

"Ian's being totally anal about loading, so there's still space for some stuff. Are you keeping this?" He picked up a lava lamp, something else that at one time Bonnie had thought was funny.

"It's yours if you want it."

"Cool. Thanks."

Feet on the stairs. The door was standing open. "Knock knock," Jane said, then she came into view, followed by Eric.

"Oh, hey. Wow." Bonnie spouting monosyllables. "Wow. You guys." What would a normal person do? She crossed the room and hugged Jane. "Hey," she said eloquently to Eric, who said Hey back. Crap. Jane held out a plastic wrapped plate.

"Oh, what's this?"

"Cookies, for you."

"Cookies," Bonnie echoed. They were red and green star shapes decked with silver trim, clearly refugees from the Christmas party.

"Don't worry, they're fresh. I had some extra dough in the freezer."

"That's great, thanks." Bonnie tried to calibrate her enthusiasm. She held the plate out to Derek, who was always a reliable consumer of munchies. "Guys, this is Derek. Derek, Jane and Eric."

"We came to help," Jane said. "Tell us what we can do." Jane looked all right, Bonnie decided. She always looked best in winter weather, like she'd just come from herding reindeer. She wore jeans and a puffy red jacket and a patterned wool scarf that had the look of a Christmas present. The cold had put some color in her face. She didn't seem exactly mirthful or high-spirited, but she was at least normal Jane, that is, some combination of repressed and depressed. Bonnie was looking at Jane so she would not have to look at Eric. The last occasion she'd seen either of them, they had both been naked. Now why for God's sake think such a thing.

"Help? Oh, I don't know, we were just getting ready to drive over with a load." The wretched condition of the apartment embarrassed her. Dust billowed across the floor. The open hall closet held a few broken backed hangers and a dumpload of old shoes. Bonnie had been cleaning out the refrigerator and the kitchen counters held the last inedible contents: jars of pickle juice, bowls of petrified leftovers. Yes, welcome to the House of Crack. "So it's not like I need a bunch of stuff packed or anything."

"We can take things in our car. See the new place," Jane said. She turned to Eric. "Couldn't we."

"Sure," Eric said, with noticeably less excitement. "As long as we pick up the kids in time." To Bonnie he explained, "They're terrorizing my parents today."

"Ah." Nodding, like this was some unheard of good idea. "OK, well, thanks. How about you take some of the lamps. Plant stands. Thanks."

There were a number of trips up and down stairs, with Ian and Derek arguing about where the center of gravity was in the load. ("Who are those people?" Jane asked, and Bonnie said they were stoner mechanics who worked for the cops.) Then Eric had to move the car seats to fit more in, which filled up their car, and Jane said that she would ride with

Bonnie and Eric could follow them. Bonnie pulled away from the curb, watching Eric in the rearview mirror. It was hard to tell anything from this distance, and with the intervening layers of glass, but she didn't think he looked happy about being part of the move.

"He's not happy," Jane said from the passenger seat, making Bonnie jump. "He was supposed to go to Albuquerque for a conference but he decided to stay and lavish me with attention."

"That doesn't sound like such a bad thing."

"Mm," Jane said, meaning, what? That it was a bad thing? Bonnie navigated through intersections, up to the Kennedy entrance ramp. Her stomach hurt.

"I don't see Eric," Bonnie said. "Do you want to call him?"

"He has GPS, he'll be all right. Besides"—Jane closed her eyes and yawned—"it's nice to have a little time to myself. It's funny isn't it, you moving into a new place. I mean it makes me think about college, when we had the apartment. Ten years? Almost eleven. It seems like longer, doesn't it? Like, when dinosaurs ruled the earth."

"Yeah." Busy with traffic, and not inclined to disagree with anything Jane said. She had not realized how hard it would be to talk to Jane face to face, or rather, not to talk to her. Jane had always been the one person to whom she told everything, and now there was this weight to drag around. She had an impulse to blurt out a confession. But it wasn't only her secret. And this was the real harm done, not that she had trespassed and made use of a body she was not entitled to, but that now and forever, there would be things not to say.

Bonnie took the Foster Avenue exit, threading through the concrete overpasses, heading west, then south, through blocks of houses built of pinkish brick, square, utilitarian, each with its own small yard, past a Jewel and a Home Depot in an elderly shopping mall, home to a dry cleaners, an upholstery shop, a locksmith, more. Past a section of overgrown park land, bare branches hemmed in by a viaduct, down a street with some older limestone houses ornamented with small porches or peaked front gables, and here at the end, Bonnie's building, also limestone, a flat-roofed cube with some staked saplings planted in the parkway out front.

The street itself was quiet, though traffic noise rumbled nearby. There was a parking lot in back, and Bonnie pulled in. She and Jane got out, and Bonnie watched Jane take the place in. "Nothing fancy, but there's a bus stop on the corner," Bonnie said. "I only have to transfer once to get to work. Look around. These are people who keep up their properties. Make sure nobody leaves their garbage cans on the curb too long. There are standards here."

"It'll be nice for you. More grown up."

"It's not as hip."

"We're not as hip. Show me the inside."

A central hallway ran from the front to the back door, and a stairway led to the second floor. Bonnie's place was on the first floor. She struggled with the unfamiliar lock, then the door opened. "Hardwood floors," Bonnie said. "Linen closet. Running water. What more could you want? That's my new couch."

"I'm glad you moved," Jane said, walking from room to room. "Your old place was getting scary. Who's your new landlord?"

"Some real estate entity. Look, I have an ice maker!"

They carried things in from Bonnie's car, and a little while later the van pulled up, and Ian and Derek brought in the boxes of books and kitchenware and chairs and mattresses. "What happened to Eric?" Bonnie asked after a time, and Jane said he probably stopped to get gas or something. She didn't seem worried about him and Bonnie decided she wouldn't worry either. You could only walk around steeped in guilt and dread and melodrama for so long, and anyway there was work to do.

It was fun having Jane there, making up a bucket of Spic 'n Span and going over countertops that Bonnie had thought were clean enough, refolding sheets, and bossing her around in ways that would have annoyed her in anyone else, but that only seemed fond and nostalgic. Maybe things would lurch on between them, only this one little hiccup to navigate.

Eric arrived a half hour later, and not in a very good mood. "Your street doesn't exist," he said. "Good trick."

"It's like platform nine and three quarters in the Harry Potter books," Bonnie told him, but he only gave her a bleak look.

"He hasn't kept up with Harry Potter," Jane said. "What do you need him to do?"

"I can't think of anything, right this minute."

"Let's get your bed so you can sleep in it tonight." Jane was full of bright enthusiasm. "Eric, can you put the frame together?"

"No, that's OK, he doesn't have to." God, no.

"Oh come on. Where do you want it? Eric?"

Eric moved grimly into the bedroom and started sorting out the different metal rails and fasteners. Jane said, "You could have it under the window, or against the wall."

"Right about here, I guess."

"Did you want the striped sheets? I just saw them. Get the mattresses set up and I can make the bed for you."

"You don't have to do that. Even my mother wouldn't do that for me."

"Especially your mother wouldn't do that for you." Jane hurried off in search of sheets, pleased with herself.

"The street really is kind of hard to find," Bonnie told Eric, attempting a tone of comradely encouragement, but he only made aggravating grunting noises. Well screw him, he wasn't the only one feeling distressed. She went back out to the living room and started opening some of her haphazardly packed boxes.

Finally the van was empty, the Ikea bookcases put together. Bonnie ordered pizza and made a beer run, and when she got back to the apartment Eric and Jane had their coats on, waiting to leave. "You don't want to stay and have pizza? You earned it." She was relieved that they were going. She hoped it didn't show.

"The kids," Jane said. "You know."

"You guys, thanks," Bonnie said. "Really, you made a huge difference."

She hugged Jane, and then Eric. It felt like the rehearsal for some overly stage-managed play.

Bonnie and Ian and Derek sat on the new couch and the new chairs with paper towels spread over everything, eating pizza. Derek presented her with her housewarming present, three tightly rolled joints. Bonnie started in on one right away. She was tired, and she didn't even want to think about the disturbing scene of Jane and Eric making up her bed for her. Ian said, "Who were those guys? They looked older than you. Like, parents."

"They're my age. They are parents, they have two kids."

"No way." Ian shook his head. "Or maybe you get married and you get all serious and generational."

"You do," Derek said. "You start thinking, 'Reproduce and die.' The guy," meaning Eric, "was kind of a bozo. He was not a cheerful worker."

Ian said, "I think we're all bozos on this bus," and the two of them laughed and snorted into their beer.

"They're friends," Bonnie said, trying to hold the smoke in her lungs. "He's a doctor, show some respect."

"You know somebody who's a doctor? Wow, you are so much more important than I thought you were."

"Screw you," Bonnie said, and then they all got a case of the stoned giggles.

It took a few more days of back and forth trips, and cleaning out the old place, and hassling with the old landlord to get her deposit back, and making sure the utilities were all on or off. Finally the new apartment began to feel, if not like home, then like more of a finished project.

She met the neighbors in two of the three apartments. Across the hall was a married couple, Mr. and Mrs. Dumpling. That was not their name, of course, but it described them well enough. Both of them were soft and pale and bottom-heavy, younger than Bonnie but, as Ian and Derek had pointed out, marriage ages some people. Mrs. Dumpling, whose given name was Fern, was most often encountered in the hallway, bringing home plastic bags of goods from Target, Home Depot, Jewel. She had a small, set mouth and was fond of household accessories like electric boot dryers and windowsill herb gardens and waterproof radios designed for shower use. The cardboard carcasses of these purchases were placed outside for purposes of recycling and envy. Mr. Dumpling, Ed, did something with computers. He had the look of an IT lifer, round-faced, goggle-eyed, and with goofy sideburns. Neither of them had much conversation, aside from the weather, before they shut themselves inside for an evening of television and, for all Bonnie knew, exotic sex. She considered them excellent neighbors.

The second floor was home to a retired bus driver, the chatty Mr. Hopkins, and, directly overhead, unseen and mostly unheard, someone the mailbox identified as C. Popek. This was a widowed Polish lady, Mr. Hopkins explained, who kept to herself. "She's been here since before I moved in and that's, what, eight years now. She doesn't speak much English. Sits inside and listens to the Polish radio station. Knock on the door, she slams it in your face. Some people! Homebodies, I guess."

"Really? How does she get by? I mean, get groceries and all. What does she do up there? Should we worry?" Bonnie had a grim, unworthy thought, Mrs. Popek dead and undiscovered until the smell wafted downstairs.

"She comes down and gets her mail," Mr. Hopkins said, indicating the mailboxes in front of them. It was a week after Bonnie had moved in. The weather had warmed and pools of slush collected on the sidewalks. The speckled brown tile of the building's foyer was marked with grime and salt melt, in spite of the mats set down at either entrance. "I keep track. And she has a daughter who shows up every week or so and checks on her. Takes her to the doctor and such."

"Well that's nice to know." Bonnie liked Mr. Hopkins. He was spindly and faded, like an old board fence, but still spry and sociable. She liked the idea of living in a place where people might look out for each other, a little mini-community of manageable size. Even the Dumplings suggested a kind of stolid respectability that seemed appealing. She would clean up her act, reinforced by social norms. She could live out her days here. Take over Mrs. Popek's apartment once she died and went to Polish heaven.

"So how are you liking the place so far? You getting settled in there?" Mr. Hopkins held his mail in one hand, the same advertising circulars that Bonnie had already thrown away, promotions for oil changes and dry cleaning. He raised the hand to gesture and the gaudy colored newsprint fluttered.

"I'm liking it. The whole neighborhood too. It seems very stable."

"That's because they don't let the blacks or browns in. You have yourself a nice day now." Mr. Hopkins tapped his mail to straighten it and started up the stairs.

Bonnie got used to her new commute, her new branch bank, learned where to get gas and where to shop for produce. There was a new training program at work, teaching the beat officers to recognize people with cognitive impairments such as autism, meaning that if someone did not make eye contact or was flapping their arms or repeating themselves, they did not necessarily need to be Tased and handcuffed. She called up an old boyfriend and they went out for some drinks and ended up having sex but they both agreed it was just one of those things and probably would not happen again. It was mildly depressing, this backsliding, if that's what it was, into the same old habits with the same old usual suspects. Wasn't she tired of casual stupid feel-good moments that left you feeling vaguely sad, yes she was, but you could also get tired of alone.

There was the usual walloping March snowstorm, just as everyone hoped that spring was finally hatching, which dumped nine inches of wet snow and snarled the roads and produced two fatal heart attacks among the city's snow shovelers. The snow began on a Thursday night and made for a slow Friday of canceled schools and people taking work off. There was a pleasant sense of holiday, with the whole weekend to dig out.

Bonnie got up on Friday morning, put her boots and coat on over her pajamas, and went out to clean off her car, in case the snow removal service wanted her to move it. The sky was low and gray and a little left-over snow was sifting down. She checked in with work, decided there was nothing worth fighting her way there for, and went back to bed. She was deep in sleep when the doorbell buzzed.

Confusion, where and why and who? She padded to the front door and looked out of the peephole. Eric stood there, half turned away, pre-tending an interest in the front door and the street.

Later she thought that she could have not answered and pretended she wasn't home. But she was still sleep-addled, and the sight of him struck her with the dread of a summons she had to answer. She opened the door.

"Hi there." He smiled, or tried to. His jaw was dark and unshaven. He was wearing a canvas jacket that looked too light for the weather, and regular shoes that had soaked through with snow. He gave the impres-sion of a man who had spent the night in jail, although she supposed that was not the case. "Sorry to barge in. You have to tell me if this is a bad time or anything."

Or anything, Bonnie guessed, meaning, she might not want his guilt-inducing and problematic presence on her doorstep and she didn't, really, but out of some reflex or curiosity or more confused feeling, she said, "No, that's OK," and stood aside to let him in.

Eric made a show of wiping his feet, though Bonnie didn't have a proper doormat yet. She had not even thought about doormats until this very moment, when her mind was casting about trying to avoid thinking other things. He looked around him. "You're all moved in, huh."

"Excuse me." Bonnie went into the bathroom and shut the door. Oh for fuck's sake. Now what? She guessed she could lock herself in here until he gave up and went away again, but that wasn't likely. She brushed her teeth, wondered whether to do anything about her creased face and rat's nest hair, decided even that much effort would be provocative. At least she hadn't slept in anything more delightful than her old pink plaid flannel pajamas. What time was it anyway?

When she went back out, Eric was examining the books on her shelves. Were they going to have to talk about books now? She walked past him to the kitchen and filled the kettle to get some coffee going. The kitchen looked out on the street in front. It had already been plowed, which she guessed was one advantage to living in a cop-heavy district.

The kettle began to whistle. She put ground coffee in a filter and poured, dividing the coffee between two cups. How did he take his damned coffee anyway? She didn't know. It was the kind of thing a wife would know.

In the end Bonnie settled for making his coffee black, the same way she drank hers. Let him complain if he wanted. She walked out and handed him the cup. "Thanks," he said. Bonnie sat down at the table and after a moment he sat across from her.

Bonnie waited. It was up to him to explain himself. He drank some of his coffee and rubbed at his eyes. Eric said, "I got stuck at the hospital overnight. By the time I got off, the roads were shot."

Bonnie didn't have anything to say to that. Absolutely no opinion. You have me confused with somebody who gives a shit.

He said, "Jane doesn't really have any friends, except for you. Not close friends."

She wasn't expecting that, and she couldn't decide if it made her feel better or worse. She said, "What about Jane, is she all right?"

"I guess so. She's taking the antidepressants. She keeps up with the kids. So things are better. But there's times she's, I don't know, she says things out of the blue, like she knows . . . She wouldn't know, would she?"

He meant, about the two of them. "I don't see how." But dread was creeping up the back of Bonnie's neck. "What does she say?"

"We were getting ready for bed"—a brief flick of his eyes made it clear to Bonnie they had actually been in bed together. Really, the man was a miserable liar—"and she pipes up with, 'Do you think Bonnie would like to spend the night sometime?'"

"Whoa."

"She meant, come over for dinner, hang out with the kids, and we'd make up the guest bed so you wouldn't have to drive home. But she had my heart going, I tell you."

Bonnie's heart was going too, just from hearing about it. Eric said, "Every so often, she'll say something, not about you, necessarily, but something, I guess, spooky. Like she's on a different wavelength. I can't figure it."

They were both quiet. Bonnie thought it had to be Eric's guilty conscience leading him to imagine things. She said, "It's a coincidence. Jane doesn't know anything."

"Yeah." Unconvinced.

"But she will if you don't get your act together. Stop looking like you murdered somebody."

"Yeah." He wasn't making much of an effort.

"Come on. It's not like you have all kinds of other things to feel guilty about." Bonnie watched him look away again and make his bad news face. "God, you're kidding. Eric!"

"You asked," he said gloomily.

"I don't believe this. How often? When?" He muttered. "No, come on. You can't tell me that and then drop it!"

"Two. I mean it was two different women. Once I was at some conference. It was practically a drive-by. The other time, well, it was actually a few times. It's over. Long over." He gave her a feeble look.

"I changed my mind, I don't want to hear about it." She felt indignant. On Jane's behalf? On her own? Because she had been only one of a series?

"Fine." He shrugged.

"But maybe you could tell me," Bonnie said, unable to stop herself, "why none of those other times were like a big crisis."

"Because they weren't you."

She had nothing to say to that. They were silent until he spoke again. "I know it sounds like some dirtbag excuse, and I don't want to be disloyal to Jane. Any more than I already have been. But she's not a very interested party, when it comes to sex."

Not only was this no surprise to Bonnie, it was something she had known about Jane from almost the very first minute of their friendship. And yes, it did seem disloyal and dirtbaggy. "So maybe I could ask you, why get married? Why Jane? I mean, you knew this, right? You could have let her be. Found yourself a real hot tamale instead."

"This is a weird conversation."

"It's a weird situation."

"I guess I didn't think anything was that wrong. With her. Us. I guess I thought most girls, women, they just kind of went along with things, it was normal. Look, this is embarrassing, I don't want to keep talking. Oh, and hot tamales? Anything cools off over time."

"Why Jane?" Bonnie asked again. "Come on. Because she was impressed with you? Because she admired you?"

"Yeah, maybe. Whatever bad motive you want to assign to me." Eric yawned and buried his mouth in his hand. "Sorry. I haven't slept much."

"She went along with things. She had her place and you had yours. You married her because it seemed like a good *plan*."

"That's not fair," Eric said wearily. "Or even if you're right, that's not the whole story. She's always had that sweetness to her. That calmness. I loved that in her. All right. I guess you don't have to throw flowers at me. But I'm trying to tell you the truth." He finished his coffee and got up from the table. "Sorry if I woke you."

Now that he was leaving, Bonnie felt, stupidly, regret at speaking as harshly as she had. She made no sense to herself sometimes. "Look, I'm sorry too. I didn't mean to give you such a hard time. I don't feel very good about myself either."

He nodded, as if he was done with saying things. She followed him to the door and opened it. He was already out in the hall when he turned back to her. "Would it be OK if . . ."

"If what?"

"If we talked sometimes? About normal stuff," he hurried on. "About work. What you watched on television. Politics. Maybe not politics."

"You want to talk."

"Friend stuff. Like we used to."

Bonnie hesitated, and he began to backtrack, never mind, and she said, quickly, "Sure. We can talk, once in a while."

"Great." He smiled a crooked smile and there was a moment when they were visibly deciding whether to hug, or shake hands, or nothing at all. Just then Fern Dumpling opened her door and stepped into the hall wearing snow boots and toting a bag of garbage. She took in Bonnie's pajamas, Eric's rumpled clothes and 36-hour beard, maybe his wedding ring as well.

"How about all this snow," Bonnie said, cheerfully. "We sure got clobbered."

Fern agreed that it was a lot of snow. Her expression took on a rumi- native quality. Unaccountably, she went back inside, taking the garbage with her.

"Bye," Bonnie said to Eric. He made the hand sign for shooting him self in the head and she closed the apartment door behind her. A little while later she watched his car round the corner and its heaps of new-piled snow, and speed off.

And now she had to imagine him headed home, calling Jane, probably, to tell her he was on his way. His tired face wearing no particular expres- sion, and then, once he reached his front door, rallying, turning into husband and daddy.

Should she feel shocked, or injured, or much of anything, that he'd cheated on Jane? She wished he had not told her, if only because it was one more bad secret. Why was she so surprised? Men screwed around, everybody knew it, Bonnie herself had done her share and more of sleazy sleeping and was not in a position to throw stones. She knew more than she wanted to about both their sexual temperaments, Jane's and Eric's. She got back into bed and willed herself to sleep, and when she woke up again it was after noon, and her head hurt from all the space that Jane and Eric had taken up in it.

Bonnie didn't hear from either of them again for a few weeks. This was not unusual, since she and Jane might go a long, busy time without talking, let alone seeing each other. Finally, hating the sense of calculation that went along with it, Bonnie called Jane to say hello and catch up and not talk about sleeping with her husband. And how was every little thing?

Jane said, "Don't ever get married."

"OK," Bonnie said. "Off the table. Care to say why?"

"I should have had the courage to be on my own. Live a solitary life. I think that would have suited me. Now there's always always somebody here. Never mind. It's too late now. Grace is having a princess moment. Everything is tiaras and twirly skirts. It's supposed to be the new girl power. I'm not so sure. It seems kind of retro."

"You don't mean that, about wanting to be solitary. Single, maybe. Not solitary."

"I meant both."

"Like what, like a hermit or something? I'm not making fun, I'm trying to understand."

Jane said, "I'm thinking. OK, not a hermit. There could be people walking around doing people things, going to work and running cash registers and mowing the grass. But I don't want to have to talk to them. I want them on mute. That's the fantasy."

"Yeah, I can see how that doesn't really jibe with family life." Not that Bonnie wanted to spend a lot of time hashing over Jane's family life.

"Eric's going to call you," Jane said.

What? "What?"

"He has some patient who got arrested for drugs, he wants to know what's going to happen to the guy."

"That's nice of him," Bonnie said, trying not to hiccup into the phone. "I mean of Eric. He's a caring medical provider."

"He's such a Boy Scout. I don't know if you can tell him anything helpful."

"Well great," Bonnie said. "Sure, have him call."

"He takes things so personally," Jane continued, as if this was a logical next thing to say.

"Don't most of us? If things happen to a person, they have a personal reaction."

"It's limiting. It means that you're confined to all these subjective things like your own experiences and opinions."

"But those are the only things that give us authenticity and validity." As always when arguing with Jane, Bonnie reached a point where she lost track of the issues and was only trying to keep her end of things going.

"I'm talking about the concept of detachment. Most people don't understand it. I've come around to embrace it."

"I'm not sure I understand it myself. Detachment?"

"It's when you can, it's hard to explain, get beyond yourself. Erase yourself, sort of. Not get hung up on your own ego. Your own little wants and needs."

"Then what happens?"

"Other possibilities open up. Other currents. Harmonies of . . . spirit."

"I'm sorry," Bonnie said. "I'm not getting it. It sounds kind of moonbeamy. New Age."

Jane sighed. "It figures. You are probably the most earthbound person I know."

"Yup, that's me."

"Moonbeamy. That's not even a word."

Bonnie told her good-bye and got off the phone. She couldn't help feeling there had been some shift or off-balance tilt in Jane since the Christmas crisis, or no doubt before then. The kind of thing that Eric called spooky. Or maybe it was only what Jane had said, detachment. Hearing the music of the spheres. Whatever.

She was nervous about Eric's phone call, but she didn't have to wait long for it. He called the next day, he might have only been waiting for Bonnie to get things rolling. "What's this about a patient?"

"It's not really for a patient."

"Yeah, I wondered." She hated that he'd come up with some lame, overcautious cover story just to make a phone call. "So what's this really about?"

"You talked to her, right? You see how things are."

Bonnie kept silent. There wasn't any point in passing on Jane's comments about the married state.

"I don't know what I'm supposed to do. Does she want me to go away? Right now she tolerates me. I tell you, there's not much worse than being tolerated. What about the kids?"

"I'm sorry," Bonnie kept saying, and she was, because they both sounded miserable, in different ways, but what was expected of her? How was she meant to make anything better instead of worse, how would she not be implicated?

"Could we have lunch or something?" Eric asked. "I'm right downtown. Up to you."

Bonnie didn't like that it was up to her. Why should she have to be the gatekeeper, the traffic cop, the one who said yes when what was really needed was no? But Eric was freaking out about Jane freaking out, and trying to get this portion of his life under something resembling control, and if nothing else Bonnie was worried about him and so she said that yes, they could meet. Not lunch, though. Lunch always sounded like an excuse, another infinitely expandable cover story. She said they could go for a drink. Meaning one.

So at the end of her day, Bonnie took a bus down to the medical campus and walked along the narrow streets between the hospital buildings and parking garages. The skyscraper that housed, among other things, cardiology, was all sleek architecture and expansive space, the lobby so grand, all glass and tile, so much clever light, indirect or blazing or pooling underfoot, the effect so precisely and solidly rendered as to make the human body seem entirely breakable and inefficient by comparison.

She found the elevators and went up to the waiting area where she would meet Eric.

Here was a long wall of couches and chairs arranged in groupings that might either facilitate conversation or allow you to avoid it, whichever your purpose. It wasn't crowded and Bonnie chose a seat off by herself. Of course Eric was not there yet. Many and urgent were the demands on his time. Who was she, or anyone, to compete with the hemorrhaging or convulsing patient, the heart struggling to manage a few more flabby beats? She thought she understood how Jane might have gotten used to the regular disappointment of his absences, might come in time to prefer it that way.

She didn't like hospitals. She didn't even like television shows set in hospitals. They were places where you got bad news, worse and worst news, where such news became routine and was routinely and briskly dealt with, when of course what you wanted, when you were in crisis, was for the entire place to stop in its tracks and indignant announcements made over the P.A. system. Here were machines that were far superior to the fallible subjects they were meant to serve, machines that made such precise and deft intrusions, which sipped blood and sorted through cells and turned everything into measurements, tests to be passed or failed. As everyone failed, sooner or later.

Bonnie told herself she was being gloomy and melodramatic. Besides, wasn't the newest catchphrase in health care "wellness," the idea that medicine was meant to coax and encourage you to make informed and positive choices? Stay fit and healthy until you die!

Eric was late, and then later. Bored with sitting, Bonnie got up and went to the bank of windows at the far end of the room. The city sky was darkening to chilly twilight. April, and still no real warmth. Across the street, looking almost close enough to reach out to, was another medical building, the dimly lit windows opposite appearing to be some sort of lab, with workbenches and a great many untidy, bulky binders and files on the shelves above them. Although she watched for some time, no one came into the room. It struck her as melancholy, a kind of abandonment.

Bonnie considered giving up on Eric and going home. His problems weren't going anywhere. They'd keep until next time. A heart doctor, such a joke! What good did it do him, rewiring everyone's cardiac circuits, unplugging their arteries, if Jane's heart had closed itself off to him? Why was anyone's happiness so hard to come by? Why not disdain the body, as Jane did, since its pleasures never lasted?

She was slipping into the kind of bad and unhelpful mood that led nowhere, only fed on itself until it consumed anything hopeful, rational, or right, and just then, reflected in the dark glass, Eric came around a corner and scanned the room. Not seeing her at first, then finding her, and coming up behind her. Bonnie saw his face, vivid with relief and wanting, wanting *her*?

The impact of this made Bonnie take a step and lose her balance and sit down hard on the nearest aesthetically pleasing sectional couch.

"Well hello," Eric said, amused, smiling down at her. He was wearing a set of blue scrubs, his picture ID hanging from a lanyard. Both the picture and his face showed his normal, friendly Labrador retriever expression. Had she seen right? Immediately Bonnie began to doubt herself. Her skirt had traveled up over her knees and she yanked it down.

"I guess I tripped over nothing. Ridiculous." Meaning herself, of course, and every wrong thing she had ever done or said. "So this is your place. Nice."

"Sorry I'm so late. I have a patient who hasn't been doing very well, we had to do a procedure."

"Of course."

"It'll take me just two more minutes to sign out and change."

"Of course," Bonnie said again, and watched him sprint back to the elevator. What was she doing here, why had he called her in the first place? She didn't like the answers she was giving herself. She had come under false pretenses.

Then he was back. Bonnie joined him and they rode the elevator down to the ground floor. Other people crowded in on them and they had to stand close together, although they did not touch, and they smiled at each other, embarrassed, comradely smiles. Eric said hello to someone, a woman. Bonnie wondered if the women he'd slept with worked at the hospital, but she shut that thought down as quick as it came.

They came out into the lobby and crossed the floors to the entrance. He said, "I'm parked in the garage. There's a place on North Clark, we can get a bite to eat there if you like."

"Eric?"

They were out on the sidewalk now. Bonnie stopped just beyond the lighted entryway, and he had to stop also and look back at her, eyebrows raised, quizzical.

"This feels like a date."

"I didn't . . ." He managed to look both irritated and guilty. "You don't have to think of it that way."

"I'm thinking we should just say good night now."

"Come on. I thought we could talk."

"Go home and talk to Jane, why don't you."

"Because she doesn't want to talk to me."

"Maybe you could try harder."

"She can go a long time without talking these days. All right, look, I'll give you a ride home. No compromising food or beverage. God."

He stalked off toward the garage and Bonnie followed, miserably. There seemed no way in which anything between them could come out right. Too many layers of hurt and sex and trouble. They walked up a long concrete ramp to Eric's gray Honda. He used the remote to click the doors open, though he didn't bother opening Bonnie's for her. Fine, be that way. She got in, settled herself, fastened the seat belt. Eric started the car and put the heat on full blast so that a whoosh of roaring air, cold then hot, blew over her. In protest, Bonnie rolled her window down.

They came out of the garage too fast, because he was driving mad, but Bonnie was damned if she was going to say anything and braced herself against the floor and the door.

He turned north on Michigan Avenue and took it all the way up to Lake Shore Drive and then they were hurtling along the lakefront, the startling darkness of the water on one side and the constellation of city lights on the other. She was ready to wait him out as long as she had to but he said, in his normal voice, "Every time I drive along the lake, I think about how it's free. The poorest, most miserable people in the city can come down here and enjoy the water."

"A lot of them do," Bonnie said. "It's made for some bad crowd control situations."

"I keep forgetting you're sort of a cop."

"A liaison. No enforcement powers. I keep forgetting you're a brilliant and highly trained cardiac surgeon."

"Sort of."

They drove on, slower now, Eric's automotive tantrum over. He said, "I'm sorry. I shouldn't keep trying to get you in the middle of me and Jane's problems."

"I'm already right in the middle. You couldn't get me any more in the middle if you measured it out."

Eric took the Belmont exit, and they passed under the viaduct and out into traffic again. They crossed the Inner Drive, and then he pulled over to the curb and shut the engine off. "Let's just sit here a minute," he said, and Bonnie didn't answer, only looked out the window to where there was nothing to see. Her own sorrowful heart beat and beat. It was as if something had already been decided. As if everything that was about to happen had already happened.

She felt his hand touch her face, turning her chin to look at him, and then they were kissing, and in spite of the impossible weight of every-thing that was wrong and would continue to go wrong, they did not stop. Who were you once you took that step outside of yourself, beyond what you had always believed yourself to be? What name did you call yourself, and to what name did you answer?

They sat on the edge of Bonnie's bed, clothed at first, taking their time. Their hands turned more purposeful. Their clothes loosened. "Let me see you," Eric said, and she stood before him to finish undressing. He put both hands beneath her breasts, cupping their weight, and she knelt between his legs. His hands pushed her hair away from her face so that he could use her mouth. After a time he pulled her onto the bed next to him and put one hand on her head, guiding it, while with the other he explored and entered her with his fingers.

She couldn't keep her concentration then and raised up off of him. "Sorry."

"It's fine. Roll over." He moved himself to one side of the bed and pulled at her hips and rearranged them so that she was face down in the mattress, her arms and legs outstretched. She tried to rise up on her knees to meet him but he spread himself on top of her so that his mouth was at her ear. "Stay still," he whispered. "Don't move."

She stayed as still as she could while he fit his penis into her. Pushing at first, then finding his path and sliding full in. It was the most extraor-dinary sensation, feeling him in her and wanting to move and having to keep herself from doing so. His breath warmed her neck. "Stay just like this," he whispered.

"All right." Nerves plucked and raced within her, ready to spark.

"Remember this. Whatever happens. Remember how good this is."

"I will," she said, and then he started to move within her and everything began all over again.

But how are you? How are you really? Are you lonely? How could you not be, how could I not be?

family time

Robbie said he was hungry right *now*, and Jane said they had to wait for Daddy. Robbie said he did not want to wait and he wanted macaroni and cheese. Jane said that he could not always eat macaroni and cheese. Robbie said what was that smell, it smelled yucky. Jane said it was dinner and there was nothing wrong with it. She cut up some apple slices and put them on a paper plate and told him he could eat them if he was hungry and Robbie said he was not hungry for apples. "Then you aren't that hungry." Jane sent him off to watch television. "You share those with your sister if she wants any," Jane told him, but she didn't hear any answer back from him, only the television's happy noise.

She supposed she could call Eric and try to find out when he might get home, but either he wouldn't know or wouldn't answer his phone. There were times when he knew he would be too late to eat with them, and then he did call, but more often Jane kept a hopeless vigil in the kitchen, monitoring the food until she judged it was just on the verge of overcooked, or sometimes past that. Telling the children another five minutes and then another, until the effort collapsed in on itself and she fed them a hurry-up meal, just the three of them, and covered Eric's food with aluminum foil so that it could be reheated later.

She was taking a different antidepressant now, one considered more suitable for moms. There had been some concern about side effects from the original prescription, meaning she had alarmed people by talking too much about the death of the self and the all-encompassing spirit. Her new pills made life both easier and harder. Easier to keep up with the things you had to do to get through a day. Harder to remember why any of it might be important. It was like living in a very busy train station with people constantly coming and going, while you yourself went nowhere.

Tonight she'd fixed halibut steaks with lemon and parsley and bread crumbs, an iffy thing for the kids in the first place, since even the blandest fish tasted like, well, fish. There was white rice (brown had triggered some memorable scenes), and a selection of vegetables served in separate receptacles to accommodate the child who would not eat carrots and the one who would eat carrots but not broccoli and there was corn, which everybody ate, and some chopped-up iceberg lettuce with the gloppy pink bottled salad dressing they liked. Sometimes she added a little flaxseed oil or pumpkin seeds because she had to be sneaky about anything hardcore nutritious. Her kids were like anybody else's kids. They'd live on Cocoa Puffs and chicken nuggets if she let them. Food in, food out. It was a constant effort to keep them fed, requiring guile and vigilance. Young humans seemed intent on either starving or poisoning themselves. You couldn't relax for a moment. Because if she did, what else might she let slip away from her?

What if the children were not properly fed? What if one were to forget to feed them at all?

When Eric asked her how she felt these days, she always told him she was better. Sleeping better. Coping better. Fewer ups and downs. And he said good, good. It was what he wanted to hear. If she had said, I am dissolving at the edges, I answer to the same name as always, but I no longer wish to be that person, he would have been alarmed, he would have felt it necessary to intervene in some unpleasant way.

Jane turned the oven down to low. The halibut could hold a little longer. She went out into the living room and watched for Eric's car. She shouldn't let herself stand there waiting and waiting, worn down by dull fretting because he wasn't home when she thought he should be, but it was irresistible to do so. It was part of her ritual of dinnertime, like a cocktail before sitting down to eat.

But on this evening, watching the long spring twilight deepen and the friendly lights coming on all along the street—wouldn't her own house look just as serene and welcoming from outside—she saw the car turn in at their driveway. It paused there a long time, and Jane couldn't see what, if anything, he was doing. Talking on the phone, maybe. Then the car moved on up the drive and into the garage.

Jane told the kids to turn off the television and wash up, and they straggled in at the same time Eric came in through the back door, and there was that pleasant bustle and confusion and warmth that made you feel, if only for as long as it lasted, that all was as it was meant to be. Mom and Dad exchanging a quick, busy-day kiss. Boy and girl setting out the glasses of milk as directed, jostling a little—"Quit it!" "You quit it!" Mildly reprimanded. Dad heading upstairs, saying he'd be down in two seconds, which of course he was not. He had to change clothes, he had to visit the bathroom, and the children had to be told, severely, to wait. Mom herself tired of waiting, but so she did, and eventually here was Dad, rubbing his hands and saying he was starved, and it all looked great.

Robbie said the fish tasted stinky, he didn't want any. Jane said he should eat it anyway, finish what he had on his plate. Eric said that if this was some places in the world, say Japan, they would be eating fish for breakfast. Robbie said he wouldn't live in Japan for a million dollars. Grace asked her mother if she could have boiled eggs instead of fish. Jane said she was not fixing different meals for everyone. Grace said her stomach hurt. Eric said Uh oh, they would have to do an emergency stomach transplant. Robbie said that was because Grace had worms growing in her stomach, and that made Grace start to whimper. Eric said that he was just kidding, she was such a silly girl, and got up to pour her some 7UP to settle her stomach. Jane objected to the 7UP on the grounds that it was empty calories, not to mention all the sugar, and why did they even have it in the house. Eric said a little wouldn't hurt her. It was for medicinal purposes. Doctor's orders. He came back to the table with a glass of ice and the soda can and reached over Jane to give it to Grace. Jane smelled the fresh, cutting scent of the aftershave he had just applied, an astringent, cedarwood scent, and that was when she knew.

She did not know the entirety of it, and she did not yet even fully understand what she knew. But she stiffened in her chair and her insides turned to gravel. Robbie said that he wanted a 7UP too and everyone waited for Jane to tell him no but she didn't, and after a moment Eric headed out to the kitchen to get him his own glass. "Eat your vegetables," Jane said, although it was unclear to whom she was speaking.

When the meal was over, Jane stood at the kitchen sink, feeding the food scraps into the garbage disposal. Its mechanical mouth the final consumer of some considerable portion of the dinner. Eric and the children were watching television together, some movie about a Saint Bernard that caused comic misadventures. Robbie wanted a dog. Grace wanted a cat. They had the names picked out already. Jingles for the dog, Socks for the cat.

Why else cover himself with scent, if not to disguise some other scent?

It should not have come as a surprise. Men were what they were and they did what they did. Did she care what he did? She wanted not to care. But even more, she had wanted not to know.

The television laughed and the children laughed along with it. Eric said something she couldn't make out, his teasing tone of voice. He'd given up on her. Who could blame him? She had nearly given up on herself. She was the frigid freak, the cold crazy he was stuck with.

She had finished with the dishes and turned the kitchen light off so that the room was dim but still watchful, its machinery humming and at the ready. Now she stood, turned the lights back on, and went rummaging through the cupboards. Of course she had purged the kitchen of anything synthetically delicious, so the options were limited. She found an old package of instant butterscotch pudding, mixed it with milk, and poured it into four small glass dishes. The glossy brown paste quivered and firmed. There was not much in it that had anything to do with actual butterscotch. It was only a chemically stabilized, edible substance. Well, at least there was milk. She found a tray and some paper napkins and spoons and carried it all into the family room.

"What's this?" Eric said. Surprised. She'd never done such a thing, a '50s housewife thing, as bring something in on a tray.

"Butterscotch pudding." She set it down on the coffee table. Robbie and Grace scooted off the couch to get to it. Eric gave her a smile that had a question in it.

"I just thought, you know, some more protein."

"Well that's nice." He reached for one of the bowls. Jane caught another whiff of bottled scent. "What?" Jane shook her head. "Kids, what do you say?"

"Thank you."

"Thanks Mom."

"You're welcome." Someday they might issue thank yous without being prodded, and with some semblance of sincerity. Right now it was only a goal. Jane picked up the remaining pudding but could not bring herself, yet, to eat. The kids were wading into theirs.

Eric ate a few spoonfuls, then set his bowl down. "I'm still full from dinner. It's good, though. I can't remember the last time I had pudding. What gave you the idea?"

"It's not some huge deal. I just felt like it." It irritated her that she was apparently so fixed and joyless in her ways, so puritanical about what they ate, that it did seem to be a huge deal. On the television, the giant dog was running down the street with the family in a car behind it, honking and calling. Then the screen cut away to a commercial. "How's the movie?" Jane asked.

"I want a dog. A puppy," Robbie said. "Not a Saint Bernard. A police dog that would bite people. Everybody else has a dog but us."

"Everybody else does not have a police dog," Jane said.

Eric said, "We've talked about this." He was using his most weighty and Dad-like tone of voice. "You need to be older so you can take care of it."

"I am too old enough. I can feed it and play with it and teach it to shake hands."

"There's a lot more to it than that," Eric told him. "There's getting home from school on time so you can walk it. There's grooming. Then we'd have to take it to the vet, get it shots and checkups. It's an investment of time and of money. A dog isn't a toy you can leave on a shelf when you're tired of playing with it."

"Would you still want to call it Jingles?" Jane asked. "That doesn't sound much like a police dog."

"Maybe Killer," Robbie said.

"A police dog, you mean like, a German shepherd?"

"I don't think you should encourage him," Eric said. "Unless you want to be the one doing all the work."

"We never had a dog growing up," Jane said. "It was like we missed out." She had a vague, wistful notion of the dog revitalizing them, providing them a rallying point, something they could all love. Rin Tin Tin, the dog that saved my marriage.

"If he gets a dog, then I get a cat," Grace piped up.

"My dog is gonna chase the stupid cat and bite it."

"Mom!"

"This is a good way to not get either one," Jane said, collecting the empty pudding bowls and piling them on the tray.

"Yes, you're fighting like cats and dogs," said witty Eric, with a smile at Jane. She smiled back.

Nothing had changed. Everything might go on as before.

And if nothing changed, if nothing either of them did made any difference, how important was this shared life?

Then it was time for bed, and all the hectic negotiations involved. Yes, they could watch the end of one video but not the beginning of another. Then on to which pair of pajamas was acceptable, how bright (or dim) the light from the hallway should be, who was not sleepy, who needed a doll, a snack, a kiss. Robbie was given permission to read one more chapter in his *Heroes of the Revolutionary War* book. Jane supposed there was a reason that the Revolutionary War was considered appropriate for younger children. No distressing subtexts like slavery or concentration camps. Grace, who was sensitive to disturbances of all kinds, especially those from the skin on in, said that one of her ears hurt. Her ear hurt and her head felt funny, which was the drill for so many previous ear infections. Grace's bedspread was pink, as was the shaded lamp next to the bed. It gave her face a hectic, reflected glow.

Did she want Daddy to look at it? Daddy was summoned and looked in Grace's ear with his big silver Ear Thingamajig, which made Grace squeal. "Hold still," Eric said. Yes, the ear was a little red. Grace could have some children's Tylenol and a warm compress.

Jane said that she'd take care of her, and Eric said, If you're sure you're OK with it. Eric could not be expected to sit up late with a sick child when he had to get to work in the morning. It was the way they were accustomed to arranging things. Jane turned out Grace's bedside light and lay down beside her, holding the wrung-out washcloth to the sore ear. Her daughter's body was still so small and light-boned, Jane could cradle most of her with one arm. Grace fussed, then slept, woke, fussed some more, slept. Jane slept for a time herself, and woke to darkness and a quiet house.

Eric must have gone to bed. Jane got up, careful not to disturb Grace, whose sleep had a damp, furious quality that spoke of fever. She used the bathroom in the hall, came out, checked Grace again. Instead of going in to her own bed, she went to the little back bedroom they used for storage and projects, cleared off the small single bed, wrapped herself in an old quilt, and slept on and off, waking to go in to Grace. She still felt warm, and her breathing had a clotted sound. Jane considered waking Eric but decided it was best to wait things out.

In the morning Grace had a temperature of 101 and threw up twice. Eric said he would take her to the pediatrician and let Jane catch a little more sleep. "Thank you," Jane said. She wondered if he was being solicitous because of his secret misbehavior. But then, any distress involving the children made them close ranks and unite and turned them, at least for a time, into better partners.

They decided that Robbie could go to school, although he said he wanted to stay home too. "You're fine," Jane said, although if one child was sick, it was usually only a matter of waiting for the other shoe to drop. Jane took a shower and made up the bed that Eric had left rumpled. Then she went back into the spare bedroom and slept there.

Grace came home with antiviral drugs and Pedialyte. Jane put her to bed on clean sheets and with a plastic wastebasket next to the bed in case she couldn't make it to the bathroom in time. Eric sat on the bed next to her and took her pulse and listened to her heart and lungs with his stethoscope. He told Grace that she was a silly monkey and that she had the monkey flu. Grace, pink-cheeked and teary, said that she didn't want to be a monkey. Eric told Jane to call Dr. Jarling if the fever didn't break or if she got dehydrated. "Call me too, I'll make sure they know to come and get me."

"How worried should we be?"

"Not worried, just cautious. Jarling doesn't think it's the flu. More like a stray enterovirus. Check and see if she gets a rash, or mouth sores. We should be able to keep her at home."

Jane, parsing this, understood that there might indeed be reason to worry, but that Eric, like all doctors, was wary of getting too far ahead of himself. He put both hands on Jane's shoulders and kissed her on the forehead. "So. Push fluids, once you're sure she can keep them down. Check for fever. And rash. Any breathing difficulties, you get on it."

"Yes," Jane said, feeling off-balance. From lack of sleep, from anxiety over Grace. And like a reflection floating over a glass door, this other condition, in which she and Eric were *husband* and *wife*, and another reflection on top of that one, what people meant when they said those words, the weight of expectations and history, and yet another layer that had to do with bodies, the curious things that people did with them, the incongruity of those private episodes compared with the public ones, just as it was incongruous to think of their tired and worried selves, she and Eric, as bodies that might come together, break apart, and come together again. So that if she tried to keep the idea of Eric having sex with another woman in focus, she had to fall through different layers of seeing and knowing, each one blurring into or obscuring the other. And what would that have to do with her sick child? How could you hold any other thought but that in your mind? Sometimes Jane thought this was what was wrong, or at least different, about her: the world broke itself into these disconnected and jarring fragments that she could not assemble into a whole.

"What is it?" Eric said, and Jane said it was nothing, which she knew annoyed him, but for now they were both intent on their daughter instead of each other, and so there was no argument.

Eric drove away. She had almost three hours before Robbie would be home from school and would have to be entertained and catered to and kept out of Grace's way. She took Grace's temperature, which had fallen by half a degree, then brought her a soft-boiled egg and buttered toast cut into soldiers. Grace said she wasn't hungry and Jane said to eat just a little of it. "Wait, first let me see the inside of your mouth." Grace obediently opened her mouth and let Jane inspect its small, smooth walls and pink scallop tongue. "Do you have any itches? Pull up your pajama top."

There was no rash, so Jane left her sitting up in bed with a picture book. When she looked in on her again, Grace was asleep. She was sick, but not in danger. One portion of her worry, at least, could ease.

Any time her daughter was ill, Jane found herself thinking back to her own childhood and the heart condition that she did not know she had. Jane told herself that Grace was her own person and she was not doomed to fragility or ill health or neurotic fussiness, was not doomed to anything at all. Nor would she have to marry a man who would deceive her, stop. Stop thinking about herself for once.

She was being ridiculous, worse, she was being one of those parents who thought of their children as some reflection of themselves. It was true that Grace resembled her, just as Robbie mostly resembled Eric. She was quiet, obedient, unassertive. She liked imaginative play, setting out her dolls or stuffed bears and constructing nests or hiding places for them while she made up stories under her breath. Just as Jane had shrunk away from all the jolly sports her father had pushed her into, Grace moped and dawdled through kid gymnastics, putt putt golf, swimming lessons, anything designed to build confidence and increase hand-eye coordination. "Come on," Bonnie had said once, when Jane had mentioned her worries. "Relax, this isn't *Wuthering Heights*. She's not doomed." Jane had acquiesced, although it was true she did not remember *Wuthering Heights* as clearly as she might have.

But no one was doomed, ever. Even herself.

While Grace slept, Jane carried some of the storage items in the back bedroom down to the basement. Most of it was outgrown toys and all the other gear you needed to raise children, the car seats and bath pillows and toddler gates, the different slings and carriers that often overwhelmed her with feeling, remembering when her babies were small, but now only spoke to her of excess and exhaustion. She cleared out space in the closet and transferred some of her clothes, the ones she wore most often. She made up the bed with a blue coverlet she had always liked and found a small lamp she put next to the bed. There wasn't room for much of anything else, and that pleased her.

When Grace woke up she said she was thirsty, and after she drank some water, Jane gave her Pedialyte and orange juice and a bowl of lime sherbet. Grace, a fussy eater at the best of times, waited until the sherbet melted and then slurped some of it up. She still had a temperature just above a hundred. By the time Robbie came home from school, Grace was tired of being in bed and so was allowed a spell of sitting on the couch in the family room bundled up in a blanket so she could watch videos. Because she was sick, Grace got to pick the videos, which bored Robbie. He escaped to the backyard, where he spent some time thunking a ball against the wall of the garage.

All day Jane carried on a silent, furious conversation with Eric, and finally he called to see how Grace was. Jane said she thought she was better, and went through the details of temperature, appetite, and so on. "Good, that's all good," Eric said. "I'll try to get home early."

"Your time management problem keeps getting more and more complicated, doesn't it?"

Pause. "What do you mean by that?"

She couldn't stop herself. "This is what it takes, a sick child, for you to try to fit us in. No promises."

"We've been through this before." They had. "There are things that are beyond my control. Surgeries go on longer than expected. Patients have problems. Patients need emergency procedures. I wish you would try not to have resentments."

"I guess I'm talking about the things that are within your control."

"I'm not in the mood for this, Jane."

"I was just wondering, when do you find time to see her?"

He was silent. After a moment Jane said, "Don't bother saying anything. Just don't think I don't know. All right, fine. See you later."

Jane hung up, feeling rattled, second-guessing herself for saying anything. She could have kept quiet, and instead she'd declared war. But he needed reminding that she was still there, not just an obstacle he had to maneuver around or evade, someone to be ignored, tolerated, lied to.

And just then it came over her. She was standing at the foot of the stairs, her hand on the bannister, damp spring clouds sweeping across the sky outside, her head aching from all her bad and poisonous thoughts. The next instant there was the floating, falling sensation of limitless white, of blessed nothingness, of peace and ease and everything else that her life no longer was, and it did not last long—Robbie's ball still made its monotonous noise against the wall—but it filled her with such longing she could have wept. She could not, she could not, she could not allow this. Eric had made that clear enough. If she retreated from them, if she absented herself, if she did not do all that was expected of her and more. Supermom! She would be taken away, subjected to more and worse therapies, her children bereft at first, then forgetting her. She had to steel herself, live alongside them without arousing suspicion.

Now she was engaged in a war with Eric. How stupid she'd been to fall into it, to have taken up the sword, to care what he did one way or the other. Why not let him carry on his secret life just as she did hers? It had been nothing but vanity and weakness on her part and now it was too late.

Eric did get home, if not early, at least on schedule. Robbie butted his head into Eric's knees and announced that he wanted to play Battleship, and that when he got a police dog it was going to be named Mike. Eric said that was a fine name, and maybe they could play Battleship later, he had to go see how his sister was doing. He had not spoken to Jane when he walked in, but once he'd been upstairs he came back down to the kitchen and said, "Her fever's 101.5."

"It's been just over a hundred most of the day. I told you."

He looked around the kitchen in an irritated way, as if the room itself displeased him. "Did you use the forehead scanner or a real thermometer? The forehead scanner's crap."

"Well that's what I used. And I've used it before and you never said anything, so I don't know why it's a problem now." He was scowling and ready to start in again, so Jane asked, "How is she?"

"She seems dehydrated."

"She hasn't thrown up since this morning. She's had Pedialyte and orange juice and ice water and I'm making her chicken noodle soup right now. I've watched her all day, Eric. I'm going to go give her some more Tylenol. There's lasagna in the oven and salad and rolls, please make sure Robbie eats." Jane left him, aware that he was picking a fight because she had picked a fight, trying to turn his own guilt inside out, to blame her for everything wrong, sad, and failed between them. She understood how that worked. But it was disgusting of him to try and beat her up over Grace's health and care. Just disgusting.

She brought Grace her soup and some soda crackers, gave her the dose of Tylenol, and sat with her while she ate and read her a story about a squirrel and a rabbit and a baby deer who all lived together in the forest. Grace's skin had a whiff of sour, bed-bound sweat to it. "How about after you finish your supper, I'll give you a nice warm bath."

"Mommy? Why do people die?"

"Honey, what a question! Is it something you're worried about?"

"I don't know." The all-purpose kid answer, half-sulky, half-fearful.

"Nobody's going to die for a long, long time. Not you or me or Daddy or Robbie. So don't fret."

"What about Grandma and Grandpa and Granny Alice and Grampy Bob?"

This was harder. Jane tried to gauge the extent of Grace's curiosity, or worry. The little girl was still flushed from fever. She looked serious but not distressed. "Well, older people usually die before younger ones. But your grandparents are fine and nothing's going to happen to them anytime soon. And you are going to feel so much better by tomorrow," she added, thinking that this had to be the source of the anxiety.

"But why do people die?" Grace repeated. Jane couldn't remember Robbie asking such a thing. Then, Robbie was a different kind of kid.

Jane said, "Because our spirits go away and our bodies aren't needed anymore." It was the best she could do when put on the spot. They weren't religious; the kids went to a Unitarian Sunday school on occasion, so they would not be ignorant of cultural traditions. "You know what a spirit is, right? The things you think and feel and believe." The Sunday school had come up with a helpful pamphlet.

"Where does your spirit go away to?"

Jane understood now, as she had not before, that one value of organized religion was that it provided answers you could dole out to children. She could hardly start in with some glib explanation of heaven and Jesus, let alone hell, even if she believed in such things herself. Grace and Robbie had been told that Christmas was Jesus' birthday and everybody got to celebrate it because Jesus was nice about things like that. Easter was for candy and colored eggs. Churches were places like school, except you went there on Sundays. Really, when it came to indoctrinating their children with belief systems, she and Eric had been total slobs.

So Jane took a breath and waded in. "Well, nobody knows exactly where, sweetheart. Some people say we go on living, but in a different place, where everybody's always happy."

Perhaps she had been insufficiently enthusiastic? Grace looked unconvinced. "Then why don't people want to die and go there?"

"Because, it's not a real place, honey. You can't get in a car and drive there or anything like that. It's more of an idea." Jane thought she heard the sound of plates, silverware from downstairs, Robbie asking something, Eric's rumbling answer. At least they were eating. She turned back to Grace, who had given up on her soup but was still pushing her spoon around in the bowl. "I'm sorry, that's not a very good explanation. It's not easy to explain."

"OK."

"Even grown-up people can't agree about it." Especially grown-up people. "You have plenty of time to think about it."

"Does everybody die?"

"All right, let's stop talking about dying. Let's eat a little more soup." Rattled in spite of herself, Jane spoke more sharply than she intended. She was going to have to come up with some better Mom-answers for some of the hard questions. And whatever was she going to say about sex? About marital discord? Would she and Eric get a divorce? Is that what happened next? She had not thought such things through.

"But do they die?" Grace prompted her.

"Yes." No way around that one.

"If I get a cat, will it die?"

"Yes."

"If Robbie gets a dog, will it die?"

"Yes."

"Celia had a goldfish and it died."

"All right, you know what? You need to concentrate on being here right now and doing things you want to do and need to do. Not worry about dying. That doesn't help. Think about getting better. Can you do that?"

An eruption of noise from downstairs, Robbie yelping in a high, wordless voice. "What is it?" Jane cried, heading for the landing. "Robbie?" She ran down to the kitchen, where Eric was boosting Robbie up to hold his hand under the running tap. "What happened?"

Robbie was still bawling, his face bright red and his nose streaming. "Eric?"

"He pulled a pot of boiling water over and burned himself. Get some ice, would you?"

"What were you—" Jane stopped herself and went to the freezer door to lever some ice into a glass. A saucepan lay on its side on the stove top in a puddle of hissing water. She wrapped the ice in a dishtowel and handed it to Eric. She didn't see any blistering, at least not yet. There would be some explanation for the boiling water, some bad decision, some lapse in supervision. As if Eric was piling up all his mistakes at once.

She put a hand on Robbie's neck, kissed his cheek, and mopped at him with a Kleenex and told him it was all right, it was going to be all right. His sobs were trailing off into whimpers now. Her eyes met Eric's. "What was it?"

"He wanted macaroni and cheese instead of lasagna. He was trying to see the water boil."

Jane didn't have to say anything. He already knew. He tied up the ice in the dishtowel and laid it on top of Robbie's burned hand. "Doesn't that feel better?" he said encouragingly, though Robbie wasn't having any of it.

"Does he need the emergency room?"

"I don't know yet, Jane, let's give it a minute, OK?"

She understood that he was angry because the accident had been in so many ways his fault and now he felt bad about it. Angry at getting called out for what he must consider his purely private screwing around. That didn't mean he had to act like an asshole.

And how she hated being a person who cared about such things! This furious, diminished self!

She turned off the stove burner and mopped up the spilled water. The pan of lasagna was sitting out on the counter and she cut a square of it and fixed Robbie a plate with salad and a roll and poured him a glass of milk. "How about you try eating dinner? You can sit right here with the ice on your hand and I'll cut your food up."

Jane helped him blow his nose and get settled at the kitchen table. "Keep the ice on it," Eric instructed. "Do we have any gel packs? I can give him some lidocaine, that should help."

Jane ignored him. "I thought you liked lasagna. Here." She loaded a forkful of it and lifted it to Robbie's mouth. He swallowed it down. His eyes still leaked stray tears. "Can you manage the rest with your good hand?" His left hand was the injured one. She guessed that was lucky. "How about some milk?" Eric watched them for a minute, then left the room. He kept his medical supplies in the upstairs bathroom. She wanted to tell him to check on Grace, but why should she have to tell him that?

Robbie wasn't making much headway on the lasagna. Jane helped herself to his portion. Eric hadn't eaten yet either. One more blown dinner. "How's your hand doing?"

"Hurts."

"Did you try to reach the stove top? You know better than that. Here." She helped him blow his nose again. "You have to learn to be more careful, sweetie." Already Jane had unspeakable visions of bicycles, automobiles, organized sports.

Eric came back in then with his medical kit and his brisk, Doctor Dad cheerfulness. "All right, buddy, let's get you fixed up." To Jane he said, "Grace says you're supposed to give her a bath." He must not have liked the look she gave him. "Tag team," he said, an attempt at lightening things up, if only for Robbie's sake.

Jane went back upstairs. Grace was fretful, all wrapped and tangled in her bedding. "What happened to Robbie?"

"He hurt himself with some hot water on the stove."

"Is he going to die?"

"No, and I want you to stop talking like that! Grace! It's not funny!"

Grace kept quiet while Jane prepared her bath. She liked it hot but not too hot. Full but not too full. A few squirts of pink bubbly soap. Jane peeled away Grace's pajamas, limp from a full day's wear. "All right, hop in. I'm not going to wash your hair because your ear's still sore. We'll do it tomorrow. Let me help you." She steadied Grace as she stepped into the tub, then squatted down. "Here's your washcloth. Scrub your feet, please."

A knock on the door. Eric looked in. "Hey there, monkey girl."

"I am not a monkey."

"I beg your pardon. My mistake. Clearly, you are a kangaroo." To Jane he said, "I'm going to give Robbie some of the acetaminophen with co-deine. It'll help him sleep."

"Fine." She didn't know why he'd bother seeking her out and telling her this. "I'd get him in his pajamas first. Here, take his toothbrush. He can get ready for bed in our bathroom." Tag team indeed.

Grace finished her bath and Jane wrapped her in a towel and helped her wiggle into clean pajamas. "You're feeling better, aren't you?" Jane asked, when she was tucking her in. Grace's temperature was below a hundred by now. Even the pink room seemed less lurid.

"Yes," Grace admitted, as if she was giving up a privilege, with re-luctance.

"And tomorrow I bet you'll feel a whole, whole lot better."

"Mommy? Do people die when they're awake or asleep?"

"Grace. What did I tell you?"

"But which one?"

"Both. Neither." *If I die before I wake, I pray the Lord my soul to take.* Some universal childhood fear? Jane couldn't remember it herself. "You don't have to be afraid to go to sleep. I promise you are going to wake up in the morning just like you always do, and you'll be fine."

"What if I have a bad dream?"

"Then you come get me." Jane stopped. "Did you have a bad dream?"

"I don't know."

"You don't know if it was a dream or you don't know if it was bad?"

"It was about Daddy."

"What about Daddy?" Jane asked, trying to keep the brittle edge out of her voice. Yes indeed, what about Daddy?

"He was crying."

This was unexpected. "Well, your daddy doesn't cry." At least, she couldn't remember him doing so. Or just the once, when they'd almost lost Grace. He was entirely too confident, which was another way of say-ing, full of himself. "What was he crying about?"

"I don't know," Grace said again, yawning.

"Then it was just a dream and you don't have to worry about it. Go to sleep now. Think about something pleasant."

"Daddy is a big crybaby."

"Good night, Grace."

Jane pulled the bedroom door closed, leaving a hand's width opening so Grace could see the hall light and wouldn't wake up frightened. In spite of what she'd told Grace to reassure her, she felt spooked, filled with free-floating dread, too many things gone too wrong, and how did you know when it was over?

She crossed the hall to Robbie's room, which was dark and quiet. His door too was open and she looked in, letting her eyes adjust. Robbie was in bed, asleep on his back. Drugged up, cried out. His white, bandaged hand lay beside him like a small pet.

Eric was in their bedroom, she guessed, waiting to tell her more of his indignant half-lies. Jane had to remind herself of the passage of time, the day and the night gone by since her suspicions, or no, her absolute dead certainty had crashed-landed on her, but Eric would not have made the same reckoning. He'd be wondering what she knew and how, and waiting to have it out with her, having already tried on this or that argument or excuse, and to Jane it was as if all of it had already happened and she had moved on past it to whatever numb and ugly part of their life came next.

Jane went to the room she'd prepared for herself, found a nightgown and robe in the closet, and changed into them. She washed her face and brushed her teeth in the children's bathroom and readied herself for sleep. She crept into Grace and Robbie's rooms and stood over them for a time, holding her own breath so that she could listen to theirs. Satisfied that they slept without distress, she returned to the small bedroom and lay down in the narrow bed and turned off the light.

Her nerves were broken glass, her head full of jumpy thoughts. She didn't expect to sleep, not any time soon at least. There was only the dry waiting to get through. For a time she dozed, or thought she did. Footsteps came toward her down the hall. Eric threw open the door to the room. "What's this about, Jane?"

The hall light made her shield her eyes with her arm. "Leave me alone."

"This is some stunt. How about, if you have something to say, say it."

"I did. Leave me alone."

"This is not the way an adult behaves, Jane." He fumbled around for a light switch, didn't find one. The room was too small for an overhead light. He'd probably never noticed. He kept reaching and thumping the wall. "Ah, crap."

Jane sat up in bed. "Do you want to wake the kids?"

"Come out of there so we can see each other."

"I'm fine right here."

"Goddamn it, Jane."

"Why are you the one who's angry? Why are you bothering? Talk about stunts."

Eric stepped into the room, a backlit shadow. She hissed at him. "Get out! What are you doing, leave me alone!"

"What's the matter with you, huh?" His face was in shadow, she couldn't see it. "What, you're afraid of me now? Christ."

"Get out of here!"

"For God's—"

"Get out!" Jane reached for the lamp and clicked it on. She and Eric stared at each other.

He had a bloodshot, rumpled look, as if he'd already been asleep and then awakened. The light made him squint.

"What are you doing in here?" Attempting a reasonable, exasperated tone. But he was still furious. And perhaps frightened, as she was.

"I'm trying to sleep. I'll talk to you in the morning."

"No, you're trying to make some goddamn point, because you think, I don't even know what you think." He shook his head, disgusted. Pretending now to be disgusted. He was trying to get her to say what she knew, what he had done to give himself away. She knew him that well. As he knew her. Nothing in their knowledge of each other made them happy.

Jane said, "You want me to just go along, go along with everything you do. Act like I don't notice."

He might have said, Notice what, but that would have given too much away, and neither did Jane wish to say what she knew, or suspected, and so they both held back. Watching him, she was aware that he had drawn into himself, relaxed for the moment, as if reassured, as if he had gotten away with something and was congratulating himself. "Don't bet on it," Jane said, which startled him back into wariness.

She could see him visibly coming to some decision. "All right," he said. "I can see I'm never going to talk you out of your suspicions. You're going to think the worst of me because you can't follow me around all the time making sure I'm behaving. So go ahead and assume whatever you want. I can't control that."

She purely hated him then. He must have seen it in her face because he took a step back and seemed to lose some of his swagger. "Bastard," she said, without heat, but meaning it.

"Please come back to bed. This is childish."

"How about, you sleep where you want and I sleep where I want."

She watched him trying to decide how he might still turn everything into an argument he could win, then she watched him give up. She'd been right. She'd been right from the very start. "I'm sorry," he said. "Really." And then they both waited to see what would come next.

After a minute Jane said, "I suppose there's some way that it's my fault." She felt calmer now, less inclined to react, but also more deeply shaken.

"No. Of course it's not."

"Who is she? Somebody at work?"

"Yes."

Jane waited. Eric said, "It isn't anything. Wasn't. It was an impulse. A bad idea. I'm sorry."

"I don't think I want to hear any details."

"Of course not." He seemed aware that he might have agreed too quickly. "I mean, that's up to you."

"No more lying."

"All right."

He was still standing there, taking up too much space in the small room. "Are you moving out?" Jane asked. And watched him look thrown off balance.

"No, why would I? Where would I go? What about the kids?" When Jane didn't answer, he said, "Unless that's really what you think ought to happen."

"I don't know yet. What I think ought to happen."

"Well please don't . . . Let's give it a little time to settle, OK? I know this is all new, and hurtful, and confusing, and I think we ought to, if only for the kids' sake, not decide anything right away."

Jane said, "It just amazes me, that as soon as there's any opportunity to talk your way out of something, you jump on it."

He said something under his breath, a quick, fast swearing, and pushed his way from the room.

Jane stayed where she was. Her armpits were damp. She heard sounds from down the hall, Eric moving around, opening, closing things. Then he was back. He'd put on clothes, a pullover shirt and jeans, and a fleece jacket. He had his keys and he thrust them into a pocket. "You win. I'm going. You don't have to hide in here anymore."

Jane raised a hand: Go.

"I said I'm sorry and I am. We could work this out. Other people do. Maybe we still can. We could talk about it. But not until you're ready. You decide."

Jane said, "You're mad because you didn't get away with it."

"Oh, now you want to talk."

"Because you just about always do, right? You're so used to being the smartest kid in the class. The guy with all the answers. The Miracle Doc."

"This is all about your own frustration and self-hatred, Jane."

"Because you are so gifted. So hardworking. I mean, why shouldn't you be entitled to a little extra on the side? Who would begrudge you that?"

"Does it make you feel better about yourself to attack me? That's sad, Jane. Really."

"This marriage thing, this family thing is just so much harder for you. I've seen you struggle with it. You need a checklist, or a manual. Something."

"I've kept this family going while you had your little mental incapacity holiday. Remember that? Huh? I'm pretty sure you milked that for all it was worth."

"And I'm pretty sure you made everybody feel sorry for you." It was as if she and Eric stood on opposite sides of a canyon, little stick figures throwing stones at each other. Nothing had to be entirely true, just close enough to land and do damage.

Eric let his hands fall to his sides, the giving up gesture. "You're the one I feel sorry for. How can you hang on to all those resentments? What did I or anybody else ever do to you that was so terrible?"

"I thought you were leaving."

He made a particularly ugly face then, a half-sneer that distorted his mouth like a gargoyle's.

"Mom?"

Robbie had left his bed and was standing outside the door, small, hunched over in his pajamas.

"Honey, what are you doing up? Does your hand hurt?" Jane got out of bed and shoved her way past Eric. "Let's see."

"Are you mad at me?"

"No, sweetheart, why would we be?"

"Because of the water."

"Nobody's mad. It was an accident."

"You were yelling."

Jane, kneeling in front of Robbie, looked up at Eric, waiting. Yours.

"Hey, buddy. I'm sorry we woke you up. We should have gone downstairs to talk."

"Are you going away?" The codeine, maybe, gave Robbie's eyes a bleared, half-shut look.

"I have to go to the hospital and take care of some people," Eric explained, and Jane thought how easily he came up with a serviceable lie. Silently, she telegraphed this. Eric didn't look at her but his mouth tightened. "How about I look at your hand before I leave, huh? Do you need to go to the bathroom?"

"Mom? Are you mad?"

"It's nothing you have to worry about. Go with your Dad, let him help you."

"Come on, Rob. Can you be a big boy for me?" Eric tended to get exasperated when the kids were what he thought of as clingy. It was one of the things they went round and round about.

Grace was still asleep. Jane listened at her door for a time, then retreated to the center of the hallway. She heard Robbie's piping voice, water running in the bathroom. All normal, at least, normal for the kind of kid crisis they went through at least once every few weeks. Not normal, the detonation of their marriage. Was that what it was, the end? How did you know? They'd never had a fight like this before, and Jane had the giddy sense that she could push it as far as she wished.

But for the moment they were like one of those blown-up buildings where the upper floors hung, suspended on nothing, while the foundation pancaked in a heap of steel and rubble.

Jane went back into the bedroom, hers and Eric's, and looked in on them. Robbie was saying his hand still hurt and Eric said it was going to hurt for a while, there wasn't any way around that. "You have to be brave, buddy. Show me what a big brave boy you can be."

The back of Robbie's hand now had a line of small blisters. "OK, try not to rub it. I'm going to put some medicine on it and give you a new bandage."

For Jane's benefit he said, "Maybe they could spare me at the hospital so I can stay here and take care of that old burn."

"No, I think you should go. Stick with the plan."

"You're going to be fine," Eric told Robbie. "It's just going to take some time to heal."

"Can I sleep in your bed?" Robbie asked. "Please?"

It wasn't anything they liked to encourage. Children should have their own beds, they were agreed on that. Jane and Eric traded a helpless, irritated look. "Maybe just this once," Eric said. "You could hop in bed with your mom while I'm at the hospital."

Screw you, Jane said silently, another telegraphed message. "All right," she told Robbie. "But I want you to try and go to sleep. Then you'll wake up in the morning and everything'll be better."

"Sure it will," Eric said, full of encouragement.

"Come on, hop into bed," Jane told Robbie. "Let's get comfortable." She lifted up her side of the covers and got Robbie settled. Eric was standing in the door, looking like the chickenshit he was, not wanting to go now but also not willing to back down. "He can't have any more of the codeine yet. There's nothing to do but wait it out."

"Bye," Jane said. "Careful driving."

He went down the stairs and she heard the sound of the back door opening and closing and then the car starting up and the noise of it pulling out of the driveway, then receding down the street.

Maybe he'd go to his girlfriend's. Maybe he'd stay there.

Robbie had made himself a throne out of the pillows, and given his bandaged hand a pillow of its own. "Can we turn off the lights and watch television?"

"No, it's late and you have to go to sleep."

"Will my hand hurt when I'm asleep?"

"No, silly. Nothing hurts while you're asleep."

He was already yawning. Jane switched off the lamp and kissed him on top of his head. Sleep, she told herself. Nothing will hurt.

But sleep didn't come. Robbie had dropped back into some motionless dream, the solid weight of him resting against her legs so that Jane had to reposition herself a few cautious inches at a time.

And then again. By now it was well after midnight—she had tried to keep herself from looking at the clock, but that proved to be even more agitating—and her heart still beat like a drum, and one bad thought after another dragged its chain on its way through her head. She would say to Eric this or that haughty or scarifying thing, and he would answer back in some infuriating way that made her go after him all over again, making him pay for his smugness and dishonesty and selfishness, oh help.

Careful not to disturb Robbie, Jane got out of bed and closed herself in the bathroom. Eric kept his stockpile of prescription medicine on the top shelf of the linen closet, in a satchel with a combination lock that was designed to keep out the children but not, certainly, Jane. She lifted the satchel down, spun the lock open, and sat on the toilet to see what she could use. You weren't supposed to combine certain things with her antidepressant—Ambien, Xanax—but there was another one that was supposed to be all right. It started with an R and she was sure she'd know it when she saw it, here it was. Little yellow pills. She swallowed one, locked the satchel and replaced it, and went back in to lie down again next to Robbie.

There were glowing patches behind her eyelids, light blue, like a neon sky, and bars of pink-violet. It was a curious kind of sleep but Jane followed where it led her, because she was so very grateful to have put her head to bed. But her eyes itched. It didn't seem right that your eyes could itch in your sleep. A phone rang, a dream phone you didn't have to answer. The sky was upside down. She fell into it and paddled around.

And then she was awake again, her eyes wide open but something urgent pressing in on her, so that she was out of bed with her feet on the floor before she was aware she'd done so. What? she said, although not out loud. It seemed that she had woken up an entirely different person. Ah, she said, nodding. She felt energized, impatient, quite wonderful.

"Do you feel like talking?" she asked the boy in the bed, but he wouldn't wake up. She went out into the hallway and listened to the night sounds, the house sailing through the dark. It was an ordinary house. Ordinary people lived here. She wanted to lift the roof and let the sky and windy stars in. Why were they asleep? This new, important person she had become was ready to make herself known. So much waiting to be seen, to be saved, to be seized!

"Wake up," she told the little girl, sitting next to her on the bed and stroking her hair. The child whimpered and buried herself in her pillow. "You're the one with the questions, right?"

The girl blinked and opened one eye to give her a fuzzy look. "Mommy?"

"No, silly." Smiling at the mistake. Nobody here by that name.

"Mommy, you're sitting on me."

She moved aside. "Ask me anything you want. Because I know everything."

"Where's Daddy?"

"Well I guess I don't know that." She tried to turn it into a joke. "Daddy must be in outer space."

"No he's not."

"OK, he's not." She was distracted by a new sound: *Whoosh* and *whoosh*. It was outer space, listening in. Perhaps the roof was off after all. The hurry came back to her then, the certainty that if she did not explain everything, the everything of everything, it would be an opportunity lost forever. "Dying is only a one-two-three jump off the end of the pier. Here we go! Last one in's a rotten egg! Dying is the body fighting back and not wanting to be not itself. And who could blame it?" she asked, which was one of those questions you came up with when you already knew the answer. "Because we only know what we know. We are dust to dust. Do you know that this is Day One of the year Eternity? Why are you cry-ing?" she asked, annoyed.

"Stop it."

"Oh you're a silly little thing," she said, wanting to coax and jolly the girl out of it, although it was aggravating, it truly was, to be treated with such disregard and inattention. So she held the child tightly round her middle and put her mouth against her ear so that there would be no chance of her not hearing. She told her that although not everyone could see it, there was a realm of being where the world fell away and the spirit flew upward like a bird and left behind all greed and fear. And this place, which was familiar to her from so many blissful, floating visits, was called love.

Love! Which she had only come to understand right that very mo-ment, was not what you thought it was, what your old constrained and tiny self thought it was. It had nothing to do with attaching yourself to this or that man, or even mother father child. That was not love. No more so than heaven was about angels and harps and halos handed out like ribbons at a school spelling bee. No, love was free and vast and limitless, and our own knowledge of it was only a slice, a speck, a single chip of colored glass in a huge kaleidoscope, the kind that shifted into new and unimaginably beautiful patterns with every turn. Everything that dazzled and sustained us, everything that saved us. It was all love! Love! she said, and then kept saying it, love! and love! wanting the word to mean every-thing that might be thought or said because she was reaching the limits of language like a bird bird too high in *whoosh whoosh* outer space—

"Mom? What's the matter with Grace?" The boy had gotten out of bed and was staring in at them.

"Nothing," she said, falling back down into language once more. "She's fine."

"Why is she hollering?"

"Is she?" She looked down at the child, who was weeping in a violent, noisy manner, her breath drawn in and in, forgetting to breathe out again. "You should stop that," she told the child, uselessly, since she seemed quite intent on screaming and you had to wait until she ran down like a clock, and in the meantime a horrible horrible idea was canceling out everything else in her head, and this was the possibility that she had gotten everything wrong.

"Mom? Are you going to answer the phone?"

The noise drilled into her. What had she done? These poor children! They had been left on their own and now she had endangered them with her reckless and forbidden knowledge or was that wrong also? Finally the drilling stopped. She said, "We have to hide in the basement," and the children, both of them, looked at her as if she had spoken in a different language. The girl ceased her crying for long enough to stare up at her.

"Hide from what?" the boy said. "I don't want to go to the basement."

"Hurry," she told them. She picked up the girl, who was heavier than she looked, and who kicked a little, uselessly, in protest. "Go." She herded the boy in front of her, all the way down the stairs and through the kitchen until they stood at the landing to the basement steps. Here she let the girl slide out of her grip until she was standing on her own feet. "You have to walk now, I can't keep carrying you."

"The basement's yucky," the boy said, but once she had turned on the stair light he started down; the girl more reluctant, taking her time with every step.

The basement was where all the lost and unloved household items ended up, the broken lawn furniture and underused kitchen appliances and outgrown toys. It was low-ceilinged and bulging with wires and piping, cement-floored and chilly. "Now then," she told them, once they had all reached the bottom. "Find someplace to sit and be quiet." There was nowhere to sit. They stared at her, lifting up first one, then another bare foot to rub against their legs, trying to warm them.

"When is Daddy coming home?"

Starbursts of light went off in the corners of her vision, confusing her.

"I don't think he lives here," she said, vaguely, since she was no longer certain of anything. She felt sick, sweaty. The children kept silent. "Mommy is having a bad dream," she told them. The boy picked at his bandaged hand. It came to her then, how he had injured it and what had come of it and all the unhappiness bound up in it. She sank to the floor so that she was sitting with her back to the wall, looking up at them. "I'm sorry," she said. "I'm at something of a loss to explain myself."

"Mom? Is it close enough to morning so we can eat cereal?"

"Hush," she said, because now there was some racket upstairs, feet walking along the floorboards above their heads. The footsteps tracked back and forth and then it was Eric calling her name and the children's voices piping up in response, Daddy, Daddy!

"What are you doing down there? Kids? Jane?" He was at the head of the stairs, peering down at them. The children ran to meet him. "What happened, are you all right?" He descended the stairs, the children crowding into him on both sides, and stopped when he saw Jane on the floor. "Jane? What the hell?"

She said, "I thought I heard something." Reaching into herself for some effort at guile. "Like somebody trying to break in."

"Did you see anything?" She shook her head, no. "Did you call the police?" Again, no. "Well next time call, all right? That's what they're for." He was only pretending to be annoyed. He was so happy to see them. He stooped over her to help her up, hesitated, until she reached up to him.

They put their heads close together and spoke so the children could not hear them.

"Sorry."

"I'm sorry."

"Don't—"

"It's all right."

"Just don't send me away. I can't stand it."

"It's all right," she said again, letting him hold her up, letting him kiss her face and carry on extravagantly and make promises he would in time forget, then skulk around feeling guilty and trying to make it up to her, let him do whatever he wanted from now on. She had seen what might happen to her if she was left on her own and it terrified her. Let it all be as before. Let them carry on and on, battering against themselves and each other.

"Daddy's a big crybaby," Grace said.

calculus

The summer of one year had gone by and now it was the summer of the next and they had given up pretending that they were going to stop anytime soon.

They stood in the parking lot behind Bonnie's apartment, saying good-bye. They were always saying good-bye. Most often they did so indoors, to avoid the extra scrutiny of Bonnie's neighbors, even though the Dumplings, certainly, and Mr. Hopkins, most likely, knew what was what. It was just easier to avoid coming face to face with them and make them a part of the farewell scene.

But on this evening of a mild, irresistible day in late June, the sky was lavender (from pollution, Eric suggested), the starlings were still chattering and whistling in the curbside trees, and even the traffic noise had a softened, indistinct sound, like an urban ocean. So they walked outside and stood for a time next to Eric's car. Bonnie wore one of her loose, bright-colored cotton shifts, garments which she hoped did not announce, "I just had sex and I'm not wearing anything underneath," but probably did.

Eric wore the clothes he'd put on at home that morning, and now, between work and Bonnie's, had climbed out of and back into twice. His summer shirts and suits were expensive and just short of dandyish. The shirts were white or mint or blue or gray, plain or checked or faintly striped. She loved the architecture of his jackets, she turned the unlined ones inside out to examine the tailoring. She loved this evidence of vanity, all the things a man might do to present himself well. She didn't have much experience with men who dressed up; she decided she liked it. Once she had asked him, in the matter-of-fact tone they used when speaking of her, if Jane bought any of his clothes for him. Eric said no, she didn't. He said that clothes weren't one of the things Jane seemed to notice.

The sky deepened another notch, one more moment of the most extraordinary lilac and deep violet tints. "I hope the traffic won't be too bad," Bonnie said, as a way of keeping him talking, keeping him there just a little while longer. "What a hassle, driving."

"Well, not everybody can take the bus." He was checking his phone for messages. She supposed it was unreasonable of her to hate his phone. He put it back in his pocket, opened the car door. Readied himself, smiling. "OK, kiddo . . ."

Bonnie took a step, reached up, allowed herself a brief, glancing hug and kiss. Break clean. She stepped back and he got into the car, started it, rolled down the window and crinkled his mouth in a smile. "Bye."

"Bye." She turned and went back inside, not allowing herself to make an affecting sight out of watching him disappear. She could never decide if leavetaking was one of the best or worst moments. Her body was still heavy and drugged with whatever mystery chemical it was that sex let loose in you. Maybe there were people who never felt such a thing, or who shrugged it off, but she wasn't one of them. Or those for whom sex was just scratching an itch, or a smutty joke. There was no explaining it, and no one she cared to explain such things to. Not Eric. She was too shy, and anyway it would have felt like bragging, risking all their precarious luck. Because she did regard herself as lucky.

And yet it was a kind of violence to be deprived of his body, to always be watching him leave.

And yet again (back inside now, wandering from one room to another, setting right all the things his presence had disrupted), how nice it was to have her own space back again, to draw breath, relax, contemplate. She wished she ever knew what she wanted for fifteen minutes at a time.

Her phone rang. It was Eric. He did this sometimes, called while he was driving home, so as to delay, once more, a good-bye. "I was thinking," he said, "that we don't do a very good job of urban planning. In general. Unless there's some opportunity, a fire, say, that levels all the old mistakes and allows for an actual plan."

"And why do you think that is?" Bonnie asked. She didn't care one way or the other about urban planning but she got a kick out of Eric's enthusiasms, his serious man-talk. Anyway, it was her job, wasn't it, to be receptive, engaged in his engagements, to be his intellectual geisha. "I mean, there wouldn't have been any such thing as planning, at first. Just people settling near the river, or the stagecoach line. I guess you could call that a plan."

"Central governments didn't develop until later," Eric said. "The whole concept of a central government having regulatory authority is fairly recent."

"That makes sense." She listened to him go on about urban sprawl, and the tyranny of the automobile, and any number of other such judgments. Bonnie provided occasional interested and encouraging noises. She didn't care about any of it. She only loved that he'd called, that he wanted to try out his important-sounding opinions on her. You could delight in a man's small affectations and flaws as you might a child's. At least, until they became tedious. She had to wonder what brought this on, this particular big idea. Urban planning not her first post-bed thought.

After a time Eric said he'd better get off the phone and concentrate on driving, the traffic was getting heavy. "Bye," Bonnie said. As before, not making any kind of goopy, huge deal out of it, because they would be thinking about everything they had done to each other while together, and that too was a part of good-bye.

They did not see each other all that often, since Eric's schedule truly was unpredictable, demanding, and crazy-making—Bonnie could sympathize with Jane here. And the children had their own absolute and unimpeachable needs. And so Bonnie occupied something like a corner of a corner, or a slice of a slice, of Eric's time. That was the deal. If she was being shortchanged of some portion of his presence and his attention, well, so was everyone else in his life. Get in line.

Besides, she was a free agent. She could come and go as she pleased. Take a new job, up and move, cut herself loose without regrets. A wild card you didn't much want to play.

A week or two or more might go by when they did not see each other, and then it might only be for lunch or drinks, that is, not for sex. But they spoke almost every day, and sometimes throughout the day. "I just never shut up," Bonnie said to him once, meaning it in a humorous, self-deprecating way that also managed to have some showing off in it. And Eric surprised her by saying that he hoped she never would. She had a vision then of Jane, and of silences as vast and lofty as a vaulted ceiling. She guessed that in conversation, as with sex, she offered a different kind of entertainment.

And was that her purpose, her function, to offer him variety and diversion? She did not like to think in this way.

Because most often things between them were fine, more than fine. They were good companions, good lovers, sounding boards for each other's troubles. She loved him. She thought he loved her. He didn't say so. Neither of them said. But regardless. Was that enough? Should it be? Then again, what kind of venal idiot was she being, allowing herself to be so used? It was a precarious balancing act, calculating, keeping score so that she might judge when it was time for her to end it. That was the only possible outcome. You could see it coming from a mile away. She would withdraw herself from him and he would return to his everyday life and he would miss her.

Or perhaps replace her with someone else.

When she was in this injured state of mind, things ceased to be fine. It was a familiar, bitter mood that spilled out in the occasional comment that she tried to make ironic and knowing but which always gave her away.

By now, at least in such difficult moments, Bonnie had reached a certain baseline level of self-loathing, in which she acknowledged that she was a dishonest and disloyal person who had no real intention of changing her behavior, and her occasional bouts of bad conscience and self-recriminations were only whatchacallit. The tribute vice pays to virtue. Hypocrisy.

If Eric went through any similar process of feeling bad about himself but not bad enough to do anything about it, or if he justified himself in some convincing way, or if he managed never to think very much about such things at all, he kept it to himself. Bonnie could not decide if he was being gentlemanly or just a typically oblivious man, but she was just as glad. Talking about the relationship, that cliché of magazines and advice columns, was overrated. It was something you were supposed to want to do, and men resisted because they did not want to lay bare their feelings, etc. They had to be led like a balky horse, with various threats and coaxing, to whatever declaration or endpoint was desired. But Bonnie didn't want to talk about unpleasant or ambiguous circumstances any more than he did. And so they did not, at least most of the time.

As for Bonnie and Jane. It seemed that it was possible for the two realities to exist side by side, one in which Bonnie was the lover of Jane's husband, and one in which she and Jane were friends. It was remarkable, the ways you could accommodate two such contradictory things. The thinking part of you, or the moral, censorious part of you, simply ceased to keep office hours. It was true that between the two of them, Bonnie and Jane, there was often a certain distance. This might have come about regardless.

They weren't kids anymore, all full of themselves—well, Bonnie had been full of herself—needing to announce themselves and their intentions and anxieties every fifteen minutes. Their lives had taken certain shapes. Perhaps they were a little bored with each other by now. Or if not bored, exactly, they were thoroughly known quantities to each other.

At least, when it came to those things they each believed they knew.

Here are Bonnie and Jane and Eric, on an outing with the children at Brookfield Zoo. This is Jane's idea, since she believes the children need a number of formative experiences, such as visiting an overcrowded zoo on a hot day and becoming tired and fretful and walking long distances between exhibits and becoming distressed at the smells. Bonnie has been invited along because she is such a good sport around the kids, plus she entertains them, they are less likely to pitch fits or fight with each other when she's around. "Should I go?" she'd asked Eric. "Is it better or worse if I'm there?" And Eric had answered, with a certain amount of irritation, that she should do whatever she wanted, it wasn't going to move the needle much. He did not share Jane's ideas about the necessity for such organized fun.

So Bonnie arrived at the zoo, parked, paid her entrance fee, and made her way to the Aviary, which was their rendezvous point. It was late morning, less than an hour since the zoo opened, but the place was already full of slow-moving crowds, family groups with children, mostly, making their straggling progress along the broad walkways, stopping to consult maps or to buy T-shirts, animal hand puppets, lemonade, peanuts. The day was bright but humid and the sun glared. Bonnie was wearing a pink summer blouse and blue cotton slacks, cork sandals that she hoped would go easy on her feet. Her clothes were chosen both for utility and to convey only an appropriate, casual attractiveness. Besides, she'd been putting on weight lately, and when she retrieved two of her favorite sundresses from the back of the closet, their front buttons had gapped. What to do? Drink less? An unwelcome thought.

She'd parked at the wrong entrance, she realized, at least if she wanted to be close to the Aviary. Now she had to walk the length of the park to get there, and it didn't take her long to turn sweaty and unfresh and decide this was a bad idea for any number of reasons. She didn't like zoos, even at their most spacious and professional. They only existed because of marauding humanity. She always felt sorry for the captive animals, sorrier than they probably did for themselves. She didn't like crowds of shrieking children, not that anyone did. And she'd grown confused about her motivations for agreeing to be here, whether there was anything genuine about them, whether she really wanted to see the children, or Jane, or even Eric, or if it was all a messy pretense in which she attempted to prove different things to different people. How natural and unaffected she was in their presence, just like always, no breath of suspicion, nothing to see here, move along.

She decided that yes, it would at least be nice to see the kids. They were good kids, and every time she saw them they had become, somehow, more and more *themselves*, as if their natures were there from the start and the hard or soft protective shell around them had only to be worn away. Was that true of people, the same way it might be true of racehorses or dogs? You were who you were and so you remained? She couldn't have said.

She passed the central fountain, with its spire of teasing, splashing coolness, and soldiered grimly on. Perhaps she was here because of Eric, although not in the way one might expect. There had been a slight, unspoken bruising of her feelings lately, a sense in which he has been rushed or preoccupied in his dealings with her. A sense in which she is an accomplished fact and no longer must be wooed or fully engaged with, an entire constellation of behaviors that fall into the category of being taken for granted.

Perhaps she wanted to be around him in a place where he would want her but couldn't do anything about it except sit and stew or flirt in some depraved way that only the two of them would recognize and yes this really was a bad stinking idea but before she could reverse course and leave and phone in with some excuse, Jane spotted her and called her over.

They were sitting on a bench outside the Aviary, that is, Jane and Eric and Grace were sitting while Robbie careened around them, imitating— an airplane? a charging elephant? The others all looked to be in some bad moods of different varieties. Grace was pink-faced and wilting from the heat, Jane was tense, and Eric was having a particularly unattractive fit of scowling. He seemed to be pretending he did not know the rest of them, and had been forced to share a bench with them because of lack of space.

Jane at least looked glad to see Bonnie. Some relief from the unhappy claustrophobia of the family unit. And Bonnie snapped to it. She knew what to do. "Hey you guys! Ready to see the lions and tigers and bears? Gracie, did you see the flamingos yet? The big pink birds? Robbie, whoa." He had jumped up on her like an untrained puppy, which made Jane scold him, mortified. "OK buddy, I'm happy to see you too." Bonnie disengaged from him and pumped up her smile. She had to coax and prod them into something resembling a good mood, since they certainly would not do so on their own. "Did you see the birds yet?"

"We were waiting for you," Jane said with a hint of grievance, but she made shooing motions to the others to get them up and in motion. Bonnie thought, not for the first time, that she liked any of these people better by themselves than in a group.

Robbie complained that he did not want to see a bunch of old birds, he wanted to see snakes, he wanted to watch them feed live rats to the snakes. Eric said, "Robbie," in a warning tone, and Robbie said that is too what they eat, live rats. "That's enough," Eric said, and Robbie went quiet and sulky from being told, one more time, to stop bothering everybody, and Bonnie knew she might not be the right one to save these people from themselves, but she wished somebody would.

Things got better once they were inside the bird house, part of the obedient crowd looking through the glass windows at the secret green worlds. Grace spotted a small rust-colored bird before anybody else did, and that lifted her spirits. Robbie, bloodthirsty as ever, wanted to know if they had any hawks or other birds of prey, but he was used to being disappointed by now and shrugged it off. Jane was absorbed in the educational aspect of things with Grace, reading the placards. Eric was cruising along behind them, and Bonnie lagged a step so that she could speak to him. Sometimes they overcompensated and practically ignored each other, when before, that is, before the sex, they might have hugged and carried on. At times like these Bonnie felt herself to be a stray explosive substance roaming around loose, ready to ignite or detonate, a walking sexual charge. No matter what half-assed good intentions she might have, no matter what the social proprieties or basic decency required, she might go off at any moment, she might willfully set herself ablaze.

So she said, "Hey Eric, Happy Zoo Day."

And granted that was a lame-o thing to say, but he didn't make much of an effort in return, just a grimacing smile. "Yeah, same to you."

She loved his shirt, a pale apricot cotton that reminded her of sherbet. She would have liked to touch it, feel the smoothness of it. She would have liked to unbutton it and slide her hands in between the shirt and his skin. There was a giddy, unbalanced moment when she was afraid she had actually done so. Reeling herself back in, she said, "Nice to see you enjoying yourself," which made him glower and wonder what she was up to, and then everyone was distracted by Robbie pounding on the glass to try and get the attention of a green heron.

They made their way to the Aviary itself, one of the habitat exhibits the zoo was famous for. Birds flew freely here through a landscape of glossy-leaved plants and ferns and waterfalls and well-engineered branches. The air smelled saturated and loamy, but not unpleasantly so. It was less crowded here, or at least less echoing, and if you worked hard at it, you might convince yourself you were somewhere real. Two splendid macaws with red heads, acid green wings, and blue-violet tails were stationed at the entrance, and they were so large and noisy and self-assured, with their flat, cracked stares, that even Robbie hung back from them.

Bonnie caught up to Jane and Grace. She was tired of having to counterfeit her feelings around Eric, and she was tired of him being tiresome. Next time she saw him, that is, next time they were alone, she was going to give him grief for it, in some way she had not yet determined. Not for the first time, she was glad she wasn't married to him, at least, glad she wasn't a wife to be ignored. If he started to treat her the same way, he might find himself surprised.

Jane was pointing out a bird to Grace, a white-crested, sharp-billed bird that looked like a kingfisher or a jay but also entirely unfamiliar. Neither Jane nor Bonnie knew what it was called, but Jane said the bird is what it is, the name was only something that people gave it. No, your father doesn't know either, don't ask him, it annoys him when he doesn't have the answer to things.

Bonnie thought this last was true. Eric did get frustrated and snappish when he couldn't provide answers, even to things nobody expected him to know, like, yes, this is the rare, white-crowned whoop de doo. It had something to do with being a doctor and needing to know everything. If their affair were out in the open, or if she and Jane were Mormon sister-wives, they could gossip about it, prod Eric in his weak places, share a head-shaking laugh. Of course this was making a lot of assumptions about Mormon sister-wives. Maybe they were closed-mouthed, private, jealous.

"How's it going?" Bonnie asked Jane. For the moment at least she preferred Jane's company to Eric's. The old comfort of their shared years.

"Good, fine, yeah," Jane murmured. "Grace, there is nothing to be afraid of, I promise. These are all friendly birds, that's why they let them fly around. Robbie, what did we talk about? About the zoo being the animals' home, and we respect someone else's home." To Bonnie she said, "I could drop them off with the gorilla moms, don't you think? They do a pretty good job."

"You'd miss them. You'd keep coming back to see them and you'd have to pay admission."

"Mom! Mom! They have vultures!" Robbie came running up to them, excited that there was something sinister available in the world of birds.

"That's great, honey. Go tell your dad he has to watch you and Grace for a minute, I'll be right back. Sinus headache," she said to Bonnie. "I have to take something. Eric?" Jane flagged him down and made a series of pointing gestures. They both watched as Eric attempted, ineffectually, to give instructions and commands to both children from too far away. "He's a gorilla dad," Jane said. "Come help me find a drinking fountain."

The two of them went through the far door and back out into the echoing hallway. Jane dug in her purse for her headache tablets and stood in line at the fountain. Bonnie thought that Jane looked tired, even frumpish, with her hair skinned back and her damp, freckling skin and her too-long shorts and canvas shoes. Summer was not her season. Bonnie had enough evil vanity to be pleased that she might look better. But what a weariness it was, all this picking, picking, picking at the same scab, what a weariness, her own stupid unworthy base nature.

Jane took her medicine and came back to Bonnie. "I hope these do the trick. We have a lot more animal kingdoms left."

"Take a break. Let Eric be in charge for a while. Come on, sit."

There weren't a lot of places to sit inside, because people were encouraged to keep moving, but they found a shallow step and rested with their backs against a wall. "Oof," Jane said.

"Double oof," Bonnie agreed.

"I just want them to have fun. It shouldn't be so hard."

"They will. It's a fun place. They're getting into it."

Jane rubbed at the bridge of her nose. "I don't remember childhood being fun."

"You were sick a lot. You had to participate in competitive sports." By now Bonnie knew all of Jane's growing-up stories. "They got mad when you fainted."

"It's more like, they were disappointed."

"Disappointed, then."

"I don't want to do that to my kids. Make them feel like we ordered different children than the ones we got."

"You don't. You won't. Go easy on yourself."

"It's harder than it looks, this parenting thing."

"It looks pretty hard to me."

Jane began to gather the bits and pieces she'd dragged out of her purse: Kleenex, comb, ChapStick, and tuck them back inside. "Tell me about the actual adult world. I miss it."

"It's no big deal," Bonnie said, cautious now.

"The intrigue. The drama. The passion."

"You'd be so disappointed."

"Would I," Jane said, and for a moment the look in her eye was as flat and cracked and crazed as those of the macaw's, and in that moment Bonnie's guilty lying self hung suspended over a chasm, and then Jane's expression resumed its familiar exasperated, wilted mockery. "Tell me about him."

"Who?"

"You know. Studly."

"He's about the same. His studly self," Bonnie said.

Because Eric was not her only lover and had not ever been.

"You should have brought him along today."

"No," Bonnie said. "I don't think that would have worked out. You ready? How's your headache?"

∽✀

L over" being perhaps too grand a term. There were other applicable words, but you might not care to use them.

It wasn't anything Bonnie had planned on, but that was no excuse. A long time ago Jane told her, "The good thing about you is that you own up to all kinds of awful behavior. The bad thing is, you think that owning up is enough. You never actually stop doing stuff."

Although Patrick, that was his name, was someone she'd known and kept company with a year or more before, that is, before Eric, so you could make some kind of a lame case that she was not transgressing, only failing to make a clean break. Except that she was too aware of her own bad intentions and her own spite, arising from one too many occasions that Eric was unavailable to her, one too many occasions of having her nose rubbed in the realities of their situation. So that if she sought out Patrick, or if he called her, and they picked up where they'd left off a few times—in fact it had been half a dozen—well, you did what you did and you had your reasons.

And if Jane asked who she was seeing these days, and if it would not do to keep saying, nobody, since this was hardly ever the case, then why not make good use of Patrick, whom Jane would never meet?

She didn't think that Jane would mention any of this to Eric. It wasn't her habit to share anything they spoke of. But there was always that chance, and Bonnie told herself she wouldn't be sorry if Jane did.

At other times she thought she should just give up and have herself committed to an institution for depraved females.

It wasn't as if she and Eric had made each other any promises, it wasn't as if she had signed over her free will. There were only certain conventions, certain unsaid expectations, namely, that he would still have Jane, for whatever purposes, and Bonnie would be his faithful mistress. Well, perhaps they should have said.

At least with Patrick there weren't any tragic subtexts. Just the usual aggravations of a certain fallible type of man. He was younger than Bonnie, thirty to her thirty-eight, a bartender at a pub-style bar off of North Kedzie. He was one of those professional Irishmen who make the most of a gabby, expansive persona, this although he'd been born in suburban Oak Lawn, two generations removed from the ould sod. Of course there was plenty of drinking and exuberance and a conscious attempt to charm, followed by more drinking and excess of feeling and the cocaine he no longer used except on celebratory occasions because it got too much of a grip on him and he'd learned his lesson. He had a mobile, handsome face, blue eyes like rolling marbles, and he kept himself from going to fat with a lot of strenuous gym work. He wasn't anybody's idea of a good idea but he was available and agreeable. In bed he was enthusiastic, if sometimes sloppy from alcohol, and largely oblivious to his partner's needs in a way that Bonnie found restful. So many men were intent on demonstrating, in the most exhausting manner, their skill set and well-studied choreography. Patrick was the sexual equivalent of a meal from McDonald's.

"You could do something else besides tend bar," Bonnie told him. "Take some classes, maybe business classes. See what's out there for you." Because he wasn't stupid, just indolent and sunk in his bad habits. Patrick shrugged this and all other advice away, saying didn't she know what they said about the Irish? They were as common as whale shit on the bottom of the ocean. He knew his limits. He was a working stiff barkeep and that was good enough for him. Bonnie was aware that she might be trying to turn him into one of those comic book heroes she and Jane used to pine after and make fun of back in the day, the lumberjack with the shelf of Great Books. Or maybe she'd just grown up with alcoholics, like her falling-apart brother (now on his second tour of rehab), and she found entirely too much familiar comfort in their antics, and in attempting to prop them up and talk them out of romanticizing their failures.

"Hey girl!" was Patrick's standard, cheerful greeting across the bar. To Bonnie and to everybody else. Bonnie suspected he used it so that he would not have to remember anyone's name. "Why haven't I seen your pretty face in here for so long?" The women ate it up. With Patrick, of course, there was no question of fidelity, no expectation of seriousness. And that too could be restful. From time to time, much younger women attached themselves to him, and then there might be some public pageant of a girl sitting at one end of the bar while Patrick busied himself at the other, and intense conversations and tears and stormings off, as Patrick smiled and attempted to look embarrassed.

And then Bonnie would tease him about being a heartbreaker and Patrick would say, "Ah, but I never thought the heart came with the rest of the goods, darlin'," and Bonnie would tell him not to talk with a brogue, it was affected.

But she thought he was right about some things, from time to time, namely, that the heart often tagged along in inconvenient ways.

∽

She and Jane headed back to the Aviary, where Eric and the children were waiting for them, ready to move on. Everyone seemed to have gotten a second wind. Jane too looked visibly cheered up. She reached out to smooth Grace's hair, while Robbie asked his mother if he could get a pet snake since they never did get a dog, and snakes were easier than dogs anyway. Jane said that they would think about it. Robbie said that what she really meant was no, and Jane said that if Robbie found out everything that was needed to know about snakes, they would seriously consider it. Eric said he was pretty sure once Robbie did his research on snakes, he would not want one, and Robbie said he would too, and the four of them enjoyed a little moment then, teasing each other about the snake they knew very well would never take up residence, still believing, some of them, in the possibility of a dog, a wonderful, big-hearted, handsome dog who would love each of them uncritically and forever.

Bonnie knew each of them so well. Perhaps better than she ought to. They were the family she'd chosen, as opposed to the damaged one she'd been born into. She was the closest thing they had to a dog. Or no, that was ludicrous. She might be the closest thing they had to a snake.

Watching them now, she felt that she was not theirs, nor they hers, not really. She might try, in ways both innocent and less so, to attach herself to them, but she was only fooling herself. She was alone, alone, alone, and that never changed.

And then, just as Bonnie was in the middle of these pitiful thoughts, Eric cruised up behind her and lightly cupped her shoulder with one hand, drawing her back in, making her a part of things once more, setting off small star-shaped explosions beneath her skin, and everything was all right, at least for this moment, this precarious balance of happiness.

They visited the reptiles, or rather, Eric and Robbie and Bonnie did so, since Grace was not a big fan of scaly, slithering things, and elected to sit this one out with Jane. They got distant and disappointing glimpses of some of the big cats, lions and snow leopards, since it was too hot for them to leave the shady spots of their enclosures. They watched the polar bears diving into their rocky pools and emerging slicked down and untidy. They took a quick tour of the fornicating monkeys. They viewed giraffes and zebras and, from underwater viewing stations, the sociable bottle-nosed dolphins.

Finally they finished up at one of the cafes, eating hot dogs and pizza slices and french fries, all the things that Jane did not usually allow the children, and this was a big hit. The children were tired but not distressed. The day had been a success. Bonnie said good-bye to them in the parking lot. "See?" she said to Jane. "You did it. Fun happened." She told the kids they were her sweethearts, she waved and said Adios to Eric, keeping everything jaunty and carefree, although it had exhausted her to do so, and she drove home wanting nothing more than a margarita and a spell of oblivion.

But when she turned onto her block, she saw a police cruiser's revolving blue lights, and an ambulance pulled up in the drive. Neighbors, those she did and did not know, stood around in witnessing clumps.

Bonnie parked on the street and made her way over to the group containing Mr. Hopkins the retired bus driver, the Dumplings, who looked more than ever as if they had begun their existence as a single cell, and a few other people she might have nodded to here and there. "What happened?" she asked, although she thought she already knew.

"Mrs. Popek passed away," said Mr. Hopkins, in a tone that managed to be both respectful and avid. "The daughter found her." He nodded at a middle-aged woman with a sturdy blond hairdo, talking to one of the cops. Bonnie thought she recognized the cop from one of her training sessions, but she didn't feel inclined to go butt in.

"What did she die of?" Bonnie asked. The others didn't know.

"She was old," offered Fern Dumpling. She and her husband wore boy and girl versions of the same khaki shorts, which extended down to their unlovely knees.

"Really old," said Ed Dumpling. "Eighty something. Anything can happen at that age."

"Well now," said Mr. Hopkins, "as a senior citizen myself I can tell you, you don't take it that casual."

"Oh nobody's talking about you, Don," said a man Bonnie didn't know. She thought he lived across the street in the house with the front yard of green-painted cement.

"You're indestructible," a woman, perhaps his wife, added.

"Oh am I," Mr. Hopkins said. "Good to know. Thanks."

"Sad, her dying alone like that," Fern said. "Just her and that awful Polish radio."

"She did like that radio," said Mr. Hopkins. "A good deal more than I liked hearing it."

Fern seemed energized by Mrs. Popek's dying. Already she'd made more conversation than Bonnie had ever heard from her. Now she said, "At least she had the daughter to check on her. Some don't even have that much."

"Excuse me," Mr. Hopkins said. "I'm going to go have a word." He walked over to the daughter, who was still in conversation with the cop, and touched her elbow. The daughter turned toward him and listened as he spoke, then folded her arms and seemed to crumple into herself.

"Now why did you say that?" Ed Dumpling asked his wife. "You know the guy doesn't have any family, anything like that." As he spoke he seemed to become aware that Bonnie too might take offense. "She didn't mean you," Ed told Bonnie. "You're not even close to old."

"Plus you do have company stopping by," Fern said.

"I'm heading inside now," Bonnie said, turning her back on them and walking away so that Fern could gossip about her.

She sat at her dining room table with the bottle of premixed margaritas, drinking them out of a water glass. She heard feet on the stairs and, overhead, someone moving from room to room, doing those things you did when someone died. The Dumplings' door opened and closed as they shut themselves in to process the day's excitement. The ambulance pulled away, and the police car, and finally everything was quiet, and the next time she thought to look outside it was dark.

Bonnie didn't call Eric the next day, or the day after, nor did he call her, which was not unheard of but not their usual pattern. He did call her the next day after work on his drive home, and that had a sense of duty and excuse about it as he detailed all of the impossible pressures and urgencies of his work life. The maddening hospital routines and short-comings that interfered with the thing you most wanted to do, which was care for your patients. They deserved better than the hurry-up, aggravated, pressurized self he brought to appointments and bedsides. He was going to make a real effort to get on top of this. Focus. Remind himself of all those things he already knew.

"That's a good idea," Bonnie said. "Admirable."

"What's wrong?" Eric said after a moment.

She didn't speak. She was crying stupid tears. "I wish you'd talk to me," Eric said. "Hold on, I have to go to Bluetooth."

That helped dry her up. She hated talking to him when he switched over to the car phone and his voice receded into a metallic echo chamber. "OK," he said in his Martian car voice, "what's going on?"

"I guess I've just been reminding myself of all the things I already know."

"What happened? What are you so upset about all of a sudden?"

"It's not all of a sudden," Bonnie said, wondering if that was true. "Look, let's talk some other time, this phone drives me crazy."

"This might be the best chance I have for a while."

"Well that right there is a good reason," Bonnie said, and waited through a space of his saying nothing. "Look, we can talk some other time if you want. It's not like I'm mad."

She hadn't managed this very well and he was the one who was mad. He said, "So what are you, exactly? If you don't mind saying."

"Tired, I guess."

"What?"

"Tired," she said loudly, but the connection scrambled and cut out.

So that was that, except of course it wasn't. It was only a tug at one end of the knot that drew the tangles into a worse snarl, and so a few days later Bonnie called Eric. She got his voice mail, as she expected she would, and left him a message saying that she was thinking of him and she hoped they'd talk soon. Eric waited a few days after that to call her back and she expected that too. He spoke as if attempting to come to terms with an exasperating child. "I don't understand, why now. What brought on this crisis of hurt feelings, if that's what it is. Because I've got no clue."

He was the one with the hurt feelings, though it wouldn't have helped anything to say so. Bonnie said, "I guess you just reach a point where things aren't sustainable. You can't predict it. I'm sorry. It doesn't mean I'm mad at you or tired of you"—except that she was, a little—"it just means things don't work anymore. Too much dishonesty. Jane's my oldest friend, for God's sake. Where are you, anyway?"

"Me? I'm in my office. Why?"

"Just wondering." He wasn't trying to fit her in during some errand run or commute, and she was glad for that. All you ever had to do for a man to take you more seriously was to up and leave.

"Can I say something that's going to sound really self-serving but it's true? I always thought it was . . . not all right, entirely, with you, but better—more genuine—than with somebody Jane didn't know. Because there's all this real feeling among the three of us. Because she loves you too."

"Yes, that is self-serving," Bonnie said. *What? What?* Was he declaring his love, was that one more advantage of ending an affair? On the way out the door you might hear the most amazing things from a man. "Look, let's leave this in some good place. Because you know we're going to see each other. We'll have to."

"Yeah, we can go back to the zoo." He sounded glum now, realizing that Bonnie might be serious and things between them had come to an end.

"Not the zoo, please."

"Did I screw up? Did I do something then, something that made you think, 'I can't stand this guy anymore'?"

"Eric."

"You're taking yourself away from me and I know I'm not entitled to you or any part of you and there's nothing I can do about it. Don't expect me to be around if Jane invites you over for lunch or whatever, not for a good long while, because I can't do it."

"Eric," she said again, but he'd hung up.

One of the sad things, though one she certainly deserved, was that she couldn't talk to Jane about the end of the affair. Couldn't blab about this or that annoying or heartbreaking development, couldn't lament and complain as she'd been used to doing for the last twenty years. Well, it was a kid's stupid habit, all those too-personal disclosures. She should be beyond that by now. Grow up.

Still, she missed her time with Jane. Missed it every bit as much as she missed Eric.

She didn't want to be alone. She never had. But every wrongheaded choice she made seemed to funnel her into the alone zone.

Bonnie spent the next week keeping busy at work, cleaning her apartment, even attempting to cook meals. All the things you did when you'd had a breakup and needed to get used to the idea and move on. Eric didn't call and Bonnie didn't expect him to. She congratulated herself on not coming up with some necessary and unimpeachable reason for calling him. Like, having heart attack symptoms, needing a sudden surgical consultation. By Saturday night, lonesome and bored with herself, she drove to the bar where Patrick worked to see if he might cheer her up.

She didn't get there until after eleven, since the evening didn't take shape until then, and if there was some other girl Patrick was sniffing around, Bonnie would find something else to do. You couldn't get your hopes up, even if your hopes were not very elevated in the first place.

She found a good parking place, right across the street from the bar. The front windows were half-covered with wooden shutters and the light behind them was a convivial red and yellow. Bonnie tried to get herself into the mind-set of an adventure, an intrigue. A night out on the town, involving certain pleasant, rowdy possibilities. But she was tired of walking into places alone and trying to look like she enjoyed it or at least didn't mind, and she almost started the car up again and drove home. Instead she fluffed her hair, got out of the car, and headed across the street for the next good time.

Bonnie locked onto Patrick right away, one of three bartenders working a busy Saturday night. He was wearing a red T-shirt that might as well have had SEX printed across it in strobing letters.

She watched him even as she took in the room, making a quick decision about where to sit. Not at the bar, she decided. Not right away. There was room at the end of a long table with a group of people she knew well enough to join, and so she settled herself there and said her hellos. It was a neighborhood place with a steady, older clientele, by which Bonnie meant, older than herself. On weekends it drew a younger, sassier crowd who pumped up the noise factor and were inclined to misbehave. Patrick's red shirt orbited in and out of her vision like a wayward erotic planet. You had to wonder how many other patrons, male and female both, were tracking him. He'd done so much lifting and other muscle work that his torso looked nearly anatomical. He did his chores behind the bar with ease and more than a bit of swagger, and Bonnie felt herself pulsing agreeably.

Had he seen her? She couldn't tell. She supposed that sooner or later she'd have to get up and sashay around, make a trip to the ladies' or something. A server came and took her drink order. Bonnie talked with the people around her in a way that did not distract her from her own thoughts. Bar conversations about the Cubs (bad), the hot weather (worse), who'd seen what's-his-name lately. Her Scotch and soda came and she drank just enough so that the alcohol could do its thing. A hard knot of sad was stuck in her throat and she guessed it was going to be with her for a while.

She missed Eric, missed the habit of him and missed him for himself. Missed him for his faults as much as his lovely and loving self. Well, pine away. She was an idiot, as she already well knew. She watched Patrick lean back from the bar, resting with his arms behind him. When he did this his shirt rode up and showed a few inches of furry stomach. Lordy Sweet Jesus. She guessed she should just keep drinking and fall into bed with Patrick and pretend he was Eric, or no. That hardly seemed wholesome. If she wanted to give wholesome a try.

Meanwhile, looky here! Patrick was waving and grinning at her, yes her, not somebody next to her or behind her, and now Bonnie was waving back and smirking like the fool she was. For her next drink, which was coming all too soon, she'd take herself up to the bar. Just to say hello.

Nothing ventured, nothing gained. Eric never liked her going out nights by herself. He disapproved, which delighted Bonnie. It was so retro, so chivalrous! "Women should be escorted," he said, severely. The idea, of course, was that they needed protection from uncouth men. It did not occur to him that society might need protecting from the likes of Bonnie.

She had to stop thinking about him. It made her melancholy. It made her feel like a bad joke to herself. She guessed she prided herself on having poor impulse control, made it into a kind of virtue. Which was fine if you were, say, a zoo animal. She reached the bottom of her drink and waited to let it settle. Patrick drew two beers, topping them off perfectly, and set them down on the bar without jostling their foam collars. Maybe he was right to call himself a simple barkeep, to want no more than what he had, be no more than what he was. So what was the matter with her, always at odds with herself, always bemoaning her faults without, as Jane said, doing much of anything to change them? Not that she wanted to think about Jane either.

Bonnie gathered her purse and stood, leaving her empty drink glass in case she decided to come back to the table. There was a space at Patrick's end of the bar where she could slide in to order. A very normal, nonprovocative thing to do. On the way she stopped to talk to somebody she knew, taking her time. In her next life, she was going to be one of those women who held themselves aloof, who genuinely did not care, and then the men swarmed all over them.

Patrick was deep in conversation with two of the old man regulars, wizened alcoholics who had grown to the bar stools like moss, and what either of them had to say that was so interesting was beyond her. Bonnie stood and waited and eventually one of the other bartenders got her drink for her. She turned to head back to her table and that's when Patrick called out to her, "Hey! Bonnie, hey!"

She pretended not to hear him and he had to call her again and then she had to pretend surprise. "Oh, hey Patrick. How's it going?"

"What?" He cupped his hand to one ear. He had a handsome, oversized face, like a movie actor's. Big jaw, craggy forehead.

"I said, how's it going tonight?"

"Crazy busy." By this time of the evening he was a little sweaty, a little disheveled. He pushed his damp hair back from his forehead with one hand and grinned. Bonnie had a wobbly moment of remembering her own wet skin smacking rhythmically against his.

"Yeah, you look busy." They had to shout to hear each other.

"Saturday." He raised his hands and let them fall to his sides. Unable to convey in words the amazing properties of a Saturday.

"Comes between Friday and Sunday," Bonnie said helpfully. Getting a conversation going tonight was like trying to strike a spark from a damp stick. "OK, well . . ."

"Hold on a minute." A waitress needed a drink order filled and he tended to her while Bonnie looked on. Another waitress crowded in behind the first. "I want to talk to you," Patrick said over his shoulder. "Why don't you . . . Here." A seat opened up at the bar and he pointed her toward it. "Let me get caught up, give me a sec, OK?"

Bonnie squeezed herself into the narrow space and perched on the stool to wait. Things were looking up, even if talking hadn't seemed to be something he'd been able to do just a minute ago. She wondered if he was going to work all the way up to three a.m. close, which would be a lot of time to kill and she'd definitely have to switch to club soda or fall asleep in a chair or both. She checked herself out in the mirror behind the bar. She thought she looked all right, that is, she looked the way she always did. The mirror was crowded with a row of bottles, things nobody ever drank, like Drambuie and Pernod and Cherry Heering. There was also a layer of postcards tucked into the mirror frame, various Cubs and Bears tokens, last spring's St. Patrick's Day green and gold garland, an old black and white photograph of a top-heavy woman in a striped sweater, a plaque containing a mechanical talking fish, more. And in the middle of all that, and further obscured by her cloud of hair, was her wary face peeking out like a forest creature from the underbrush.

Then Patrick was leaning over the bar and beckoning to her to lean forward too. Now what, he needed privacy? The place was so loud, you could plot murder without anyone overhearing. "Hey cutie," he said. A whiff of his hot breath reached her, a not entirely pleasant sensation. "Can I ask you something? A favor?"

"What kind of a favor?" Wary.

"I have a chance to buy a little blow." He leaned back to see what she thought of that.

"Not the best idea you ever had. What do you mean, a favor?" Although she thought she already knew.

"If you could loan me, say, a hundred and fifty. I can get an eight."

"I don't think so."

"Come on. Fun. What do you have against fun?"

"Patrick," she said in a tone of sorrowful disapproval.

"It's only once in a moon. I can't afford it more often than that."

"Sounds like you can't afford it now."

He made an impatient face, then somebody farther down the bar needed a refill and he went to tend to them. Bonnie was left alone to sit and feel dismal. Patrick had a bit of a history with substances and if he was going down that road again, she needed to back off and leave him be.

Not that she had anything against the occasional drug holiday. The occasional cocaine-fueled fuckathon.

But why did he have to ask her for money?

Patrick must have had his own second thoughts. Here he was again, planted in front of her.

"Look, I'm sorry. I shouldn't have—"

"Yeah, it's all right."

"I thought maybe . . ."

"It's all right," Bonnie said again. "It's your business, not mine."

"No, I can't argue with you. Moment of weakness." He reached for a glass and fixed Bonnie a new Scotch and soda. "This one's on me."

"You don't have to—"

"Please. Least I can do."

"Thanks," Bonnie said, and then he was gone again, working the bar, talking up a customer, making change, wiping down the bar surface. When he got back to Bonnie, he said, "I'm getting too old for this job."

"You're not old."

"I can't keep up the pace like I used to. I need to figure out something else I'm good for besides having my first heart attack at forty-five, like my old man."

"That's just Celtic doom talk. It's maudlin, cut it out. You could do anything you set your mind to."

Patrick didn't answer right away, only scanned the bar briefly, watching for empty glasses, troublemakers, whoever it was that wanted to sell him an eightball. He did seem tired tonight. His eyes had a dry, abraded look that aged him. He saw Bonnie staring at him, smiled, shrugged.

"Did I tell you I applied for a manager's job? You know Kevin, the guy with the red beard? He's moving to Texas. Don't ask me why anybody would do that. Anyway. I tell them I want a shot at it, I want to step up my game, not to mention a real salary. You know what they come back with? I'm a valued team member. My skills are a great match for my current position. Meaning, I'm too stupid to run the place. They don't want to give me the keys and let me hire and fire and schedule."

"I'm sorry. They're not being fair."

"Yeah, but that doesn't mean they're wrong."

"So apply for a manager job someplace else. They're stuck here, they only think of you as a bartender."

"I'll do that," Patrick said. "Just as soon as I update my résumé."

They looked away from each other then and out over the room, which was packed with people at the tables, and in between the tables. People stood two deep at the bar, everybody working on their best Saturday-night drunk, all loudy rowdy and crowdy. The old timers getting cross-eyed, the young kids in their punk T-shirts and half-scalped hairdos and little hats. Patrick turned back to her.

"You ever get so sick of yourself, you might as well run headfirst into a wall? Or maybe not a wall. Maybe it's a . . . mattress." Here he made such a funny, mugging face, his eyebrows arching like a lecherous comedy villain's, that Bonnie giggled in spite of herself. "Oh yeah, party time! What the hell. It's not like I'm saving myself for anything."

"Come on," Bonnie said. "It's not so bad, being you. You're like, lord of all you survey."

"Yes, and it's all of it lovely." He wriggled his eyebrows again and went off to fill another drink order.

Bonnie sat for a time, calculating. She finished her drink and looked at the one Patrick had bought her, took a few sips, put it down again. He'd mixed it extra strong and it sent a new current of loopy merriment through her. Good idea, bad idea, fun idea. She thought she could afford it, and she thought she could keep from telling herself it was some selfless gesture designed to cheer Patrick up at a low point. Although she guessed it would do that too.

There was a convenience store around the corner with an ATM and it wouldn't be too hard to get herself there and back without being mugged. She slipped off the bar stool and waved down one of the other bartenders, told him she was coming back in a couple of minutes, don't get rid of her drink, OK? Now that she'd made up her mind, she was excited and in a hurry, wanting to get it done before she changed her stupid mind or lost her nerve. She pushed her way to the door, past people who didn't want to let her through, and she was a little under the influence or maybe more than a little but not so much she couldn't manage a simple, semi-criminal transaction.

Once she was outside she had to stop and get her bearings in this whole different night time—this gliding sliding darkness and its smears of light, the cars thumping by, the sidewalk requiring some concentration and effort on her part. The convenience store was thisaway. Or thataway.

She set off for it. A man passed by and maybe he said something to her, she couldn't be sure. Asshole.

The convenience store looked like an armed robbery waiting to happen, a grim place with the cashier behind a plexiglass shield and coolers full of Keystone and Busch and headache in a bottle of wine. Slim Jims and bagged snacks that were already half-dust, cigarettes in a cage, a Middle Eastern clerk who'd seen it all. Someone was already using the ATM, a boy and girl having trouble getting their card to work and giggling about it. Hurry up, Bonnie told them silently. You didn't want to absent yourself for too long when it came to barroom intrigues. Things were, in all senses of the word, fluid.

She was still in line behind the couple when her phone buzzed. She fished it out and stared at it. Eric, it said, or rather, WALGREENS, the code she'd used for him in case Jane ever happened to get her hands on Bonnie's phone, and wasn't she clever. The phone buzzed again. What the hell was he doing? It was after midnight. "Hello?" Bonnie said, squeezing the phone up against her shoulder in a pretense of privacy.

She couldn't hear anything. "Hello?" she said again, as the couple finished their business and she fumbled for her own card. Two men walked in behind her, crowding the space and making drunk noise.

"Bonnie? Where are you?"

"What?" It was hard to hear with the racket of the store.

"I said, where are you?"

"Why do you—wait, you better not be at my place. Are you at my place?"

"Calm down. I'm at home, where else would I be."

"What do you want?" Bonnie said, trying to fathom the machine in front of her, watching the men behind her in the reflections of the glass window. Her heart was making rabbity thumps. "It's Saturday night, I'm out, where else would I be."

"All right, look, I just wanted to say hello."

"Yeah, hello." Bonnie swiped her card and the screen lit up with expensive options. Did she want to accept the bank fee? Get fast cash? She tried to enter a hundred and fifty but the machine balked.

Eric said, "OK, I guess you're in the middle of something. I guess you don't have to be overjoyed or anything. But I don't like the way we left things." He waited. "Bonnie? What are you doing, it sounds like you're in a street fight."

Getting money for cocaine so I can get myself laid, she didn't say. "That's exactly what it is, a street fight. I really can't talk right now." She punched in a hundred dollars fast cash. That looked like the best the machine would let her do.

"I wish," Eric said, "that I could find some right way or right time to talk to you, but maybe there's no such thing. So look, you were loved. Still are. That counts for something. It's worth something. I wish there wasn't this blazing heap of wreckage all around it, and I guess you don't have to help me feel better about myself. But there it is."

Bonnie didn't answer. Eric said, "You're the most intense person I ever met, you know that? Always full steam ahead. Always restless. It's scary to watch sometimes, it's like, I don't know, some really scenic natural disaster. I don't know what you're looking for. But I sure hope you find it."

The machine was shooting twenty-dollar bills into a stack, making its whir and chunk noises. Bonnie held the phone away so he couldn't hear it. "Hey, Eric . . ."

"Just don't ever sell yourself short," Eric said, and then the call ended.

Bonnie gathered up the money and headed back out to the street and the humid, jittery darkness and *fuckety fuck*, there was nobody to tell and what would you say anyway, why was he not here, if he cared so much, meant so much? Why be angry for no reason/no good reason, why answer the phone in the first place if she hadn't wanted to hear what he had to say? Well she had, and it hadn't helped anything.

Walking back into the tavern was like walking back into a mouth. It closed over her and mumbled her this way and that while she tried to get back to the bar. Once she reached it, her drink was gone and somebody else had taken her seat, no surprise, so she looked around for Patrick, didn't see him at first. The fizzy part of drinking had gone out of her and left her with a headache just starting up like an itch in her brain. Where was he? It was too crowded to move freely. She nudged her way along the bar until she spotted him sitting at one end, taking a break, it looked like, with a beer in front of him.

"Patrick!"

He didn't see or hear her and Bonnie said, "Excuse me," over and over as she advanced. She waved at him and now he did notice and waved back, still absorbed in conversation with two girls with dyed hair (one pink, one shoe-polish black), both of them as scraggly as stray cats. Now what? How was she supposed to get him the money, was there any way that didn't scream drug deal?

First, of course, she had to get to him. She'd stalled out and wasn't going to come any closer unless she climbed over the bar. Bonnie got an elbow in, planted it on the bar and ordered a 7UP, and stood sideways waiting for it. She asked the bartender to tell Patrick she needed to talk to him. Watched as the message was conveyed, as Patrick had another pull of his beer, put it down, all cool and unhurried and like to drive her crazy, then sauntered along the back of the bar until he reached her. "Hey Bon."

No way to be subtle. "You remember when you loaned me some cash? Well I have a hundred of it for you." She held out the twenties, folded over in an effort to look at least half-assed discreet.

"Yeah? Really? Thanks, sweetie." He leaned over and gave her a smacking kiss on the forehead, grinned.

"I hope it helps."

"It sure does. I'll get it back to you real soon. Promise."

"Not a problem. You working till close?"

"I'm thinking I can get away early."

"Excellent," she said, nodding, beginning to relax, her skin warming as if it had been polished.

Again he leaned in toward her. "Want me to save a little for you?"

"Ha ha," Bonnie laughed. "You better."

So funny. He gave her a wink and took his slow time getting back to the far end of the bar. Finished his beer. Stood and reached behind him to make sure he had his keys and wallet. Bonnie watched him pocket the twenties, roll his neck around to loosen the kinks. Then he put an arm around the girl with the shoe polish black hair and the two of them, walking unsteadily since the girl was so much shorter, made their round-about way to the door. The girl's face was set in a half-smile of private amusement, and although she kept her gaze fixed on the floor and did not look at Bonnie, it felt like the girl had managed somehow to know everything about her.

ordinary, again

She didn't *know* know. But there was a way in which things came to her.

Once the certainty settled, Jane thought, of course. Of course it had been Bonnie. It was such a reckless, wrongheaded, Bonnie-type thing to do. Not that Jane had gone looking for guilty e-mails or anything distasteful like that. The notion just slid into place in her brain and clicked. In the same way she was sure that, for whatever reason, things between Bonnie and Eric had ceased. It was as if the air around them had changed, lost some of its charge.

She guessed she should be furious at Bonnie, hurt, betrayed, disappointed, etc., but really it was more like exasperation. Did Bonnie never learn? Never check herself, talk herself out of anything?

As for Eric, if she was not disappointed in him, it was because she was not capable of any further disappointments.

She didn't care to think about how it might have come about. She did not picture such things. There was a sense in which she could be said to have no imagination, and there were times this might be considered fortunate. Whose fault, who to blame? What did it matter? People who let sex push them one way or another never wanted to believe they could do anything to stop it. You might as well go all the way back to the snake in the Garden of Eden. The irresistible apple. Yes, apples, red and green and yellow, tawny or shining, all the colors and tastes you might imagine because this was paradise and there was no need to confine yourself to just one apple, just one woman.

Apple apple apple. Then Bonnie said, "Somebody should tell her he's not worth it," and Jane struggled through layers of cottony panic and realized that she was looking at actual apples right in front of her. Spacing out again in the middle of conversations, television shows, and now, grocery shopping and she could not let that happen. Where had her list gone? Why so many apples? Think!

Her mind chased itself around in scurrying circles. Oh, because. Because it was that time of year, the harvest. What a relief, to come up with a reason. If you could entertain any such quaint notion as "harvest" in the vast, efficient commercial process that brought the apples from tree to market while outside it was still late summer and miserably hot, something gone wrong with the sequence of growth, the seasons, the entire planet, they said, no, too much, stop. All the things she had to put herself through in order not to think about Bonnie.

But here was Bonnie herself, whom she had forgotten about, or wanted to forget about, standing in front of her with an expectant scowl on her face, needing an answer.

"Who?" Jane said. "Tell who?"

❦

What was Jane thinking? What was she ever thinking? Entranced by the ingredient list for make-ahead casseroles? Writing poems in her head? You never knew. Bonnie had been carrying the conversation by herself for some time now, trying to strike a spark. Going on about the weather, about which vegetables one might, or might not, wish to eat, about her car, for God's sake—the last, desperate throw of the dice. Hello, hello, anybody home?

Not that Jane wasn't often spaced out, not quite on target. It was her medicine, all that brain candy. There were side effects. The medicine got her turned around, Jane said, and led her to trip over her own feet, if your brain had such a thing as feet, which was foolish but perhaps Bonnie knew what she meant? And Bonnie did, from long experience with the overmedicated population. But you had to wonder if Jane was not entirely unhappy to be skimming just above the surface of her day's chores, her day's routines, gaining a peculiar kind of power by absenting herself. Who would have thought it? Jane being Jane was a force to be reckoned with.

Meanwhile, Bonnie was moping around being Bonnie. Her dismaying episode with Patrick had been two weeks ago, and she had not been able to resist compounding her humiliation by calling him, by arguing with him, accusing and berating and weeping and raging. Which never helped anything, only left you feeling weak and empty. Patrick had brushed her off at first, then turned annoyed and defensive. He'd never promised, etc. It was not his fault if Bonnie had misunderstood. He was going to pay back the money, she didn't have to worry about that, OK? Just as soon as he got a little bit ahead. Since when did she get so touchy anyway, so . . . Bonnie heard him trying to come up with another word besides "bitchy." So needy. Possessive. His voice took on a plaintive note. She was always such a good sport.

Yes she was. And that was her whole problem. A good time good sport and way too careless about the damage she did to herself and to everyone else. "Screw you," Bonnie said, and hung up on him.

She stomped around the apartment, swearing a little more. Then when she trailed off, she called Patrick back and got his voice mail, and who could blame him for not picking up. "Look, I'm sorry," she said, into the waiting hum. "You're right. I overreacted. I've been feeling . . ." Her turn to come up with a word. "Vulnerable. Not your fault. Never mind." She almost said that he should keep the damned money but she didn't want to let him off that easy. "Take care."

She'd hung up, feeling she'd reclaimed at least a bit of her equilibrium, if not her dignity. Of course the one she really wanted to talk to was Eric, but that wasn't going to happen. She missed him. He missed her too, he'd said so. Well, it had run its course. Adios. She was having a hard time leaving it be. It was as if something had been torn out of her, root and branch. Some idea of herself that had grown up alongside Jane and Eric and was now sundered. Well, suffer in silence, since she could hardly expect Jane to listen to a bunch of lovelorn blather about her own husband. And so by default, she was forced to complain about Patrick. As she had been doing for much of today's visit.

She had not planned on coming out to see Jane on this Saturday, but here she was, and maybe it was just as well. Sooner or later she'd have to resume some semblance of normal relations with them. Come to dinner. Go back to the zoo. Jane said that Eric had taken the kids to some organized funland, to atone for his many late hours and many missed family dinners. "How about I stop by," Bonnie had said, seeing an opportunity.

So here she was, trailing after Jane in the everyday boredom of a suburban grocery store. Not that she had anything much better to do. Why not ruminate over root vegetables? Love among the cabbages. She would make herself ill with wisecracks.

She would do better from now on. Be better. She could hardly help but improve, given this particular low point. Try to operate on some other level besides gratification, selfishness, vanity. There had to be some more worthy effort you could make, even if, you had to admit, it might not be as much fun as orgasm.

Trailing after Jane, she had to maneuver around a cart full of cardboard produce boxes, grapefruit, it looked like, and, of more interest, the young couple next to it, engaged in a low-key but public argument. The boy worked here. One of the produce guys. He was supposed to be unloading the grapefruit but the girl had come to track him down and confront him. That much seemed clear, and he was plenty pissed off about that. He kept looking around and jamming his hands in his pockets, not wanting anyone he knew to witness. Bonnie caught some of it as she passed them, all ears but not wanting to seem obvious about eavesdropping. "I can't talk now," the boy was saying. "I'm working, OK?"

"Well when can you? It's not like you ever . . ."

Bonnie moved on, but turned around once she'd reached the end of the aisle and pretended to be sorting through the packaged carrot and celery sticks. She could still hear them, from time to time, and now she had a good view of them. Oh honey, she wanted to tell the girl. Give it up. There was nothing about the boy to recommend him, nothing at all, just another sweaty loudmouth—even trying to keep from being overheard, he was loud—who would continue to treat her badly, out of indifference or arrogance. The girl was too pitiful. That beseeching, heartbroken face. As if that would soften him, make him change his ways. How old were they anyway? Not old. A year, maybe two, past high school. Bonnie hoped to God they didn't have children. Or maybe this was what the quarrel was about. She was pregnant, and he was saying it was her problem, not his. Maybe she had gotten pregnant on purpose. Girls did that sometimes, thought their boyfriends would go all mushy at the idea of babies or at least come around in time, or maybe it was just stupid vindictiveness, or some peculiar process for preserving the species. Bonnie herself had never done such a thing, set a pregnancy trap. And thank God, because imagine all the dreary men she would have to be reminded of on a daily basis, long after the man himself had lost all appeal.

∽⑤

Earlier that day Jane had said, out of nowhere, "Kids can really tie you down. You do know that, don't you?" Bonnie wondered why Jane would say such a thing.

The girl was trying to keep her voice low. Some of the tone came through, some of the desperate or whiny things she had hoped not to say. Whatever convincing case she had hoped to make was falling short. The boy smirked and tried to move past her to the work cart. He said, loudly, "If you say so. Makes no nevermind to me." Because nothing she did made any difference to him, couldn't she see that? Couldn't anyone ever? The breathtaking dumbness of lovelorn girls, herself of course and always included!

Bonnie caught up with Jane, who had moved on to the apples. Positioned herself at Jane's elbow so that she was certain to be heard: "Somebody should tell her he's not worth it."

∞

A lthough Jane knew well enough that she was standing right next to her cart of food items, looking into the unexpected complications of the grocery's expansive ceiling, with its systems for lighting and ventilation and support all laid out like a blueprint or perhaps a skeleton, there was a moment when up and *down* reversed themselves, a dizzy, sick-making lurch. Was it her medicine? Or one more episode of Crazy Jane, suburban madwoman and unsuitable mother?

Her vision steadied. The intricate wires and piping and metal bracing, the braided cables and vents fit together like puzzle parts. What if you had everything wrong? Upside down, backwards, and inside out. What if she ceased to apologize for herself? Ceased to worry what they thought of her? Give crazy some room to grow, if that's what it was. She guessed Eric wouldn't much like it. He didn't get a vote anymore. As for Bonnie, here she was again, what was she even doing here?

Why had she come around, full of the same old moping and complaints that Jane, her straight man, was meant to take seriously, meant to ignore everything else? How stupid did Bonnie think she was?

And then she saw from Bonnie's startled face that she had let her thoughts betray her, as they said in old-fashioned books, and because she was not yet ready to tip her hand, say what she might have said, know what she already knew, she composed herself and said, "I never noticed how big this place is. Warehouse big. I mean, you know it from walking around, but . . ." She nodded at the ceiling. "It's just a long way down."

"Don't you mean, a long way up?" Bonnie asked, and Jane closed her eyes and when she opened them again the ceiling was turned around where it was supposed to be, and Jane agreed with Bonnie, yes, of course, she meant up.

∽

Bonnie would cut back on her drinking. There were so many good reasons to do that anyway. Focus on her work, where she was valued and needed. It was time to clean up her act. Make a fresh start. Build a Better Bonnie.

Just that morning she'd received one more hilarious e-mail from the industrious spammers of Taiwan, "Do you have ploblems with your loving life?" Yes, that was it exactly! She had ploblems! Never had it been laid out so clearly to her! Bonnie enjoyed a little ha ha at that one, because you might as well see the humor in life when you could, and set off to find whatever it was Jane had sent her for, oh yes, the olives.

∽

Jane set her groceries out for the checker and waited for the belt to advance them down to be scanned. The bright, overpackaged boxes of cereal, the plastic sheen of the meat trays, the frozen items. Of course you could not really predict the future, not exactly. But you could make other people wonder what was going to come rolling down the line next.

crisis intervention

The woman in the third floor apartment had locked herself inside after an escalating encounter during which she waved a kitchen knife and threatened to cut her stupid bitch neighbor if she did not shut her stupid bitch ass up. There had been some trouble over a man, although the man himself was long gone. A case of purloined affections. The police had been called, and upon their arrival Mrs. Jackson, Luella, had announced that the representatives of law enforcement could kiss her black ass. Now the two cops were at the apartment door, trying to get her to come out. She was not the sort of woman to open her door to police in a welcoming way.

Bonnie stayed outside, waiting to see if the officers upstairs would get tired of talking, splinter the door, and go for it. Her function was to encourage a less confrontational process. She wore a CPD vest but no uniform. Other neighbors had gathered, standing around and waiting for any entertaining developments. The day was fine and very hot. Some of the crowd had draped wet towels around their necks to cool off. Children were making the most of the last free days before school started, playing elaborate sidewalk games, taunting and whaling on each other, then ceasing combat and starting all over again. "I expect she drunk," one woman told Bonnie. It was not quite noon. "She drunk all the time."

Bonnie asked if anyone lived in the apartment with her. "Nah. Too mean and nasty."

"She run her mans off," another, younger, woman volunteered. "Nobody want to live wit her big head self. Sorry-drunk woman."

"She cause any problems like this before?"

"Mosly jus run her mouth. Whooee. She would slap Jesus, she get in a mood."

Through her shoulder mike, Bonnie could hear one of the officers talking outside the apartment: "Mrs. Jackson? We need to talk to you. Just open the door." He wasn't putting much energy into it.

Less distinctly, Bonnie heard the woman's enraged, high-volume ranting. The officer spoke into his mike. "We're kind of at the end of a conversation here," he told Bonnie.

"Can you keep it going a little longer?"

"Yeah, we can all talk about our feelings."

"Just a minute," Bonnie said. She asked the neighbor woman, "Where does she get her alcohol?"

The woman pointed toward the end of the street.

"Corner store? What time does she go there, usually?"

"Like, now times. Prolly why she so mad."

"Does she have any friends? Anybody who runs with her, who would help her?" Meaning, anybody who was on her side and might interfere.

"Not nobody. Pitiful."

"OK," Bonnie told the officer. "How about, shut it down. Tell her you'll come back later."

"You're kidding, right?"

"Just come down and talk to me." She heard some muffled talk between the two cops, no doubt agreeing what a big drag she was. "Oh, tell the neighbors to clear out. Tell them not to bother her. Walk wide."

"Yeah, that'll work. They're a peace loving bunch."

"Please," Bonnie said, "let's just try it."

A few minutes later the two cops came out, pausing on the building's stoop to talk to the people congregating there. Then they came up to Bonnie, still squinting from the sudden daylight, crescents of sweat beneath their arms. "Now what?"

"Those are her windows, right? Get in the cruiser and pull out. Make sure everybody can see you leave. Then, I'm not going to point, but down there's her neighborhood juice bar. Give her twenty minutes. I bet she'll head out to buy some of her favorite beverage. I'll stay here and watch out for her."

"Yeah? What if she comes out swinging her knife?" one of the officers asked. He was white and his partner was black. Bonnie didn't really know either of them. They were young guys, full of muscles and boys'-club arrogance. Bonnie knew their type. Oh did she ever. They were required to undergo this course of training and were facing it with a heavy dose of cop-skepticism.

"I'll be fine."

"You will," said the black cop, not impressed.

"Twenty-five yards east, in that alley. In my vehicle."

"So then we have to come save your . . ." The white cop wanted to say, ass, settled for "bacon."

"I promise I'll keep the doors locked. Low risk." She waited. They didn't have to do anything she told them, or rather, suggested. It was all advisory. They didn't want her to get knifed because then they'd have to call it in and get hung up on a lot of bullshit paperwork. The two cops traded looks that said, Let's get this over with.

"What if she doesn't come out?"

"You can always go back up there and kick in her door and drag her down three flights of stairs."

"Too hot for that."

"So give it a shot. So to speak."

They weren't inclined to do anything she said, but they didn't mind getting back into the air-conditioned cruiser. And so they climbed in and took off, while Bonnie got into her own unmarked motor-pool car and circled the block. She eased through the alley and idled at its entrance, scanning the sidewalk for Luella Johnson, and not finding her, kept her eyes fixed on the building's entrance.

It was only Wednesday and she was already dragging herself through the week. She felt restless, off her game. She'd made a point of asking to shadow Officers Hardee and Watkins, not because her shining example was going to keep them from cracking heads the next time they lost patience with somebody giving them attitude. Just to try and keep herself sharp, occupied, something other than a useless, mopey woman.

She was losing her touch. She used to be able to kid along with guys like this, show them she was on their side. Flirt and coax them into doing what she suggested. Now she guessed they looked at her like she was the high school English teacher they hadn't been able to shake.

In the end they did not have long to wait for Luella. She came out to the stoop and stood there a minute, blinking. She was tall and whip skinny, a face and body that looked wasted, as if pieces had been gouged out of her. She had ashy skin and burnt-orange hair that stood out in stiff hanks. She wore tight pink jeans and a black sleeveless shirt that had stretched itself loose at the armholes. With care, she navigated the way to the street and took a few teetering, delicate steps along the sidewalk. Prolly drunk.

She wasn't carrying a knife, or any kind of purse or bag that could contain a knife, but just as Bonnie went to radio this in, the cruiser pulled up behind Luella and both cops got out to confront her. Even taken by surprise like this, Luella put up a good fight, windmilling her long arms and twisting out of a shoulder grip, running her mouth at high speed until she was taken down and cuffed and with some effort bundled into the cruiser's backseat.

Hardee and Watkins weren't going to linger, Bonnie knew. It was always best to get yourself out of neighborhoods where arrests might prove unpopular, where hauling away even somebody like Luella could remind people of all the things they didn't like about the PoPo. By the time Bonnie was able to edge out of the alley, the cruiser was two blocks ahead. It took a while for one of them, Hardee, the white, smart-mouth one, to acknowledge her on the radio.

"Any more suggestions?"

"Nope. Just wanted to say, well done."

"Yeah, I think we achieved a real, you know, rapport with her." In the background Bonnie heard Luella, who had turned sorrowful and was howling, *Hunnh, hunnh, hunnh.*

"At least you didn't have to deal with the stairs," Bonnie said. She would have liked a little bit of grudging credit for that at least.

"Have a nice day," Hardee said, and clicked off.

Asshole. Someday he was going to manhandle the wrong suspect, somebody deaf, disabled, somebody who didn't speak English. And then there would be more of the headlines nobody wanted, and attorneys with microphones, and big money payouts, and it wouldn't do her any good to say she told them so.

By now she was in a lowdown bad mood. She would have bought Luella a drink, if she'd had the chance. The sky was the hazed-over urban gray of pollution and heat. You breathed in asphalt and chemical stink. The air-conditioning in her shitbox vehicle made the engine run hot, so rather than get stranded in this choice neighborhood next to the Dan Ryan, she switched it off and opened the window to let the rush of hot air blow over her. Good times.

Her phone rang. She snarled at it. Reached for it on the seat, fumbled, came up with it. It was Eric. What the hell. She hadn't talked to him in a month and she didn't want to talk to him now. She let the call go to voice mail and tried to maneuver from out behind a panel truck with a bad paint job that was belching clouds of evil exhaust. Would he leave a message? Bonnie waited, then the ping sounded, and she guessed she didn't have to listen to it but she knew she would.

She waited until she was back at her office and she had the place to herself, everybody else gone to lunch, to call up his message. "Bonnie, hi,

I don't know if Jane's called you yet, but she wants to meet with us. Both of us. Yeah, I know. I mean, I don't exactly know. So . . ." A pause while he did not say some number of things. ". . . I guess we'll see. OK. Talk to you later."

There it was. She put the phone down and let herself sit without thinking or moving, letting dread rise in her. Whatever Jane had to say or do, she guessed they had it coming. It might even be a relief to get it out in the open. But not right away.

First she'd have to get through whatever confrontation Jane wanted to have. Or a meeting? Why did he say meeting? Like, an ambush? Jane wasn't the type to go after anyone with a kitchen knife, at least, it was hard to imagine her threatening to draw blood with her wedding present Wusthof Classics. She would tell Bonnie she never wanted to see her again. Heap some names on her. Fair enough. She was accustomed to heaping those same names on herself.

Or maybe it was something entirely different. Jane was going to open a yoga studio or some other exciting plan, she wanted their blessing.

Eric had not said that she should call him back, and Bonnie didn't want to do so. Nor could she call Jane and say, I understand you'd like to set up a meeting, possibly to discuss my behind-your-back affair with your husband. There was nothing to do except wait for Jane's call. Which came in the form of another voice mail message the next day while Bonnie was in a conference and had her phone off.

"Bonnie? Can you come to dinner on Sunday? I'm thinking around seven. I'll feed the kids ahead of time, they really can't wait that late. Let me know if you can't come, otherwise just show up. Oh, no need to bring anything. Bye."

No need to bring what, lawyers? Armaments? Reparations? Jane had sounded the way she always did. Sunday night dinner, as they'd done any number of times before. Maybe it was the yoga studio.

She went back and forth, thinking about calling Eric, calling Jane, fishing around to find out what was in store, or launching a preemptive apology. In the end she did not. Partly out of cowardice, partly because she figured she deserved whatever was coming to her.

Sunday came and Bonnie got herself as ready as she could and drove out to the suburbs. A spell of rain had broken the heat. Her tires made a whisking sound on the wet pavement. In spite of what Jane had said, she equipped herself with a bottle of decent red wine that could serve as a peace offering, or an anesthetic, or even to help disguise bloodstains.

She parked on the street, as she always did, and stopped to look around at the pretty houses. Even with the recent rains the lawns looked bleached out from the dry summer. The sun was setting earlier now, the kind of thing Bonnie never noticed until she was in a place where you might actually have a chance to see the horizon. What if she took herself out to the wilderness? A mountaintop or a seashore? Would she activate some preindustrial portion of her brain, learn to navigate by the stars and gather edible plants? But now she was procrastinating.

Jane met her at the door. "I told you not to bring anything," she said, taking custody of the wine. "Come on in, I've got to . . ." Trailing off, leading the way back to the kitchen. Normal Jane, preoccupied with getting the meal on the table. Bonnie followed. The house was quiet. No television. The children otherwise occupied. Eric not in evidence. Sound of water running upstairs.

Jane stood at the counter, chopping something. She was always careful and precise about her kitchen work and the knife made methodical *snicking* sounds. The oven was on, but Bonnie couldn't detect any smell from it. "What's for dinner?" she asked.

"It's a surprise."

"Oh, sure."

"Or more like, an experiment." Jane left the heap of radishes she'd been turning into thin rounds and opened the refrigerator.

"Can I help?"

"Open the wine, maybe."

"Sure." Bonnie found the corkscrew. "Want some?"

"Not right now. Take some to Eric, why don't you, he's out back."

"Sure." Bonnie poured out two tumbler-style glasses and maneuvered carefully past the open refrigerator and Jane's contemplation of it. It was hard to tell if she should feel more or less nervous after this normal-seeming encounter. Jane still had not really looked at her. But maybe she was just intent on whatever it was she was cooking. A pig's head. A par-boiled bunny.

Eric was sitting in a lawn chair on the paved patio, surrounded by a summer's worth of sports equipment and outdoor toys. He looked up as Bonnie came out, then away. "Hi," she said, handing him the glass. "For you."

He took it without speaking. Bonnie sat down in a chair angling away from his. It was still damp from the rain and she felt the plastic webbing soak into the seat of her pants. Eric appeared to be contemplating Grace's pink bicycle, resting up against the garage wall. Pink streamers had been affixed to the handlebars and there was a white basket ornamented with daisies over the front wheel. After a moment Bonnie said, "So what—"

"I really don't know."

They sat in silence. Eric drank half his wine in one pull. Then he got up and climbed the steps to the back door.

Stay or go? She could walk right around the house, get into her car and drive off, never see either of them again. Or no, she could not, be-cause she had left her purse and keys inside on the kitchen counter. She swore under her breath, although there was no one there to hear her. Having come this far, there was no retreat.

The back door cracked open. "Dinner," Jane called.

Bonnie took a fortifying drink of wine and rose to go inside.

In the kitchen, Jane's voice floated back to her. "Go ahead and sit down, I'm just going up to get the kids settled."

Eric was already in the dining room and Bonnie took her usual place to one side. The table was set with one of Jane's flowered cloths and the earthenware dishes she favored for everyday dinners.

Eric turned to look at her as she sat down, without expression, then went back to kneading his chin with one hand and staring out the front windows. A green salad was to the side of each plate, and a loaf of brown bread, unsliced, was in the center of the table. A stick of butter and a small pitcher that was probably salad dressing.

Bonnie might have made a joke about the unpromising look of the meal, but it didn't seem like a jokey situation. They heard Jane upstairs, telling one of the kids to stop doing whatever it was they were doing. Then her feet descending. Jane came into the dining room in a rush. "All right, then. Let me just . . ."

She went into the kitchen and they heard her opening, closing things. "Eric? Would you put down a trivet? There's one in the silver drawer." Eric got up, placed a circle of cork on the table, sat back down. Jane came in with a casserole swaddled in hot pads. "Oh, the bread. One second." She maneuvered the casserole onto the cork and returned to the kitchen.

Bonnie and Eric regarded the casserole. It was brown, with the lumpy surface of an unplowed field. It was hard to identify the ingredients. Something white and weblike that might be cheese. "Christ," Eric said, to himself, not Bonnie.

Jane came back in with a wicker basket of the sliced bread. "All right, everybody can serve themselves."

Nobody did. "What is it?" Bonnie asked, trying not to sound like one of Jane's children.

"Feta and Chili-Vegetable Crumble. Here." Jane took the serving spoon, pried up a corner of the casserole, and deposited a helping on Bonnie's plate. "It's butternut squash and sweet potatoes. And the feta. And sriracha sauce, that gives it a little kick. Eric?"

Jane handed the serving spoon to him. Eric used it to put a scant portion on his plate. He reached for two slices of bread and buttered them thickly.

"What's in the topping?" Bonnie asked.

"Wheat flour, thyme, ground walnuts, some of the cheese. Oh, and oatmeal."

Bonnie used her fork to push aside the brown layer and tried some of the vegetables. They were orange, with the melted cheese adhering to them here and there in white curds. She tasted and got a blast of hot garlic. "Wow," she said, fanning her mouth. "Spicy."

"That's the sriracha. I have extra in the kitchen if you want it."

"No thanks. Wow, I really got a good hit there, I think I need some water. That's OK, I'll get it."

Bonnie got up to run water in the kitchen sink and, since the others could not see her, put her scorched mouth to the faucet to drink directly from it. Then she filled a glass with water and returned to the dining room.

"You all right?" Jane asked when Bonnie came back in.

"Yeah, it just landed kind of funny." She sat down, picked up her fork, and started in on the salad. Her eyes were still stinging. She didn't dare look in Eric's direction.

Jane got up then. "You know, I've got a whole different dish of it without the sriracha. I made it for the kids, I'll bring it out."

Out of reflex politeness, Bonnie started to tell her not to bother. But she stayed quiet and took a slice of the bread, for something to do. She was scarcely hungry. "Here you go," Jane said, putting the new casserole down on a folded kitchen towel. "This should go down a little easier."

"Thanks." Bonnie spooned up some of the new glop. She was aware of Jane watching her.

She lifted a forkful. "Oh yeah, this is better, I can tell." Nodded, yum yum. The vegetables had a peculiar, slippery texture in her mouth, like something that did not wish to be swallowed.

Bonnie's stomach roiled. She had a sudden stupid panicky thought: Jane had poisoned her.

It was all a set-up, a monstrous plot, this new dish prepared just for her. The hot sauce a ploy. Jane would sit back and watch her eat, then later that night Bonnie would start to sweat and heave and kick. . . .

With an effort, she swallowed. "Yeah, much better," she said, and took another bite.

"Like I said, it's an experiment." Jane ate a bite of her own portion, considered it. "You know, trying out some vegetarian options. But less sriracha next time. Definitely. It's a little too punchy."

"It's slop," Eric said. "It's completely inedible. I don't know what you're trying to prove."

Bonnie kept her eyes on her plate. In the corner of her vision she saw Jane take another bite of the casserole, chew, swallow, put her napkin up to her lips. "I suppose it proves that everybody has different tastes. Different appetites. I think it turned out fine."

Eric pushed his plate away. "Slop. A possum wouldn't eat it."

"Well, I'm not a possum, am I? I'm sorry you don't like it. Bonnie's not a fan either, she's having a hard time with it. But she's trying to keep up a good front, aren't you, Bon?"

Bonnie said nothing. "You two," Jane began, then she reached for her water glass and drank.

They waited. Jane put the glass down. "You both seem to have a taste for any number of things that I don't share. Fine. I've thought about it and I decided I don't care. You should do whatever you want. Just don't think I don't know. And keep the children out of it. I shouldn't have to say that, but maybe I do."

Jane stood up and cleared her plate. She ran water in the sink, then she called back to them. "I made dessert. Brownies." Then they heard her climbing the stairs.

Bonnie and Eric looked at each other, haggardly. "What happened?" Bonnie asked.

"This is how she's been. I can't stand it."

Bonnie felt herself shaking, the tension coming out of her in rippling, hiccuplike waves. "I'm sorry."

"Everybody's sorry."

"Does she know we're not . . ." Bonnie stopped, embarrassed. She didn't want to say, "Not sleeping together anymore," although that was what she meant.

"I don't know what she knows. Or how she knows it. She just does. It's creepy."

"I guess we're . . ."

"What?"

"Not as smart as we think we are."

Eric waved this away. "I haven't felt very smart lately."

Bonnie wished he'd unbend, let himself be something other than furious and ashamed and hostile. But she was not allowed to expect anything of him now. She guessed she never had been. "I should go." She stood, steadying herself on the table edge. "I hope," she began, but trailed off, because in fact she did not know what she hoped for.

She was already out the front door when he came up behind her and pulled her inside and held her body against him and kissed her face and hair and then released her and walked back into the house.

Bonnie tried writing a letter to Jane. She never got very far. Dear Jane, I know how you must feel. Except that she didn't. Maybe she never had. Good old anxious, long-suffering Jane, so reliably preoccupied with so many small challenges. Now she was through with that, or no longer cared. No longer cared about her husband or about Bonnie. She'd said so. Friendships didn't always last forever. Sad fact of life. People moved on. Things came to a bad end. So Bonnie told herself. But losing Jane was—and this was a dopey thought, but it came to her—like losing a tooth, when your tongue kept rooting around in your mouth, just to feel the hole.

And then Jane called her. It was a couple of weeks after the deadly dinner. Bonnie looked at Jane's name on the caller ID with dismay, but in the end she answered.

"Eric's miserable," Jane started in, without preamble. "I can live with that, but it's hard on the kids. They keep asking if Daddy's mad at them."

Bonnie muttered something about that being too bad. She'd thought she was out of the business of being responsible for Eric's well-being.

"I meant what I said. I have no objections to the two of you—being together. In fact I can see where there would be advantages."

"Correct me if I'm wrong," Bonnie said, "but last time I saw you, it hardly seemed like you were perfectly OK with the concept."

"I was angry. Hurt. I had to process that. Get beyond it."

"I don't think I can ever eat squash or sweet potatoes again."

"Oh come on. It wasn't that bad."

"Yes it was."

"All right, look, it's taken me a while, but I've made progress, you know, emotional and mental progress. Set aside a lot of my insecurities and come up with what's best for everyone. You, me, Eric, the kids. That's why I'm calling."

"You're calling because you think it would be better for your children if I went back to having sex with their father."

"Do you always have to say things in the crassest possible way? But yes, something like that."

"That's really white of you."

"I hate that expression, you know better than to use it even when you're making fun of it."

"Really Caucasian of you."

"What were you like when you were actually in the eighth grade?"

"I was hell on wheels," Bonnie said. "A worldbeater." She allowed her mood to lift ever so slightly at this hint of their old back and forth, needling humor. She said, "Look, you know I'm—"

"Yes, I know you are all those things. Sorry and all. Let's not dwell."

"No, you have to let me say it. I apologize. We thought we could avoid hurting you. It was just easier to be dishonest." Unworthy tears formed in her eyes. She had to stop feeling sorry for herself. It was one more unattractive character flaw.

"All right. Noted. I'm more interested in how we can . . . move forward."

Bonnie thought she heard a hesitation, as if Jane might still be trying to talk herself into this particular idea. She said, "Could I ask you something? Why don't you just separate. Divorce. I mean, if you really don't care what he does. It would be tough and scary, but that's what people do when they come to this particular fork in the road." It occurred to Bonnie that it sounded like she just wanted Jane out of the way. Impure motives. Not that her motives were ever particularly pure.

"Divorce came up. Not until the kids are older. We can tough it out. People do. But . . ."

"I don't think I want to be in charge of babysitting your husband until you're ready to get rid of him. No thank you."

"Listen to me. It's not that. Or it's not all that. He needs, he deserves, somebody who loves him. In some . . . way I don't."

Bonnie was silent. Then she said, "I don't know if you can expect things to work out that neatly."

"But you do love him, don't you? That's how it works for you, isn't it? Hormones. Biochemical processes."

"Thanks," Bonnie said. "You make me sound like a spawning salmon."

Jane sighed. "But that's exactly what the whole sex thing always seems like to me. Like a bunch of wriggling, copulating fish."

"Why did you get married, exactly? Remind me."

"I guess I thought you were supposed to. I was lonesome. And it's not like I didn't care for Eric." Bonnie noted the past tense. Jane went on. "It's better to get all this out in the open. A relief, really. The two of you gave off such a guilt vibe. Should I have Eric call you?"

"This is a totally weird conversation."

"That can't be helped," Jane said, briskly. "At least now we don't have to keep having it."

"Well . . . what does Eric think about all this?"

"Who knows what he thinks. Mostly he's been sulking and feeling sorry for himself. I have to go, the kids need to return their library books."

Bonnie tried to wrap her mind around this new circumstance. There was something incongruous and off-putting about it. She and Eric would now be paired off like rabbits or racehorses, and the entire distressing problem would thus be solved. It would only make sense to someone like Jane, who by her own admission did not understand such things, did not know the nuances. Had the words but not the beat. It reminded Bonnie of hearing a group of Chinese people singing, with gusto, John Denver's "Take Me Home, Country Road," in which "road" became "roar," and so on. John Denver, it seemed, was very popular in China.

And how would Eric feel? Maybe he would not like being given permission, or told what to do.

Maybe he would no longer want her.

This was her most shaming fear. He would take a new, cold look at their time together, decide that it was based on the cheap romantics of secrecy and betrayal, and if that was gone, not much else was left.

Bonnie spent an unhappy few days after Jane's call. She didn't hear from Eric but then she hardly expected to. It was possible that he felt as embarrassed as she did. *That's how it works for you, isn't it? Hormones. Biochemical processes.* As if love was only a matter of falling on her back some endless number of times. Something she had no choice in.

It made her angry to think how shallow and mindless she might be made to seem. A grubby pleasure-seeker, not to mention all the other choice language that got hung on women who had too much enthusiasm for sex. Although it was true that her enthusiasm had gone a bit downhill lately.

Thank God! Maybe it was age, some kind of menopausal early warning system. She could relax and lead some chaste and useful life. Take up beekeeping, like Sherlock Holmes. She would have to explain it to Eric, and now, perhaps, to Jane as well. Sorry. Hormone depletion. One of those inevitable biochemical processes.

Because that did happen. Not that there weren't randy senior citizens out there. But everybody slowed down. So we'll go no more a roving by the light of the moon, etc. The body failed and fell.

Then what happened to all that leftover love?

She didn't want to believe it came to nothing. Amounted to nothing. Had no worth. But the more she went round and round, trying to come to some wisdom, the more scattered and inconclusive she felt. Yes, she would have said she loved Eric, and whether she ran hot or cold, dishonest or true, it was nothing you could simply wish away.

That was as close as she came to sorting things out. And then the call from Wisconsin came.

∽❦∾

Claudia had gone into town for her morning yoga class, then stopped at the grocery for the items on her list. And at the bank to deposit a check that Stan had recently received for an installation in Connecticut. This had been a difficult project involving a difficult client, and Claudia had labored to smooth and soothe and to keep Stan from swearing into the phone and threatening to enforce the legal terms of the contract by extralegal means. But now it was over and done with. The check was a relief and a validation, a testament to her patience and her skills. And to Stan's vision, of course, but she was the one who had steered it to its happy conclusion.

Stan simply lacked self-control. Not that he couldn't be entirely charming when he wanted to be. And not that he wasn't sorry— eventually—when he lost his temper and ranted and raved and insulted the very people whose goodwill and cooperation, not to mention money, he needed. He was incapable of thinking strategically, of using the right people smarts in difficult situations. Claudia liked to say, "I've raised three children and one artist!"

Arriving home, she put the groceries away and went through her cookbooks for a recipe she wanted to prepare for dinner, baked chicken dressed with a lemon-cream sauce and allowed to cool to room temperature. It was September but there had been a spell of sunny warmth, and she thought the chicken would taste summery but with a hint of richness, like the coming autumn. Alongside the chicken they could have artichokes and a rice pilaf and a simple green salad with garlic croutons.

And then there would be another dinner after that and another after that and so on and on, not to mention the meals that came in between, and lately the thought of all that needed to be done made her tired. She loved it but it made her tired, and there were times she could have slept for a week, and leave people to feed themselves! That was not a nice impulse. But then, she was sixty-three and not as young as she used to be. You were allowed to slow down.

Of course you were supposed to eat low-fat and the chicken was hardly that, but the rest of the meal was virtuous enough. Besides, Stan sulked and was difficult if she reminded him about his cholesterol, his blood pressure, or anything else that spoke of moderation and prudent habits. He was old-school, and believed that artists expended themselves in a blaze of reckless glory, mortal limits be damned, like Icarus flying toward the sun, etc.

Claudia went back to the bedroom to take her shower. She pulled off the unfriendly elastic of her yoga gear and stepped into the steam and spray, used some of the eucalyptus shower gel that she favored, dried off, and wrapped herself in her white terry robe. Then, because the mild air from the open window was so sweet and welcoming, and because she felt, once more, so unexpectedly tired, she sat down in the little upholstered chair next to the bed and closed her eyes.

This was how Stan found her when he came in from the studio in search of his lunch. Dead of a heart attack, with her hair still clean and damp from the shower.

∞

Bonnie picked up her brother Charlie, since he no longer drove. They hugged but they didn't talk much at first because their grief was a sodden and lumpy thing that did not give rise to graceful words, only stale and stupid ones of the sort they'd have to hear at the funeral service. I can't believe, so sudden, such a shock. But as they approached the state line and the road opened up, Charlie said, "Stan should have gone first. The old bastard deserved it. She didn't."

"That's a lovely thought."

Charlie didn't answer. Bonnie said, "Just get it out of your system now. I don't care, but it won't go over big at the house."

"He'll find a new woman to cook and clean up after him and put up with his bullshit. I bet he's already interviewing them."

Bonnie thought this was probably true, or mostly true, but there was no need to chime in. She said, "Haley's there now. Her and the kids. They got there day before yesterday. She's making a lot of the calls and setting things up."

"How about what's-his-name?"

"Scott? He couldn't get away." Bonnie waited to see if her brother would comment on this, but he was looking out the car window at the fading green of the roadside fields. She'd already had one long conversation with Haley. She expected there would be a few more. "I didn't know that Mom had heart disease. I guess she didn't either. We should probably get our risk factors and all that checked." More silence. "Are you still drinking?"

"Do you want me to lie to you?"

"Only if you think I'd believe it." She wouldn't. He had an alcoholic's grainy skin and even, from time to time, a perceptible case of the shakes.

He'd taken to wearing his hair slicked straight back with some kind of grease that showed comb tracks. It gave him an elderly, wasted look, like those photographs of farmers in the Great Depression.

"I'm keeping it under control."

Bonnie figured that meant he was drinking at home, or mostly drinking at home. "Good."

"Stan's going to cut me off, isn't he?"

"Cut you off, how?"

"Mom sent me checks. But it was Stan's money." Charlie gave her an irritated glance. "I didn't ask her to, she just did. She felt bad because of my accident."

Bonnie hadn't known. A muddled anger rose in her. "Just how bad did she feel? I mean, how much money are we talking?"

"It wasn't a regular thing. A few hundred here and there. Nothing Stan would ever miss."

Bonnie let a mile go by before she spoke. "Unless you think that Stan's going to keep giving you money for sentimental reasons, then, no, I wouldn't count on any more checks."

"There's probably some money that was hers. That would go to us, not Stan, right? I'm pissing you off."

"During your time in rehab, did anybody ever introduce the concept of enabling?"

"I shouldn't have brought up the money thing. My bad."

"Mom always liked you best."

Bonnie had meant it sarcastically, or rather, as bitterness taking sarcastic form, but Charlie surprised her by saying, "Yes, she did, but she always liked boys—men—better. She was just built that way. She was always, not flirting, not exactly, but always so tuned into them. What they were doing, what they were saying, what they wanted. You know how she was with Stan. The sun shone out of his ass, as far as she was concerned. Yeah, my ass too, I guess. Funniest thing. Pretty sure nobody else ever will."

Charlie's voice wobbled. Bonnie didn't speak. She kept her eyes on the road in case he started crying, but when she did look, he had sagged against the car door, his mouth hanging open in unlovely sleep.

She didn't want to feel any sorrier for her miserable brother than she already did. She wished he had not told her about the money. She wished he had not said any of it. Now she had to wrestle with this new, bruising knowledge (or rather, confirmation of what she already knew or guessed), on top of her already complicated feelings about Claudia. That mix of exasperation, guilt, loss, a child's need, all the difficult love that had never managed to thrive in her. The last time she'd spoken to Claudia, more than two weeks ago, Claudia had told Bonnie that Stan's work was going to be featured in yet another advertisement-heavy publication devoted to expensively gracious living. Claudia was disappointed that Bonnie had not expressed more excitement about this. Bonnie hated that their last conversation had been about Stan.

She woke Charlie up as they approached the house. There were times when the homestead and its collection of oversized structures looked grand or austere or at least whimsical. At other times, like today, it brought to mind an abandoned junkyard. Maybe she was seeing it through some dense refraction of unhappiness. Maybe with Claudia gone, some part of it would now always seem diminished.

Charlie sat up and began to tug at his clothes and try to set himself to rights and look around. It wasn't yet high season for fall color, only a few tarnished softwoods and yellow maples. The house came into view. A lone Toyota sedan with the look of a rental was parked out front. Bonnie pulled in next to it and she and Charlie got out and stretched and tried to work out their kinks. Neither of them noticed the boy and the girl until they started up the path to the front door.

They were perched in the circular cutouts of the long, barrel-shaped entryway. These were not designed for sitting and the children had to maintain their balance by bracing themselves with their feet. When Bonnie and Charlie approached, they let their feet skid away from the wall and stood, as if they had been caught at something.

"Hi, you must be Leah. And Benjamin. I'm your Aunt Bonnie! I bet you don't remember me. I haven't seen you since you were, what, five?"

"And I'm your Crazy Uncle Charlie. The one you've heard so much about."

The children only stared at them. They were both freckled and taffy-haired, dressed in jeans and sneakers and T-shirts. Bonnie said, "How old are you now? Let me guess. You must be nine."

"Yes ma'am," the boy said. "Her too." The girl didn't speak, only scratched a spot on her bare ankle.

"Your grandma was always talking about you. How smart you are. All the books you've read."

The children did not acknowledge this, perhaps because it did not involve a direct question. They studied the ground at their feet with interest.

"Well," Bonnie said again. They did not seem like the sort of children who could be successfully chatted up. "It's nice to see you again. Is your mother inside?"

"Yes ma'am."

"We're going to go look for her. We'll see you kids a little later."

"Yes ma'am."

When they were inside, Charlie said, "I forgot, they've grown up in a cult, haven't they."

"Quiet." The great room was empty. Firewood was piled in a tidy stack in a brick recess, but the fireplace itself had been swept clean for summer. On the dining room table, a number of florists' arrangements were lined up, sympathy cards tucked among them. Some of them were autumn-themed, with orange lilies, chrysanthemums, sunflowers. Others were more unconventional, with bird of paradise and protea. There was one fruit basket encased in green-tinted cellophane.

"Stan? Haley?" Bonnie passed into the kitchen, also empty. This was Claudia's domain, with its ceramic pots of herbs on the windowsills and pretty dishtowels and the display cabinet with the ornate porcelain hot chocolate pot set in its ring of cups. It made the idea of her death into something impossibly sad.

"Bonnie!" Haley came in from the bedroom wing then, and they hugged, and both of them cried and patted each other's backs, separated, shared a box of Kleenex, sniffed some more. "I didn't hear you drive up. Where's Charlie?"

"I think he's in the bathroom," Bonnie said, thinking that he had probably already found his way to the bar cabinet. "We said hello to the kids. They're huge! I mean, they've grown so much, they used to be little peanuts."

"Yeah, that's what happens when you feed them. Are you hungry? I know it's early, but we might as well eat. People keep bringing food. Hot dishes. It's a Wisconsin thing. There's three potato and cheese casseroles. Venison. Pea salad. Half a ham. Apple cake. It goes on and on."

Bonnie looked into the refrigerator. It was crowded with plastic ware, and serving dishes stacked one on top of the other. "Maybe a sandwich."

"Go sit down, I'll bring everything out. I thought that's what we could do for dinner. Just kind of graze. It wouldn't seem right to start cooking in her kitchen. Though I guess sooner or later . . ." Bonnie took a 7UP from the fridge and went back into the dining room. She found a chair between two of the flower arrangements and removed the cards to read them. One appeared to be from somebody in Claudia's yoga class. The other was a name she recognized as one of Stan's old collaborators from the early days. When Haley came back in with the food, Bonnie asked where Stan was.

"Out in the studio. I wouldn't say he's doing so good. There's been some alcohol involved. I guess it's hardest on him. Not that we need to have a contest."

"I'm glad you've been here," Bonnie told her. "Now tell me what needs to be done. With the service and all."

"Not that much. It's coming together." The funeral would be in two days, at a Lutheran chapel that would allow Claudia's spiritual advisor to conduct the service. Bonnie said she did not know that Claudia had a spiritual advisor and Haley said it was the woman who ran the yoga studio and gave mindfulness seminars. Close enough.

"There's going to be music, old Judy Collins songs, Leonard Cohen songs, things she enjoyed. There's some great pictures of her we can set out. It's going to be nice. It'll be something she would have liked."

"It's not fair," Bonnie said. "She was way too young." She guessed she meant, she felt too young to have lost her mother. She found herself going back and forth between tears and anger. Both made her feel stupid and ineffectual.

"She didn't suffer. She didn't see it coming. That's the best way to go."

"That's the horseshit second prize for having to go at all. Sorry. I forget, you have the consolations of religion."

"Maybe I'm not all that consoled anymore."

Bonnie filled her plate with ham and macaroni salad and cherry cobbler. She was suddenly very hungry. She thought that people who brought food when there was a death were onto something.

The dining room window had a view of the side yard. Charlie and the two children were engaged in some game that involved the throwing of stones. Charlie had a thermos of the sort used for coffee, although it was doubtful that it held coffee, and with his free hand he was pitching stones at one of Stan's smaller constructions, a ten-foot-high tower made of hubcaps. Every time his throw connected it made a shimmering, metallic sound. With Charlie's encouragement, the boy and then the girl also heaved their own stones and landed them.

Bonnie said, "I don't suppose Stan would be entirely happy to see that."

"Let them. The kids need some distractions. It's hard on them, being here. They're scared of Stan, he cries and rages and drinks and slobbers over them, all in about the space of ten minutes. I'm going to enroll them in school here," Haley added, as if this was an ordinary thing to say.

"Really."

"We could be around for a while. Stan needs looking after. Him and the kids will get used to each other."

Bonnie supposed this was at least possible. She said, "What about Scott?"

"He has the whole Fellowship to look after him."

"What happened?"

"I guess I gradually fell off the belief bus. Oh, not entirely, I mean, I still pretty much go along with God. With Jesus. But all the day-to-day, exalted, pray every time you can't find your shoes? After a while it didn't seem to make any difference, and everybody kept saying it did. Well, everybody in the Fellowship. You're supposed to keep burning with this white-hot intensity, and if you don't, if you're just having an ordinary, so-so day, that's a lapse, and you have to pray about that too. It's this constant hectoring to be filled with the spirit. It's like cheerleading camp. Or the way I imagine cheerleading camp is. It took so much damned *effort*. I started to resent it. And Scott." She brooded, darkly. "I don't think he's ever had an original thought in his life. He's like a vending machine. Drop a quarter in, Scripture comes out."

"Does he know you're not coming back? I mean, the kids . . ."

"We didn't talk about it. We don't exactly have a lot of deep conversations. Or much of anything else. Ever wonder why we don't have more kids? Uh huh. He can see Ben and Leah whenever he wants. But they're not going back there."

Bonnie thought that Haley might have a fight on her hands with that, but she kept her mouth shut. Haley went on, "I want to start over. I was so young and stupid and full of it. I want to finish college. I'm not that old. Thirty. I could take classes at Eau Claire or Menomonie."

"Sure you could."

"Like you mean it, please."

"I absolutely mean it. I think it's great."

"I know it looks like, Mom died and so I'm going to turn it into some big opportunity for me, but I need this. I need to turn things around. For the kids too. Big changes. People can change."

"Absolutely," Bonnie said. Haley was wearing a flowing, hippie-style top in an ethnic print. Her blond hair, the same color as Claudia's before it went gray and was chemically revived, had been cut in bangs straight across her forehead, like a child's. She'd never lost the baby weight and her face was going soft at the jawline.

"Don't worry," Haley said. "I'm planning on dieting."

Bonnie shook her head and looked out the window to the hubcap tower. She could no longer see Charlie or the kids. She hoped he hadn't led them into the woods to track bears or something else stupidly dangerous.

"Tell me about you," Haley said. "Tell me what's going on with you."

"Oh . . . work, mostly. Same old."

She'd called Jane to tell her about Claudia. Jane would want to know. The conversation went all right, in a somber sort of way. A mother's death, after all, trumped whatever transgressions had gone on with a husband. It reconnected them, at least for a moment, a sad, sentimental moment, and reminded them of how far they went back. Jane said she would come to the funeral if Bonnie wanted and Bonnie said no, she didn't have to. It was bound to be a bloodbath.

"She was always nice to me. Your mom," Jane said.

"Yeah, she wasn't always that nice to me."

"She fussed a lot. It was just her way of caring. Not the easiest way, I know. I'll sure be thinking about you, hang in there," Jane told her. They hadn't said anything about Eric. Maybe they could keep on not talking about him.

Haley said she'd gone through Claudia's address book and called everybody. "I found a number for your father."

"My who? BioDad? You're kidding."

"Rizzi, that's him, right? Like somebody in *The Godfather*?"

"Carl Rizzi. In New Mexico?"

"No, someplace in Ohio. Claudia had three or four addresses for him, old ones she'd scratched out."

"Huh," Bonnie said. "Double huh. I had no idea she kept up with the guy."

"She was sentimental, you know that. She saved all our report cards. Our artwork from grade school."

"That's different." Bonnie was still trying to get her mind around the idea of her father as an actual real person, someone her mother might have had some secret contact with over the years. "It's not like she ever talked about him. He was, you know, a closed chapter." Their father was only invoked when she or Charlie did something wrong or disappointing, and their paternal genetic heritage was said to be at fault, because God knows they did not get that from her. He was a drunk, they were given to understand, a drunk and a loser. Well, Stan was a drunk too, just a successful one. It was something of a pattern.

"They kept in touch? Wow, the mysteries of Claudia." It was almost as much of a shock as her death. "So what did Pop have to say?"

"I didn't talk to him, I had to leave a message. That's what I did with a lot of people. I had a little speech about how sorry I was to be calling with the news, and when the service was going to be, and the contact for the funeral home. Do you think he'll show up?"

"No clue. I don't think I've seen him since I was four years old." Bonnie remembered a game they might have played, a loud game that involved chasing. He might have carried her on his shoulders. Fragments, memories of memories. She said, "Maybe it's best not to mention any of this to Stan."

"Stan's not exactly being a good sport right now," Haley said. "Just so you know what to expect."

Stan came in from the studio at dusk. He moved slowly and his eyes were a smeared red. He hugged Bonnie but seemed to forget about her midway through. Haley asked him if he was hungry and he lifted one hand in a leave me alone gesture. Haley ignored this and brought him a plate of beef with noodles. She put a tray of rolls with butter next to him. "Here, try some of this."

"Where'd it come from?" Stan glowered at the food. "Who the hell brought it? One of the yoga witches?"

"A perfectly nice lady from Mom's book group. Eat it."

"She wasn't in any book group."

"Yes she was. They read a lot of mysteries with female sleuths."

"Female whats?"

"Detectives," Bonnie said. "Crime solvers."

Stan gave her a bleary look that might have been menacing or maybe he was just unable to keep his eyebrows raised. He picked up his fork but before he got it to his plate he was distracted by Benjamin and Leah, who had finished eating and were sitting next to each other, not fidgeting, technically, but poking at each other under the table and lifting up from their chairs with a kind of stealthy delicacy. Of course, it was how they got away with fidgeting in church. "Aren't they supposed to be in school?" Stan asked.

"We don't go to school," Benjamin said.

"While you're here you go to school," their mother said. "It doesn't start until next week."

No one said anything to this. Benjamin asked if they could be excused. Haley told them yes, and to clear their plates. "Do we say blessings while we're here?" Benjamin asked, and Haley said yes, of course. Benjamin and Leah bowed their heads and mumbled something in unison that could not be deciphered. Then they got up and took their plates to the kitchen.

Stan watched them go. "There's something not right about those kids," he said.

"They're perfectly fine, Dad. You're just not used to children with good manners."

Stan surveyed the table around him. "What did you do with my drink?"

"You didn't have one. You don't need one. Come on, eat something."

Stan got up and went to the bar cabinet in the corner of the great room. He came back with a fifth of Jameson's Irish whiskey. He dumped the contents of his water glass into one of the floral arrangements and poured out three fingers. "Want any ice?" Bonnie asked him.

"You're a good girl," he told her.

"Thank you."

"Even if you can't find yourself a man."

"Drat. I forgot to get married."

Stan took a pull of his drink. "Go ahead, make fun. You're missing out on the most important . . . most, I tell you your mother was the most . . ."

They heard feet ascending the stairs from the basement, where Charlie had been taking a nap.

The refrigerator door opened, closed, and Charlie came into the dining room with a piece of cold fried chicken in one hand.

He and Stan stared at each other. Charlie pointed to the Jameson's. "Can I have some of that?" His mouth was full of fried chicken.

"Get your own. Better yet, get a job so you can afford your own."

Charlie went back to the refrigerator and returned with a beer. "You can put this on my tab," he said. He surveyed the food on the table, lifted the top from a baking dish. "Is this Tater Tot casserole? Awesome."

Haley said, "Get a plate, don't stand there and pick at things."

"No, that's OK, I'll just eat some scraps off the garage floor."

"Sit down," Stan said. "And stop being an asshole."

Charlie sat. Haley said, "Dad, I really need for you to watch your language while the kids are here."

Stan made a show of looking around the room and beneath the table. "Kids? I don't see any kids."

"You know what I mean."

Charlie said. "I believe that what we have going on here is an asshol-ery contest. Who has the biggest, hairiest—"

"You both win," Bonnie said. "You both get a prize. Now please. Mom would be really unhappy to hear this."

That shut them up at least until Stan finally ate some food and went off to bed, and Charlie took a six-pack with him to go watch television. Bonnie and Haley put the food away and cleaned the kitchen. Haley said, "Mom wanted to be cremated. Did you know?"

"I think I do too. As soon as possible."

"They're both lost without her and they don't know what to do except have tantrums."

"I don't want to keep refereeing them, it's exhausting."

"They just have to get through the service. Then they never have to see each other again."

They worked in silence for a time, then Bonnie said, "About the cre-mation. It's not like I enjoy thinking about these things, but when do they . . ."

"After the service. We'll get to see her, then they take her away. We'll get the, I think they call them cremains, later. I know. I don't like think-ing about it either. We have to pick out clothes for her, Stan's no help. Something pretty. You know she'd want to look pretty."

Charlie had fallen asleep wrapped in a blanket in the den, and Bonnie took the basement for herself. She slept and woke up an hour later, sud-denly, her heart knocking, as if something had alerted her. The dish-washer rumbled in the kitchen overhead, but otherwise the house was quiet. Nerves, or bad dreams, maybe, although she could not remember dreaming.

She got up, went to the bathroom, drank water from the tap. She thought about calling Eric. It wasn't all that late, not yet midnight. She had lost her mother, she was allowed, she had even been given permis-sion to do what she would with him. How had she gotten herself to such a desperate place, wanting to use poor Claudia as some horrible excuse to cozy up to her illicit lover? But Eric was another loss, an emptiness, a bereavement, and there seemed no cure for this. Why should she always be alone? Always cast aside? Oh goddamn you Stan, who said she couldn't find a man? She'd found any number of them. She just couldn't keep them around. Then she was ashamed of herself and her unending black-hearted desires.

Her phone pinged. It was a text from Eric: **So sorry.** Bonnie texted back: **Thanks.** She was weak with gratitude. She fell asleep with the phone cradled next to her and slept until morning.

There was another day to get through before the service, and they managed by keeping out of each other's way, by keeping busy with preparations. There had been a brief death notice, and now there was an obituary to write. Stan insisted on having a hand in this, and since he could hardly be told no, Claudia was memorialized as "a beautiful and classy lady who knew a thing or two about a thing or two." The house kept filling up with flowers. Stan and Claudia's connections in the world of high-end art went in for dramatic arrangements of orchids, curly willow, anthurium, and bear grass. Charlie said they looked a lot like Stan's sculptures. "You know, ugly on principle." But at least he did not say this in Stan's presence.

On the day of the service, Bonnie and Haley got to the chapel early to see to things. They met the yoga instructor/spiritual advisor, a tall blonde dressed in clothes that resembled origami constructions. It was unexpected to see so much high style in the middle of rural Wisconsin, but then, Bonnie reminded herself, there was a bit of an artist's colony that had grown up in town. Jewelry makers, potters, even a theater group that staged experimental plays. The yoga woman said that she had in mind some remarks that would be spiritual, though not really religious. They nodded. They had not wanted the Lutheran pastor and his Bible verses. "And then, if family members or others want to speak in remembrance of her . . ." The yoga woman lifted a blond eyebrow, waiting for them to volunteer.

"We didn't prepare anything," Bonnie said, panic fluttering in her. She didn't think it had occurred to any of them.

The yoga woman said it was better to speak from the heart anyway. Sure, unless your heart, like Bonnie's, resembled the lint trap in a dryer.

The man from the funeral home led them to the side room where Claudia's coffin lay. It would not be displayed in the chapel. They had all, miraculously, agreed on this. Bonnie hung back. She felt fizzy, light-headed. She didn't want to look, she was squeamish about the dead. They brought her no comfort. The man from the funeral home stepped aside, discreet, professionally sympathetic. Bonnie allowed herself a quick, blurred glance. Claudia wore the pale blue wool dress they'd chosen for her. The funeral home had used too much hair spray on her and made her eyebrows too dark. There was something wrong with her jaw. Bonnie seemed to remember that they wired it shut so it wouldn't fall open. Haley murmured something to the funeral home man, yes, very nice, thank you. Claudia did not look pretty. She only looked dead.

Once they were back in the chapel, it felt as if the worst might be over, but that feeling didn't last long. They set up the guest book and the pictures of Claudia on tables in the vestibule. Claudia as a pretty blond child in a homemade Easter dress. High school graduation. Holding babies. Riding in a motorboat with Stan. Nothing with Carl Rizzi. Bonnie and Haley had agreed on that. They'd found a few photos but they all seemed to have been taken with the same bad camera. They made both Claudia and Carl look dark and shifty, like somebody else's immigrant grandparents.

Out of necessity, Stan and Charlie and the children had driven there together. It was a ten minute ride but they arrived looking as if they had traveled cross-country. People began to file in and the family, that is, Stan and Haley and Bonnie, stood at the entrance to greet them. Old neighbors who had made the trip, some of Stan's art world friends, Claudia's friends from different places. Haley started the music, and Steve Winwood's "Higher Love" came out of the chapel's speakers. It helped to have music, gave everything the feeling of a ceremony. Higher love, higher love, yes, there had to be something out there less confounding, less selfish, less of everything that you had tried and failed at. Steve Winwood was succeeded by Leonard Cohen, and then, as the family and others took their seats in the pews, Judy Collins. The yoga woman mounted to the pulpit, and Haley cut the music and took her seat.

Leah, who was sitting next to Bonnie in the front row, tugged at her sleeve. "Is she a real witch?" Bonnie shook her head. Leah looked disappointed. "Dear friends," the yoga woman began, her amplified voice clear and assured from much practice in exhorting people how to breathe. "We are here today to remember and to celebrate a wonderful soul. A wife, mother, friend, and lover of life in all its beauty and variety. An unfailing source of kindness. A seeker of peace and wisdom."

So far so good. Standard spiritual boilerplate. It would be harder to sit through anything personal. Bonnie was relieved to see that the chapel was nearly full, and that Stan and Charlie had chosen to sit in different pews and ignore each other. The chapel was a new building, with a great many high windows, white surfaces, and blond wood. Her eyes closed against the glare, lulled by the yoga woman's well-modulated urgings to view our earthly selves as merely containers for the precious spirit within. Like milk cartons, maybe. Stale dated. Stamped with expiration codes. Or no, she had not said all that. One by one several women with Kleenex wadded in their fists came to the pulpit and offered their tributes.

Bonnie tried to pull herself out of her fit of dozing, fell back again. She should be thinking about Claudia, she should be actively mourning. She guessed that would come later. She was so weary. Stress catching up to her. The body perished, the spirit took flight. Birdybirdybirdy. The darkness behind her eyelids was so pleasant and so welcoming. A nudge in her side from Leah. Her head had drooped forward and she had begun to snore, a buzzing sound. Bonnie jerked awake, righted herself, and when she opened her eyes she was dismayed to see her brother mounting the steps that led to the pulpit.

The yoga woman stepped aside politely. Charlie positioned himself at the lectern, gripping its sides. He did not seem drunk. Neither did he seem sober. Ill, perhaps. The skin beneath his eyes looked bruised. He'd been mistreating his body for so long, and now it was beginning to give out. Charlie cleared his throat. "Death," he began, and paused for a too-long beat. "Sucks."

A few people tittered, as if hoping to find this funny, but most of them stayed silent. "I mean," Charlie went on, "I know we're in the business of finding the silver lining here, but why kid ourselves? Death. Let the idea roll around in your head for a minute. It's the end of the line. Finito. There's no upside."

Bonnie turned her head to scan the length of the pew and saw Haley staring back at her. Haley looked shaky. Bonnie expected she did too. Charlie had stopped speaking. It did not give the impression of a rhetorical strategy, only mental vacancy. Then he came to himself again. "She wasn't even that old. She took good care of herself. It's not like this is what, Africa or someplace. Where people die all the time. Kids. Ebola, even. I mean, whoa."

Please stop, Bonnie told him silently. She tried to make eye contact with Charlie but he was not looking at her, or, it seemed, at anything in the room. Maybe he was drunk. The people in the pews were stony quiet, waiting for it to be over. It kept not being over.

"We have doctors here. Why didn't some doctor see this coming? Well it's too late for that. Nobody was paying attention. I wasn't paying attention. I guess I thought she was always going to be around. Always be my mom. Always doing things for everybody else. Keeping the, what I call the art-industrial complex going."

Stan's voice rumbled from across the room. He said something that included the word "crap."

"Because she sure bought into all that. Look where it got her. Behind every great man is a dead woman."

At some point in Charlie's monologue, Bonnie had made frantic signals to Haley, mouthing words until Haley got it, rose from her seat, and went to the sound system on the back wall, so that Charlie's last words had to compete with Judy Collins launching into "Amazing Grace."

Bonnie got to her feet and signed for Leah and Benjamin to do so as well. "Amazing Grace, how sweet the sound," Bonnie began, and the children looked at each other, then joined in with their wavering trebles. Haley came back to the pew and stood alongside them. She had a good clear voice and it carried. "That saved a wretch like me." Across the aisle, the front pew stood, raggedly, and tried to catch up. "I once was lost, but now I'm found."

Charlie said, "What is this, like the Academy Award speeches? You only have three minutes?"

"Was blind, but now I see," Bonnie sang, and stepped out of the pew. "Go," she said to the children. "Keep singing."

Obediently they set off down the aisle to the back of the church, singing, two identical blond angels. Haley came to the end of the pew and she and Bonnie followed them, an impromptu recessional. Charlie gave up, came down from the pulpit and sat on the step beneath it, rubbing at his eyes.

"'Twas grace that taught my heart to fear." Everyone stood and sang along or tried to. Nobody knew all the lyrics. They came in a beat or so behind the singer, but they chimed in on "grace," and by the second verse the recorded choir was backing Judy up, by the third the sound was strong and swelling. People stood and waited their turn to leave. The song was so entirely beautiful in its perfect sadness and its promise of consolation. A series of lifting phrases that raised the heart along with them. Bonnie, passing the pews, saw people crying new tears.

Once they were safely in the vestibule, Bonnie and Haley leaned against a wall, shaking with nervous relief. "How did you hit on 'Amazing Grace,' or was that just luck?"

"It was either that or the Rolling Stones."

"Would have been tricky, but we could have made it work."

"Maybe not 'Brown Sugar.'"

Bonnie tried to catch her breath. It was still running a block ahead of her, "The kids were great. Where's Stan? We have to keep him from killing Charlie."

The rest of the crowd was coming out behind them now and there was a confusion of voices and people wanting to talk to them. Stan was on the other side of the room with his art friends, his money friends. He looked sad but Stan-like, his usual talky self. Bonnie supposed she ought to worry about Charlie, but she was tired of worrying about Charlie just now.

A group of Claudia's friends were offering condolences to Bonnie and Haley when Bonnie stiffened and touched Haley's arm. "Look, I have to . . ."

"Excuse me," she called after the man who had pushed out of the chapel's doors and was walking to the parking lot. He didn't turn around. "Excuse me," she tried again, but he only quickened his pace.

"Hey, Rizzi!"

He stopped then and she caught up with him. She said, "I get that you don't want to talk to us. But once every thirty years or so isn't asking a lot."

Carl Rizzi shrugged. "Didn't want to intrude."

Now that she'd stopped him from getting away, she didn't know what to say to him. They both looked out over the sunny afternoon. The wind had blown a few dry cornstalks in from a farm field and they scraped across the sidewalk. Carl Rizzi said, "I didn't think anybody would recognize me."

"You look like my brother." That is, he looked like Charlie would if he lived long enough to put in thirty more rough years. How old was he, close to seventy? Carl Rizzi was a tall man with a hunch in his back. His face had a leathery quality, especially around his eyes, which had receded into folds of skin. Some ghost of good looks still lived on in him. He had a full head of silver hair, going thin on top. His shoes had seen better days. His sports coat fit like something borrowed. He smelled like a million million cigarettes. She could see why he might not have wanted to intrude.

"Yeah, your brother. How's he doing?"

"You saw how he's doing."

"Charles," he said, as if uncertain he had it right.

"He goes by Charlie."

"He's named after me, you know? Carl. I'm named after my dad. Carlo. There's times I can't place things right away. There's a few holes in my brain. But I haven't had a drink in five years. Almost six. Just so you know."

"Good for you."

"Something your brother ought to think about."

"Maybe you could help him with that," Bonnie said. "Talk to him."

"It's not something someone can do for you." Carl Rizzi looked over his shoulder at the parking lot, then back to Bonnie. "So how's everything with you?"

"Fine," she said, meaning, no thanks to him. "Look, I'm not trying to be obnoxious. But really, why are you here? You and my mom, you hadn't been together for like, forever."

"We talked some. Every so often. Once the dust had settled." He shrugged. "We were just kids when we got married, you know? She still had a soft spot for me."

"I guess you had one for her too."

"Just because things don't work out, that doesn't mean you lose all the feeling. She was a good woman. Too good for me. She had a good heart."

Not good enough, Bonnie thought. Carl Rizzi said, "Look, I really do have to get back."

"To Ohio."

"Yeah, Ohio." He held out his hand and they shook. His hand was spare and hard. "You have my number, right? Tell your brother he can call me if he wants. We can talk the drunk talk. See if it takes."

"Thanks. I'll let him know."

"You look good," Carl Rizzi said. "All dressed up and everything. You dodged the drunk curse, right?" He smiled. He was missing a tooth up front, in one corner of his mouth.

"I've been thinking I should quit drinking. At least cut back." She didn't know why she told him. It wasn't like it was any of his business.

"If you think you should, then yes, you should. But your mother said you were all right. I did worry about you kids. The genetic predisposition. That's what it's called. I'm glad you didn't inherit that godawful misery. All right, I'm out of here. Take care."

Bonnie watched him walk away across the parking lot. There was a slight hitch in his step, one leg gone stiff. She didn't know if what she felt was loss, exactly, because how could you lose a father you never had in the first place? He had bequeathed her a different misery, a hunger for men who never stayed around.

g p s

Jane was not unhappy with the way things were working out.

At night she slept in the little spare room she'd arranged for herself. She told the children it was so she could hear them better if they needed her. Eric did not make objections. They no longer argued. They spoke about their children's schedules and who would be where (at the dentist's, at soccer practice), they conferred as needed about household accounts and taking the cars in for maintenance. Jane fixed Eric's dinner along with everyone else's and sometimes he was there to eat it and sometimes he was not. But he almost always arrived home by the children's bedtime and read them their good-night stories and played good-night games. He was a fun daddy. Jane went to bed soon after the children and left Eric looking over paperwork in the den, his feet up, a drink beside him on the table, the television talking quietly to itself.

She assumed that Eric saw Bonnie on those evenings when he arrived home late. Or some of those evenings. Maybe called her after Jane went to bed. Talked about whatever it was they talked about in between screwing. Jane didn't pretend to know and she didn't ask. Maybe they talked about Jane from time to time, although she hoped they had something more interesting to discuss.

If Eric was detached, he at least seemed to be on an even keel. Life might go on like this for some time. Was it the normal way of arranging things? She supposed not, but you never knew how other people lived, how they really lived, even in the placid suburbs. People sent out Christmas cards, they kept up their lawns and waved to each other when they hauled garbage cans to and from the curb. But every so often you heard stories. Even someone as disconnected to gossip as Jane was might hear stories. A neighbor caught in a prostitution sting. A grown son moving back into his parents' guest room, trailing failures. A wife and mother who was said to be away, visiting relatives in another state, and who never came home.

Surely more people carried on in day to day boredom, or day to day contentment, than got caught up in scandals. But who were people behind their closed doors, and how did they treat one another? How did they navigate love, spite, sex, grievance, and all the rest of it? Jane had no idea. Human beings were a mystery to her, as she was often a mystery to herself.

It was not unusual for a married person to stray from the marriage, for partners to go outside the boundaries. She told herself this. And there were places in the world, and times in history, where people practiced polygamy, or it was understood and permitted that husbands might keep mistresses, and wives, have lovers. But how were such things managed, and did you ever get used to them? Was one system more natural, or unnatural, than another? She did not know if she had failed at marriage, or transcended it out of some accidental wisdom. She had no real guide, either within or outside of herself. She understood there was such a thing as passion, and that often enough it drove people to some brink, but much in the same way that she understood there was such a thing as arithmetic.

Bonnie was just one of the topics she and Eric did not discuss. There were times when Jane was tempted to ask how Bonnie was, or to tell Bonnie she said hello. But they weren't at that casual point yet, if they ever would be. It was hard to imagine the three of them sitting down to dinner together, as they had so often done over the years. At least, not after the last time.

She and Bonnie had talked when Bonnie's mother died. Jane knew all about Bonnie's crazy family. She knew that Bonnie had not really lived up to Claudia's expectations, and vice versa. But you only ever had one mother. It had seemed like the right thing to do, calling. "How was the funeral, did everybody behave?"

"Charlie was drunk."

"Well, yeah."

"My father was sober."

"Stan?"

"No, BioDad."

"Who? The actual, real—"

"Uh huh."

"You're kidding," Jane said. The BioDad was a practically mythic figure, the king of bad fathers. Like Darth Vader, but Italian. "So what was he like? What did you say to him?"

"We didn't talk that much. He didn't exactly want to rejoin the family circle."

"But he came to the funeral, right?" Jane was conscious of a reticence on Bonnie's part, things she might have said if not for the inconvenient awkwardness of the whole Eric situation. "At least you got to see him."

"Like I said, he was sober. I guess that's a relatively new development."

"Good," Jane told her, with more enthusiasm than was required, to make up for Bonnie's lack of it. "It had to be good to see what he's really like, after all this time."

"'Good' is stretching it."

"All right," Jane said, after waiting for Bonnie to say more. "At least you can cross it off your list. BioDad, revealed."

"You don't want to think your life turns out one way or another because of your parents, you know? You want to believe you're a free agent and you made your own choices. Aside from things like eye color or freckles. You want to think you're self-created. At least I always did. I wasn't going to be a big sack of crazy, like the rest of my relatives."

"You aren't. You didn't."

"Yeah, maybe. All right, look, I should—"

"Sure."

"I'll talk to you some other time," Bonnie said, and got off the phone while Jane was still trying to formulate ways to both say and not say the rest of it. Bonnie was the person she knew best in the world, and now there would be a divide between them.

Grace had started kindergarten, Robbie was in the second grade. Now Jane had the mornings to herself. She drove the children to school, came home, tidied the kitchen, started the laundry. Once her chores were finished, time sifted over her like dust. She sat at the kitchen table and watched light track across the window. No visions came to her. Maybe they had bled out of her after too much exhausted worry, too much kid noise, too many nincompoop arguments.

Eventually it would be time to pick Grace up again and hear about her day at school. At least Grace got to color and sing nursery songs.

She missed Bonnie. She began to consider that she'd made a mistake in the way she'd behaved, that she'd shamed Bonnie to the point where the two of them had no clear space in which to speak or stand. Jane had been angry then and she'd wanted to force things out into the open. But maybe she should have kept her peace. Should have left Bonnie and Eric to carry on their furtive affair until it wore out or blew up in everyone's face. She'd been angry, and now she was only lonesome.

She picked out a sympathy card and wrote a brief, careful note. But rather than mail it, she chose a Saturday morning when Eric had taken the children on one of their Dad excursions—these were officially cast as fun, rather than guilt-driven—and set out for Bonnie's apartment. She'd baked peanut butter cookies for the kids and she packed some of these in a wicker basket. She didn't call ahead so as not to give Bonnie a chance to make excuses not to see her. Bonnie would probably be home, but even if she wasn't, she could leave her offerings.

How long had it been since she'd driven into the city by herself? Although Bonnie's neighborhood only technically qualified as urban. Jane told herself she'd become a total stick-in-the-mud, never leaving her small, safe zone. She was nervous about the expressway at first, all the high speed bad drivers, but then she got the hang of it and increased her speed to keep up with the rest of the mayhem. She allowed herself a bit of cautious confidence. The city's hazy skyscrapers approached on the horizon. Once upon a time she used to live among them.

The closest she and Eric had come to a conversation lately was when he'd asked her, as if it were a casual thought, something that had just come to him, if Jane had considered going back to work. Now that the kids were in school.

She hadn't. "Doing what?" she asked him.

"I don't know, what you used to do. Public health. Clinics. Research studies. Or something else entirely." Eric ran out of ideas and encouragement then and waited for Jane to say yes (or no), what a good (or bad) idea that was. He looked hopeful, even a bit timid. As if he might not be allowed, at this point, to give her any sort of suggestion.

Jane said, "I expect it would help to have some extra money coming in. We have to start thinking about college."

Eric made a certain kind of face that she recognized, an impatience at being misunderstood. "Sure, but I was thinking, something that would really involve you. Speak to you, be important to you. Because I don't think you've ever had that."

Oh but she had. Except the visions had failed her, she'd worn them down with too much ordinary spite and grief. She said, "I guess I should think about that." Hoping she didn't sound too droopy and defeated. She did not believe that Eric was only proposing a way for her to keep herself occupied while he and Bonnie entertained each other. He still cared about her welfare. Or at least felt responsible for her. "I can look for things online."

"It wouldn't have to be public health. It could be anything. You could take classes. See what they have at the community college." His enthusiasm rose, encouraged by his ideas.

"I could volunteer," Jane said, meaning it sarcastically, since that seemed like one more thing that suburban dilettantes did. But Eric said that by all means, she could volunteer. There were so many great organizations out there that needed volunteers. She was bound to meet some interesting people. It was a long time since anyone had found her interesting.

Here was Bonnie's exit. Jane took it, drove a ways, then had to double back when she got confused. She never thought about using GPS until she was already at a place, or already lost. She guessed she should have asked Eric for directions, ha ha. Everything looked the same to her here, the bungalows on their narrow lots with their old-fashioned awnings and brick chimneys, the middle-aged shopping centers. Once Bonnie had moved in, Jane had only visited once, and that was to drop off some curtains Bonnie thought she might be able to use. Jane felt bad that it had only been the once. As if she was always the busy one, and she guessed she was, but nothing that kept you busy seemed like anything that ought to keep you housebound. Maybe she really should get a job.

Jane came to a street she thought she recognized, and then another, and here was Bonnie's building. She parked out front, after studying the signs that threatened you about snow routes and street cleaning. Leaves had been raked and set out on the curb in brown paper lawn bags. Bonnie's front blinds were half open and there was no way to tell if she was home or not. Jane retrieved her basket of cookies and the card from the seat beside her. It seemed stupid to have brought the cookies.

At Bonnie's door she rang the bell, waited, knocked, waited again. "Bonnie?" she called, in case she might be mistaken for a Jehovah's Witness or someone selling meat off a truck. No answer. Jane walked out

back to the parking spaces. Bonnie's car wasn't there. It was a disappointment, but also something of a relief.

When she came back inside, a man was standing at Bonnie's door,
knocking. He looked up at Jane when she came in, then away again. "I
don't think she's home," Jane said.

"Uh huh." Not interested in conversation. He was tall and oversized,
with a big square handsome face and ruddy skin. He was dressed in jeans
and a leather jacket and a black T-shirt. Jane felt the inner commotion
that Bonnie used to call Jane's Spidey Sense.

Jane said, "You're Patrick."

He left off knocking then and gave her a mistrustful, startled look.
"Do I know you?"

"I'm Jane. Friend of Bonnie's."

"She's told you all about me, is that it?"

In fact Bonnie pretty much had. "Like I said, I don't think she's home.
I don't know where she is."

"Huh." Patrick considered this, knocked again, so as not to appear
that he was paying any real attention to Jane.

"She wasn't expecting me." Jane waited to see if he'd volunteer his
own information, but he just kept knocking and looking pissed off. She
turned to go, then remembered her card and the cookies and hesitated.
She didn't want to leave anything at the door as long as this large and
glowering man was hanging around. She said, "Maybe I'll call her now."

Jane stepped outside, went out to the sidewalk, and stood next to her
car. She dialed Bonnie's number and got voice mail. "Hi, guess what, I'm
over at your apartment. I just stopped by. No biggie," she added, in case
Bonnie might think she was there for a throwdown or a catfight. "I miss
you. Well OK, talk to you later."

Patrick came out then and walked up to her. Hands in his pockets,
looking from side to side. A bit of a strut in his step. "Sex on wheels,"
Bonnie had called him. Or one of the things she had called him. "So, you
reach her?"

Jane said she had not, that she had left a message. "You didn't say I was here, did you?" His speech had a lilt, or maybe a tilt, to it. Echo of Ireland, filtered through a layer of South Side. Jane shook her head no. "Ah," Patrick said. "Just as well. We had a bit of a dustup."

That was one word for it. Jane raised her eyebrows politely. "Oh, that's too bad."

"Misunderstanding. Clearing the air." As if he cared what Jane thought, that is, he so clearly did not care.

"It was probably the money that really got her mad," Jane said.

He stared at her. Unfriendly. That wasn't going to stop her.

"I hope it wasn't all that much. She wouldn't tell me. She was embarrassed. But when you get money involved, it can throw such an ugly light on everything."

For a long minute Patrick's face stayed frozen in its menacing stare, and then it crumpled into a grin. "Ah well. Get a woman mad enough and she runs her mouth."

Jane was unsure if he was referring to Bonnie or to herself. "She was angry, yes."

"You know what? I came to give her the money back. So we'd be square." He took his wallet out of his back pocket, opened it, and fanned the bills at her. "See?"

"Not really my business."

"Well, now that you've made it yours, or she made it yours, you can go ahead and tell her I was here. With her money."

"I'm not sure when I'll talk to her."

"And I'm not sure when I'll have money in my pocket again. Just tell her."

Jane didn't answer. She was waiting for him to leave so she could go back inside and deposit the cookies and card. Instead he stood alongside her and leaned against the car. "This is yours, right? You mind? Some people are tetchy about their cars."

"No, feel free."

"Toyota," he pronounced. "That's a girl car. At least it's not a minivan."

It was Eric's car. He had the kids, so today he had the minivan. "What do you drive?"

"I'm in between cars right now. No wheels."

"I guess you can get by without in the city. Public transportation."

He shook his head at this and looked out to the street. He did not seem excited about the merits of public transportation. Since he didn't seem to be going away, Jane said, "So what's a boy car?"

"A manly car," he corrected. "Dodge Ram 1500. With a Hemi V8. I used to have a '98. It was only a V6. But it drove like a bat out of hell."

Jane couldn't think of anything to say to that. No opinion. Patrick said, "Or you could go hog wild and get a Hummer. You're not much of a car person, are you? I can kind of tell. What did you say your name was?"

"Jane."

"Jane. Right. Where do you know Bonnie from anyway?"

"College. We were roommates." She relaxed some now that Patrick did not seem likely to do anything violent or alarming. Bonnie had painted him in the blackest colors. But now that she'd met him, Jane thought he was harmless, maybe a bit on the simple side. And, as advertised, quite the physical specimen. If you gave him a handlebar mustache, he could have been one of those Irish boxers of the last century, posing barechested in fighting stance.

He said, "You're the one with the kids, right?"

"That's right." And the husband. She didn't want to think about the timing, Patrick and Bonnie vs. Eric and Bonnie. Although it seemed pretty obvious. The two of them and the two of them. They must have overlapped. It made Jane queasy, she didn't want to think about it. Except of course you had to think about it.

She held out the basket of cookies. "Do you want some of these?"

"What are they, peanut butter? Awesome. Thanks." He took two and popped them into his mouth. His jaw slid back and forth and his lips smacked. He saw Jane staring at him. "What?"

"Nothing." It was like watching a horse eat. "I was going to leave these for Bonnie, but she doesn't need them all." Patrick was eyeing the basket. "Go ahead, help yourself."

"You're sure?" He took two more cookies, then two more with his other hand. "You make these? Outstanding. Bonnie don't know what she's missing."

She could still leave the card. "Excuse me," Jane said. She walked back inside and slid the card underneath Bonnie's door. Behind her she heard the sound of a door opening, then clicking shut, but when she turned around, no one was there.

When she went back outside, Patrick was still making himself at home, sprawled on the hood of her car. Really, he was comical, a big, cookie-eating kid. He couldn't have been more unlike Eric. Bonnie wasn't one to limit herself. But once in a while, for God's sake, couldn't she at least try? Eric wasn't one to deny himself. She was tired of both of them.

"I'm not going to wait any longer," she told Patrick. "Do you want a ride home?"

He did. He didn't bother to pretend polite reluctance. He got into the front seat and tried to adjust it so he fit. "I guess you really do need a manly car," Jane told him.

"No, I love riding with my knees up in my face. I don't live super far. Lincoln Square."

He told Jane he had plenty of room, honest. And he did, but he pretty much filled the space. She was not accustomed to having so much, well, manliness all up in her face. It was going to take some getting used to.

This time she did use the GPS. This amused Patrick, who said he could tell her where he lived, but Jane said she would have to get herself home again, and so kept it on. They didn't say much as Jane tried to keep up with the synthetic chirping voice. She would have been entirely lost without it. Whenever she thought she might be heading east, she found herself going south. Buses clogged her lane, intersections confounded her. Patrick tapped his fingers on his leg, shifted his weight, sighed. He could at least not convey boredom and impatience so clearly; she was doing him a favor, after all. Or maybe he was ADD? Bonnie hadn't said so, but then Bonnie wouldn't much notice or care. Not as long as she could get his clothes off. Somebody's clothes off. There were things she had to stop thinking about. Except that she could not stop thinking about them.

Patrick said, "That's really cool, you and her being friends for so long. It's kind of not usual for girls."

"Why is that?" Jane asked, busy with navigating a left turn against traffic.

"I don't know, girls seem to fight over stuff more. They get jealous more. Stupid stuff. Whose hair is bigger. I guess that's important to you all, I can't figure it."

"That is not what women fight about. Women, OK? Not girls."

"Ah." He shrugged. "You say potato, I say potahto."

The GPS was giving her a new set of directions, telling her to turn when she'd thought she was done with turning, and Patrick had begun some annoying explanation of how "girl" was really a compliment, a term of endearment, and most girls, excuse me, *women*, understood that, when he said, "Hey! Where you going? It's right here." And Jane stepped on the brakes in mid-turn and the next instant was hit from behind, hard, in a thudding crush of metal.

Both of them jolted against the dash. The seat belts threw them back again. A moment of shock when Jane chose not to believe what had just happened. A horn was sounding, the driver of the car that had hit her laying on the horn in angry bleats. "Whoa, you all right?" Patrick asked, and she said she was, because nothing obvious was broken or bleeding, and he said he guessed he was all right too. "I didn't mean, stop dead in your tracks, you know?"

Jane reached up to fix the mirror, which her head must have knocked against. The view was unfamiliar because the red hood of another car now filled the back window. The driver, a pissed-off–looking young guy, was already out of the car, waving his arms and talking into a cell phone. At least he didn't seem to be hurt. She supposed she would have to get out too. She opened her door.

"Hold up," Patrick said. "You should sit a minute. Breathe."

"I'm fine," Jane said, unhooking her seat belt. She wasn't quite fine, since her head seemed only loosely attached to her neck, but she thought she'd do.

"How about you turn the engine off before you do anything else."

Good idea. She shut off the car and stepped out to the street, holding on to the roof for balance. "I'm sorry," she said to the other driver. "How bad is it?"

"What the fuck were you doing, huh?" He had one of those simple-minded haircuts, the sides shaved and the top all flopping curls. His car, a late-model red Mazda, appeared to be trying to mate with Jane's Toyota, crawling up its back end. Jane couldn't tell what her car looked like beneath it.

"I said I was sorry."

"Yeah, being sorry doesn't keep you from being stupid." He was busy taking pictures with his phone. He wore a red T-shirt with a drawing of a skull wearing a bandana headband over long hair and sunglasses, pointing a gun. OUTLAW, it read, in block letters. "What's your problem, huh, you drunk or something? You stopped in the middle of the fucking intersection!" He wasn't very tall. He didn't look much like an outlaw.

"Sorry," she said again, uselessly. "I wish you wouldn't use that kind of language."

"Oh, sorry, heavens to Betsy!" he said, in a hateful, mincing voice. "You mean, fuck? Fuck fuck fuck fuckety fuck. Stupid bitch. You better have all kindsa insurance. I'm calling the cops."

"I have my insurance card," Jane said, hoping that she really did have it. She kept it in her wallet but she couldn't remember the last time she'd seen it. She guessed she would have to call Eric too.

"Screw your card. My whole front end's messed up." He tried to jiggle the Mazda's bumper to free it, gave up, and kicked at Jane's car. "What?" he said to Jane.

"Nothing." She had been staring at his hair and turned away, embarrassed. Why would anybody want to look like that?

Traffic clogged behind them as people saw what had happened and had to stop and back up.

There was more horn honking. A small crowd had assembled for the purposes of admiring the wreck and trading opinions. Jane turned away from them. She felt tears starting in her eyes from helpless, stupid weakness.

"Hey Richie." Patrick had squeezed himself out of the car door. "What the hell, man?"

"Oh, hey Pat." Richie did a confused double-take.

"What's the big hairy deal? Be nice to the lady. There's a reason they call them accidents."

"Why'd she stop, huh?" Richie said, less furious now, but unwilling to give up his grievance. "Stopped cold. Don't say she didn't."

"Well you hit her from behind. That's not so good."

Some shut-down part of Jane's mind flickered back to life. She recalled that this was true, it was not, generally, a good thing to hit somebody from behind.

"It still run?"

"I don't know, I can't even move it. It's all hung the fuck up, see?" Richie said, slapping at the hood. "Ow."

"The bumpers are locked. Help me lift it off. Hey!" he called into the crowd of onlookers. He seemed to know a number of them.

Patrick took off his leather jacket and tossed it into the Toyota's front seat. They conferred together, then some of them began pushing and bouncing on Jane's trunk, while Patrick and the others tried to lift the Mazda's front end. They made a great deal of grunting and heaving noise, broke off, conferred again, and tried once more. The rest of the crowd cheered and shouted their suggestions. Patrick's jaw clenched with effort. Metal scraped against metal. It was as if she had blundered into some terrifying ceremony of men, who roared and swore and sweated and strained and egged each other on.

A police cruiser drove up, its blue lights revolving. An officer got out and made his way over to the two joined cars. He was one of those slow-walking policemen. The men working on the cars sounded more urgent now, hoarser. "Chrissake, wait till I . . . You got it? All right, PUSH!"

Finally there was a metallic groan. The Mazda bounced loose and its front wheels landed on the pavement. A cheer went up. Richie started the Mazda and revved the engine. Jane went to see what the Toyota looked like.

It wasn't as bad as it might have been. A deep, V-shaped crumple to one side of the license plate and some long scrapes across the length of her trunk. Patrick joined her, breathing hard and looking pleased. His face was red and his shirt was tracked with sweat. The veins stood out on his throat and forearms. It occurred to Jane for the first time that this was what people meant when they said they were "pumped up." They meant it entirely literally. The extent of her ignorance about ordinary things still amazed her. "Tires seem OK," Patrick told her. "You might want to get the suspension checked."

"Thanks," Jane said, although that seemed inadequate, given all the muscular effort that had gone into the production. "I mean, thanks to everybody. I wouldn't have known what to do."

"Ah, it was kind of fun," he said modestly, and Jane understood that this was true. They had all enjoyed the chance to hurl themselves against heavy objects and work their will on them.

Richie and the police officer stood a little distance away, talking. Richie had worked himself up again and was waving his arms around.

"Uh oh, here comes trouble," Patrick said in a jolly tone, as the police officer left Richie and approached them. Jane felt twitchy and nervous, the way she always was around police, even when she was being the most blameless of citizens.

"This your car?" he asked her. One of those silly questions that you still had to answer. Jane said that it was. "You know you aren't supposed to move anything at an accident scene, right?"

"I've never been in an accident before," Jane said. The officer gave her a brief, sizing-up glance. She hoped she looked as pitiful as she felt.

"Oh come on, Dougie," Patrick said. "We were just trying to clear the way for traffic. Anyway, it was my idea, give her a break."

Did Patrick know everybody? He was a bartender, he probably did. The policeman did not look like a Dougie. He was middle-aged, square-faced, with small, staring blue eyes. Maybe he was one of the cops Bonnie knew. She didn't want to think about Bonnie right now.

Officer Dougie asked Jane for her license and insurance card. She handed them over and he went back to his patrol car with them. Richie backed the Mazda up against the curb. He popped the hood and some of the men who had helped push gathered around to lean over the engine. "I think I need to sit down," Jane said. Some adrenaline that had propped her up until now was draining out of her. She felt hollow, shaky.

"Sure, hey, let me pull your car over to one side, OK? Then you can wait there. Don't worry about these guys, I'll talk to them."

These guys, Dougie and Richie. Was everybody here called by a kid's nickname? Jane watched Patrick start her car, move it to the side of the street. Even at such a short distance, he drove the way he walked, with a swagger. He got out and opened the door for her. "There you be. Rest easy, now. Don't worry about Dougie, he's a peach. The worst part's over."

Was it? (And what, if anything, about Dougie suggested peach?) She still had to get herself home and decide what to tell Eric ("I was giving one of Bonnie's lovers a ride home when . . ."), file an insurance claim, get the car repaired. Oh, and fix dinner. She hoped the GPS hadn't gone haywire, since she still had no idea where she was. Some welter of bars and check cashing stores and Thai restaurants and signs offering tattoos, phone cards, credit counseling, and everyone but her with purposeful, important places to go. She watched in the rearview mirror as Patrick, Richie, and Dougie conferred on the sidewalk, Patrick acting as her representative, she guessed. They spoke their own language of hierarchy and casual violence, they understood the ways in which the world worked, its machinery of laws and money and power. Wasn't this always how it went for her? Wasn't she always excluded by her own fear and weakness? Sitting and waiting while men decided what would be done to her, for her, on her behalf. And she let it happen. It was as if she had never before really noticed, or found this remarkable.

After a time, Patrick came back to the car and climbed into the passenger seat. "So here's the deal, Dougie's going to write up an accident report, but nobody gets a ticket. Which is so very, very good. You and Richie get to fight it out with your insurance companies." He waited for Jane to say something.

"Thank you," she said, since he was that pleased with himself, and she guessed he really had saved her from at least one layer of trouble. "That's great." She was noticing all the things about him that were alien, male: his sweat smell, his enormous hands, the creased, mysterious territory of his crotch. She said, as if this followed from their conversation, "I've never trusted men. Never understood them. My whole life."

"Yeah?" He had no idea what she was talking about. And why should he? "Well, a lot of guys, they're the same way. About girls. Women," he corrected. "No clue. All right, you know not to tell anybody you stopped. OK? He just hit you."

"Bonnie's sleeping with my husband. So she and I had a, what did you call it, a dustup too."

"You're kidding."

"Not kidding."

She felt him staring at her. "When, like, now?"

"Probably not right this minute." If only because Eric had the children with him.

"But, wow." He contemplated this in silence. "For how long?"

"A while."

He was busy asking himself his own questions. "Good old Bonnie," he said, finally. "She does get around."

"Doesn't she though."

"So, I have to ask, not that it's really my business, but why is it you were taking her cookies?"

"Because I felt . . . bad. There was a scene. I said some things."

"Yeah, I bet."

"No, I should have handled it differently."

"You were upset," Patrick suggested. "Sure. Finding out a thing like that."

"I already knew. I told them to go ahead. That neither of them mattered that much to me."

Patrick nodded, making a visible effort to understand.

Jane said, "But it wasn't really true. Not for her. Him, maybe. We have kids. You don't want to rock the boat."

"That's messed up."

Jane said yes, it was. She looked behind her to where Dougie was still sitting in his squad car, taking his sweet time about the paperwork. What happened if they had an actual, serious accident, would they move any faster? Richie had taken himself off already in a blast of acceleration.

Patrick said, "Hey, do you think I could have the rest of those cookies?"

Jane retrieved the upended basket and handed it over. Patrick ate with one hand cupped beneath his mouth to catch the crumbs. Once he'd swallowed he said, "If you don't mind my asking, what's your husband like?"

"He's very smart. He's a doctor, a surgeon. People like him, he's fun to be around."

"A doctor." He shook his head, marveling. "Now that's something the likes of me could never do. He's not so much fun for you though, huh."

"No," Jane said. "Not lately. Not for a long time." She looked behind her again. No Dougie. No one paying them any attention. "Would you do something for me? One more thing?"

"I kind of have to get ready for work."

"Oh, sure. Never mind."

"No, what?" Smiling, but already thinking of the next thing he had to do. Ready to move on.

"Would you let me kiss you?" Instantly and horribly embarrassed. "You don't have to if you don't want to. Never mind."

"Wow. I wasn't expecting that one." He was looking at her with more interest now. "I mean, no one ever comes right out and asks. That's so cute."

"Never mind," Jane said again, feeling both shamed and irritated. He could have just said no. "Forget I—"

He leaned over and wrapped around her, lifting her out of her seat, and then he was on her, his big face pinning hers down, his mouth working on hers as if it wanted something, wanted something, insistent but soft, and then he drew away and set her back again.

"Oh." She touched her mouth. "Thank you."

"You're welcome."

They both laughed and looked away. Then they both spoke at the same time.

"I hope that was—"

"I wanted to—"

"You first," Patrick told her.

"I don't know anybody like you." She didn't want to say, anybody as sexually healthy as you seem to be, so she said, "It's great the way you jump right in and take charge of things. Thanks for helping me out."

"Hey, no problem." He seemed relieved that there might be no more to it than gratitude. "Yeah, it's my neighborhood, so I know these guys. Of course."

Of course, she would not have been in his neighborhood to begin with if she had not been taking him home. "Well, I appreciate it." She wanted to kiss him again.

"Yeah, I've been here four years? Three. One year I lived in Lakeview, I thought that was really far north. My whole family's back in Bridgeport. They think I moved to Alaska or someplace. It's like they have their feet in cement. Don't get me wrong, I love em to death. I just don't need to see them every morn, noon, and night."

Hadn't Bonnie said something about his family? Something about them living next door to the Daleys, back when the Daleys had lived in an ordinary house. Patrick said, "I actually do think about moving to Alaska. First I need to take a trip there. Check it out. Like, a camping trip."

Jane agreed that a camping trip in Alaska would be a real adventure. Bears, Patrick said. They had actual, real bears. You had to watch out for them. He seemed energized by the idea of bears, of going up against one. There was a movie, it had Brad Pitt in it, and at the end he went off into the woods and fought bears. Did she know that one? Jane did not. The movie had not been in Alaska but it was someplace wild like that. Patrick said, "There's times I think I'd be better off where life is just, you know, the basics. Food, shelter. Survival. I mean, I'm a city boy born and bred, but I get these flashes. Like, maybe I'm supposed to live some other way. You know what I mean?"

"Yes," Jane said. "And you have to pay attention to feelings like that." It seemed that once she decided to make a man into a mindless sex object, he started confiding his heart's desires.

"Ah well." Patrick raised one hand and let it fall, dismissively. "Alaska, what would I do there anyway? All I have on me is a strong back and a weak mind."

His brogue, Jane noted, grew stronger whenever he said something self-disparaging. "Don't give up on it," she said. "Why shouldn't you go there? Who says you shouldn't?" In her side mirror she saw Officer Dougie approaching with papers in hand. "Here comes your friend."

"He's not exactly a friend. It's more like, professional courtesy."

Jane rolled down her window and Dougie handed back her license and insurance. He went through the accident report with her. He still looked like he would have liked to arrest her for something. Jane did not have to appear in court. She should notify her insurer. Here was the file number they would ask for. Here was the time, date, location. She should call her insurer without delay. She should be careful about making sudden stops unless it was necessary to avoid hitting a pedestrian or another vehicle. Did she understand that?

Jane said that she did. Dougie leaned down to put his head in the window. "Pat. Keep your nose clean."

Patrick gave him a mock-salute. "Yessir, Officer sir, and thank you for your service."

Dougie shook his head and walked back to his cruiser. Patrick said, "I could tell you stories about that guy. He knows I could."

Jane decided not to ask. She started the engine. Patrick gathered up his jacket and opened his door but didn't get out. "Thanks for the ride. Sorry about your car."

"It's all right. It's actually my husband's car. I don't mind it getting knocked around."

"Ha ha." Still he wasn't leaving. "Look, would it be all right if I called you sometime? I know you're married and all, but it sounds like, well, special circumstances." When Jane hesitated, he said, "Just to talk. This sounds corny and all, but I feel like I already know you."

Jane found a pencil and a note pad in the console and wrote down her cell phone number. Her name too, in case it didn't stay with him. "Here. Oh, don't forget the cookies."

"Cookies, right." He gathered them up, hesitated, then turned back and kissed her again. Slower this time, more inquisitive and exploratory. Then he drew away, stepped out to the curb, and shut the car door. "See you."

Jane watched him until he rounded the corner and disappeared. Small explosions, like static electricity, went off in her skin. She turned on the GPS and waited for the bright mechanical voice to guide her home.

the language of flowers

Eric sent her flowers. Actual flowers. He had never done this before. Nor, with a couple of exceptions, a couple meaning exactly two, had any other man she'd ever known. She had not been a flower kind of a girl.

Bonnie studied the bouquet, first from the chair she drew up next to it, then getting up and moving around the apartment, trying out different angles and distances. There were roses, lots of them, big champagne-colored blooms of a sort she had not seen before. Also some ferny stuff and smaller, trailing sprigs, white and fragrant. The flowers came in a tall vase that was sprayed gold to go along with the general magnificence of the thing.

Bonnie tried to decide what it meant, sending flowers, especially ones as extravagant-seeming as these. The card said *Love, Eric* and it was written out in his own handwriting. He'd gone into the shop himself rather than ordering them over the phone or online. You were meant to pay attention to such flowers. She guessed she was meant to look upon his suit with favor. Take him back into her bed. Which she had not yet decided to do.

She was at a low point and by now nothing she might do or not do seemed like a good idea. She missed him but she didn't know if the two of them made sense anymore; in fact, she was pretty sure they did not. By now there was so much difficult history between them, their affair had become almost like another marriage. They'd had their honeymoon of sexual ecstasy, their doubts and bruised feelings and reconnections. And now they seemed to have circled back to courtship.

Or maybe she was reading things wrong? Maybe when Jane had outed and shamed them, that had been a final and insurmountable blow, and the flowers were meant as a kind of kiss-off. A sentimental (and expensive) farewell and thanks for the memories. Maybe he had decided the question for her, and all her back-and-forth, yes-or-no, should-or-shouldn't drama was beside the point. Maybe they would never see each other again. Except perhaps in some safe and sexless territory that would never be anything other than glum and awkward, everything over over over.

She bounded up from her chair. She couldn't stand it, she had to talk to him. It was the end of the workday, of her workday at least. There was no guarantee of reaching Eric, who often enough stayed late at the hospital. Or else he might have gone home on time for once and was already in the bosom of his family, doing penance. Maybe Jane had gotten flowers too.

Bonnie punched in his cell phone number and listened to it ring, once, twice, three times and the fourth meant voice mail.

Eric answered. "Hey there." A distant, tin can sound to his voice.

"Are you on speaker?" She hated the speaker phone.

"Sort of. I have a rental car, it has Bluetooth. So the call goes through the car."

"Why do you have a rental?"

"Ah, Jane was driving my car and somebody hit her in a parking lot. So it's in the shop."

"Oh, sure." It was not how she had planned to begin. She tried to regain her momentum. "The flowers are beautiful, thank you."

"You like them? I thought they were pretty."

"They're this wonderful color." It occurred to her that they were the color of fancy lingerie. She hurried past this thought. "Kind of a peachy, pale gold. Very elegant."

"Good, that's good. I wanted to . . ." His voice cut out, then back in. ". . . for you."

"I can't hear you."

"I said, I thought they'd brighten your day."

That was not what he'd said, but there was no getting it back now. "Where are you anyway?"

". . . home."

"Why don't you call me sometime when you're not driving, OK?"

"Wait, I'll pull over. Hold on." There was some scattered, ambient noise as he put the phone down and maneuvered the car. Bonnie waited. One of the things you could really get tired of was never being able to have an uninterrupted phone conversation. Either Eric was trying to juggle the phone while he drove or else he was getting calls from home or his pager was going off. "All right, sorry." At least he'd turned the Bluetooth off. "What were you saying?"

"Nothing. Just, thanks. Have a good evening."

"No, wait, I do want to talk to you. How've you been?"

"Fine," Bonnie said, still feeling difficult and pissy, roses or no. "I bet you're fine too."

"They gave me a pretty cool rental. A BMW."

"Uh huh."

"Want to see it? It's sharp."

"How am I supposed to do that, exactly?"

"Look out your front window."

"What?" Bonnie took the phone away from her ear and stared at it. Put it up to her ear again. "What are you talking about?"

"Just go look."

Bonnie went to the window and pulled back the curtain. A car at the curb flashed its lights.

"What are you doing here?"

"I miss you. I wanted to see you."

"No, what are you doing here right now? Did you think the roses would soften me up?"

"You called me," Eric reminded her.

"Were you out there waiting to see if I'd call? Huh?"

"I was hoping you'd call," he admitted.

"Ha," Bonnie said. She had him dead to rights. "Sorry, that's a little too cute for me. When I was a kid, Charlie and I used to set rabbit traps. We'd get a cardboard box and prop it up with a stick and put a carrot on the ground. So the rabbit would go for the carrot and knock the stick and the box would fall and trap it. Needless to say, it never worked. You didn't use a carrot, you used roses. Nice try." She felt idiotic looking out the window at him and dropped the curtain.

Eric cleared his throat. "I drive by here a lot. On my way home from work."

She was incredulous. "You've been *stalking* me?"

"That's such a melodramatic word," he said, sounding annoyed. "It presumes all these hateful motives. Was Romeo stalking Juliet when he showed up under her balcony?"

"Now you're Romeo."

"I don't know what I am." He coughed and tried to suppress it. "Sorry."

"Sorry for what?" For coughing, maybe.

"For being stupid and miserable and missing you."

There was a space of silence. Then Bonnie said, "I'm not going to let you inside."

"Yeah, OK." He sounded droopy and hopeless, in a way she found irritating.

"But I'll come out and talk to you. Give me a minute."

She ended the call, went to the bouquet, and extracted one of the roses. She rummaged around in a bathroom drawer for bobby pins. Of course there were none. Victorian ladies probably had all sorts of hair pins and miniature vases for such purposes. In the end she settled for braiding the stem into her hair and securing it with a paper clip. She didn't bother to change out of her sweatshirt and jeans. She thought she looked badass.

She locked the apartment door behind her and stepped out into the early dusk. The passenger side of the BMW was at the curb, and Eric reached over to open the door for her. Bonnie got in and shut it behind her. "Nice ride," she said. "I'm all sorts of impressed. Take me, I'm yours."

He touched the flower in her hair with one finger. "Pretty."

There was enough of the last daylight for her to get in a sideways look at him. "You look tired," she said, although she had not intended to say anything. In fact he looked worse than tired, he looked worn down. Old, even.

"I'm always tired." Not a complaint, just a statement of fact.

"You do have the original high-stress job."

"I'm used to that by now."

"You don't sound convinced," Bonnie said, who was happy to keep the conversation away from herself. "More like a punch-drunk fighter."

"I'm used to being tired," he corrected. "But I'm not tired of the work. Not most days. Most days you feel like you're doing something almost nobody else can do. And it's important, it's needed. Although there are times I wish everybody could just be . . . healthy. Let the body do its work without all these violent interventions."

Bonnie looked at him, wondering. Eric was famous for his annoyingly positive attitude about his profession. It was practically an article of faith that he loved medicine and everything to do with it. If he was getting a case of burnout now, that was something new. Or maybe admitting to it was something new.

"But listen to me go on," Eric said, as if he was aware of a lapse. "Tell me how you are. I really was sorry to hear about your mother. I'm glad I got to meet her, I liked her."

"Thanks. I'm fine. There's always family stuff to get through, but everybody's coping." Haley and the kids were staying in Wisconsin, which suited Haley since she wouldn't have to go back to her marriage, and suited Stan since someone would be there to run the house and be an audience for his tantrums. The kids could go to a normal school and learn swear words and how to play video games. Charlie was supposed to be doing another stint in rehab, though no one was too hopeful by this time.

"Death of a parent," she said. "It's one of those milestones everybody gets to experience." She didn't want to talk about meeting Carl Rizzi. It was a sore place in her heart that she didn't like touching. "This really is a sharp car," she said, wanting to move the conversation along.

"I had to put down some of my own cash for it but I thought, why not. A little self-indulgence."

Another thing that was not really in character for him. He seldom spent money on himself. Bonnie found this new, restless version of Eric interesting; severely, she damped her attraction down. She listened to him recount the car's many luxury features. The 50/50 weight distribution. Zero to sixty in some ridiculous time measured in seconds. Heated seats, blind spot detection. Speed limit information. Automatic door closers. She'd heard it said that men regarded cars as substitutes for women. Or had it been the other way around? Regardless, she would be at a disadvantage. She was not very well equipped with top of the line options.

"I'm thinking, even when I get the Toyota back, I could lease this." He shrugged, looking glum, which she knew translated into embarrassment, probably at his own excitement over a fancy car. He would regard it as one of those guy things he was supposed to be immune to.

"You should do that, if you want. Go for it." She almost said, "Live a little," but she did not want to sound too encouraging.

"We could see each other," Eric said, as if this was the conversation they'd been having all along. "There's no obstacle now with Jane. She doesn't care what I do."

"Oh yes she does. And she cares that I'm the one you were doing it with. Don't be mistaken about that."

"She's done with me."

"Well you're not done being married, are you? Or living under the same roof, or raising children together. It's a screwed up situation. I can't do that kind of thing anymore."

"Since when did you—" He stopped himself. "Sorry."

"Since when did I get so scrupulous? Fuck you. Like, sincerely."

"All right," he said, meaning, he gave up. Which made her, perversely, more angry with him. How dare he send his giant extravagant roses, cruise her neighborhood in his ridiculous extravagant car, if he was only going to weakly concede?

"Let me try and explain it to you. Why I can't go back to what it was." She still didn't want to talk about Carl Rizzi, but maybe she could talk around him. "You want to hear it or not?"

"Of course I want to hear it."

Now she wished she hadn't said anything. But she guessed she owed him this much of an explanation, after all those damned roses. "I'm a slow learner," she began. "I always thought I was pretty crazy-adventurous, you know, a thrill seeker. That's who I was. Prided myself on it, actually. Venturing where others dared not."

She paused, waiting for Eric to say something, but he wasn't about to interrupt. Nowhere to go but onward. "So you do all these outlandish things, you carry on with all these bad idea men, no, let me finish, and you get this romantic notion of yourself as, I don't know, passion's plaything? Shipwrecked on the wilder shores of love? I don't even want to think about the crap I used to tell myself. Then one day, the short answer is, I figure some things out. I was raised with all these addicted people and I grew up addicted to chaos and drama and I guess, acting out to get attention." She stopped, feeling depleted, even a little nauseated. "So that's the deal. It's all sickness. And I have to try and get better. Bonnie 2.0."

It was entirely dark by now, the cool light of the many dashboard gizmos the only illumination.

Bonnie looked out to her own apartment windows, her hand already on the door, ready to take her leave. Then Eric said, "I don't think I'm a bad idea."

"Oh?" Disbelieving. "Come on, you're the ultimate bad idea. You're like, original sin."

"Maybe at the beginning. Not now. Now we're the best thing each other has. Or you are for me."

He waited, but now it was Bonnie's turn to keep silent. He went on. "You think you're the only one second-guessing yourself? Exhausted with yourself? OK, we shouldn't have. But we did. And where we are now, it could be pretty great. I wish it wasn't sideways and upside down and backwards. In spite of all that, here I am. Up to you."

He was done with talking. Bonnie reached out and took his hand. "I think I'm going to need some more flowers."

∽⚘

Why take him back? Why start up all over again, in spite of all the good intentions and sadder-but-wiser speeches, everything that was complicated and hurtful? Because she held out hope that Eric was right, and that they were a good thing, not a wicked, or a furtive, or a crazy-making thing. Their own version of a marriage, messy with compromise and complications, but like any other marriage. She was lonely, she loved him, he felt the same. Start with that.

They returned to each other with all the old feeling. But something had changed. Their lovemaking was steady, comfortable and comforting, but no longer filled with desperate erotic violence, as before. No longer provoking and submitting, no more the particular sexual delirium that they had previously inhabited. They did not speak of it. Bonnie thought it was likely that neither of them wanted to embarrass or blame the other. And she did not blame him. It was just how things progressed, for them and for everybody else who lived long enough.

They still had their share of reliable pleasure. Were still at ease with each other's bodies. One could hardly complain. It might even be a cause for a certain kind of celebration, since this new and calmer state was surely a part of what she had claimed she wanted: a life not built around ridiculous extremes of feeling or behavior. Anyway, there was still enough of the unconventional and the outlandish in their situation, wasn't there? How much, exactly, of tameness and sameness did she have to complain about?

But there was a way in which the diminishment of sex was the exaltation of death. Bonnie did not put it to herself in quite these words, but she felt its truth. You gave up dancing one jig and took up another. The body failed. Flowers wilted and so did you. If anything, she loved him more dearly now, and more sadly, because of what had been lost, what was broken, and now what remained.

What to do. Push the dread and doubt to one side and enjoy what they could of their shadow marriage. The time they managed to spend together, squeezed in between and around other obligations. Their cautious plans for how they might, in time, come to spend an entire night together, go on trips together. The matter-of-factness of checking in and checking out, the foreseeable exasperations. All this might have gone on for quite some time if Jane had not up and fallen in love.

jane writes a poem

Jane and Patrick walked along North Avenue Beach. The beach had been closed to swimming for a month, since Labor Day. The long, boat shaped beach house was closed as well, and the vendors of Sno Cones and Pronto Pups, of wakeboards and paddleboards and kayaks and Jet Skis, sandals and sunglasses and T-shirts had all gone away, the summer long over. But the sky today was blue, as was the rolling lake, and any number of people were walking along the paved paths or on the sand itself. Bicyclists and runners streamed past them, keeping up their single-minded pace.

It was always cooler near the lake and the breeze off the water was strong and chill. Patrick had taken off his leather jacket and given it to Jane to wear. She hugged it to her. It gave her the most extreme and solemn pleasure that he had done so. There was the jacket itself, with its good smell and its silky lining and the zone of warmth within it. A man giving you his jacket was the kind of thing you might see in a movie, all right a not very good movie, but still.

"You been here before?" Patrick asked her, and Jane said she didn't think so. She might have driven past it, or been driven past it, or perhaps that had been some other beach. She couldn't remember. She'd been raised instead around suburban pools and compulsory swimming lessons.

"No? You should bring the kids next summer, they'd love it. Bring Eric too." They had been speaking as if hers was still a functioning marriage. It made things easier.

"Oh, I don't know. It's so hard to take the kids anywhere." Not to mention Eric and his limited enthusiasm for family outings.

"So come by yourself and play beach volleyball with us."

"Ha ha, right." Only slightly less implausible. "No thanks. I always got picked last for everything, you wouldn't want me."

"Sure I would," he said gallantly. "There's all kinds of teams, some of them are just for fun. There's coed and a women's league. I bet you'd find one you liked."

"I don't know if I'm the beach volleyball type," Jane said, thinking of the girls you saw wriggling out of their bikinis as they jumped and lunged. Not to mention the sport itself, which she remembered from her miserable gym-class days.

"Don't be a wuss."

"I am a wuss. But I could come watch you play. Be one of your groupies," she teased. She was sure he had groupies. Bonnie had said as much, muttering darkly.

He looked away, his expression one of distaste. He didn't like being teased, she had to remember that. "Sorry," she said. "Just mouthing off."

"Everybody acts like I'm some kind of slut."

Could men be sluts? She wasn't sure. "I didn't mean it that way. I'm sorry. I meant, girls notice you, that's only natural. It's not your fault if some of them act silly." Jane reached for his hand and after a moment he squeezed her hand back and they walked on that way, content.

It was only their second date. Jane called it that to herself, date. Of course that was counting the day she'd smashed up Eric's car as a date. Talk about acting silly. They'd talked on the phone a lot since then, mornings when Jane had the house to herself and Patrick was waking up after his late nights of tending bar. "Hey," he'd say, still yawning, still in bed. Naked? Jane let the pictures roll around in her head. He yawned again, stretching. "So what are you doing for fun today?"

And Jane would insist that she didn't know what fun was, she was washing up the kids' cereal bowls, or folding laundry, or some other dull chore. And Patrick would say they were going to have to do something about that, her lack of fun, and there would be a pause while that open-ended promise hung in the air.

Jane told him about things the children had done, about Robbie getting chewing gum so matted into his hair that the barber had to shave a patch of it, about Grace's allergy tests. "See? No fun."

"You're a great mom," Patrick would say, on the basis of no actual information, except what she told him. She liked hearing it anyway.

He said, "My mom was the same way when we were growing up. Anything for the kids. She still lives to knock herself out. Don't tell her there's an easier way to scrub a floor than with a brush and a bucket, or you don't have to iron sheets."

"She irons sheets? Who irons sheets?"

"You know her favorite thing to say? 'I was so busy today, I didn't have time to go to the bathroom.'"

He was the youngest of seven. Seven, that was nothing, he'd grown up with families that had ten, eleven, twelve kids. Real old school. Thank God people had wised up. His brothers and sisters had normal sized families themselves. He was the only one who wasn't married. Don't think that didn't come up at every family get-together. There was the smart-ass brother-in-law who made the crack about being gay. Yeah, and he only ever made it once.

"Not that I have one thing against gay people. But come on, show some respect."

He wasn't really that Catholic anymore, even his mom had given up on him. His dad had died when Patrick was fifteen. Pancreatic cancer. Which was why, whatever else he did, he tried to keep in shape and eat a salad once in a while. He worried about stuff like that.

"Of course you'd worry," Jane told him. "But that doesn't mean you're going to get that particular cancer, or any cancer." She wasn't sure how people got pancreatic cancer anyway.

"Ah, we all have to die of something, we do." The brogue again. It came and went. It seemed neither entirely genuine nor entirely fake.

"You can't dwell on it," Jane told him, aiming for a tone that did not sound like one of his female relatives. "Keep it in perspective."

"Perspective," Patrick repeated. "Good concept. I should make that my next tattoo."

"No you shouldn't." Jane wasn't sure how she felt about tattoos, except that her own kids had better never get any. She'd caught a glimpse of the two Patrick had across each enormous bicep: a stylized arrow and an angel that managed to look like a pinup girl. It was likely there were others.

"On the back of my hand, so I can smack myself in the face with it." He was the one teasing now.

Jane almost said he should put it somewhere she wasn't going to see it, but that remark might have seemed too racy, so she only sighed and said he should suit himself, he was the one who'd have to walk around wearing it, she was too old to understand such things. Patrick protested that she wasn't old, anyway not all that much older than he was, what, five years?

It was eight or maybe closer to nine, but Jane didn't bother correcting him. She was smitten with him. Two kisses and a heavy dose of phone flirting and she was as goofy as a teenager, more so, since even as a teenager she'd never done such a thing as flirt. The boys she'd known then had not inspired it. Now she played music when she had the house to herself, old Fleetwood Mac and Joni Mitchell, singing along and imagining—what, exactly? Scenes of corny romance in which he rescued her from car crashes (likely, if she kept trying to drive in the city), or armed assailants, or perhaps a log jam in a frigid river. Because he was certainly the comic-book lumberjack that she and Bonnie had hooted over all those years ago, minus the elevated reading habits you weren't meant to believe in the first place.

They didn't talk about Bonnie. Patrick either didn't have much to say about her or else was trying to be tactful. As for Jane, she thought Bonnie already took up too much space in her life.

She felt sorry for Patrick, even in the midst of mooning about him. He didn't seem happy doing what he was doing, living as he was living, but he had no clear plan to do anything different. He wasn't the sharpest knife in the drawer, as Jane's father used to say about, well, about a great many people.

Not much had been expected of him, youngest son of a big, hectic tribal Irish family. Just as, in different fashion, not much had been expected of Jane.

They reached the northern terminus of the beach, turned and headed back to the parking lot.

They'd dropped their joined hands, but continued walking side by side, taking their time. The beach had been Patrick's idea. He had to work later that night, and Jane had only managed this free afternoon by arranging a play date for Grace. So there was only this brief window of time for all her foolishness, and that was reassuring, since she would hardly have the opportunity to do anything seriously stupid.

Anyway, it was just her trashy unbalanced daydreams. Nothing real. Unless she climbed out of her fantasy and made it real.

They reached the parking lot, but neither of them wanted to leave yet, and so they found a spot on the grass to sit. "You're not too cold, are you?" Patrick asked, and Jane said she was fine. Of course she would have sat on a block of ice if she'd had to. It was so unlikely, the two of them being anywhere together in the first place. Talk about two different worlds. She'd even had to pick him up in the minivan, although Patrick had refrained from repeating his opinions about minivans.

Now he looked out to the blue bar of the lake and the edge of tawny sand, then behind them at the rushing lanes of traffic and the city skyline, which even on a clear day was wreathed in haze and golden shimmer, as if it was some zone of impossible glamour. "This is great," he pronounced. "Being outside and all. Something different. I spend too much time in the damn bars. Ah well, it's a living."

"It's a nice change for me too, from my routine. Not that I go to bars a lot."

"No I guess you wouldn't." Jane felt him watching her, enumerating her deficiencies and lack of verve, then he said, "Not with kids and all. You wouldn't want to." And Jane agreed that this was so.

After a moment he said, "That's messed up, Bonnie and your husband. Sorry. Maybe you don't want to talk about it."

"No, that's all right. I can't really talk about it with anybody else." This was true. It was a dismal thing to realize.

"People step out on each other all the time, I'm not saying it's good, but when it's your friend? No way."

"They knew each other for years and years, we all did. They were attracted to each other and they crossed the line. You can understand how it happened."

"Yeah, but it didn't have to." Patrick shook his head. He had a head like a sculpted bust, something made out of marble or granite, and it looked just as heavy. "You oughta hire a hit man."

Jane shrugged. She didn't want to kill anybody. She just wanted them to go away.

He said, "All right, not a hit man. But you don't have to put up with it. Jesus, I wouldn't. You're a pretty woman, you know that? And you're smart and you're nice and you deserve a lot better. If you don't mind me saying so."

Mind, oh no. If she hadn't been already sitting down, her butter legs would have melted and collapsed with gratitude. She wanted to put her hands on him, on his skin. She wanted to touch his hair. She wanted him to climb on top of her and turn her inside out. She dropped her eyes so she would look all sad and he wouldn't see how shameless she was. "Thanks."

"I mean, I always got along fine with Bonnie; sure, she could be a little out there, but . . . OK, sorry. She's like, dead to me. Her name is now a swear word."

"But you liked her, right?" In spite of herself, she had to ask. "You liked going to bed with her? It's none of my business, I know that, go ahead and tell me so. But she was always the one who ended up with all the guys."

"Ah." Patrick nodded. Then shook his head. Embarrassed. "Well she was, I mean it was fine. A normal kind of fine."

"I was never like that. I never figured out sex. Not in all this time." Once she'd begun, she couldn't stop.

"Oh yeah?" Embarrassment replaced by a new attention. Some male Pavlovian response. Say sex. Ring bell. Arf arf.

"So I can't really blame my husband. I mean I can, but why wouldn't he want that. Someone who has more enthusiasm. Who's better at it. It's only natural to want that."

"Huh," Patrick said. He appeared to be working through a particularly knotty thought process. "That's really tough luck. For everybody, I mean, especially for you."

"I shouldn't have brought it up. I guess I wanted you to know, because you've been so nice about listening to me. I wanted you to know there's this whole other part of the story."

"Huh," he said again, making it sound more contemplative this time. "Do you think maybe it's because you haven't been with the right guy?"

"I've thought that. I have."

He leaned over and kissed her, a brief, grazing kiss. "Is that OK? I mean do you like it?"

"Yes."

They kissed again, and this time there was more intention behind it. "How about that?"

"Yes. I like that too."

She guessed you'd call it making out, the touching and rubbing and more of the kissing too. He put his hands inside the jacket and made himself at home there. She liked it and kept liking it and she had to be careful not to let on how much she did, so that the exercise did not lose its pretense of instruction.

They drew back from each other and laughed. Patrick said, "This is a little weird, you know? I don't mean you're weird; I meant, the situation."

"The other parties involved," Jane agreed. She had trouble catching her breath. She set about making some necessary adjustments to her clothing.

"Because, maybe you're trying to get back at them? I could totally understand that."

Jane thought about this. "I guess that's part of it. Maybe I wouldn't be here in normal circumstances. But now I'm glad I am."

"Well I guess that's going to have to do," Patrick said cheerfully. He leaned in to kiss her again and worked one of his hands around to the back of her pants and slipped it inside her waistband.

When they broke apart again Jane felt blurred or smudged, as if she were a drawing that had been partly erased. "I have to get back home."

"Right now?" Jane nodded. "Bummer." He stood and then pulled Jane to her feet. It felt effortless, as if he could just as easily send her flying over his head.

Jane drove him back to his apartment and, with some reluctance, returned his jacket. They kissed again. She was growing very accustomed to that part of things. "You could come up if you want to," he said, his voice buzzing her ear, and Jane said no, she really had to leave. And she did, that was true enough, but what if she stayed? The idea horrified her. The idea fascinated her.

"You can call me," Jane said, feeling more and more like a teenager in an old song on AM radio. What if he never called again? Decided she was too freakish and unappealing, too much trouble? She would just up and die. No she would not, she was at least old enough to know that.

"Of course I will." He gave her nipple a quick, friendly tweak. "Drive safe, now."

So he wasn't the most conversationally gifted or sensitive guy around. Did she even care?

Jane got herself home and picked up Grace from her friend's house and thanked the other mother for watching the girls, and said that next time Katie could come over to their place. The woman asked if Jane had gotten her shopping done and Jane had a moment of blankness before she remembered that this was the reason she'd given for the afternoon, shopping. "I mostly looked around," Jane said, and for the briefest moment the other woman's expression showed a flicker of interest or disbelief or mockery, and it filled Jane with sober fear.

Jane drove Grace home and told her she could watch one video but first she had to bring her dirty clothes down to the basement. Then Robbie's school day was over and the whole house took on the particular quality of his energy.

Eric was home on time, or rather, on time for him, and the four of them ate the chili mac casserole with sufficient good cheer, and Jane thought how strange it was, landing back in the everyday, serving a meal, herding the children through their minimally required manners, and all the rest of it. This must be how it was for Eric, coming home after his time with Bonnie. Holding himself apart, watching himself as he eased back into the life of his house and became the ordinary, expected self who lived here. He saw Jane watching him. "What?" he asked.

"Nothing." He wouldn't be able to tell if there was anything different about her. He didn't pay enough attention to know.

Once she lay down at the end of the day, her real first alone time, she tried to locate and hold steady any one idea or impulse, such as wanting to have sex with Patrick. But then, she also did not want to. She wanted him to be a means to an end, an obliging body, but his inconvenient human personality kept intruding. Her motives were both straightforward and not so. She wanted to get even, take something from Bonnie as Bonnie had taken from her. As if you could think of people in terms of belonging and stealing. But you did. There was no use pretending you were any better than you were.

She hardly owed Eric fidelity, she had no reason to feel guilty. She felt guilty. "I am a mess," she said aloud, though nobody outside the small room would have heard, and that seemed like the one true statement she could make.

Bonnie was better at this sort of thing. Bonnie and all her sexy drama. Well, maybe she could pretend to be Bonnie. Just this once, be the wild and crazy one who everybody wanted.

Then Patrick didn't call. And didn't call. If Jane had wanted to be crazy, here was her chance.

She worried and suffered, suffered and worried, imagining every bad and worse possibility. He was ill, injured, hospitalized, with a rotating troupe of Irish relatives camped out in the waiting room. Ha, no. He was with some other girl. He'd lost her phone number. It was no big deal to him. He didn't care.

Jane could have called him, she almost did, but every time she came close she sank into her familiar gloom and self-doubt. She was the least sexually interesting person on the planet, both in and of herself, and as a rapidly aging suburban mom. Why would Patrick or anyone else want to pursue her? She was romance-proof.

Finally, he called. "Hey, how you been? How's my beach buddy?"

"Your what?" Jane said, but he was already talking past her.

"Listen, sorry I've been out of touch, I had to fill in for somebody at work and it totally wiped me out."

"Really." She was not inclined to listen to any breezy excuse he tossed her way. Should she hang up? Say something spiteful? Not if she wanted to see him again, which she did. It was one of those stupid dilemmas you thought you were done with once you got married.

"Yeah, it was killer." He didn't bother sounding killed or even particularly weary. Presumably he had recovered. "What's new with you?"

"I can't think of anything." Stay mad? Invent an interesting anecdote? She said, "I guess I've been busy too."

"Yeah?"

"Mmn."

"All right then! So, did you get your work done?"

"My what?"

"Your work that was keeping you busy."

"No, I'm still in the middle of some things." Big fat lie.

"Ah."

Jane didn't offer anything more. It was going to be up to him. He said, "I've been thinking about you."

"Have you." He must have all kinds of practice at getting women mad at him, and then talking himself back into their good graces.

"Hold on a minute." There was a sound of rustling, then unidentifiable small collisions, then liquid swallowings and smackings. "Sorry. Bit of a dry mouth this morning."

"Why's that," Jane asked, careful not to sound very interested.

"Debauchery," he said, and Jane giggled in spite of herself. "You didn't think I had such a big vocabulary did you?"

"No, I figured that's a word you might know."

"Oh, good one. I didn't know you had a mean side."

"You haven't seen mean yet."

And just that fast she was happy with him again, and carrying on like a rabbit in heat. Which was pretty much how she'd wanted to be, wasn't it? Except with a little more dignity. Farewell to dignity. "We should get together sometime," Patrick said, and Jane's rabbit heart went thumpity thump, and an agreeable agitation, a kind of sexual washing machine, started up in her. Then the dread settled in.

"That would be tricky," Jane said, thinking of Katie's mom, and how she could hardly call up and beg another favor, not after her lame shopping story. "I don't know."

"If it's easier, I can come there."

Instantly Jane envisioned every small or large disaster, beginning with the erotic unsuitability of a house decorated to withstand two young children, the ringing phone or doorbell that would require answering, the unexpected arrival home of her husband/children/neighbors who would be greeted by the sight of Jane entertaining Patrick in some naked fashion. Was she actually going to do such a thing? It was beginning to seem that she was. "It would be pretty hard without a car."

"All right. I guess—"

"A weekend might work." Eric could watch the kids. Evil alibis occurred to her. She would say she was going to a museum. The opera. "I mean, if you didn't have to work."

"Ah, they owe me. Or they could do me a favor and fire me."

"I need a couple of days to try and set things up." She wished she didn't sound so cold-blooded and businesslike. Set things up, she sounded like she was in charge of a catered luncheon. A phrase came to her: my heart misgave me. What did that even mean, how could your heart give or misgive? But she knew what it felt like. "Look, I'm still not sure about this."

"That's my job, isn't it. Convincing you."

Eric was mildly surprised when she told him she had a chance to see an Edward Albee revival with an old friend from her blood-bank days. No one he knew. It did not occur to him to suspect her of anything transgressive because it did not occur to him that she might be capable of doing so. It was as if her entire life had been camouflage, and now she might rob banks or hijack planes. She might be a little late, she told Eric. He was not to worry.

Should she go shopping for a new outfit? She decided not to, out of a combination of guilt and thrift, plus confusion as to what, exactly, she wanted to look like, suburban sex kitten or virgin sacrifice. In the end Jane settled for a plain white V-neck shirt, pencil skirt, and modest heels. Her black trench coat over that, both because of the blustery weather and to add, she hoped, a bit of rakish glamour.

There were also certain mortifying decisions regarding underwear.

They were supposed to meet at a bar in Patrick's neighborhood so that she could be plied with liquor, although this had not been stated outright. It was just after sunset when Jane arrived and circled the block looking for a place to park. Here was the intersection where she'd had her accident. (She was driving the Toyota again, now repaired. Eric had leased the extravagant BMW, which Jane thought was a billboard for a midlife tantrum, although she did not tell him this.) She found a space at the curb where it looked like she might not get towed, and was about to get out when she saw Patrick across the street.

He was walking with his phone to his ear, slowing to talk, now stopping entirely and tucking his chin, as if for privacy on the busy street. His forehead churned, listening. He was wearing his leather jacket, which Jane understood was an important garment, both utilitarian and a token of vanity. His hair was a darker, damp color and it still showed comb tracks. Jane watched him. Again an agitation filled her, both pleasant and not pleasant, and she gave herself over to it, letting herself imagine a first and a second and third thing, and then Patrick put the phone away and it came to her, in the way such certainties did, just who he had been talking to.

Jane waited for him to walk on. She got out of the car and followed him down to the end of the block and watched him open the glass door of the nice-looking bar he'd selected. She dawdled for as long as she could, then she too went inside.

Although she was only a couple of minutes behind him, already Patrick had a drink in front of him at one end of the bar and was chatting with the barmaid, a tall girl with a brutal haircut dyed a shimmering orange. He turned to look at Jane as she approached and she saw from his gaze that at least she looked all right.

"Hey." He stood and leaned in to put a hand on her shoulder. "Let's get a table. What do you want to drink, wine? White wine?" He picked up his glass. "Sheila, why don't you bring us some of that Pinot Grigio. How's that sound?"

Jane said that sounded fine, thanks. She let him fuss over her chair and with hanging up her coat. The barmaid arrived with Jane's glass of wine. The cropped orange hair elongated her neck and made her seem even taller, like a giraffe who'd learned to serve drinks. Patrick settled himself in the chair across from Jane and leaned over the table toward her. Jane said, "How's Bonnie?"

"What?"

"How is she?"

"I guess she's all right."

"Weren't you talking to her? A little while ago?"

"What?" he said again, attempting puzzlement. "What, she said that?"

"I saw you on the phone and I guessed it was her."

"Well that's, I don't know why you would think that."

"Not that it's any of my business. Except actually it is. I don't need to get any more into the middle of things than I already am."

"Honestly, I was talking to—"

Jane held up her hand. "Did she say anything about my husband? You can tell me that, at least."

"No," he said, defeated, drained of good cheer. "She called me, OK? I guess she's still mad at me about, you know, that money. Other stuff too." He shrugged, picked up his drink, put it down again. Suspicious. "Were you listening to us? Did she call you too?"

"It was a guess. Or a feeling, call it. I get them sometimes."

"You're into surveillance, aren't you? You have those eavesdropper things. You do phone hacking stuff. A buddy of mine, that's what his ex did."

"No, it's more like intuition. A really strong sense that I know something. I can't explain it."

"You mean you have superpowers?"

"Yes."

He stared at her. "Or, not super," she qualified. "It's not like I can fly, or start fires with my mind or anything. I know, it's a little weird." Jane waited to see how he'd react. She watched him visibly consider, trying out one idea, then another.

"That's real interesting," he said finally. "In a disturbing kind of way. Can you read minds?"

She thought there were probably times she could read his. She shook her head.

"Good, because that'd make me nervous."

"Ha ha." They relaxed, they offered up small bits of conversation. Jane drank her wine and nudged herself back into carnal mode. Should it matter if Bonnie called him, for whatever reason? She didn't want to be thinking about Bonnie but it could hardly be helped, with all their crossing of paths and sharing of men. Fine, now forget about her. Jane let the wine slide through her. It left a trail of glowing heat. She smiled at Patrick. "Tell me more about your softball team."

They ordered a second drink but Jane left most of hers behind. They strolled out onto the dark street, Patrick's arm draped around Jane's shoulders, and how ordinary and how amazing it was to be nothing more than a body, an amorous body yearning toward another body. For just this moment she had no history, no resentments, no agenda. She was only a normal woman looking forward to normal sex. All right, she wanted it to be a lot better than normal. Small geysers of sensation erupted within her. She and Patrick kept lurching and knocking against each other. He was so oversized, it was hard for her to get in sync with him, and not for the first time Jane imagined herself flattened, crushed, obliterated beneath his weight, oh Lord yes.

"This is it." He stopped at a doorway in between two unidentifiable dark office fronts and unlocked the outer door's many and serious locks. Inside, a landing and stairs, on the worn side. "No elevator, sorry."

He was on the third floor. Jane labored up the stairs, wishing she had drunk either more or less of the wine. Patrick was saying his place was nothing fancy, really. As if she was there for the decor. He said he'd tried to pick it up a little, but he hadn't been home much, you know? "Ta da," he said, ushering her inside, and Jane thought the apartment wasn't any worse than she'd imagined, rather like the back room of a sports bar, and right away she asked for the bathroom, overcome by an ignominious need to pee.

Any cleaning efforts had not reached the bathroom. It was inhabited by swampy towels and a number of end rolls of toilet paper lined up along the sink. Jane had seen worse, but probably not since college days. The light was too bright and she squinted at the mirror, thinking she didn't look too bad, and anyway she'd gotten herself this far so she must look good enough.

When she came out again she passed the bedroom, empty, the covers pulled up on the unadorned bed in an attempt at neatness. She'd imagined him waiting there for her but no. She made her way back to the main room. Patrick was seated on the oversized couch with the television remote in his hand, clicking through the stations. Jane, confused now, stood in the doorway until he patted the seat next to him and she sat.

"Want something to drink? A beer? That's all I have, sorry."

"No thanks." He was still fiddling with the remote, leaning forward and trying to get something on the screen to advance. They should just, you didn't want to say, get on with it, but that was how she was thinking, get on with it before she talked herself out of it, before she had to start worrying about driving back home, had to think of her innocent, needy children, had to go back to being Jane the uptight frigid dope. She looked around her at the unpromising furnishings, the bookcase with no books but the line of sports trophies, the magazines on the coffee table (automotive, football), the sweatshirt hung over a doorknob, the stack of newspapers under a chair, and the edge came off her desire.

"OK, wait a minute . . . wait a . . . here we go." He settled back and put an arm around Jane, drawing her in even as her muscles tensed. The television screen brightened and the sound track started up in scratchy mid-note.

"What are we watching?" Jane asked, because the picture quality was uneven, both shadowy and washed out. A woman was making a phone call in a kitchen. Cut to the doorbell ringing and the woman opening the door and inviting the young blond pizza delivery boy inside. She couldn't find her money, or maybe it had somehow fallen on the floor? She bent over and her short skirt rode up to reveal her bare behind and a nether costume consisting only of a garter belt and black stockings.

"Hey," Jane said, meaning it as protest, but Patrick's hand was working around the side of her bra to the front, even as the pizza boy grasped the situation, and then the lady, dropping his pants to reveal his erect, dark red penis. "I don't want to watch this," Jane said, even as Patrick divided his attention between Jane's left breast and the action onscreen, where the woman was now on her knees, her mouth busy, and the pizza boy's face took on an expression of writhing agony.

"Patrick!" Jane succeeded in detaching his hand. She pushed away from him and stood up. "Cut it out!"

"What's the matter, huh?" He had a visible erection, Jane noticed.

"Turn that off, please."

"You don't like this one?" He picked up the remote and the couple froze in mid-groan. "There's all kinds of others. There's one in a swimming pool, it's really hot."

"No, why do you think I want to watch that, it's gross!"

"Really?" He seemed uncomprehending, as if she had announced that she was neither a Sox nor a Cubs fan. "I thought it would, you know, help you. Get you in the mood."

"Well it really doesn't." She didn't know if she should be angry, or if it was the kind of thing you could laugh at. "I'm sorry, watching other people have sex, that does nothing for me."

"Oh." He aimed the remote and the screen went dark. He looked around the room, considering. "You want me to light some candles?"

"No. I mean that's all right, I don't need candles." It was funny, she decided. In a despairing kind of way.

"Come on and sit back down. Jeez, I'm sorry."

Jane sat, but at some distance from him. Her mouth was dry from the wine. She didn't feel angry, just disappointed and dreary at this latest failure. Maybe you were supposed to like porn. Maybe Bonnie did. "I should probably go."

"No, come on. What's the problem, huh? It's no big deal, it's a stupid movie. Relax."

It really wasn't a big deal and Jane told herself that and tried to send the Relax command to her central nervous system. The message wasn't getting through. She knew she wasn't being fair to him, backing down like this, and that made her feel even worse. She tried to explain. "I guess I've never been very good friends with my body."

"Friends," Patrick repeated, uncomprehending. "You can do that? Be friends with yourself?"

"Comfortable with your body. Natural."

"Yeah? How come, you think?"

He was trying, gamely, to follow along. Jane said, "I've always been more of a . . . spiritual person."

"You mean, religious?" He was wary now. "Because I gotta tell you, I've done my time with girls who got totally messed up by nuns."

"No, don't worry, I'm not Catholic, or anything else. I meant, living in my head. Not being very physical."

"You have a really nice figure, you know? Especially for having kids."

"Thank you." She guessed you had to take your compliments where you found them.

"I mean it, is that the deal, you think you don't have a good body? I like a tall girl, they don't go to fat. Is that all right for me to say? I don't want to get you mad again."

"No, that's OK." She'd been thinking of her mom boobs and her stretch marks. Maybe you had to get over things like that.

"I wish you'd come sit a little closer."

Sitting closer did not commit you to any particular course of action. Without standing up, she moved herself along the cushions, stopping just short of his reach. He made a mock grab for her, failed, and fell back against the cushions. "She's hard to get," Patrick said, as if to an audience. "She's making me work for it."

"I'm not making you work for anything," Jane said, although she was beginning to like the idea of doing so.

He was studying her now, pretend-solemn. "So will you help me out here? I need, like, spiritual enlightenment."

"You're making fun of me."

"Naw." He was trying, and failing, to keep a straight face.

"Yes you are."

"Maybe a little. But you have to tell me, seriously, is there some way you like doing it better than others?"

Jane shook her head, embarrassed all over again. Was there? She didn't think so. But then, she had not spent much time considering the matter.

"Fantasies," Patrick suggested. "Give me a clue. Work with me here. Think of me as your friendly neighborhood sex therapist."

Her fantasy was that she was Bonnie. Someone who knew exactly what she wanted and how to go about it. Jane reached behind her, unhooked her bra, and let the straps slide down her arms. Unbuttoned the top three buttons of her shirt and leaned back. Crossed her legs and let her skirt ride up.

"Whoa." Patrick took a measuring look at the space between them. "You're not going to sit over there all night, are you?"

She was such a tease. She liked that he was excited, that he acted like she was worth putting up with, worth pursuing. "Would you turn off the lights?" she asked, and he got up to do so.

You could be anybody in the dark. She stood, stepped out of her panties; took off her stockings, skirt, and bra; put her shirt back on. There was a bit of dim light from the hall, enough to see the shape of him moving toward her and she guessed he could see her too, her white shirt, her hair, maybe, because he went right for her and everything began to happen fast.

He had her lie back on the couch and there were the sounds of his belt buckle loosening and the sounds of unzipping and the next minute he was inside her. He was standing in between her legs and holding them apart and he went slow at first, holding back. "You're so big," she murmured, because he was, and because she knew he would want her to say it, it was the kind of thing you said to a man, and she was the kind of woman who said such things, at least she was now, wasn't she? He let go of her legs and put both hands beneath her to pull himself even farther in and come at her harder and it hurt, at least until she got used to it, but she thought this was how it was supposed to feel.

Because Bonnie had liked it. She'd said so. Said she'd liked fucking him. The word she used. What Jane was doing this very minute, and it was quite extraordinary to think this was really her, it was *really happening*. It went on and on. It was her, Jane, but it was also Bonnie, this confusion of bodies the strangest thing, but how else would she have come here? How else allow herself this cresting pleasure? She had come close to such feeling a time or two but for once it was in reach and she let go, let go, let it shake her all the way loose.

"How you doing?" he said from somewhere next to her ear, because he had collapsed on top of her. He balanced his weight on his elbows and raised up. "You OK? Huh?"

She couldn't talk yet so she nodded. She was still wearing her shirt; it was all wadded and crumpled around her. When she could speak, she said, "How did you do that?"

"Do what?" Her eyes had adjusted to the dark and she could see his face, big and pale and too close up, as if the moon had come in through the window and fixed itself on her chest. The angel on his right bicep fluttered as he moved.

"What we just did," she said weakly. There was a slick of sweat all along her stomach, turning chill.

He gave her a smacking kiss on the mouth. "It all comes natural, darlin'. Scuse me."

He hoisted himself up and took off down the hall to the bathroom. Jane got up too, shivering, and put on the sweatshirt hanging on the doorknob. She searched the floor and found her panties and put them on too. She was wet between her legs and that felt strange, soiled, and what she wanted most now was to leave and find some quiet space to be alone and put the pieces of herself back together again.

But she couldn't leave yet, you had to go through the awkward part first. She heard Patrick come out of the bathroom and then he must have been in the bedroom, opening and closing things. "All right if I turn on the lights?" he asked, when he came back in.

Jane said yes. The light came on and she saw that he was wearing a pair of basketball shorts, the silky kind, blue with gold striped up the side. "You checking out my fat belly?" Patrick asked, striking a pose that made his stomach stick out. Jane shook her head and dropped her eyes. She thought the shorts were ridiculous.

She didn't want to get dressed with him watching so she took all her clothes into the bathroom. She'd seen cleaner toilets in gas stations. When she went back out, he had the television on again.

"Relax, it's just SportsCenter," he said. "Come here."

Jane sat down next to him and he patted her knee. "You OK?" Jane nodded. "You sure? You're not going to get weird on me, are you? Sometimes girls do that."

"What do you mean, weird." She guessed she knew what he meant.

"They act like this is some kind of sad occasion. Like we just murdered somebody."

Jane started to tell him it had to do with insecurity and anxiety and whatever cocktail of sensations the body served up before, during, and after. Then thought and words and everything else left her and she floated free in blissful white space and here was Patrick calling her name and shaking her.

"You all right? Hey!" He was standing over her, so that she opened her eyes to the ridiculous shorts, the cheap synthetic fabric with the perforations for ventilation and the elastic stitching at the waistband and the piece of white net lining working its way loose, and she had an impulse to pull the shorts aside so she could examine his penis with the same degree of intensity and wonder, but that would be a different kind of weird or else taken as an invitation for some new carnal activity and she didn't mean it that way. And so even though she felt extraordinarily fine, clear-headed and refreshed, she made a show of fluttering her eyes and breathing small sips of air as if she were coming out of a swoon.

"Wow," she said. "I guess you really did a number on me."

Which was the truth, but not in the way he would imagine.

"You OK? Really? How about I get you some water."

Jane allowed that water would be nice. She closed her eyes. She heard him in the kitchen, running the tap and opening cupboards. Lord save her from having to look at the kitchen. She tried to recapture the feel and the memory of that floating white space but it got confused with the feel and memory of the recent sexual climax, which was not a bad thing at all.

Patrick came back in and she opened her eyes to find him carrying a bowl and a tall glass of ice water. He set them down next to her. "Chocolate ice cream," he said, indicating the bowl. "Actually it's frozen yogurt, it's better for you."

"Thanks." Jane drank the water and started in on the frozen yogurt. She didn't think she was hungry but it tasted better than she expected and she liked that he was fussing over her. "This is good," she told him, waving the spoon in the air.

"Yeah, it's not bad for healthy. So what happened, did you pass out or something?"

"What did it look like?" She had a dread of making weird noises or crossing her eyes or worse.

"You went kind of limp. Your eyes were still open. Like you were having an attack. I'm glad you came to, I wouldn't know what to do if you were dead. Does that happen a lot to you? Do you have some condition or something?"

Jane guessed she couldn't blame him for not wanting to end a date with body disposal. "It's nothing dangerous. Sometimes I zone out. It's like I was talking about, living in my head. It's like . . ." She hesitated. "Like an orgasm in my brain."

"You're kidding." His eyes grew round, trying to fathom this. "Wow, you should teach people how to do that. Can you do it whenever you want?"

"No, it sneaks up on me." She wasn't used to talking about her episodes—orgasm in the brain, how had she come up with that?—and she hurried to change the subject. "Anyway I'm fine now. Better than fine. You're . . ." She searched for a compliment. ". . . I think you have superpowers too."

"Yeah?" He was pleased. "Yeah, the Amazing Dick Man!"

Jane shook her head. "Eww. Too much."

"Sorry." He took the empty bowl from her and set it on the floor. "Come here," he said, pulling her onto his lap.

"I have to go home."

"One for the road."

"Patrick, I'm already dressed and everything."

"And I bet you can do it all over again."

This time she was on top of him while he put his hands on her hips and bounced her up and down. It took him longer this time and she started to get sore and chafed and she didn't think she could manage to come again but he had her turn around so that she was still on top but with her back to him, and he reached around with one hand to tickle it out of her. This one was different, almost painful, her insides clenching and unclenching, and there was no rest because now she had to hold on while he took his turn, a hard ride to the end.

They rolled apart and let their hearts and breathing calm, and Patrick got up and fetched a blanket from the bedroom and they wrapped up in it, and in each other, and slept.

Jane woke suddenly, not knowing what time it was but judging from the quiet of the street outside that it was late, probably very late. She rolled away from Patrick, who was on his back, snoring lightly, made her way to the bathroom, and tried not to think any hard thoughts.

Back in the living room Jane found her purse and pulled out her phone. It was twenty after two. She'd turned the phone off at the start of the evening and now she saw that she had two texts from Eric: **Where are you?**, and, **Are you all right? Call me**. There were also three missed calls and two voice mails, the last one an hour ago. Her first guilty thought was that something had happened to the children, but she recognized this as something she had fabricated, and anyway, Daddy Doctor could handle a crisis on his own for once.

Jane got dressed, all except for her shoes, which she carried to keep from making noise. She crouched down next to him. "Patrick?" she said, but softly, since she didn't really want to wake him, only wanted to admire him, lying there as if he were dead, this beautiful dead thing she had killed. She let herself out the door, managed the stairs as best she could. Her legs felt weak, as if she was a puppet come unstrung. Her car was where she'd left it, and there was no one on the street to waylay or distress her. She was glad when she got as far as sitting in the driver's seat, the doors locked, the engine starting up like a champ; she thought that after this achievement, everything else might be managed. She was a mess indeed, but she was beginning to get used to being a mess.

The radio news station played the same ads it always did, the GPS announced the route in miles and hundreds of yards, everything was the same except herself. Her skin seemed to be dissolving into molecules, her head was full of clouds and ache, and every so often her secret parts sent out a tremor. Maybe she should have called Eric at some strategic point, made up some story he'd have to believe; well, too late for that.

Too late also to have any hope of slipping inside and climbing the stairs to her own bed, because the lights were on downstairs. She pulled the car into its space in the garage and came in through the back door. Then opened the refrigerator, took out the orange juice, poured herself a glass and drank. She heard Eric coming down the stairs and then he was in the doorway, trying to decide what sort of unpleasant face to make. "What happened to you?" he demanded.

"Nothing." Which was not really true, but was true in the sense he meant. "I'm fine."

"Where have you been all this time? Don't tell me the play went on this late."

He was wearing one of his sleep costumes, plaid flannel pants and a gray T-shirt printed with the Beer Nuts logo, something he'd thought was funny back in med school. Jane allowed herself a detached thought about the clothes men wore for lounging. As Eric's hair receded in front he'd taken to growing it longer in back, which seemed like the entirely wrong sort of vanity. Jane was aware that she was comparing him to Patrick and for a moment she felt sorry for him, then all that went away. She said, "Since when did you care what I do?"

"I care that you said you'd be home at a reasonable hour, not three in the morning."

Jane finished her orange juice, rinsed the glass, and put it in the sink. "I believe I said that I might be late."

"The play got out at ten thirty. I checked. What did you do, close a bar?"

He'd folded his arms, an absurd posture given the plaid pajama pants, the shelf of belly he'd developed over the last year or two, his untidy hair, everything she no longer loved about him.

"I didn't go to the play. I went to see my boyfriend."

Jane waited but it was taking him some extra effort to speak, to choose among his options, anger or disbelief or scorn, and she took advantage of this to leave the kitchen through the other door and so not have to pass by him. "His name is Patrick," she said, on her way out of the room.

∽

H ere is the poem Jane wrote a week later:

The angel on his arm
rising from her scrolls of purple ink
her wings her twirly hair her angel gown all drawn
in curves, said:
Darlin', sweetie-o
pretty pretty pretty
oh honey babe
you two, you and him, should go for a ride
without a car. All alone
except for of course, me.
Because I go everywhere with him.
I am the angel of taverns and bottles and dollars left on the bar.
I am the angel of last call
in charge of sobering up and good intentions and bad days
when my name is Screw It All To Hell
or Who Cares.
But remember, skin is where I live
and sometimes
sugar bear, sis, ladyface,
I can make you fly.

true confessions

S he said Patrick? Patrick Doyle?"

"Just Patrick, that's all."

"And you're sure about that."

"It's the one thing I'm sure about," Eric said, irritated and glum. It was Monday night, almost nine, which was late for them to be meeting, and ordinarily they would be in bed together instead of sitting at Bonnie's kitchen table. He'd called and said he needed to talk to her. He needed to talk to her about Jane. Jane told Eric she was going into the city to see a play and instead had come home looking like something the cat dragged in and announced that she had a boyfriend. Whose name was Patrick.

Bonnie said, "I doubt if . . ." and then stopped herself. She didn't want to get into the saga of herself and Patrick. Specifically the part where she'd had sex with him not so very long ago. Or the part where she'd called him two days earlier. Which had been a mistake she didn't want to be reminded of. Anyway, for Eric, the important part was "boyfriend."

He said, "I mean, Jane? Where would she even find somebody? It's not like she has some big social life. And when? She's almost always with the kids."

Bonnie did not point out that even busy surgeons were able to find such opportunities. She said, "I guess she wants to get even with you. With me." Patrick? No way. It was Jane making things up, throwing out the name for a reason. Though she didn't care to think what that reason might be.

She didn't want to think about Patrick either, and now she had to. She'd called him because she was still angry, and because she never could get over things, and always wanted the last, or at least the loudest, word. She didn't want to sleep with him anymore, she really didn't (unless perhaps, immediately afterwards they could both be hit in the head hard enough to forget all about it), but maybe she had wanted him to want to so she could tell him to drop dead.

The conversation had not begun well and then had gotten worse. He'd answered, at least. Bonnie had not been sure he would. "Hey, listen, it's not a good time for me to talk, I'm trying to get someplace."

"Oh. Work?"

"No, just out." He wasn't going to tell her where. Bonnie heard street noise. He'd be walking since he no longer had a car. His not having a car now seemed like one more thing to hold against him.

"Well, I won't keep you. Just wanted to know how you've been."

"Fine." After a moment, he said, "How about you?"

"Great. Well, normal. I guess nobody says they're normal, huh? It's always 'great.' I wonder how come?" Bonnie waited but he didn't register any opinion. "How's work going?"

"Yeah, it's busy. Real busy. Nuts."

"Lots of job stress in those executive positions," Bonnie said. It came out sounding meaner than she'd intended.

"What? Listen, I can't talk now, I've got too much going on."

"Uh huh. Being busy sure comes in handy when you owe people money." She had not meant to bring up the money. But he wasn't paying any attention to her.

"What's that supposed to mean? Look, I'll pay you back. I tried to. I had the money but I couldn't find you."

"I'm sure you looked real hard." It wasn't all that much money. But she didn't want to feel used, ripped off, although that was exactly how she felt.

"If I get you your money, would you leave me alone? Because I don't think this is such a good idea, you and me seeing each other."

The hurt part of that didn't reach her right away, like stubbing your toe and the nerve taking a moment to twinge. She said, "We're not 'seeing each other.' This is a phone call."

"Whatever you say."

It infuriated her that he didn't care enough to fight with her. "I know it's not a good idea. You were never a good idea, I hate to break it to you. Just a really available bad idea. Have fun with whatever lucky girl's buying your drinks tonight, I'm sure you found one."

"Yeah? I hear you've been keeping pretty busy yourself."

In the space of silence before she could come up with a response, he said he had to go and hung up.

Why had he said that? She'd raged and wept, thinking too late of all the hateful things she might have said. It served her right; calling him was the kind of thing the old crazy Bonnie would have done, the addicted-to-drama Bonnie she'd been trying to leave behind. Calling had been backsliding, falling off the wagon. How many different, tangled ways could she feel guilty? Now, trying to navigate between explanations and lies, she told Eric, "I know a Patrick but Jane's never met him. I can't imagine it's the same guy."

Eric had not been listening, she realized to her relief. He was still preoccupied with Jane's declaration. But now she had at least inoculated herself against possible accusations. Eric said, "I can't get over it. I know it seems kind of hypocritical of me—"

Here Bonnie made her face of polite disbelief: Come on. "OK, really,

really hypocritical of me, but this is going to take some getting used to. If Jane has somebody too. Go ahead, tell me I'm a pig and a jerk."

"You can't really blame her. That's not fair."

"It's not about fairness. It's not really rational. But it changes things."

"How, exactly." She didn't have much patience for whatever male prerogative he was attempting to access. Though you had to admit, it wasn't anything you could have seen coming from Jane. Maybe Jane was really through with Eric, and the two of them would go their separate ways.

Maybe Bonnie and Eric could then have a life together: patched together, imperfect, happy. So her mind raced ahead with devious, hopeful plans, when she ought not assume any such thing. Because everything between them was balanced as if on the edge of a blade. "How does it change things?" she repeated.

Eric didn't answer right away. Bonnie waited him out, sick with foreboding. Then he said, "It's one more fault line. One more piece of instability my kids shouldn't have to put up with. She's their mother, I know it's not fair to expect more of a mother, but that's the breaks. Kids may not know exactly what's going on but they're intuitive, they know when something's not right."

When he didn't say more, Bonnie said, "So what do you think you should do?"

"I guess some of that's up to Jane. Let's see how far she wants to carry this boyfriend thing. Maybe she was just trying to get back at me, out of spitefulness. She has that side to her, you know?"

"She does," Bonnie agreed, thinking of the Casserole of Death. "Do you want me to talk to her?"

"Is that smart?"

"I don't know. I guess she could tell me to go to hell, or refuse to take my call." Now that she'd voiced it, the idea solidified and began to summon arguments for itself. There was no reason they couldn't talk once in a while, and after all, Jane had called her after Claudia died. Jane might have come up with the name Patrick just to aggravate her. There might, in fact, be no boyfriend and this was just another of Jane's productions, and there would be nothing, really, to worry about. "I could at least try." And if somehow, in the name of wonder, Jane had managed to align herself with Patrick, didn't she want to know how? The idea began to glow with the certainty of not just a good but a necessary course of action. "I mean, I'd be willing."

"Well . . . I suppose you could call and fish around."

"No. It's better to ask straight out."

"If you think so." He stood up. "Ask me how my day was."

"How was your day, honey?"

"I repaired two mitral valves and chewed out a resident for not following up on his postop patients."

"And you didn't leave a scalpel in anybody's chest," Bonnie said, which was something they often signed off with, a lame joke—except when such things really happened—which had become a kind of shorthand for cheer up, it's not so bad.

"Pretty sure I didn't."

They embraced and Bonnie let herself rest against him. "We're OK, aren't we?"

"More than OK."

And then they drew apart and he left and Bonnie watched from the window as he got into his car, flashed the lights as a signal to her, and drove off. She thought they were OK, at least for now, and it was better not to look too far down the road since it was not as if he had promised her, well, anything.

Bonnie waited a couple of days to call Jane, and of course by then it was not feeling like such a great idea at all. But how else to learn what Jane might or might not be up to? Bonnie needed to be able to talk Eric out of any bad second thoughts he might be having. They'd managed their little bit of precarious happiness so far, but how easily it could be threatened.

She'd imagined Jane not answering, but she picked up right away. "I thought you'd probably call," Jane said.

"Hello to you too."

"Hang on a minute." Jane put the phone down and there was the racket of some household machine starting up, the clothes dryer maybe. When you called Jane, her appliances were usually included in the conversation. She came back on the line. "OK, sorry."

"So, can we talk?"

"Sure, why not."

"All right, well." Bonnie ran through and discarded the different scenarios she'd rehearsed. Jane sounded noncommittal, almost breezy, and there didn't seem any point in guile. "Why don't you tell me about your boyfriend."

"You know what's funny, the whole time we were in school, and even later on, we never went out with the same guy. Never liked who the other came up with. And now here we are."

"Where are we exactly, Jane?"

"You remember those stupid comic books you used to love? Remember the story about the guy who was a big galoot? That's who he is, isn't he. A big galoot."

"Who is?"

"Patrick," Jane said, and Bonnie felt something settle inside of her. She had not really wanted to believe it.

"How did this happen? I'm not understanding."

"I don't think that's really important."

"We're talking about the same Patrick, right? My Patrick?"

"We should probably steer clear," Jane said, "of expressions of ownership."

"Did you go looking for him? Were you trying to get back at me? Is that what this is about?"

"No," Jane said after a moment. "No and no. But if it upsets you, I guess I don't mind that."

"What's the plan here, huh? What does that mean, he's your boyfriend, you think he's going to take you on movie dates or to the prom? He's not that guy. He's not anybody reliable."

"I know that," Jane said, sounding patient. "But thanks for looking out for my best interests."

That shut Bonnie up. Jane said, "I see no reason why I can't live my own life while you and Eric are busy carrying on with each other. I'm in love with Patrick. I don't expect you to understand—"

"Oh, now it's true love," Bonnie said, wanting to mock Jane, laugh her out of it. A kind of panic was rising in her, beating against her ribs.

"I don't know about true love. But it's some kind of love. Bodily. Erotic. Of course it came as a total surprise. A shock, even."

"You don't even sound like yourself," Bonnie said, meaning it as an accusation.

"Really? That would be so interesting. You know what else is interesting? I've been doing some writing. I've never done that before. Poetry, mostly, but some journal odds and ends too. It's as if all of a sudden, I have all these ideas and feelings I need to get down on paper."

"I can't believe this," Bonnie began, trying to imagine the two of them, Jane and Patrick, even having a conversation together, let alone sex. "You don't have one thing in common with him."

"Well sometimes that's what you need," Jane said, again with her irritating patience. "And I'm going to keep seeing him. That's what you're trying to find out, isn't it?"

"It won't last."

"However long it lasts it's fine with me."

"Are you going to leave Eric?"

"Why would I want to do that? Leave and go where? I guess he's not very happy with me. Well you can tell him, since he doesn't want to ask me himself, that I'm going to see Patrick whenever I can. Eric should get used to the idea that we have one of those zippy, modern marriages."

"He doesn't want that," Bonnie said, aware that she was arguing not just a losing cause but an indefensible one. "I think he'd like everything to just calm down."

"I'm being perfectly calm," Jane said. "I feel, I guess, energized, and sometimes I get a little swoony, a little giggly about the whole thing, but I wouldn't say I'm, what's the opposite of calm. Rowdy? If you're all of a sudden jealous, that's your problem."

"I don't care about Patrick."

"You sure about that? Because it wasn't all that long ago you were going on and on about him."

The panic rose up in her again. She shoved it back down. "That was nothing. Patrick's nothing. I love Eric."

"Well that's nice. That makes everything all right."

"Look, I don't blame you for feeling raw about things, and nobody's seen more of my sketchy behavior than you, all right? But this is different, I need it to be different. I'm done with all the crazy stuff. It's not good for me. It never was." Bonnie considered bringing up Carl Rizzi, and the way you thought something was normal, because you grew up with it. But she only said, "I need to settle down."

"With my husband."

"Yes." Defeated.

"And you're worried that if I'm not playing along, if I'm not the long-suffering idiot I've been all this while, it's going to disrupt the status quo. I guess I'm not very invested in how tragic that would be. You know? But if you get in my way, I'll tell Eric all about you and Patrick. Then you can explain to him about how you've settled down and this is different for you. I have to go, Grace has another appointment for her allergies."

Bonnie told Eric that Jane had been noncommittal, hadn't said much.

It seemed best to let things ride for now. She couldn't imagine any blissful idyll with Patrick going on for very long.

Then Eric called her. "She brought him to the house! She introduced him to my kids, for Christ's sake!"

"Who?" Bonnie asked, although she knew.

"Her loser boyfriend. She let him borrow one of our cars. I came home and asked her where the Toyota was and she said, 'Patrick has it, he needed to do some errands, he'll bring it back tomorrow.' And Robbie told me he met Mommy's friend and he was really really big and he showed Robbie how to match quarters."

"Oh no."

"This is just way, way out of line. We had a big fight about it. Well, I had the fight. She just stood there looking puzzled. She said she didn't understand what the big deal was, since you came to the house too."

"And what did you say to that?"

"I said that was different."

"It is and it isn't," Bonnie said, wanting to calm Eric down. She couldn't tell if he was most upset about the car, or the children's involvement, or . . . "How long was he there? Were they . . ."

"I guess he was there just long enough to pick up the car and pollute my children. He came in on the train. Tomorrow when he brings the car back, excuse me, if he brings the car back, who knows. Maybe this will turn into a regular thing. Maybe I'll come home some night and find him in the shower."

"Jane wouldn't do that." Or perhaps she would. The new, sexy version of Jane might be one who had simply lost her mind. It was creepy, it promised ill, to have Jane bring Patrick into the family sphere. And the car would come back with an empty gas tank and the backseat full of fast-food wrappers. "What do you think she's trying to do," Bonnie asked. "Goad you? Get back at you?"

"It's really been a long time since I could account for any of Jane's motives."

"I know you're upset, but I'm not sure what you can do about it."

"I can go talk to Loverboy and tell him to stay the hell out of my house."

"That's not a good idea," Bonnie said, too quickly, before she could come up with all the reasons it was a bad, catastrophic idea. "Honestly, I'd just try to wait it out."

"This is nuts. It makes my head explode. I can't live this way."

Then divorce her and make a life with me. But she couldn't yet say that, not yet, and not over the phone, and not while Jane was being this wild of a wild card. What did Jane want, besides living out some stupid fantasy? Bonnie said, "Maybe there could be some house rules. Ones that would apply to me too."

"No, that's bullshit. Rules for screwing around? Please."

Bonnie kept silent, and Eric said, "I'm sorry. That was a crummy thing to say. That's not how I think of us."

"All right."

"I'm just floored by this thing with Jane."

"All right," Bonnie said again. Eric might be having some primal, jealous response. She never understood why men were so protective of their bad relationships.

"We'll be OK," Eric said. "It doesn't matter what Jane does."

"I don't want it to matter."

"You have to understand, I need a certain amount of calm. Predictability. Otherwise I can't get through my day. I can't do what I have to do for patients. And now it's like I have Jane on the brain. She's used me up. Even before this boyfriend stunt. All her mental health issues. Her constant, exhausting misery."

But he didn't seem to want her to go away, at least not anytime soon, and that was the wall Bonnie kept running into, but she could not imagine giving up on him now, or ever. "I love you," Bonnie said, and waited.

"I love you too."

"Where are you?" She thought that if he was still at work, he could come over, they could make love and close some of the sorrowful space between them.

"I'm at the liquor store, in the parking lot. Crap. It's starting to rain, and the goddamn windshield wipers aren't working. I have to get back now before the kids go to bed."

It was not her fault that he could not make a call from home, or that his windshield wipers were not working. He had not said it was. But she had become part of some central, messy problem he might soon get tired of grappling with.

What should she do? What should she not do? Bonnie went round and round. It was late, after eleven, although that was not late for Patrick, when she decided to text him:

Her husband is really pissed about the car

She didn't expect to hear back from him, but she did:

He should worry more about his woman

What a jerk. She wrote:

You aren't helping anything

He wrote:

Like you ha ha

She couldn't even tell what he meant. Even in person, he could be borderline incoherent.

Whatever just stay away from the kids

Her phone rang a minute later. "What's that about the kids, what did he say I did to them?"

"He doesn't want you around them. You can understand that, right?"

"What, I'm some child molester now? That is total bullshit. I only have like, thirty nieces and nephews, you think I'm not good with kids?"

"I think it's more like he doesn't want to have them asking about Mommy's special friend. And he said you taught them some drinking game."

A pause while he tried to remember. "Quarters? That's a drinking game?"

"I'm just telling you. Back off. Try some discretion. Try not to wreck their car."

"And you're so concerned about this why, exactly?"

"They're my friends, I care about them."

"Sure. Daddy's special friend."

Bonnie said nothing. After a moment Patrick said, "Yeah, she told me. Real nice. So quit pretending you're the good guy. Back off me and Janie."

"She doesn't know you the way I do."

"Wrong. She knows me exactly the way you do."

"Fuck you, Patrick. Really."

"No thanks. Kind of busy."

By the time Bonnie could manage any words, he'd ended the call. None of her interventions were turning out the way she wanted, as if she'd lost some instinct or judgment or maybe she had never done anything right to begin with and was just now figuring that out.

Four days later and Patrick still had not returned the car. What was he thinking? Was he trying to be a jackass or was he just clueless? Bonnie would have liked to ask him but she was through putting up with him and his fathead insults. Instead she fielded a series of increasingly pissed off messages from Eric. Jane, it seemed, was untroubled. Detached. Jane told

Eric that they had too many cars anyway. Eric relayed this, incredulous. Who was this guy, a con man? (He did not expect Bonnie to answer, although she could have.) What was Jane going to do next, start giving away his clothes? He would call the police. No, Bonnie told him. You will not. The car's title was in both their names, there was nothing actionable there. She did not say that whatever cop took his complaint would have trouble keeping a straight face, that he would be mocked, openly or behind his back, for allowing his wife to give a car to her boyfriend.

"Then what am I supposed to do, sit back and let her carry on like a . . ." He could not come up with a name for the rampant perfidy that was Jane.

Bonnie told him she was sure the car would be returned. And the next day it was. There was a half-assed explanation and a half-assed apology. News like this reached Bonnie indirectly, through Eric, and after the fact. She was relieved that Patrick was at least avoiding any outright criminal acts. He had always been good at skating right up to the edge of serious consequences, then retreating. The infuriating luck of the Irish.

A week went by, then two. Bonnie kept reassuring Eric that Jane's infatuation (or Patrick's part in it) wouldn't last, although she did not wish to tell him why she thought that. She waited for things to run their course, for Patrick to act like Patrick, that is, oblivious and faithless, for Jane to get tired of it. And that kept not happening. It was well into October, and Eric reported that Jane was still making trips into the city and not bothering to hide it from him, although she was at least circumspect around the children. Probably because it was the one thing she knew Eric would not tolerate. Bonnie told him, "It's not good for you to get so worked up. I wish you could . . ."

"Get over it? Get used to it?"

"No," she said, although she had meant something close to that. "Get the right perspective, maybe."

They were in bed, although they had not yet made love, because Eric was still going on about Jane Jane Jane. He had taken off his shoes and tie, and his feet in their black socks kept knocking together as he spoke. Bonnie was curled up next to him, attempting patience. She was tired of hearing about Jane, worrying about Jane, analyzing Jane. She did not understand how Jane had made herself so interesting just by sleeping around. It hardly ever worked that way. Let Jane go, let her live her own life, she wanted to tell Eric. Take advantage of this really swell opportunity to untie the knot. Pay attention to the here and now. That is, herself, her more than willing body. She was aware of the evening slipping away minute by minute, she knew at what time he was accustomed to sigh and say he had to be getting home.

Not that they had to make love every time they saw each other. She only felt that way because of the stupid limits of their stupid situation, and everything meaning too much.

Eric said, "She could run off with this guy."

Bonnie kept silent. And this would be a bad thing why? she wanted to say.

"How would the kids feel? Or what if she tried to take them with her? I don't trust her. I don't trust her to make good decisions. And this character she's hooked up with, who the hell knows? That's the kind of thing that's driving me crazy."

She almost told him then. Told him not to worry about Patrick, he wasn't anybody who would entertain thoughts of settling down with a wife and children, especially someone else's wife and children, and then she would tell him how she knew. Get it said, get it out there. But she could not find a way to begin, and with any luck she wouldn't need to.

"I'm not going to let this go on indefinitely," Eric said, and Bonnie shook off her worries for this new dread.

"What do you mean, you won't let it? What do you think you're going to do, punch the guy out and wreck your million dollar hands?"

Right away she was sorry she'd said it. Eric's face closed down. He might have a surgeon's borderline-arrogant pride in what he did, but he resented being reminded of the downsides. There was a kind of male vanity that Bonnie knew she should not underestimate. Although, punching out Patrick? You would not do that unless there were two or three of you. She said, "You have to think this through. You don't want to make anything worse."

"I don't know what I'll do. Tell her she has to cut it out. For the kids' sake."

"And what do you suppose she'll say to that?" Bonnie asked him, and that ended their conversation, but not her sense of time running down and down and down.

Bonnie stretched herself along the length of him and rolled over so that one of her legs was between his. Her ear was against his chest and she heard his heart bumping along, and then she slid her hands down to his stomach and took hold of him. His heart seemed to beat, not faster, but louder. He rolled over so they faced each other. He pulled her clothes loose and then his own, though they did not bother to undress entirely. There was always a moment, or a series of moments, when one of them might ask, with or without speaking, Do you want? Like this? And the other would answer, yes. But on this night the questions went unasked, or unheard, and what they did felt uncomfortable, furtive, perfunctory, something they might have done while asleep or otherwise not entirely in their bodies, and when it was over Eric said, "Sorry."

"It's OK." She was disappointed in him. In the two of them.

"It's this thing with Jane. It feels like she's taunting me. Like she wants to mess with me."

"I'd say it's working."

"Let me make it up to you." He reached for her but Bonnie said no, that was all right. She didn't want to come in that lonely way, as an afterthought. She rolled away from him and after a moment he said he should be thinking about getting home.

Neither of them wished to leave on an unhappy or unquiet note, so Bonnie dressed and walked out to the car with him. It was a warm night with a damp wind blowing through a sky of low clouds and bits of grit in the air. Bonnie wrapped her sweater around her. Her hair blew into her eyes and she pushed it back, then it blew and tangled itself again and she resigned herself to looking unkempt. Eric started his car and came around to the sidewalk to say good-bye. They kissed and he said, "I'm sorry I let this whole thing with Jane get to me."

"No, don't be. I mean it. You'll think this is weird but—"

He waited. "What's weird?"

She shook her head. She wanted to say she was almost glad. That she loved him in spite of their disappointments, or maybe because of them. Normal people had disappointments, and disappointing sex, all the time. She so wanted to be normal, to lay down the sword and shield. Stop fighting the same losing fights, chasing after one or another dumbshit sensation, imagining herself in love when she was only desperate and needy and foolish. And he was her best and possibly last chance of something finer, more generous, a chance to be something other than what she had been. In spite of everything flawed and failed and sad between them.

But since she could not say any of this, she told him that they were just tired and stressed, and who would not be, and what she meant by "weird" was, how weird to think that the three of them had known each other for so long, she and Jane even longer, and what a long strange trip it had been, right?

She did not call Patrick again, nor did she call Jane. But the next night and the night after that she drove past Patrick's apartment, circling the block, hoping to see him, or the two of them together. Which was more backsliding and hardly fit into any scenario of higher love, but left on her own she relapsed back into fever and impatience and worry. The streets and sidewalks jigged and jagged with lights, cars, motion, with everything urgent and dangerous that she could not keep away from unless Eric would claim her, come to her, save her from herself. What would she do if she found Jane and Patrick? She didn't know. Her head hurt with not knowing, and with rehearsing all the things she might tell them, begging or threatening, whatever might get them to cease and desist, or else to run off together, if they really were each other's own true love, which she found so, so hard to believe, in any case to get out of the way. Or there might be some daft scheme where she inveigled Patrick in a cocaine buying sting and then got him busted. Or maybe Jane could be arrested, or committed? There had to be some way to solve the four of them like a math problem so that Bonnie equaled Eric minus Jane minus Patrick, some way to nudge Eric into realizing the rightness of the two of them. Why could he not see it? Why would he not take that next step and cross over to her?

And then she would think of his children, his and Jane's, who were entirely innocent when it came to their mother's and father's unhappiness and who could not be made to fit into any mathematical formula. They deserved the parents they were born to, not some bogus arrangement with Aunt Bonnie or Uncle Patrick and why had she ever imagined otherwise?

The next week was Hallowe'en, the season for loony crimes and costumed drunks, when everybody at the cop shop kept track and kept score: how many bar fights with Elvises, how many batshit Batmen, how many zombies urinating in public or OD'd witches? How many actual or fabricated reports of poisoned candy given out to trick-or-treaters?

For a few nights it would be difficult to tell anyone with actual mental health issues from the rest of the population, and so Bonnie's schedule had some slack in it. She had a lot of vacation days she'd saved up and needed to use. She could leave town, take the kind of trip she was always waiting to take with Eric. Hiking in the desert, fishing in Montana, renting a cottage on the Oregon coast. She supposed if she went by herself she could do the cheap version of these things. Then he would miss her and she would come back and everything would be better than before. But she did not entirely believe that and anyway she was too anxious about what Eric might do if he got mad enough in some idiotic way, and besides, she could never stand to be away from the scene of the action so she could insert herself into things at the absolutely worst time, yup, she was still that girl, no matter what elevated intentions she harbored.

Hallowe'en was on an inconvenient Monday this year, and most of the parties and carrying on took place over the weekend. So that when Eric called Monday evening and started shouting about trick or treating, Jane screwing up the trick or treating, it took her a moment to sort it out.

"Slow down," she said. "What happened, what did she do?"

"I was supposed to take the kids out, we had it all set up, and I'm going to be, not even a half hour late." He was in the car, Bonnie could tell. The phone echoed and turned his anger shrill. "I just talked to her and she says she isn't going to wait, she and Loverboy are taking them. Now he's like, part of the family. She can't even wait a few goddamn minutes. You believe it?"

"Taking them where?" Bonnie asked, then realized he was talking about some organized suburban Hallowe'en ritual, the day and hours set aside for the procession of costumed children from door to door. "You're sure she said that? About Patrick?"

"I'm on my way there now. I'll see—"

The phone cut out then, and the call was lost. Bonnie tried calling him back, got voice mail. Tried again, nothing. She called Jane's cell phone. It rang and rang. She was not going to call Patrick, no matter what happened. Eric had not said where he was when he called, but if he'd just left work she might be able to get to Elmhurst ahead of him. Traffic would be bad for both of them.

Go.

It was not yet six and there was still some fading light in the sky. The weather had cleared and turned cold and the sky was wide open, cloudless, one of those times when driving west was, for some moments, to enter a kingdom of tarnished gold. Then the horizon dimmed and the light grayed and Bonnie stepped on it, cut people off, blasted cars out of her way in the passing lane. The trick-or-treat hours probably started at six so the littlest kids could get back home before dark. Not for the first time she wondered what Jane was thinking, if she really believed that Patrick would make a swell substitute daddy, or if she'd loaned him the car again, or if there was some other reason for Patrick to be hanging around the house, other than to piss Eric off mightily.

It usually took her twenty-five minutes to get to Elmhurst but for once in her life she caught a break and was there in twenty. She slowed down to observe the posted village speed limit. At Eric and Jane's house the porch light was dark, meaning No Sale to the trick-or-treaters, although there was a light on from somewhere inside. The minivan and the Toyota were in the driveway, but not Eric's BMW, which was a good sign. Bonnie parked and rang the front bell, then went around to the back. The door was open, the kitchen lit, the children's supper dishes in the sink. "Hello?" she said to the empty house. "Hello?"

Back out on the sidewalk, she saw a group of trick-or-treaters being herded along by an adult with a flashlight, and another group farther down the block. She watched them until she was certain that none of them were Robbie and Grace, then got in the car and cruised around the block, and then around the next block and the next, in a widening circuit. Creeping along so she would have some chance of seeing them and so she wouldn't hit and flatten any stray, sugar-crazed child. Where were they? She couldn't imagine they'd go too far from the house. It was completely dark by now and she was afraid of missing them. The streetlights were on and some homeowners had decorated with strings of orange lights or cobwebs draping their hedges, wispy ghosts suspended from porches, jack-o'-lanterns, silhouetted black cats. The excited voices of children carried through the cold air as they ran from house to house, a

pretty, festive scene that Bonnie could not appreciate since she was waiting for Eric to arrive in full meltdown mode.

Finally she spotted them, or rather, spotted Patrick, who was never
inconspicuous, passing under a streetlamp. Other, smaller figures trailed
after him. Bonnie parked the car across the street and hurried to catch up.

They had stopped outside the next house and Jane was adjusting the
collar on Grace's costume. Grace was dressed as some Disney figure in
a puffy blue dress, while Robbie, in a head to toe costume with a hood
and a tail and all-over spikes and splotches, resembled some particularly
repulsive stuffed animal. Remarkably, Jane and Patrick wore costumes
too, or at least some attempt at them: Patrick a green derby he was
accustomed to wear for St. Patrick's Day, and around his neck a kind of
lei made of gold foil harps, of the same provenance. Jane wore a cat hat,
that is, a fur hood that tied under her chin and had two pointed ears.

Bonnie skidded up to them. "Hi guys." It had not occurred to her
what she would say.

They all stared at her. "Where's your costume?" Robbie asked.

"I'm not going trick or treating. What are you supposed to be?"

"I'm a dinosaur."

"Of course you are. I see that now."

"I'm a *Tyrannosaurus rex*!"

"That's the best kind of dinosaur to be. What are you, Gracie?"

"Cinderella." Grace looked down at her shoes, turning them this way
and that to admire them. They weren't glass slippers, but glitter-coated
mary janes.

"What are you doing here?" Jane asked Bonnie. Looking more closely
at her, Bonnie saw that she'd drawn cat whiskers on her face and a small,
triangular cat nose. "Kids, go on up and ring the doorbell. Grace, here,
put your coat on, you're getting cold."

They waited for Grace and Robbie to run up the front path. "So?"
Jane asked.

"Eric called me. He's on his way home, he's really mad."

Jane and Patrick looked at each other. Patrick's green derby was at least two sizes too small. Perched on his head, it made him resemble the sort of cartoon character drawn to be a recognizable fool. "Well," Jane said. "I don't know what I can do about that at this point."

Patrick said, "Should I take off? You could pick me up somewhere, I don't mind."

"Too late," Jane remarked as the BMW pulled in behind Bonnie's car. Jane turned her cat's face to Bonnie. "Happy now? You're such a drama queen. That should be your costume, really."

Eric got out of the car and strode up to them. "Where are the kids?" Jane pointed. "I told you I was heading home, you couldn't wait?" He looked at Patrick in his ridiculous hat and shook his head. "Jesus."

"Hey, excuse you," Patrick said. "You got a problem? Let's discuss your problem."

"I can't believe," Eric said to Jane, "that this is who you choose to take up with. Have you lost your mind?"

"Hey." Patrick said.

Jane said, "I can't decide which is the worst thing about you, Eric. Being a hypocrite or being a snob."

"You guys, the kids will be back in a minute," Bonnie said, and the other three looked at her.

"What are you doing here?" Eric asked her.

"I'm a UN observer."

He looked as if he would have liked to say something to that, but just then three little boys dressed as a skeleton, a pirate, and a football player raced past them, intent on loot. Jane walked a little ways down the sidewalk. Robbie and Grace were moving on to the next house. Patrick followed her. "You know," he said to Eric, "I'm not real impressed with the looks of you either."

"Eric, come on," Bonnie said, uselessly, as Eric took after them down the sidewalk. "Let it go."

What kind of a fight was he hoping to start, or finish? And why was she so unimportant in the whole stupid scene? It was too dark to see very far ahead. Her feet tangled on something, a branch or a stick, and she half-fell into a hedge, the scratchy kind. Got up again. Ow. "Eric, wait for me."

Going forward, she blundered into Patrick, or rather, the back of his leather jacket. "Uff."

He turned, raising his arms as if to shield himself. "Whoa there, darlin'. This isn't the time or the place."

"You're disgusting, Patrick."

"You didn't used to think so."

"Why don't you just leave Jane alone? She doesn't need you screwing up her life."

"Oh, did I screw up yours? Didn't think that was possible. Maybe you're jealous? Want a little more screwing up, for old time's sake? Sorry. Not into a threesome. Leastways, not with you."

"Disgusting."

"Bonnie?" Eric stepped out of the darkness. "What the hell?"

"Oh, we were just . . ." Dead stop.

"Who is this guy? Huh?"

"It's not important. Don't pay any attention to him."

"Yeah, man," Patrick said, tipping the derby. "What can I say? I get around."

"God," Eric said. He looked around him, as if deciding where best to spit.

"I told you I knew him," Bonnie said miserably. "I really did."

"I don't understand you. I don't understand any of this."

"Slow learner, isn't he?" Patrick remarked.

"Shut up, Patrick."

"He should take better care of his hens, you know?"

"Eric, let's get out of here. Let's just be by ourselves."

"Hey Eric, buddy, she might find that a little dull. Just sayin'."

"Shut up, you big Irish clod, or I will buy a gun and shoot you."

Eric stepped into the street, fishing in his pocket for car keys. Bonnie called after him. At the same time, Jane came running up, dragging Grace by her wrist. "I can't find Robbie, he took off somewhere. Eric!"

He did turn around then. "Grace, where did Robbie go?"

"With the boys."

"What boys? Where did the boys go?"

"I don't know." Grace pressed her face into her mother's legs.

"Jane, why weren't you watching him?"

"Do not put this on me. Just don't."

"Robbie!" Eric called out, but there was no answer from the dark street, and even the noise of the marauding children seemed to have vanished. "Robbie! Oh for Christ's sake, Jane. Why didn't you wait for me?"

"Stop it, Eric. Wait for you to do what, exactly? Go look for him, I have to take Grace home, she's freezing."

"I can help," Bonnie said, and Eric looked her over, visibly trying to overcome his distaste.

"All right, why don't you drive around the block? He probably didn't get very far."

Patrick said, "I can help too. Come on, man, it's a kid."

The four of them separated and headed off in four different directions. Bonnie started her car and set off. She didn't want to think about anything but Robbie now. The rest of the night's disasters were ripening like a bruise, but they would have to wait their turn. Robbie was just the kind of kid to run off, oblivious, and need retrieval. He was probably trying to get his hands on all the candy in the world. The other little boys would peel off for home and he'd do the same. Then they could all put aside the nightmares of lost or stolen children, creeps out patrolling for the holiday, or a front door opening, inviting a child inside, someone you never would have suspected. Or a child in a bulky costume, not paying attention, not watching, stepping into the street at just the wrong moment. In fact Bonnie's car windows were frosting over, making it hard to see the road. She ran the defroster and rolled down her window.

She saw a mom and pop shepherding a small, duded-up cowboy, stopped and asked them if they had seen a little boy in a dinosaur costume. They had not, but they would keep an eye out. She stopped two groups of trick-or-treaters and asked them the same and got the same answer. She wanted to be the one who found him. She wanted to find him so that Eric would be grateful to her and forget all the crummy, sketchy things she'd done, and once you admitted that you were willing to use a child's safety as a means of shining yourself up, there was not much more to say.

She thought of calling someone, Eric or Jane or their home phone, but no one was calling her.

It was getting later and trick-or-treat hours were drawing to a close. Surely they would have called her if Robbie had been found? Or maybe they would not. Finally she returned to Eric and Jane's house, which was now lit up inside and out, which meant that Robbie was still out there. Eric was not back either.

Bonnie let herself in the back door. Patrick and Jane were seated at the dining room table.

They'd taken off their costume items and Jane had scrubbed the cat off her face. Grace, still in her blue dress and sparkly shoes, sat on the living room floor, sorting through her bag of candy.

Jane said, "Eric went to the police station." She was pale, remote, suffering. Patrick slumped in his chair, giving Bonnie the stink eye. He hated her and she hated him right back.

"I can go out again," Bonnie said. "If there's anywhere we haven't looked yet, just tell me."

Neither of them answered. Bonnie didn't want to sit with them, nor did she want to leave again just yet, so she joined Grace on the floor. "Wow, you got a lot of candy. What's your favorite?"

"Where's Robbie?"

"He's still trick or treating. He'll be along later."

A car door slammed. Eric came in through the back door, alone. He didn't seem to want to sit at the table either. "They're sending the squads out to look for him. They'll call us. Grace, don't eat any of that tonight."

"I told her she can have three pieces," Jane said.

"All right, three. No more."

"Can Bonnie have some?" Grace asked.

No one spoke. Bonnie said, "I don't need any candy, sweetie, but thank you anyway."

They waited, minute by minute. It was almost nine and Robbie had been gone for more than an hour. Bonnie got up to use the bathroom, embarrassed at having to do so. When she came back downstairs, Eric was in the kitchen making phone calls. Jane and Patrick were still at the table. Jane was saying something about a taxi and Patrick said No way, he wasn't going anywhere, and Jane reached out and held his hand. Bonnie went back to her seat next to Grace. None of them wanted her here. One minute kept sliding into another. How long could she remain here, if Robbie didn't come back and didn't come back? To get up and leave would be to allow for that possibility. And so Bonnie stayed, and was allowed to stay.

Eric said, "I'm going out again. He could have ended up downtown, somewhere a lot farther away."

"He knows his address and phone number," Jane said. She was crying, quietly so as not to upset Grace.

Patrick kneaded her hand in both of his. "He's a fine, strong little boy and he'll come through for you," he pronounced.

Eric picked up Patrick's green derby, held it out with one hand and with the other drove his fist through the crown.

The front doorbell rang. Jane reached it first, Eric a step behind. Jane cried out, a choked sound, and there was a confusion of voices, Jane's, Eric's, someone else, a woman, and then they all, including Robbie, stepped into the room. Robbie still wore his dinosaur costume but the hood was off. Jane bent over him with a smothering hug that he tried to wriggle out of. The strange woman said, "The babysitter thought he was another one of my son's friends. I am so sorry. My husband and I only got home ten minutes ago. They were playing video games and I'm afraid they probably ate quite a lot of candy."

"I bet I still have more than Grace," Robbie said, escaping his mother and plopping down on the floor.

"That's because you cheated and went to a bunch more houses."

"It's because you have a really stupid costume."

"All right," Eric said. "Cool it. Don't eat any more candy, either of you. Thank you so much," he said to the other woman.

"Boys," the woman said, "they never know when to quit, do they?" The three of them moved back out to the porch, talking, then the door opened and closed and they said good night.

Bonnie stood when Eric and Jane came back in. "I think," she began, but Jane was talking to Patrick and she was cut off.

"We can still do this," Jane said. "There's just enough time."

Patrick reached across the table, picked up his hat, and wiggled his fingers through the broken crown. "I don't suppose I can get some compensation for this."

"Patrick."

"All right OK." He stood, displacing a couple of chairs in the process. "Let's do this."

"Do what?" Eric asked.

"Get to the airport," Jane said. "Patrick has a red-eye flight."

"To where," Bonnie put in. The others looked at her as if they might have forgotten she was in the room.

"New York, Dublin, Donegal," Patrick said grandly. "Reverse migration. Back to my roots. A fresh start. A cousin's going to take me on at his car lot."

"Don't look that way, Eric," Jane said. "This has nothing to do with you."

"When are you coming back?" Bonnie said, hoping that did not make it sound as if she wanted him to.

"I give it a year or two. More, if I like it. If they like me. I'm thinking they will, I mean, why wouldn't they?"

He waited for Jane to find her coat and purse and to hug Robbie and Grace and then Robbie again, then the two of them headed toward the back door. On his way past Bonnie, he picked up the broken derby and clapped it on her head. She swiped it off. Asshole.

"Would you get the kids settled in and ready for bed?" Jane asked Eric. "I won't be long, I'm just dropping him off. Robbie, your dad and I are going to talk to you about some things." Her eyes flicked over Bonnie. "And I think it would be nice if we had the house to ourselves."

Bonnie waited until she heard Jane's car start up and pull away. Then she too got up and put on her coat. "Bye kids, Happy Hallowe'en." And then to Eric, "Bye."

He followed her out the front door and held it shut behind him so the children would not hear. "I'll call you tomorrow and we can talk."

"No, don't."

"You don't want to talk."

Bonnie shrugged. The night was frosty and she could see her breath, and the houses along the block had gone dark now that all the candy had been handed out. The Vigil of All Hallows. A time for lonesome ghosts and broken love. She hugged herself against the cold and told herself not to get all wrapped up, for once, in the stupid romance of her third-rate, sloppy, sentimental heart. The weather was the weather. And it didn't matter what day it was.

He didn't understand. "Look, tonight was just, tonight. I got upset. Is that it? You're mad because I got mad. You can't exactly blame me for having an initial poor response."

"No, Eric."

"Then what?"

"It's too much crazy love."

"What, you mean that guy? He's leaving. Yeah, and if he misses his plane, I'll buy him a ticket on the next one. What is he anyway, some kind of God's gift to women?"

Bonnie didn't answer that, and Eric must have realized he did not want an answer. He said, "Look, we can sort this out."

"I can't do crazy anymore," Bonnie said. He shook his head: what? "I kept telling myself I could turn it into something different. Less selfish. More, well, worthy. Boy did I get that wrong."

"You're not making sense. If anybody's crazy, it's Jane. I'm sorry if I overreacted. If you hadn't come out here tonight—"

"But I did, didn't I? Jumped right into the middle. Couldn't help myself. I never can. And that's bad for me. I don't mean you're bad for me, you by yourself. But you're not by yourself, are you? I think I need to be in some kind of detox program. A detox for the lovelorn."

The more she said, the more confused and angry Eric was becoming. She had at least hoped to end things well. A clean break and a meeting of the minds. Nope.

She tried once more. "I'm not saying I never want to talk to you again—"

"Yeah, well that's not entirely up to you, is it?"

He turned and went back into the house. Bonnie heard him speaking to his children. And because she knew him as she did, knew the quality and reach of his anger, and that before very long it would burn itself out and he would allow himself to be coaxed back into some other mood, she recognized this as her chance to go. Almost she wanted to offer it up, this deep and tender knowledge they had of each other, tell him, See, there is this good, this very good, splendid part of us that I will never regret. And neither should you.

But that would make it too easy to linger and change her mind. And so Bonnie followed her feet down the stairs and out to the sidewalk and onward, and a part of her heart broke off and scattered and left a trail of longing like spilled candy.

j a n e

I've burned my boats. Is that what they say? Burn your boats?"

"It's bridges," Jane told him. "You burn your bridges so you can't go back again."

"Well I've burned those too," Patrick said, and laughed. He was nervous, but in an excited way. "This is only the second time I've been on a plane. You believe that?"

"I've never flown across an ocean. So you'll be way ahead of me." She was just now recovering from the fright over Robbie. It had left her feeling weak and languid, so that Patrick's leaving had an unreal quality, like a disappearing trick. But it was all settled, she had helped to bring it about, and sometimes you had to make yourself make sense.

It wasn't a long drive to O'Hare and at this time of night the Tollway traffic wasn't anything to slow them down. Up ahead, a plane was coming in for a landing, lowering itself over the highway so dramatically that you imagined, for a moment, the crash, the fireball, the shrieking unreal Hollywood moment. And then the plane passed on, headed for the runway. Patrick had been leaning forward, watching. "Whew. What keeps planes in the air anyway? How does that work?"

"The engines," Jane said. "Propulsion. What keeps birds in the air?"

"What if I don't like it there? What if it's too, you know, foreign for me?"

"If you really don't like it, you can come back. But you have to give it a real chance. You need to move on to the next thing. Set yourself a challenge."

"You're right. Sure you are. I'm just spinning my wheels here. I mean, aside from you, Janie. You're the best."

"You're pretty great yourself."

He put one hand between her legs, exploring, and they drove on that way for a time until their exit came up and he took his hand away. He said, "I'm sorry if I was kind of a jerk. You know, earlier."

"You were provoked."

"Eric seems like a pretty nice guy. I mean normally. I wouldn't want him to have an entirely negative impression of me."

"I imagine if you'd met under different circumstances you would have gotten along just fine," Jane said, and that seemed to please him.

"Oh yeah, and Bonnie. I wasn't much of a gentleman."

"There's a history there," Jane said. "So it's understandable."

"I guess. Why are you always so nice to me? Nobody else sticks up for me like you do."

Jane didn't answer, only pointed to her cheek, and Patrick leaned over and kissed the spot.

She took the deck for Departures, and slowed the car as she looked for a place to pull over by the United signs. It was cheaper for him to get his Aer Lingus flight from JFK, and he said he could catch some sleep at the airport, he could stretch out right on the floor. He was like, a champion sleeper. Jane said he should tell somebody to wake him up, she was worried he might sleep through the boarding announcements, and Patrick said he would be fine. They talked this way so as to avoid saying anything too mushy or difficult. Jane found a place at the curb and Patrick got his backpack and suitcase out of the trunk. They stood next to the car and hugged, conscious that time was short.

"I'll call."

"It's expensive."

"I'll figure out how to text or e-mail or something. We can Skype too. All kinds of stuff."

"You know I'll want to hear from you," said Jane, and she did, although she was not sure Patrick was the staying in touch kind. "I'll want to know you're doing all right."

Patrick took off his leather jacket and handed it to Jane. "Here you go."

Jane thought he needed her to hold it and so she was confused when he said, "Go ahead, try it on."

"What? What for? Patrick."

He helped her take off her own coat and then slide her arms through the jacket sleeves. It was large on her but not hugely so. "I want you to have it."

"No, Patrick, come on. You're going to need this, it's cold over there."

"I'll get a new one. Take it. I don't have anything else to give you. You really helped me work some things out, you know? You cared about what happens to me. You took an interest. Nobody's done that before. Talked to me the way you do."

"This is really, really . . . You're sure?" The jacket was heavy on her shoulders. The leather enveloped her, its rich smell filling her head. Jane was touched. And she could not help thinking that talk was not, perhaps, the only important thing they had done together. "Thank you. I will love wearing it, I'll think of you every time I put it on."

"That's the idea. I got something to show you. Look."

He held up his left arm. On its inner surface, between the wrist and elbow, was a line of flowing blue ink: **PRESPECTIVE**.

"See?" he said. "Prespective." Or close enough. "So I won't forget to stay cool."

"I know you won't. Now you'd better get to your gate. Do you have your boarding pass? Passport?"

They faced each other and he drew her up into one of his huge, smothering hugs. "Bye, cutie."

"Good-bye."

He lifted his backpack and suitcase and walked through the automatic doors into the terminal, and turned once more to wave, knowing she would be watching.

Jane got back into the car and set off for home, and she shed a few tears, but they had more to do with sentiment than loss, as you might cry at the end of a sad, but satisfying, movie.

The house was quiet when she let herself in the back door. All the Hallowe'en candy had been transferred into a bowl in the middle of the dining room table, a lurid heap of Tootsie Rolls, lollipops, peanut butter cups, toffee, red hots, Skittles, miniature wrapped Milky Ways, more. Robbie's dinosaur costume hung over the back of a chair like something that had been trapped and skinned.

Upstairs, Eric's door was closed. The hall light was on and Jane stepped into both the children's bedrooms and watched their quiet sleep. Then she returned to Eric's bedroom and knocked.

He opened the door, still dressed in his day clothes from the hospital. He said, "I put the kids to bed, they were both ready to crash." His eyes took in Patrick's jacket, registered it.

"We need to talk to him, to both of them, really, about safety issues. A little more plainly than we have up to now."

"You mean about sexual predators?"

Jane gave him a hush sign, and Eric motioned her inside the room and closed the door. He said, "Maybe you don't want to use those exact words, but some kind of stand-in. People who do bad things."

"And their next question would be, what kind of bad things."

"We could work it into a more general discussion, things like traffic safety."

"I suppose," Jane said. It had been a long time since they had both been in this bedroom together, and it felt queasy, too intimate, the space now entirely his with its pile of bedside reading and the unfresh sheets and the rings on the dresser from his soda cans and coffee cups. She had refused to clean up after him in here but maybe it was time to relent and do for him whatever unremarkable things might make for calmer waters between them. Then she looked again at Eric. "What?" she asked.

"I didn't say anything." Jane kept her gaze on him. "What?" he said, irritated now.

"Nothing." Although it seemed clear to her that something had distressed him, beyond the already distressing events of the evening, that he was suffering and only with an effort speaking, standing, keeping the sense of himself together. But if she were to insist on asking, there were too many other things that might be asked. It was late and neither of them knew where or how they might begin. "Nothing," Jane said again. "Let's try and come up with some gentle way of saying 'child molester.'"

Eric groaned. "Maybe there's an instructional video."

"I expect there is."

They stopped talking, and there was a moment when they looked at each other with—curiosity, perhaps—and then looked away, and Jane said good night and went out into the hall.

She visited the bathroom and got herself ready for bed and checked once again on her son and daughter, thankful that certain nightmares would not visit them, at least not tonight. Then she got into bed and turned on her small light and took up the pen and yellow legal tablet she kept within reach. She had filled several similar tablets with her neat, scratched handwriting. They were stacked along the wall next to her shoes and purse. They contained the poems and the odd thoughts that came to her, in no particular order. She had not yet gone back and read through them but she would do so as soon as she filled this latest tablet.

And then at some point she would spread all the pages she had written out before her and put one next to another and then another, and move the order around and write more pages to go in between. And the result would be a book, which against all odds would find someone to put it between two covers and send it out into the world, where it would claim a certain amount of unexpected, surprised attention. It would not make her a celebrity, oh no, nothing like that, but it would allow her to shed certain assumptions that might have been made of her.

All this came to her as a certainty but without fanfare, as her visions always did. She held the pen above the paper and then let it touch down. She wrote:

There was a game I used to play with my daughter when she was younger, one that we turned to at the end of a disappointing day when she needed cheering up. I'd tell her to close her eyes and imagine a door, any old kind of door, and she had to guess what was behind it. Sometimes she was sulky and didn't want to play, but once she got going, her guesses, or wishes, turned enthusiastic. Behind the door might be a birthday cake, or a kitty, or someone from a favorite cartoon, come to life. Like all magic, it only works if you aren't too greedy with your asking.

"What do you see behind the door, Mommy?" she'd ask me, and I would always say that she was behind the door, her and her brother and Daddy. And on some days they were. But there were other days, or perhaps other doors. Here was my own childhood and its paintbox green grass and blue skies. Here was sleep when you needed it most, and an ocean you had never seen. Behind one door was a lover who spun you round and round and who polished your skin like an apple.

And one door opened to what seemed like nothing at all, a space of white and tender light and buoyant joy, and only over time would you learn that this was love for all things within yourself and all things beyond it, and one name for that was heaven.

b o n n i e

They made it way too easy to jump out of an airplane. You'd think there would be more to it than watching a video and signing a waiver and hearing a pep talk. The pep talk was delivered by one of the jump instructors, who went by the name of Rocky and whose hair had been so bleached and skin so reddened by the desert sun and wind he resembled a photographic negative. Rocky told them that they should be proud of themselves for having the nerve to do something that most people never did. He said they were going to have an amazing experience. He said he wanted them to be excited about it, could he hear a little excitement? A little enthusiasm?

The room tried to oblige, but there were only five of them, and it was early for enthusiasm, not yet eight in the morning. Bonnie was sitting next to a young newlywed couple, Honey and Babe. They must have had other names, but this was how they addressed each other. Babe hooted, and Honey said Yay! The other two jumpers, a middle-aged man and his wife, said nothing. Bonnie settled for clapping politely.

"Now some things you'll want to know," Rocky continued, "because everybody wants to know them. First of all, is it safe? Well folks, it's just about safer to jump out of a plane than to ride in one. When it comes to tandem jumps, the kind you'll be doing today, the statistics say there are only three deaths per million jumps."

No one seemed reassured by this. Whose statistics? When did they start counting? Bonnie imagined that like herself, the others were thinking that somebody had to be one of those three and there was no guarantee it wouldn't be you. Then there was the problem of three, when you jumped in pairs. What had happened to the fourth jumper? Had they survived but smashed or smeared themselves into some tragic condition?

Rocky changed tactics. "Anybody want to guess how many dives I've done? Solo, tandem, exhibitions, the whole enchilada?" No one did. "Almost five thousand," he said, raising his invisible eyebrows for emphasis. "And once I hit that number, I'll start working on my next five thousand."

Honey leaned in and whispered to Bonnie, "He's kind of cute. I hope I get him for my jump partner."

Bonnie thought she probably would, since Honey was young and cute and frisky, and perhaps it was just an excess of honeymoon high spirits that was making her giggle and roll her eyes, anyway, Babe didn't seem too troubled by any of it. He was a hulking young man with a shaved, military-style haircut and a wrestler's neck. Once Honey and Babe completed their jump, they were headed to Flagstaff and the Navajo Casino. They were having the best time!

The older couple were acting older. They drank coffee from styrofoam cups and paid attention to Rocky as he went on to talk about all the safety features and precautions, the many inspections and requirements, certifications, and so on that were in place. There were probably people who chickened out, although there was no doubt a point when you no longer got your money back.

Bonnie felt a little sick. She guessed she was going to do this thing. No one was making her. No one had made her put in for vacation time, scramble around looking for airfares and hotel deals, then come up with the notion of heading out to the desert because, why not? The Chicago winter was closing in with its usual sullen cold. She would go back home with stories of enormous pink sunsets and swimming in hot springs and riding a horse through a red rock landscape and, if she lived to tell about it, one minute of free fall at 120 miles an hour, followed by the blissful floating. Along the way, she might accidentally have a good time. A part of her always knew that she would end up taking such a trip alone.

The lights in the room dimmed. It was time for the instructional video, with its cheery music and ecstatic testimonials from newly minted survivors. Then there were the parts you had to pay attention to, having to do with the rigging of parachutes and how to secure the harness with its chest and hip straps. The procedures aboard the aircraft, which included, oddly enough, wearing seat belts. Above the guaranteed minimum altitude of ten thousand feet it was bombs away, although of course they did not say it like that. The instructors hooked themselves up to the clients, the jumping pairs positioned themselves in the specified fashion, the doors opened, and it was READY, SET, GO!

The parachutes billowed and blossomed. The music let out its breath. The lights came on again.

Rocky reappeared. "Any questions?" The middle-aged man raised his hand. "Yes sir."

"Anybody ever try to commit suicide on one of these jumps?"

"What do you mean?" Rocky said after a moment.

"You know, not pull their chute, or cut the lines, something like that."

"No. Some reason you're asking?"

"Just curious," the man said. His wife looked away, impassive.

Rocky steered them back to the script. "All right! Last thing, we have a little more paperwork for you to fill out."

The paperwork was a waiver stating that you (or your estate) would not hold the company (or its employees, pilots, the maker of the aircraft, the maintenance personnel for the aircraft, the manufacturer of the parachutes, the riggers of the parachutes, and so on) responsible in the event of your injury, disability, dismemberment, or death. Bonnie signed it, since if you were already set on going through with this, you might as well renounce your rights in a fit of bravado. There was a place on the form for an emergency contact. Honey and Babe were having a mock-argument about whether they should each list the other as their contact. After a hesitation, Bonnie filled in the form with Jane's name and phone number.

∽

She had gone out to Elmhurst to see them, or rather, to see Jane. Jane had called and said they might as well get back to talking, they were probably stuck with each other, at least for this life.

The family had recently acquired a golden retriever puppy which the children had named Stevie, for unclear reasons of their own. Bonnie should come out that weekend and experience puppy joy. She didn't have to worry about Eric; he was on his way to some big deal conference.

Bonnie said yes before she thought too much about it. She guessed that Jane was right, and the two of them had traveled so long in the same orbit, there was no point in avoiding each other, even now. Besides, she missed Jane in the way you can miss a long friendship, even one with such difficulties. And she was curious, more than curious, to hear about Patrick, that is, hoping to hear any really bad news about him. Not to mention how in the world he and Jane had done . . . whatever it was they had done.

And so on a Saturday morning, Bonnie made a stop at a pet store and bought puppy treats and puppy toys of the sort that she hoped would not be immediately shredded and ingested. Then she headed out to the suburbs. The weather was bright and clear and cool. The sky was a thin blue and the breeze was fresh and it seemed possible to believe in new starts.

She took the Elmhurst exit and stopped at a traffic light. On the other side of the intersection she watched a BMW inch forward, waiting for the signal to change, and when it did and they passed each other she thought it might have been Eric and then she told herself it didn't really matter.

When she arrived at the house, she heard the puppy and the children in the backyard and walked around to join them. Robbie and Grace were each calling the puppy from opposite sides of the yard, "Here Stevie, here Stevie," and the excited puppy was racing from one to the other, or sometimes tearing round in a circle and tripping over its own feet.

Bonnie let herself in at the gate. "Hi guys, who's this?"

"It's Stevie, he's our dog."

"He's mostly my dog," Robbie said, but Grace wasn't going to let him get away with that one.

"Can I pet him?" Bonnie squatted down and let the puppy mouth her hand. It was small but sturdy, a compact blond fuzzball with a black triangle nose and brown eyes. "This is the cutest puppy in the world," she announced. "Where did he come from?"

"From the puppy farm. We picked him out."

"Daddy's going to take him to obedience school."

"I'm thinking it'll be more like Mommy," Jane said from the back door. "Kids, Stevie needs a break. Make sure he pees, then bring him inside so he can rest for a while."

Robbie said, "When you have a dog, you get to say pee and poop."

"Yes, those are important vocabulary terms." Bonnie started up the stairs to the back door.

"Want coffee?" Jane asked, and Bonnie said Sure.

Jane went back inside. When Bonnie reached the kitchen, she handed Jane the bag of dog items. "Things Stevie can chew on besides shoes and furniture."

"Thanks. He likes houseplants too." She set Bonnie's coffee on the table and Bonnie, since she had not been invited to sit, drank it leaning against the counter.

"Stevie's?" Bonnie said, pointing to the dog crate and the cushioning inside. She was glad there was a puppy to talk about. She thought maybe that was one reason he'd been acquired, as an occasion for marital discourse and family bonding.

"He has another crate and bed in the upstairs hall. We tried making him sleep in the kitchen. Big mistake. They're just babies, they don't want to be alone. And that way I can scoop him up and take him outside if he needs to go at night. And he does."

"So you get stuck with the dirty work."

"Oh I knew that would happen." Jane looked out the window, checking on the children. She'd cut her hair, not to the punishing extent of some suburban moms, but chin length. And there was some evidence of professional gilding, as if she was trying to match the puppy. "Do you like it?" Jane asked, without turning around.

"Like what?"

"The hair."

Bonnie was reminded all over again of Jane's occasional weird intuitions. Or maybe she had just been staring. "I do. It's subtle, but forward-looking."

"That's me."

"So, listen—"

Jane faced her and held up her hand. "Let's not do this. Not today. Baby steps."

"All right," Bonnie said. She was relieved not to have to take up the whole roiling business of accusation, apology, explanation quite yet. "But could I just ask you about Patrick?"

"What about him? He's doing well. I guess Ireland's full of big, big-talking characters just like him. It took him a little while to adjust and settle in, but he's a hit over there, it's like he went home. He sells lots of cars to lady buyers. And he's joined a soccer league. As for your next question, I encouraged him to go. He really wasn't happy here, you know that."

"But—"

"And your question after that, I'm not going to answer."

"Whatever," Bonnie said. She guessed there were some things she would never understand.

"Don't you miss him?"

Jane considered this. "Yes. But I knew it wasn't going to last. Not the . . ." A very pretty flush colored Jane's cheeks. "Not with Patrick, at least. I mean, he is who he is."

Bonnie thought that even with her new introduction to blissful sex, there was still something detached and cautious and self-protecting about Jane, something that made her hold herself back, and that was one difference between them, and one Bonnie was glad for.

"Anyway," Jane went on, "I knew he'd be happier if he left. If he made some changes. We can all work a little harder on ourselves, right? Well, maybe not Eric. He already thinks he's perfect."

"That's kind of harsh."

"I wouldn't expect you to agree." Jane crossed to the back door and opened it. "Kids! It's time to come in!"

"Well I don't think I'm perfect," Bonnie said. "Duh. I guess I should . . ." Bonnie began, then stopped. There was probably a whole list of things.

"Should what?" The children rushed in then, the puppy running between their legs and yipping, and Jane had to raise her voice. "The one thing you could do for yourself? Try not to be so *heartbroken* all the time."

The plane was a blue and white turboprop, distressingly undersized, but then, they were only going to jump out of it anyway. Bonnie waited as Honey and Babe were loaded in. Then it was her turn. The other, middle-aged couple were not coming, and everyone was OK with that. They had left the room with the rest of them when the orientation was done, but when they reached the hangar and the equipment locker, it was discovered that they had not followed. Through a glass door, Bonnie saw them out in the parking lot, standing next to their car, engaged in what looked like intense conversation.

Rocky said to Bonnie, "I was definitely not going to jump with that guy. No way. Pass."

"Maybe he just wanted to scare her," Bonnie said. "Or maybe he was showing off."

"Isn't it great that we'll never have to know." He was checking out Bonnie's harness and his own gear with as much care as if they were astronauts. The harness straps were uncomfortably tight, like some sort of unsexy bondage gear. Rocky was going to be Bonnie's tandem jump partner, which surprised her. She would have thought that all of Honey's carrying on would have gotten results. Instead it was likely that they were paired off by weight class, since Babe was headed out with the largest of the instructors, and Honey the smallest while Bonnie and Rocky measured up in the midrange.

Rocky said, "Now tell me you're not a suicide risk."

"Not consciously." And then, because he did not know her and was not familiar with her particular kind of bleak humor, she said, "No."

She was glad she was jumping with him. She didn't care about cute; she wanted somebody like Rocky, a weatherbeaten veteran who shoved people out of airplanes all the time, like sacks of mail. The skin around his eyes was pale, from wearing goggles, probably. He was looking at her, sizing her up. "You're pretty nervous," he stated.

"If I throw up on you, it's nothing personal."

"Try not to do that. But really, you should relax. You're paying good money for this, you need to enjoy it. Otherwise, why go to the trouble?"

"Because I'm trying to redirect my risk-taking behavior into less destructive activities."

He thought she was joking. "Ha! I'll have to remember that one. Now let's go over the jump sequence again."

The plane was loud, and already crowded enough, even without the missing couple and the instructors that would have gone with them. There wasn't much point in talking, so Bonnie watched the desert beneath them, its vast brown expanses, receding as the plane rose. It looked pillowy, soft, like something you could bounce off of. The altimeter Rocky wore on his wrist was at three thousand feet and climbing. Three thousand seemed plenty high enough for her. Across the narrow aisle, Honey and Babe were holding hands. There was a GPS-equipped vehicle that was supposed to pick you up afterward. But what if the gadget didn't work and you were stranded, how long could you last without water? What if Rocky had a heart attack and she had to figure out how to open the chute herself? What if her harness broke, or the chute didn't open?

The altimeter went to five and then eight. Bonnie tried to steady herself, imagine herself safe on the ground, laughing with relief and amazement. But she was never any good at seeing into the future. That was Jane's department. That morning in her hotel room, Bonnie had woken up early, showered, dressed in the recommended sweatshirt, jeans, sneakers. She tied her hair severely back and decided there was no point in makeup. When she checked her e-mail, one of the spam messages caught her eye, one of the endless ads for dubious potency drugs: Lift your lady to the heavens!

And here she was, lifted. That had to be some kind of a sign, didn't it? Something about heavenly sex? Or maybe you would have great sex and die? Never mind. She didn't believe in signs anyway.

They had reached ten thousand feet. One of the instructors stood up and beckoned to Honey. "Ladies first!" he shouted. Honey shrank against Babe then stood, waving her hands fretfully, as the instructor hooked their harnesses together and helped her adjust her goggles. The door of the airplane opened with a battering rush of wind and noise, and the two of them duck-walked over to the door, stood there for only a moment, then dropped off. There might have been a thin shriek from Honey, but it was snatched away in an instant.

Babe went next, looking around him as if there might be some escape, like the emergency stop cord on a bus, but there was not, and so he too, along with his instructor, stepped out into the nothing and was gone.

Rocky beckoned to Bonnie and she stood and allowed him to hitch the two of them together, then, guided by his hands on her shoulders, approached the plane's door. Her mouth was dry, her stomach liquid.

What if you landed right on top of a rattlesnake? What were you supposed to do then? Moment of truth! Go or no go!

The wind whipped at her. She gave Rocky a thumbs-up and raised her feet, as they had been told to do, so that he could propel them both out the door. Although she knew that she was falling, she was confused, in that first moment, to find herself looking up into the pure sky and thinking that Jane had been right, it really was a long way down.

ACKNOWLEDGMENTS

It's time, once again, to thank some people. My wonderful, smart, relentless agent, Henry Dunow. David Rosenthal for his enthusiasm and support. Sarah Hochman, peerless editor. And the Blue Rider team.

To my readers, those I know and those I do not, my gratitude. You are the driving wheel of the engine.

ABOUT THE AUTHOR

Jean Thompson is the author of six previous novels, among them *The Humanity Project* and *The Year We Left Home*, and six story collections, including *Who Do You Love* (a National Book Award finalist) and, most recently, *The Witch*. She lives in Urbana, Illinois.